CHASING THE GHOST by Bob Mayer

Who Dares Wins Publishing
www.whodareswinspublishing.com

Fiction Books Available by Who Dares Wins Publishing

Books by Bob Mayer
BLACK OPS: THE GATE
BLACK OPS: THE LINE
THE OMEGA MISSILE
THE OMEGA SANCTION

BODYGUARD OF LIES
LOST GIRLS

Books by Robert Doherty
ATLANTIS
ATLANTIS: BERMUDA TRIANGLE
ATLANTIS: DEVIL'S SEAL
ATLANTIS: GATE
ATLANTIS: ASSAULT
ATLANTIS: BATTLE FOR ATLANTIS

Bob Mayer is the Best-Selling author of numerous books, both fiction and non-fiction. He is a West Point graduate, served in the Infantry and Special Forces (Green Berets): commanding an A-Team and as a Special Forces battalion operations officer; and was an instructor at the JFK Special Warfare Center & School at Fort Bragg. He is the CEO of Who Dares Wins Publishing.

His books have hit the NY Times, Wall Street Journal, Publishers Weekly, USA Today and other best-seller lists. With over 3 million books in print, he's the author of *Who Dares Wins: The Green Beret Way to Conquer Fear & Succeed* and *Hunting Al Qaeda*. He has appeared on/in local cable news around the country as well as PBS, NPR, the Discovery Military Channel, the Wall Street Journal and Sports Illustrated as an expert consultant.

Bob is an honor graduate of the Combined Arms Services Staff School, the Infantry Office Basic & Advanced Courses, the Special Forces Qualification Course, the Special Warfare Center Instructor Training Course and the Danish Royal Navy Fromandkorpset School. He is Master Parachutist/Jumpmaster Qualified and earned a Black Belt in the Orient and also taught martial arts and boxing. Bob also earned an MA in Education. He's spoken before over 1,000 groups and organizations, ranging from SWAT teams, Fortune 500, the University of Georgia, IT teams in Silicon Valley, the CIA, Romance Writers of America and the Maui Writers Conference. He brings a unique blend of practical Special Operations Strategies and Tactics mixed with the vision of an artist.

www.bobmayer.org

CHASING THE GHOST

by

Bob Mayer

CHAPTER ONE

Years ago, Horace Chase was told that an effective sniper was a man who could shoot another human being on nothing but an order and stop; also on order. The stopping is important.

He'd been told he was one of those people.

Which was why, years later and several shots in between, he was currently sitting on top of his rucksack, on top of the snow, on a foothill leading into the Medicine Bow Mountains of Wyoming, looking through a night-scope mounted on top of a sniper rifle, scanning his new kill zone. The chopper that had just dropped him off flew away to the north. It was just after dark and the moon had not yet risen.

Chase felt almost at peace for the first time in a long while.

He turned off the scope, pulled his head back and looked up at the stars and then the surrounding terrain. The High Plains were off to the east; the Rocky Mountains leading north up to the Grand Tetons behind him. Closer at hand was a rock spur, behind which he was hidden; and laid out below him was a valley, running perpendicular to his position. According to the map there was a road running through the valley.

The road was only noticeable because it ran straight and level next to a small creek. It was unplowed and nothing had moved on it since last snowfall, which he had checked over the radio on the chopper flight here earlier today. To the right/south the road came up a wide valley. To the left/north, it climbed to the pass and the valley narrowed to an opening between two peaks, both taller than the one Chase was on. He had about five miles of visibility to the south and less than a mile to the north. There were a network of trails beyond the pass that he knew his targets if they came through his kill zone could turn onto. This would make observation and tracking from the air near impossible.

The intelligence on the targets he'd received on the flight up from Boulder, Colorado, had been terse and to the point: A Larimer County Sheriff's Deputy had pulled over a truck on north-bound Route 287, about eighty miles south of where he was sitting. According to witnesses, the deputy had been shot several times with an automatic weapon by one of the occupants of the truck. It then sped away, leaving the deputy on the side of the road, like so much road kill. An update just before exiting the chopper reported that the deputy was DOA at the hospital in Fort Collins.

There was a crackle of static, and then a voice spoke in the small receiver in Chase's right ear hooked to the satellite radio in his ruck. "All team members, this is Hammer." Chase recognized the call sign and the voice: Fortin, his team-leader. "The latest. The dashboard camera in the deputy's patrol car was checked. It confirms Wyoming plates on the truck. The passenger used an automatic weapon. AK-47. We ran the plates. The registered driver is in the FBI database; a Patriot."

Chase knew that the Patriots were a small, but dangerous, militia group in central Wyoming that had defied both the local, state and federal authorities' dozens of times over the past decade.

His team-leader's voice continued. "We have no idea why these Patriots were in Colorado, but we want to make damn sure to catch them before they got back to their stomping grounds or else they'll just hunker down in their bunkers in the Mountains with their heavy fire-power. Vehicle is a red Chevy Blazer. Two men inside. According to the video camera on the sheriff's dashboard, the driver shot the deputy first as he approached. Then the passenger got out and finished the job with a burst of AK-47 fire. The passenger is a big man, approximately six-two, large bushy black beard, wearing khaki pants and a black windbreaker."

There was a brief moment of static, and then Fortin continued. "The Wyoming State Police thought they had the border sealed up tight, but the truck just ran a roadblock on the Wyoming border. Three state troopers wounded. They're ours now. Out." The radio went silent.

Chase pulled a pair of binoculars with a built in laser range finder out of his pack. He got the distance to the road. Eight hundred and ninety two meters. He adjusted the sniper rifle's scope for the distance. He checked wind. He'd been on enough ranges and parachute drop zones to be able to estimate wind speed within a mile an hour. Five or six miles per hour out of the north. At the distance, Chase was from the road, which meant a three-click adjustment left on the scope.

Chase put the M-21 to his shoulder, turned the scope on and sighted in on the road. He held it there for a few seconds, and then scanned left and right, the scope illuminating the view. Nothing moving. There were no headlights, no sign of civilization along the road or anywhere within view for that matter. There wasn't even a phone or power line. Chase could have been on the dark side of the moon. He pulled back the charging handle, letting it slide forward, loading a round into the chamber.

Chase put the crosshairs on the two-inch thick branch of a pine tree on the far side of the road. He cleared his mind, letting go of everything other than the sight-picture inside the scope, the press of the stock against his shoulder and cheek, his finger lightly resting on the trigger. Chase could feel the steady beat of his heart, a rhythm that he picked up. He let out a breath and then didn't inhale. Right between heartbeats, his finger gently squeezed the trigger.

The 7.62 match grade round splintered the branch.

The rifle was zeroed.

Now the wait. One of the tenets on his counter-terrorist team was to always play a wild card. To do something, anything, that the bad guys wouldn't expect. Chase, freezing his ass off on this mountainside, was certainly the unexpected.

There was a crackle of static, and then Fortin spoke again, this time directly to Chase. "Snake Eater, this is Hammer. Rest of the team is on the ground in their positions. We've got the FBI HRT team on the ground. They can be at your location in ten minutes. Your mission is to delay if the targets come by you."

Ten minutes could be an awfully long time, Chase knew, but it was better than being two hundred miles behind enemy lines.

"Hammer, this is Snake Eater. Roger that," Chase acknowledged, the mike wrapped around his throat picking up the words and sending them to the satellite radio. "I'll be hanging around."

"Out here."

It was going to be a long and cold night even for late April. Chase pulled a parka out of his pack and put it on underneath his combat vest, then sat the pack between his butt and the cold ground. He'd managed sixty-eight hours in a similar situation with two other men on his Delta Force team on the Afghan-Pakistani border, deep in bandit country before some drug smugglers stumbled across his element. That led to a ten-hour long firefight before a Night-Stalker chopper got them out of there, all three bleeding but alive.

Chase closed his eyes. He rolled his head on his shoulders. He didn't like the situation. A good sniper needed surveillance in position well before having to take a shot, usually at least twenty-four hours. If the bad guys came up the valley, he'd have scant minutes to react with only an hour or so of surveillance.

He put the night-scope back to his eye and scanned beyond the road, to the ridge on the other side. He worked in small sections, left right, from the top of the ridge down. He paused when he saw a line in the snow coming over the ridge, directly across. Slight, but visible even at over a mile's distance.

It could be a deer, he thought, as he followed the line down about thirty yards. It disappeared into a copse of trees.

And no line came out of the copse.

Something had gone into those trees. And not come out. Since the snow fell during daylight. Chase scanned the dark patch of woods but saw nothing. His kill zone was the road, but he kept his attention on the copse for almost ten minutes, only occasionally shifting back to the center of the valley.

Chase blinked. A pair of headlights appeared to the south, moving north on the closed road about five miles away. Chase spoke: "Hammer, this is Snake Eater. I've got movement on the road. Coming this way."

There was a long silence. Too long. Chase looked through the night-scope. A Chevy Blazer, two figures inside.

"This is Hammer. Go ahead." Fortin sounded distracted.

"I've got the target closing."

"Shit."

Now Chase knew he truly was in trouble, as he'd never heard Fortin swear.

"Need back-up," Chase prompted.

"The HRT team is up around Casper, near the North Platte. State troopers got called on a possible sighting."

Four miles.

"They're in the wrong place." The North Platte, if he remembered rightly from the map, doubled the distance the support team was from Chase. Twenty minutes. The truck was moving slowly through the snow, but not that slowly. They'd pass by in about ten.

Bob Mayer

"They're also low on fuel," Fortin added. "They have to land in Cheyenne to top off."

Chase didn't say anything. It was his situation, but Fortin's problem. Chase could sit still and let the truck pass and he wouldn't have a situation, then Fortin would. They could always say nothing; no one would have expected Chase to be here.

"How long?" Chase asked.

"They're reporting twenty-five minutes."

"The target will be out of sight by then. There are other roads once they cross the pass. We might be able to track them in the snow, probably not. They might split up. Or they'll go to ground and cover up."

Three miles.

Chase shifted from the truck to that track on the far ridge and then to the copse of trees. He could feel his pulse picking up and he closed his eyes briefly and forced his breathing back to normal.

The radio was silent. It occurred to Chase that the State Patrol might well have been called in after a Chevy Blazer near the North Platte, but that it was a decoy. Contrary to many, Chase had a lot of respect for the capabilities of some of these militia groups. The really hard-core ones had a lot of ex-military men in them. There were some guys who weren't too happy about being double-crossed about going into a war in Iraq.

Chase shifted left and immediately saw a second pair of headlights carving into the valley from the north, coming over the pass. A black HMMWV with a plow had cut a path through the deep snow in the pass. Chase didn't believe in coincidences. More Patriots, meeting their buddies, clearing the way for them. He twisted the focus, not thrilled with what he was seeing. The HMMWV had been modified with the rooftop used on military versions, meaning it had a circular hatch, which was now open. On the ring around the hatch, a machine-gun was mounted.

"Hammer, this is Snake Eater. I've got a second contact," Chase reported. He knew Fortin was probably on the radio, trying to get more help, permission to proceed, etcetera, etcetera, but Chase didn't have time for bureaucratic bullshit right now. "HMMWV came up from the north with a plow and a machine-gun in a turret. These are definitely our people."

"Wait one."

Chase needed more from Fortin than that but he held his tongue, knowing his boss knew that. Or hoping he did.

Someone was now standing in the HMMWV's hatch, holding on to the machine-gun, which Chase recognized as an M-60.

The numbers for that gun had been drilled into Chase as a plebe at West Point: length 43.3 inches; weight 23 pounds; maximum effective range mounted 1,968 yards; rate of fire 550 rounds per minute cyclic. It fired the same 7.62 mm NATO round that Chase's rifle did, but a hell of a lot faster, rattling off hundred round belts while his magazine held twenty rounds and only firing as quickly as he could pull the trigger.

There was a flag tied off on the large radio antenna poking up from the rear of the HMMWV. Chase stiffened as he recognized the shape and image on it: a Cavalry guidon with a large shield in the center. The First Cavalry Division. That had been Chase's first assignment in the Army, when he was still in the Infantry.

Chase turned off the scope and glanced over his shoulder. No way could he make it over that ridge under fire and he didn't have much cover here. And there was that trail in the snow across the way.

Chase pressed his eye against the site and turned it on. He sighted on the man in the hatch. He wore a heavy coat and black watch cap. A scarf was covering the lower half of his face. Chase knew the smart thing to do would be to take him down first. Take out the most dangerous threat.

"Can you stop them?" Fortin finally asked.

"I can stop the Blazer," Chase acknowledged, "but they can make it on foot to the HMMWV. And I would be engaged by the M-60." Which meant he'd have to take them all out.

Chase had been school-trained at the Special Forces school where it wasn't called sniping but SOTI: Strategic Observation and Target Interdiction. Most people who didn't know better thought that was army-bullshit for blowing someone's brains out from long range, but actually, they really did focus more on shooting things than people. One well-placed shot can ground a hundred million dollar jet fighter or take out a microwave relay tower. Occasionally a person might be a strategic target, and they were trained to do that too. In fact, Chase knew shooting people was easier than shooting things, with the objects; you had to know the vulnerable points. With people, a round through the head did the job.

7

"The HMMWV is another story," Chase added. "Might be armored."

"Stop the Blazer," Fortin ordered.

"And then?" Chase asked.

"The HRT team will be there in twenty-one minutes."

Uh-huh, Chase thought to himself. The Blazer was less than a mile away, the HMMWV the same distance the other way. Chase looked at the copse of woods and in the glow of the night vision sight, he saw a flicker of light. The smallest of things and it was gone as fast as he saw it. Someone else might have wondered if they saw anything at all, but Chase had no doubt.

Someone was in the wood-line. Someone was looking through a night-vision scope just as he was and had pulled their eye back from the scope for just a moment, revealing the glow. Mirroring him. Chase turned off his scope and crawled to his right ten yards, taking a new position in case he'd been spotted by whoever was over there. He put his eye back to the scope and turned it on.

Chase swung back to the pick-up. The driver was flashing the high beams, greeting the HMMWV.

"The FBI will be too late," Chase told Fortin.

"I'm calling off their bird then. You have free fire."

The two vehicles were less than half-a-mile apart.

Chase did the math. Two at least in the HMMWV, if not more out of sight. Two in the Blazer. That was a lot of fast shooting at long range. The guy on the machinegun was the pressing threat.

Except for the ghost with the night scope in the woods across the way.

Chase took several deep breaths. He swung back to the Blazer. He could clearly see the silhouette of the two men in the front.

The two vehicles met. The man with the beard got out of the Blazer, AK-47 in one hand as he went up to the HMMWV. He shook his head and looked angry. Chase sighted on the murderer's face, his finger on the trigger.

He could feel the rhythm of his heart.

He exhaled.

He shifted the sight back to the copse of woods.

He could see nothing.

But someone was there. Mirroring him. Waiting.

For what?

A ghost in the machine, Chase thought. Gumming up the works.

Chase exhaled once more, finger on the trigger, then he pulled his finger away from the thin sliver of metal that dealt death and wondered for a moment if perhaps he wasn't part of that narrow slice of humanity any more.

Then where did he fit?

CHAPTER TWO

Two mornings afterward, Chase woke just before the alarm went off. He always did, without a single exception, yet he still set an alarm every time he went to sleep. He lay there, eyes closed, awaiting the noise that would announce the start of his day.

The alarm on his watch started beeping and it took a few seconds for him to remember that it was probably somewhere under the debris cluttering the camouflage poncho liner he used as a blanket. He pushed his way through the discarded clothes, beer cans, gun magazines, maps, and piles of books until he found the offending device, turned it off and strapped it on.

He didn't have a real bed or a nightstand. He used to. He used to have a lot of things. That was before he got served with a divorce eighteen months ago while deployed in Afghanistan. Anne had kept the bed and nightstand because she knew he'd never get another on his own and he'd have to start every day remembering she took them. He didn't think she was being particularly vindictive—she also knew he didn't care much about stuff like that and she did.

He crawled out of the windowless room. It was more of a stonewalled cave he called his bedroom. It had originally been the coal storage room in the basement of the house, into another small room, actually an overly wide hallway, which he called his den when he was feeling positive, where his weight bench was crammed. He started his standard exercise routine. Fifteen minutes of stretching and stomach work and then some upper body weights on the rig. He did reps until he felt the pain deep in his muscles. After the sets of curls and presses, he slid off the sweaty surface of the weight bench. He walked barefoot and dressed only in his shorts into the backyard onto the small stone flag patio outside his screen door. The early morning chill cut into his skin and the sweat turned into steam.

A battered heavy bag, repaired many times with duct tape, dangled from a bolt Chase had drilled into a crossbeam holding up the deck. Chase started the timer on his watch, and then began to work the bag. His arms were heavy from the weights, but he kept them up, pummeling away. He interspersed the punches with snap kicks, turn kicks, sidekicks and the entire repertoire he'd learned over the years, all kicks below chest height on the bag; everything else was just movie bullshit, plus he was too damn old to get his hamstring muscles that stretched out to do Hollywood spinning high kicks to the head any more.

The watch finally began beeping after five minutes of non-stop action and he stopped, bending over, trying to cough out the previous day's cigarettes. Still breathing hard, he walked over to an upright two by four that had coarse rope wrapped around it. He began hitting it at half-power, knuckles, knife edge, open palm, with all the striking surfaces of his hands, feeling the calluses years of such work had built onto them smash into the rope. He did that for two minutes, and then stopped. His hands tingled when he stopped, and he was still breathing hard.

He walked across the grass, still wet with dew and knelt next to a large square of turned up dirt. He gently ran his fingers though the surface, searching for new growth, but there was nothing yet.

Chase went back inside to take a shower, picking up his hand-cruncher on the way. It was a small rubber ball that he squeezed. It built forearm strength. He took it everywhere with him.

On the way to the shower, he stopped at the half-length cracked mirror on the bathroom door, still needing to catch his breath. Tucked in the upper right corner of the mirror was an envelope addressed to him with an APO address in Afghanistan, stained with mud, sweat and dried blood. In the upper left was a faded black and white photo of a young man in jungle fatigues with a green beret on his head bearing a Vietnam era Fifth Special Forces Group 'flash' sewn on the front, tilted at a cocky angle. He had a wide smile and he looked ready to go off and conquer the world. It hadn't quite worked out that way, Chase thought.

Chase shifted his gaze from envelope, to picture, to his image between the two. He always thought it strange to look older than the father he'd never met every time he passed the mirror. His dark hair was cut tight on the sides and flecks of gray were already sprinkled there.

He took a moment to raise his right hand over his head and stretch that side out. There were a dozen various sized pockmark scars on the right side of his body, running from his waist to just below his armpit. He'd had the arm raised when the Taliban grenade had landed fifteen feet away and produced the holes. Signaling for the other guys on his team with the classic Infantry 'follow-me' hand signal, just like the Iron Mike statue outside of Building Four at Fort Benning. What an idiot he'd been, Chase thought.

There was another scar on his stomach, left of center. A round puckered mark. He shifted his eyes from that because thinking about the events surrounding that was guaranteed to ruin his day and he already felt like shit.

The phone rang while he was in the shower, so he stood naked and wet in the kitchen while he got a call from his partner, Porter, telling him they had a body. Porter gave Chase the location and told him to forget about the office and get his butt over. Porter told him the corpse was in Mount Sanitas Park, less than eight blocks from where Chase lived.

"It looks like a homicide, Chase," Porter added just before he hung up.

Chase dressed quickly. He grabbed the photo of his father and the letter from his mother and put them in his jacket pocket before leaving. He slipped out the backdoor, letting the screen door back quietly so as to not alert his upstairs landlord, as he wasn't in the mood for a 'reading' today. It didn't work.

"Good morning!" a shrill voice echoed across the back yard and floated down the street until Chase was sure Porter must have heard it up in the park.

"Good morning, Louise," Chase returned in a more normal tone. Her dog, Astral, an extremely dumb Collie, was already running her dripping nose up and down his pants leg.

Louise was his upstairs neighbor and landlord. The house was an old Victorian on Pine Street between ninth and tenth. There was a dirt alley behind the house that ran the length of Pine. Alongside the alley was a ditch, the Farmer's Canal, which old time Boulderites had dug to get water from the mountains to the fields in the Plains. There was about three feet of water in it now that the Spring run-off was beginning.

"It's going to be beautiful today," Louise gushed.

CHASING THE GHOST

Every day was a good day for her, Chase now knew, whether it was twenty below and snowing or the most perfect summer morning. She was somewhere in her sixties, gray-haired and supported herself with a network of rental apartments. She supplemented that by 'readings'. She ran a group of local psychics out of her house and the people that came and went, well, strange would not begin to describe them. Astral was an old dog and lounged in Louise's back yard day and night.

"Looks like it," Chase said as he pushed his way past Astral.

Louise touched his shoulder. "I saw you looking at your garden. It's still early, but it will happen."

Chase kept moving. Louise followed him to the Jeep door. She put her hands on Chase's shoulders and peered into his eyes. "Have a most wonderful day and be open to the powers. I sense something important coming for you."

"I'll be open," Chase assured her. The last sentence was what he took to be part of the psychic scam: important could cover a lot of ground. Hell, something was sure to happen today and then she could always claim it was important.

"I can see through your eyes into you," Louise continued. "You've spent your life making your heart like your hands, all tough on the outside, but it's a good heart, Horace. The world needs good hearts that do good deeds."

Chase stared at her, and then simply nodded, unable to think of anything to say to that. He got in his Jeep and drove down the alley seeing Louise in the rear view mirror when he glanced at it. She was staring at the Jeep, smiling. The image disappeared as the alley curved slightly.

It was less than a mile from the house to Mount Sanitas Park, but traffic on 9th Street, which he had to turn left onto, was heavy. And not just cars, there was an endless stream of bikes heading toward downtown and the University, all screaming downhill on the steep slope from Mapleton School, a hundred year old elementary school that had a great view of the city.

Chase considered using the red bulb light plugged into the cigarette lighter, but what the hell, since it was a body he figured there wasn't much of a rush to get to the scene. To be somewhat productive he checked the basics with his partner on the department issue cellular phone while he waited for an opening in the traffic. Porter was on top

13

of everything. He had a warrant en route and the area was closed down. The warrant was important, Chase had learned during training, just because a body was there didn't mean the cops could just waltz in and start counting bullet holes. Americans got rights after all, although sometimes Chase wondered.

This location, at first glance, appeared simple for the warrant because it was in Open Space, which meant the city owned the land. But the way politics went in Boulder, Porter had made sure he requested the warrant, because one never knew, the wacko Open Space people could sue the police department for trespassing if the cops happened to step on a few bushes while checking out the murder scene. Sounded crazy, but Chase had seen crazier things happen in Boulder in his short four months there. In fact, he knew Open Space was the most powerful branch of the local government. They had their own funding from a special sales tax where the money went directly to their coffers, no stopping and skimming at City Hall. To get someone fired up in Boulder, just mess with the Open Space. Or try to get rid of some prairie dogs. Or smoke a cigarette, Chase thought, getting more and more irritated as he waited for an opening and his headache grew. Here in Boulder, the number one capital crime in terms of citizen outrage was smoking. It was illegal just about everywhere.

Just thinking about it made Chase's blood boil, so he quickly lit up a smoke to calm himself down, earning a disdainful look from the spandexed bicyclist stopped next to him at the stop sign. Chase was two steps toward the grave in the biker's eyes, in a car and smoking a cigarette. Chase had started again a couple of weeks ago and it had wreaked hell on his daily runs, so he'd stopped running. Chase had never smoked in his life until he'd gone into Afghanistan for the first time. After a couple of month's in country, everyone on the team had taken the habit up. He felt like telling the citizen-cyclist to take a tour over there and see what kind of health he came back in. If he came back at all.

Chase spotted an opening and gassed it, leaving the bicyclist sucking his exhaust fumes. He went up 9th a block and turned left at Mapleton Elementary. He drove past the Mapleton Center for Rehabilitation. There was a thought Chase quickly pushed away and was abruptly at the end of civilization. Open Space. Boulder was surrounded by it, an attempt to have a "band of green" between the city and the rest of the world. Chase had always meant to ask Louise, who was native to Boulder, if that band of green had some sort of mental effect on the good citizens of the town, because never had he lived any place as loony. He'd fought in loonier places, granted. But bullets, bombs, blood, and guts tended to do weird things to the psyche, Chase figured. He didn't get how green space and white-capped mountains and bubbling creeks did it.

When Chase finally got to where Porter had said to get to, he was thirsty, hungry and slightly hung-over. Before he could wallow completely in his self-pity, he had to deal with Porter who was at the Jeep door before the parking brake was set.

"Chase, you look like crud. You need to get more sleep."

Chase closed his eyes at his partner's words. "So much for sympathy. You got a wife who loves you enough to iron your shirts and get your beers and you go and make fun of a man fending for himself in this cruel world."

Porter dressed well, courtesy of his wife, but that couldn't hide the fact that he was short and had an ample beer belly to go with his receding hairline. Contradicting the scarcity of hair in the front, he had a graying ponytail in the back that he proudly snapped a colorful band about every morning. He looked like a Harley biker fifteen years past his head-busting prime. Porter fit right in with the rest of the strange people of Boulder, Colorado in that he didn't fit in anywhere else. Chase noted that for some reason his partner had a set of mechanics coveralls on over his suit. Chase was in his usual outfit of cheap suit and wrinkled shirt.

Porter snorted. "I got a wife who'd iron the dog before she touched my shirts. Ever heard of a drycleaner? Stop whining, Chase. You sound like one of my kids. Speaking of the kids, I got a call last night from Bennie's teacher. She says he's gonna flunk kindergarten. Can you believe that? How the hell can you flunk kindergarten? Is he napping wrong? I asked her. Maybe sleeping upside down instead of right side up? Or not washing his hands with soap? Jeez, Chase, how the hell can you screw up kindergarten?"

Chase nodded his head and remained silent. The last time he'd seen Bennie, the kid had loaded the cuff of his pants with potato salad.

Porter was still on it. "Know what this teacher says to me then, Chase? You're not gonna believe it: She says I'm insensitive! Typical Boulder bullshit." He shook his head in disbelief, ponytail wagging. "Well, let's check the stiff. I'll show you how to do a murder scene seeing as you're busting your cherry on this one. I already did a prelim."

Chase didn't say anything and wasn't surprised his partner hadn't asked about the other night. The word must already be out, he figured. Porter was hooked in tight with the police grapevine. But Chase knew Porter was a good partner, which was why he hadn't asked right away.

Ben Porter was eight years older than Chase and the senior major crimes investigator for the grand City of Boulder. Since there were only six investigators, that wasn't saying too much. One night over beers, Chase had learned that Porter had come to Boulder from the mountains of middle Colorado with a guitar and a dream. Instead, he'd picked up a wife and family and had to get practical. He'd opted for the sure pay of being a cop combined with the theory of doing society some good. Occasionally Chase could see a certain wistful look in his partner's eyes when he was probably remembering what had blown away with the years. Porter wasn't brilliant but he was very, very thorough. Chase was partnered with him because the powers-that-be figured Porter would keep him in line and from screwing anything up too badly since no one took Chase seriously as a cop, least of all Chase.

"You need to cover up," Porter advised Chase, leading him to his car trunk. "Everything that enters a crime scene can become evidence and I know you don't want to give up that finely tailored suit. I brought extra."

Chase took off his jacket and put on the set of faded coveralls his partner held out. He took off his low quarters and slipped on a pair of $2.99 K-Mart-special sneakers, which, given that Porter was always prepared, were his size. Porter and Chase moved out, but he'd noted the glance his partner had given him when he was changing. Porter's opening comment had been true. Chase knew he did look like crud and he knew it was more than having a rough night of sleep.

Chase looked around. They were parked in a small area just off Sunshine Drive, which is what Mapleton turned into once it hit the foothills. There were two black and whites there along with Porter's car. Chase looked up, which was a pretty common thing to do when in the western edge of Boulder. He could see two uniformed cops standing in the grass about a hundred yards up the gravel-walking path, but no sign of a body. Behind them, a rocky ridgeline ascended over a thousand feet. And that was just a 'foothill' as they called them here.

Along the way to the crime scene, Porter told Chase the particulars he'd gotten from his prelim, no more humor or joking his voice. Female, Caucasian, about mid-thirties. Looked like her throat had been cut. The medical examiner was on the way, and she was lying as she'd been found.

As Chase had noted when he looked from the lot, the body couldn't be seen from the road. The elevation and grass were too high. She was lying on her back in the wild flowers, hair splayed around a pale face that still showed something despite the lack of animation and blood. Incredibly deep blue eyes stared up lifelessly at the bright sun that was crawling up out of the eastern sky.

She was nude and the front of her body had been bathed in blood. The rigid lock at her elbows and knees gave her body a stiff, rubber doll appearance. Despite that, Chase sensed that she had been lithe and graceful in life. Chase looked around, trying to get a feel for the area.

Porter glanced back from where they'd come. "The killer probably parked just off the road and brought her up here."

Chase was examining the immediate area. "How many people have been up to the body?"

"The jogger, over there, who found her, and the responding patrolman. And me."

Chase pointed. "The jogger came from that way. You and the patrolman came up the same way we did. There's no blood other than what's on her, so she was killed elsewhere and carried here. But I don't see any other tracks."

Porter looked about, apparently trying to see what Chase was seeing, and failing. "You can read tracks?"

"After I was in Special Forces a couple of years, I was sent on a training exercise to Malaysia, to the tracking school run by their military."

"A tracking school?"

"Run by ex-headhunters." Chase could see the look Porter was giving him. His partner was wondering if he was joking. "No shit," Chase continued, realizing he was going to have to explain. "The instructors at the Malaysian Army tracking school didn't speak a word of English and myself and the other three SF guys going through didn't speak a word of their language, but it didn't matter. What they were teaching us didn't require talking.

"The first three days all they had me do was sit still in a blind and watch a waterhole. The point the instructors were making was that tracking is not as much about finding broken twigs and footprints in the dirt. Although they did move on to that, but more about understanding the habits of whatever creature one was following. If the tracker could understand the prey, he could predict what path it would take, where it was going. Sometimes one could even get to where the prey was headed before it got there. Sort of like those FBI behavioral science guys profile killers. Except this was out in nature, where even men become animals."

Porter was just staring at him.

"I watched the animals around the waterhole for three days, then moved into the rain forest and trailed them. The last week of the course, I tracked the most dangerous animal, man. By that time, I was part of the jungle. I followed other instructors from the course and they used all their techniques to lose me. And did. Then they tracked me and found me every time, no matter what I did to cover and confuse my trail. I learned a lot."

"OK. Headhunters." Porter slowly nodded. "How'd she get here then, if there's no other tracks?"

"That doesn't mean someone didn't carry her here and dump her," Chase said. "You can avoid making tracks for a short distance or cover them up."

"So you're thinking a headhunter did this?" Porter asked.

Chase looked at him. "Funny guy. She still got her head."

"But someone sure tried to take it off," Porter said. "Check it out. I'll touch base with the reporting officer again." Porter went over to talk to one of the patrolmen.

Chase knelt for a closer look at her face; her short hair was so dark and thick that it obscured most of her neck. He pulled a pencil out of his pocket inside the coveralls and used it to lift some of the hair aside. One thing stood out immediately: a thin red line around her neck, the source of the blood. Chase stared at it and frowned.

"Don't touch the body. Didn't they teach you anything?"

Chase turned to see the owner of the voice. Doctor Hanson pushed the words around the cigar butt he had tucked in the corner of his mouth. The voice didn't go with the cigar though; high and squeaky. He was a short, fat man who looked more like St. Nick without a beard than a coroner.

18

"Sorry," Chase said, backing off.

Hanson looked at the neck. "I'd say the neck incision would be a good guess on this one. But how about letting me do my job and you do yours?"

Chase walked away since Hanson was ready to do the on-site on her and he'd already made one mistake. Chase was supposedly trained to investigate murders but he knew, and the people he worked with knew, that wasn't the real reason he was here and his police training was minimal at best. He wasn't a real cop, at least not according to the other real cops. His paycheck was cut by Washington because he was a Federal Liaison Investigator, FLI for short, which when pronounced, had gotten him more than enough sick jokes over the past four months—assigned to the grand city of Boulder, in the Rocky Mountain State of Colorado. Lucky him. He was a bastard stepchild, born of some whiz kid's bright idea high in the Federal Government and crammed down local governments' throats with the almighty lever of federal dollars. They thought they were killing two birds with one stone. Sometimes Chase wondered what kind of bird he was supposed to be.

Chase was one of the five hundred counter-terrorism experts the new president had promised to put on the streets, while at the same time; he was part of a Federal Agency Counter-Terrorism Team, specifically the High Plains FACT Team. They couldn't just have all those highly paid specialists like him sitting around doing nothing, waiting for terrorists to strike, so the whiz kid had reasoned. So let's shlock them onto the local police to earn their pay, day in and day out, the numbers sounded good in the President's speech and be in the right area ready to go when needed. Plus they had their 'ear to the ground' or so the reasoning went, picking up 'intelligence' at the local level.

Thus, Chase worked with the Boulder PD, just like one of their own cops, even answered directly to the chief of detectives, but he also carried a red beeper with him everywhere he went. When it went off, he went wherever he was ordered, Boulder PD be damned; like he had two nights ago. Chase also attended refresher training with his CT, counter-terrorist, team, one weekend a month and for four week-long sessions yearly. At least that was the idea. Four months in and he wasn't sure how it wasn't going to work out as it hadn't been thoroughly tested yet, although to judge by the other night, not exactly too great.

Chase's paycheck was cut by the Feds, which was fine with the local politicians, and, he assumed, the taxpayers in Boulder, but didn't thrill his superiors in the police department. It was sort of like the deal the Feds used to get extra teachers into classrooms, an analogy that didn't impress Chase or his co-workers too much.

Chase rejoined Porter. "What do you think?"

Porter shook his head. "No ID. No rings. No nothing. I don't like it. No sign of the murder weapon, but I've put out the word to check the area for a knife."

"I don't think it was a knife," Chase said.

Porter raised an eyebrow. "What cut her throat then?"

"I think she was garroted. Thin steel wire."

Porter frowned, the worry lines etched on his face getting deeper. "We'll let Hanson determine cause of death."

Chase shrugged. "Roger that."

Porter nodded toward the crime scene. "Come on."

Chase stood perfectly still for a minute, feeling Porter's impatience to get started, then tuning it out. He imagined the place at night when the body had been dumped here. Stars overhead. Chase felt the hair on the back of his neck tingle and he turned toward the ridgeline, eyes searching the tree covered slopes.

"What's the matter?" Porter asked.

"I feel," Chase began, but then realized he'd already freaked his partner out enough for one morning. "Nothing." Chase walked over to join his partner, but he looked over his shoulder once more at the mountains. He shook his head. Fucking ghosts were getting to him. He thought for a moment about the VA shrink in Denver he'd gone to. She'd made light of his ghosts, but then again, she was a shrink and a civilian. Chase knew from experience that some monsters were real, although they appeared human. Chase hadn't gone back and he hadn't taken the pills she'd prescribed.

Chase followed Porter's lead. A hundred yards from the body, they began working their way in, checking the ground. It was slow, tedious and warm under the rising sun.

There was nothing after two hours of careful searching. They'd searched in to the body and Porter called for Hanson's ghouls to come and take her. Chase and Porter took a smoke break waiting for the wagon to get back out, neither of them saying anything, lost in their

20

own thoughts, getting dirty looks from people getting turned around from their daily run/walk on the Mount Sanitas trail.

Chase knew there would be letters to the editor about closing the trail in the Daily Camera in the next couple of days. And their smoking. Chase always felt like he could tell the pulse of a place by the letters to the editor. In Boulder, they were mostly about protecting animal rights, protesting nuclear weapons, and basically getting in other's people's stuff on a large scale. Nobody ever sent a letter saying they needed to stop doing something themselves.

Chase looked around, taking in the area. It was a good drop spot for a body. On a bend of road where one could see either way for a distance, yet not be seen. He had a feeling the spot wasn't chosen randomly or in the heat of the after-murder. He looked up once more at the ridgeline and shook his head.

They had her sealed up in the rubber bag, but Chase could still discern the outline of her body. She had been tall, but they moved with an ease that told Chase she wasn't heavy. He figured it wouldn't be very long before they identified her, maybe even before the coroner ran her prints. She looked like a woman somebody would miss.

"Let's head on back," Porter finally said. "We'll see if anyone matching has been reported missing and do the honors with Donnelly."

****

Chase thought the best thing about the office was that it was in a new building with a nice view of Boulder Creek and the bike/run path that was next to it. Chase always enjoyed sitting there watching people huff and puff their way by. He'd also enjoyed running on it before he decided it interfered with his smoking. The path stretched from three miles up Boulder Canyon to the eastern end of town where the Great Plains met the Rockies.

Porter was away, briefing Lieutenant Donnelly, then checking the front desk for information. Putting his feet on the desktop, phone on lap, Chase leaned back in the chair. He hit speed dial on his cell with eyes closed.

Her voice sounded confused; she had been asleep. "What?"

"Noon. You're mine." Chase hung up.

He was watching two female joggers headed west to east, when Donnelly arrived at his desk while Porter was still away, now checking

21

on messages. Chase had worked for him for four months now, since arriving in Boulder after his FLI training. The first few months Chase had just thought he was an asshole. After another couple of months of Donnelly regularly affirming that initial impression, Chase got so used to it he couldn't hate him anymore. Donnelly was a politician covering his ass, looking for promotion, and eventually retirement at a nice pay grade, something Chase had also seen too often among the officer corps in the army. Chase didn't have the energy to fight that any more.

"Looking a little rough today," Donnelly said, his fingers playing with his police-badge tie clasp.

"Yes, sir," Chase said automatically. Coming out of twelve years in the Army and four year at the Academy, Chase had little idea how to dress in the civilian world and frankly, he didn't give a shit. He did what he was supposed to do, who cared what he looked like doing it?

"I heard you were alerted the other night for that shooting in Larimer County."

"Yes, sir," Chase said. He noticed that everyone within earshot, and those beyond, were trying to listen in.

"I didn't get a report from Agent Fortin."

That's because he doesn't report to you, Chase thought but didn't say. "I suppose not." Chase noted Porter coming into the squad room, a piece of paper in his hand.

"Well," Donnelly said. "Seeing as this is your first homicide, you're in good hands with Detective Porter."

"Yes, sir."

"Follow his lead," Donnelly advised.

"I certainly will, sir," Chase said.

Porter walked up, almost stepping between Chase and Donnelly. "I've got a name. Her husband reported her missing. Mrs. Rachel Stevens." He looked at Donnelly. "We're going out there to interview him, sir."

"Good," Donnelly said, as if he had thought of that course of action himself.

22

CHAPTER THREE

"You up to this?" Porter asked as he drove.

Chase shrugged. "We dealt with this in the Army by writing a letter from the other side of the world, not going and ringing a doorbell. Of course, we also usually knew and saw the person dying. So it's hard to say which is more difficult."

Porter nodded as if he understood. "The husband's already identified the body. He's back home. Doc Hanson doesn't want to see us until later this afternoon after lunch. We need to talk to the husband ASAP because you always have to look at family first in a homicide. Most murders are crimes of passion."

Chase didn't think there'd been much evidence of passion, but he kept his mouth shut, deferring to his more experienced partner. They'd stopped at Moe's on Broadway, and Chase was eating a pizza bagel and drinking a coffee, trying to quell his rebellious stomach. They were on the way to Pine Brook Hills. Even in Boulder where a run-down two-bedroom house could sell for a half-million, the Hills were expensive. The area was northwest of downtown in a section of the foothills with great views in every direction, particularly overlooking the town and the peons who lived there. There wasn't a dwelling in the Hills that went for under a cool million and most cost several times that. Their mountain road also got plowed first in the winter; so much for equality and democracy, Chase thought.

Chase's back was stuck to the vinyl seat and the open window encouraged the dull roar of the city to exacerbate his hangover. He was trying to wipe a small dab of pizza sauce off his tie when they got to the Stevens' neighborhood.

"The body bother you?" Porter asked, glancing over.

"I've seen lots of dead people," Chase said, taking another bite of his bagel.

"Right."

The silence lasted until they turned in the driveway of the victim's house.

"What does the husband do?" Chase asked as they pulled up to the sprawling mansion.

"Urologist," Porter said.

"Must be a lot of prostrate trouble in town."

Porter smiled. "Actually there is. Boulder has the highest rate of prostate cancer in the entire country. There was an article in the paper last year saying it's all the bike riders. Those thin seats can be hard on the anatomy."

Chase snorted. "You don't think it's Rocky Flats?" he asked referring to the sprawling government compound eight miles to the south of Boulder where the Rocky Flats Nuclear Munitions Plant had churned out big, dirty bombs for decades and was still in the middle of a massive cleanup effort. Chase's FACT team had already done one training exercise down there and they'd been fully briefed on the facility. It wasn't as clean as people thought.

"They've shut that down," Porter said.

"They're shutting it down. Big tense difference." Chase shook his head. "They call it an 'Environmental Technology Site' now, like that changes the history of the place. I spent enough time in the army to know government double-speak."

Porter glanced at Chase as he turned off the engine. "You don't trust the government?"

"Do you?" Chase asked.

Porter shrugged. "Let's keep our focus here. I'll question, you watch and listen."

Chase got out of the car and took in the house. It had more levels than he could count and enough glass to make the Hubble weep with envy. The sprawling home screamed money. He followed Porter up to the door and waited while his partner pressed the doorbell.

The woman who answered was early fifties, well groomed, and saddened. She told them she was the maid and that Doctor Stevens was waiting on the back terrace. The inside of the house as Chase walked through was a little much for someone who didn't have a nightstand and slept in a converted coal bin.

Doctor Stevens looked terrible. After a few seconds, the doctor finally acknowledged their presence, and told them to sit down. The doctor didn't stand, but Chase estimated he was about the same height, a little over six feet. He was in his late thirties but looked older. Probably all the silver in his dark hair and the worry lines around the eyes. Chase imagined he worked long hours. This house looked like it demanded it.

Porter took point. "Doctor Stevens, I wish we didn't have to do this now, but we need to talk a little about your wife. Most particularly where she was last night."

Stevens was twisting a small paper napkin into a roll. "She was at school."

Porter had his small notepad out. "School?"

The doctor was staring vacantly over at the view of the foothills rising up behind the house. "This is probably not the best time to talk; the reality of her death hasn't touched me yet. I was just sitting here wondering when she would be back."

Chase figured if they waited for a good time, the killer could walk to Canada or Mexico. He wondered for a moment which one he would head for if he had to?

Porter pressed on. "What time should she have returned last night?"

"Around ten-thirty."

Porter was writing. "What time did you call the police?"

"About eight this morning."

Chase's eyebrows raised a notch but it didn't matter because Stevens wasn't looking at him or Porter for that matter. Porter asked the obvious: "Why did you wait so long?"

Doctor Stevens put the napkin down and finally looked at Porter. "I was just so positive she would be home. Bad things simply did not happen to Rachel."

Right, Chase thought. Even money and living in Pine Brook Hills couldn't protect a person from the vagaries of life. Stevens finally looked up and must have seen something on Porter's face because he continued, trying to amplify his comment, explaining his lack of action.

"I know it sounds strange, but she was so in control and so structured that when she was gone so long I just presumed she had a good reason. Rachel doesn't--" With great control he stopped and then continued. "Didn't do stupid things. It is simply impossible for me to think that she's really gone."

Porter nodded as if he understood. "Could you just give me an idea about your wife's school schedule?"

"She goes two nights a week. Wednesdays and Thursday's. CU. She was working on her masters in clinical psychology."

That was something, Chase thought. A starting point at least.

Porter moved on. "What kind of car did she drive last night?"

"A white BMW 330CI." Stevens suddenly stood and motioned for them to follow him into the house. "Rachel was a very organized woman. Why don't you take her address book and calendar? It will tell you more than I could."

Chase followed the doctor and Porter through the house, crunching the ball he kept in his pocket, until they reached the upstairs master bedroom. To the right was a large alcove; Stevens referred to it as Rachel's sitting room. It was bright and colorful and facing east, which meant Rachel Stevens, had preferred to look out over the Plains than the Rockies. Chase briefly wondered what that meant about her.

The stuff the Doctor wanted was in the desk. Stevens got it for Porter, while Chase scanned around. Everything seemed to be in drawers. It wasn't one of those homes that had lots of personal things lying around for prying eyes to see. It seemed rather cold and sterile. For a moment, Chase wondered what someone would figure out looking at his apartment—he put the brakes on that line of thought quickly, because it wasn't pretty.

Porter asked for a picture of Rachel and Stevens reluctantly pulled a small wallet size photo from his billfold.

"I have the portrait of this at my office." Stevens seemed to feel a need to go on. "Rachel didn't like photographs of herself and it took a lot of pleading to get her to sit for this one."

Porter took the picture without looking at it, handed it to Chase, thanked the doctor for the other stuff, gave him a receipt for the property, and they left him standing in that room alone and saw themselves to the door.

"What do you think?" Porter asked, as soon as they were outside.

"The house seems a bit much for just two people. Conspicuous consumption like a lot of Boulder."

"About the husband," Porter said wearily.

"Seemed pretty broken up," Chase said.

"Or he's a good actor," Porter commented as he got in the car.

Chase got in the passenger side and smiled. "You don't trust people."

Porter nodded. "Not in murder investigations. Trust no one, especially family, and never, ever, fucking pray with them in front of their damn Christmas tree."

"Say again?" Chase asked, slipping back to Army radio lingo.

"The first detective on the Ramsey case did that," Porter said. "I was in uniform then. The body was still in the damn basement of the house and the detective was upstairs praying with the family, thinking it was a kidnapping. I learned a lot watching all the fuck-ups."

Chase nodded. "Same here, partner. You wouldn't believe some of the shit I saw in the 'Stan and Iraq. Never underestimate the power of stupidity."

"Amen." Porter frowned. "You know, it's weird he didn't call her in missing when she didn't come home. Didn't go drive over to the school to look for her. He just went to bed."

"Marriage," Chase said, shaking his head.

"You can't judge everyone by your experience," Porter said. "You aren't exactly center of the bull curve."

Chase pretended to look hurt. "Hey."

Porter ignored him. "I don't like the doctor's story. He's a surgeon. He could have done that cut."

Chase thought about mentioning it had been a garrote once more, but kept his peace. He'd never seen anyone's throat that had been cut with a scalpel so maybe Porter was right. Scalpels were not standard Taliban combat equipment.

Porter checked the time. "We'll see what Hanson has for us after lunch, but I want to focus on the husband for now. Where do you want to eat?"

"I've got an appointment for lunch," Chase said.

Porter stared at him for a second, and then nodded. While Porter drove them back to headquarters, Chase pulled the picture of Rachel Stevens out of the address book. The likeness was small, but he was struck by her just the same. There was something in the eyes. He wanted to see the larger portrait in the husband's office.

"What do you think?" Porter asked, glancing over.

"I think you don't trust me driving," Chase said, passing the photo over to his partner. "I might not be able to do murder scenes, but I can drive at least."

"Last time you drove, you got all squirrelly on me," Porter said.

You drive along roads with IEDs for a while, Chase thought but didn't say.

Porter pulled over to the side of the road short of headquarters, to look at the picture Chase thought, but he was wrong.

His partner turned to him. "What happened in Wyoming?"

"What did you hear?" Chase asked.

"Your team got alerted, you deployed but the killers made it back to their land in the mountains."

"That's it?" Chase pressed, wondering how good security was on his FACT team.

"There's some rumors," Porter allowed. "But I'd rather ask you than listen to rumor."

"I had clear long-rifle shots at the killers, but I didn't take them. They got by me."

When Chase fell silent, Porter nodded, and started the car.

"You don't want to know why I didn't shoot?" Chase asked, a bit surprised.

Porter turned to him, looking equally surprised. "Jesus, Chase. I'm a fucking cop. We don't shoot people in cold blood. We arrest them. You'd have shot them, I'd have left you standing there on the side of the road and you'd have needed a new partner."

* * * * * * * * * * * *

The door to the apartment was unlocked. Chase opened the door and quietly walked in, shutting the door behind him and locking it. From the sheath tucked into the small of his back, he drew the double-edged commando knife. He held it at the ready as he entered the living room. The shades were pulled and it was dark. He stood perfectly still and took almost a minute to let his eyes adjust. She was on the couch, covered with a blanket, her eyes closed.

With his other hand, he pulled out his handcuffs, being sure not to make any noise. He went over to the couch and put the blade just a scant inch from her neck. Her eyes opened and widened, but she didn't scream as he pressed the knife against her throat.

He efficiently cuffed her, then used them to pull her off the bed, the blanket falling aside. She was naked. He looped a scarf that was lying on the coffee table underneath the chain connecting the cuffs, pulling her across the room to the bedroom door. He tossed the free end of the scarf over the door, reached around, and jerked down on it, stretching her arms over her head. Taut.

Then he shut the door, pinning the scarf in place, leaving her exposed in front of him. She was watching him, still silent, but she was breathing hard. He stepped closer and she closed her eyes as he brought the knife back to her throat.

Chase slid the knife down from her throat, to the swell of her breast to her right nipple. The edge of the blade pressed into the flesh enough to be felt but not draw blood. It flicked over the nipple to the underside of her breast. Her breathing was coming faster, her ribs moving. As he moved the knife lower, across her tight stomach, he leaned forward and put that nipple in his mouth. He caught it between his teeth and exerted pressure.

Her body tried to move away, but only had a few inches of slack. Her hands had wrapped around the scarf, taking the weight off the metal cuffs around her wrists. He could see the whites of her knuckles as she twisted the cloth in her hands.

The knife reached the thin sliver of red pubic hair. It scraped over the hair, producing a slight crackling that he sensed rather than heard.

He knelt in front of her, sliding the blade over the lips between her legs, then he reversed the knife, pressing the handle against her. He leaned forward and his tongue snaked out.

She was wet.

He pressed the top of the handle against her and her lips parted. He slid it in halfway. Then he pressed his mouth against her, his tongue finding her clit. He gently moved the knife handle in short strokes, putting slight pressure toward him, while his tongue moved, finding the rhythm of her body.

She was gasping now. He could hear it and feel it through his tongue. He moved the knife handle faster, his tongue slower, his free hand grasping her ass, holding her tight in place.

He lost track of time, focused only on the body he now controlled.

She was moaning, whispering something to herself, something he couldn't make out.

Then she shuddered, her back hitting the door, his hand crushed by her tight ass pushing against the wood. She was on her toes, and as she slowly came down to put her feet back on the ground, he slid the knife handle out of her and slowed his tongue to a halt.

Bob Mayer

He put the knife back in the sheath as he got to his feet. He opened the door, releasing the scarf, letting it fall to the floor. He uncuffed her and put those back in the case on his belt. Then he lifted her in his arms and carried her to the couch.

She still had not opened her eyes, but she was smiling.

He put her on the couch and slid the blanket back over her body. He leaned over and kissed her on the forehead. She sighed contentedly.

Then he left, making sure the door locked behind him.

****

Chase had had to go in cold rooms like this in Kandahar and Baghdad to see his men and claim their effects and make sure their remains were taken care of. Then he went and wrote letters. But this was different. Rachel Stevens hadn't been a soldier. She was a civilian.

The coroner was standing over an autopsy table, which held the remains. Chase didn't think of her as a person for now. Chase stood next to Porter and waited patiently. Hanson was talking into a microphone hanging from the ceiling while his assistant measured, portioned and weighed the parts he was removing.

"I'm almost done here." Hanson pointed at the neck. "Cause of death was loss of blood from trauma to the neck. Her nails are clean. No apparent struggling." He frowned. "No defense wounds."

A clean kill, Chase thought, but didn't say. Hanson rolled the head to the side so they could see the wound. Chase tried to look interested, but all he could see was the big gaping hole on top where Hanson had scooped out the brain. They usually didn't do autopsies after combat action.

"What kind of weapon made the cut?" Porter asked.

"That a strange thing," Hanson said. "I've never seen a wound like this. It's too narrow for a knife."

"Scalpel perhaps?" Porter asked.

Hanson frowned. "Maybe. But it would have to be a perfect cut with a very steady hand."

"Like a doctor might do?" Porter pressed.

"That's a possibility. But the wound is deep. Not a scalpel, though. Maybe a bone saw."

Hanson's lack of commitment must have gotten to Porter because he glanced at Chase, then asked: "A garrote?"

30

Hanson nodded. "Maybe. A garrote would make sense."

Hanson removed his mask, immediately popped the unlit stub of the cigar in his mouth and motioned for the assistant to relieve him.

Chase and Porter followed Hanson to an office and waited while he peeled off his gloves and used the sink in the corner of the room. He had a strong fan going. Chase remained standing. Porter took a seat. "That's it?"

Hanson looked at Porter in the mirror above the sink. "No, there's more, but it will take some time to get all the results. I'm estimating the time of death between ten and midnight based on rigor mortis and her stomach contents, but I'd like a more accurate time on her last meal."

Porter nodded his head while he made notes. "What about blood alcohol and drugs?"

Hanson sat behind his desk and started leafing through a folder. "No obvious signs of drugs. I'll get blood back from the lab early tomorrow." He put the folder down and looked up at the two detectives. "I did find semen in the vagina."

To Chase, Porter seemed a little put out by that information. "You mean she was raped?"

"That I don't know. There weren't any lacerations or bruising. I've seen raped bodies and this one doesn't look like it. There's just semen in her vagina."

Porter shifted in the hard wooden chair across from the coroner. "Then she had willing intercourse sometime before she was killed?"

Hanson pulled the cigar out of his mouth. The wet end looked like something Chase used to dig up when he was a kid getting ready to go fishing during his time with his mother in the Low Country when they went on their yearly vacation. "That's my guess. Or she was raped and didn't struggle for some reason—maybe threatened and acquiesced. It'll take some time to get the DNA tests back on the samples."

Porter tapped his pen on his notepad. "Would you say she had sex where she was killed?"

Hanson shook his head. "No. Wherever she had it, she stood up sometime afterwards. She probably had the sex somewhere else. And she was killed somewhere else since there was no blood on the ground, only on her body." He slid a slim folder across the desk. "Here's the initial report that I wrote up on the scene. I'll call you when I get the autopsy results put together. Now, I have some more work to do in

Denver so I have to hit the road." Hanson glanced at Chase. "Does he speak?" he asked Porter.

"When he has something intelligent to say," Porter said, looking at the contents of the folder.

"You have anything intelligent to ask?" Hanson said.

"Nope," Chase said.

"That's intelligent," Hanson said.

Chase followed Porter out. When they got to the car, Porter handed Chase the keys. "All right. There are no explosives along the road, Chase. Don't get squirrelly. Let's go back and brief Donnelly. He's not going to like this one bit. The housewife, CU, the sex. Bad. Bad. Bad."

CHAPTER FOUR

It took about ten minutes for Porter to bring Lieutenant Donnelly up to speed on what had happened so far in the case, which wasn't actually worth more than two minutes in Chase's opinion, but Donnelly was kind of slow and Porter had to repeat himself several times. Chase remained quiet, figuring he was on a roll with one compliment.

Porter's hunch had been right: Donnelly was real upset about the CU-Pine Brook Hills connection. Academe and wealth; that was going to mean a double load of pressure. Reporters from the Daily Camera and a Denver TV station were already flitting around downstairs looking for the story. When Porter mentioned the semen information, Chase could see Donnelly become even more agitated. He took his glasses off and cleaned them nervously. "Oh, God. Not a campus sex-killing."

Chase winced. Sometimes Donnelly drove him right up the wall. The LT shouldn't have been in a profession dealing with death; he didn't have the temperament. Chase always felt that a person had to be a little crazy for this type of work. Chase had been to war in two different countries on the far side of the world and now he was in the streets with a badge in his wallet. He never doubted what the human animal was capable of. He figured that was a plus on his side.

Chase saw Donnelly in his tweed jackets with their suede elbows as one of those people with a center-out view of the world. He had a hard time realizing he wasn't one of the original molds for mankind. Maybe he just wanted people to be better than they were, or maybe he just wasn't as cynical as Chase. Donnelly's four years in civilian college and two decades working in Boulder showed as surely as Chase's time in the army and years in combat.

Chase sensed this was going to be an ugly case, the kind where all involved pondered the future of their career every time there was a downturn. Chase's brief police career wasn't doing too hot anyway so he wasn't that bothered, plus he trusted his partner's abilities as an investigator.

For Chase, the bottom line was that Donnelly was just going to have to accept the facts. Besides, Chase knew he was going to be the shit magnet if things went wrong even though he wasn't saying a word and Porter was lead investigator. That was another unexpected aspect of the FLI program. The locals could blame the Fed in their office, and the Feds could distance themselves from their guy working down in the local trenches. A win-win for everyone but Chase.

Perhaps to justify his existence as boss, Donnelly gave Porter and Chase the benefit of his supposedly hard-earned police wisdom. "Put the heat on the street, men. It was probably someone from the neighborhood where she was found. Maybe some Denver punk joyriding over to CU."

What neighborhood? Chase thought. She was found in open space. Should they interview the wildlife? Roust a squirrel or two? God forbid they hit up a prairie dog. Chase had a bad feeling about this case, beyond his partner's misgivings. Donnelly was looking for the easy way. Chase had already experienced a few bitter lessons about the easy way. He'd learned in the army about Murphy's law. Whatever could get fucked up, would.

Donnelly stood up, effectively ending the meeting, and gave his version of a pep talk. "Men, you've got to wrap this case up quickly."

No shit, Chase thought to himself. *Unlike all the other cases that we dawdle over.* But Porter nodded. "We're working on the car next, Lieutenant. If we could figure out how she was nabbed, and where she was killed, we'd have some clues. So far, all we have is a rich, naked lady, found dead, who had just had sex, whether willingly or not we don't know yet. Not a lot to go on. We're waiting on forensics to give us the complete report from the site and for Hanson's final results." Porter opened the door. "But no problem, lieutenant. We'll get it wrapped up."

Chase slipped out, followed by his partner. "That was pretty upbeat," Chase noted as soon as the door was shut.

Porter led the way to their desks. "It always pays to leave things on a positive note with Donnelly. No need in bursting his bubble prematurely. I've got a feeling we're probably going to be doing that soon enough." He looked at Chase across their desks, which faced each other. "Why do you think it might have been a garrote?"

"I've seen that kind of wound before," Chase said. He started to say more, but paused.

"Go ahead," Porter prompted.

"The cut was clean, which meant it wasn't a butcher job," Chase said. "Most people wouldn't know how to use a garrote correctly."

"There's a correct way?" Porter asked.

"Most people are amateurs, but for the best, killing can be an art form just like everything else."

Porter opened his mouth to say something, then stopped.

Chase stood up and walked around the desks. He pulled his belt off and showed Porter the piece of steel wire that was held on the inside of it by several strands of thread. Two small loops were at either end. "That's a real garrote."

"You carry a garrote inside your belt?" Porter said, staring at him.

"Ever since I went into Special Forces," Chase said. "My first team sergeant showed me how to put this inside a belt. Gets missed on most searches."

"What other hidden weapons do you have on you?"

"Main gun in belt holster, back-up gun in ankle holster, knife in middle of my back, the garrote." Chase said all of this matter-of-factly, because they were just facts to him. He realized that the others in the room were staring at him. "Everyone on my team carried the same," he added, as a sort of explanation. "Anyway, the correct way to use a garrote and not have the person you're killing get a piece of you or get covered in blood, is to use their own weight to kill them. Stand up. Face away."

Porter did as instructed. Chase looped the smooth outside of his belt over Porter's head, then around his neck. "Most people think you loop the wire over the neck and then pull. But what you really do is flip it over the head to the throat, hold tight, then quickly spin yourself back-to-back with the victim, crossing the wire to tighten it initially, and lift them—" Chase spun about, the belt pulling tight and he easily lifted Porter onto his back as he bent forward. He heard Porter gasp.

"If it was a wire instead of a belt, it would have cut through into your neck by now, severing your carotid arteries and your wind pipe." Chase straightened, let go and stepped away. Porter pulled the belt away from his neck, rubbing the skin. "And you'd be on the ground now, dying and I'm clear. No blood spatter on me, no screaming and yelling. Clean kill."

Everyone in the squad room was staring at them.

"What?" Chase asked, staring back.

"Have you—" Porter began, then stopped. He handed Chase the belt. "I'm going over to CU to track down the car. You write up everything we have so far. I'm leaning toward the bone saw and the doctor-husband."

Professor Plum in the library with candlestick. Chase sat at his desk. Briefing the LT had certainly been a waste of time and he had a feeling Porter wasn't too happy with the garrote demonstration. He wanted the easy answer. Hell, Chase thought, Porter could well be right.

So he began typing in everything they'd done into the computer. Porter had decided that Chase could use a computer and let him do their reports while he escaped the office as much as possible. Chase figured it was a fair trade since he didn't contribute much in police experience. So he typed away.

And when he was done with morning reports, Chase began to search through the files for any information on the Patriots. There were a few news reports of brushes with law, all relatively minor stuff and then, of course, the news coverage of the cop-killing two nights ago. Chase had just brought up an article on them in Merck Magazine—for 'mercenaries and professional soldiers' when Porter called with good news. He had found the BMW.

The truth of the matter was that Porter had pushed the right buttons with the people who could find the BMW. After flashing his badge and rubbing elbows with the campus security chief over at CU, a retired Denver metro cop, it had taken them two hours to locate the car in one of the parking areas on campus. Porter was waiting for Chase at the municipal impound lot to open it. He'd already had forensics do an outside run-through at the spot where the car had been prior to towing.

Chase shut down the computer and headed out.

****

Porter had a mechanic from the local BMW dealership standing by when Chase got there. The grease monkey was a guy who enjoyed this aspect of his job: breaking into cars legally. Chase guessed they could have gotten a spare key from the husband, but Porter said he wasn't ready to go back there. Chase tuned out the mechanic's boasting about how he was getting past all the security things the BMW people put on the car to keep the bad guy from getting in.

The door was open in about a minute and a half. Porter shooed the mechanic away. Before they touched anything inside, Porter used the digital camera and took shots as they opened the other doors and trunk. Then they gloved up.

After making sure they had a good set of pictures, Chase slid in the driver's side and looked around. A leather book bag was on the seat on the passenger's side. Chase unsnapped it and looked inside. Two textbooks: "Life Cycle and Human Development" and "The Theory and Practice of Group Psychotherapy." Great, Chase thought, psychobabble.

A large binder was in there also. Chase flipped it open and looked through. Course syllabuses and notes. The book bag in the car was a little confusing to him. Had she been nabbed before or after class? And why hadn't she been carrying it?

Porter came around the car. "Nothing exciting in the trunk. A spare. An umbrella. Doesn't look like a body was transported there. I'll have the lab guy go over it just in case."

The glove compartment yielded meager fare: the owner's manual; vehicle registration; paper napkins; a stub of a pencil; a broken pair of sunglasses.

Chase reached under the driver's seat. Pay dirt. Her purse. What the hell was her purse doing in the car? He wondered. This was even more confusing than the book-bag. Chase opened the clasp. Lying on top was her key ring. He flipped through. A key with the BMW logo. He tried it in the ignition and it worked. Then he got out and tried it on the door. Worked again. He checked with Porter: the car had been locked when they found it. Chase tried the doors. He couldn't lock them without the key. So she must have had a spare with her?

Chase went back to the other contents of the bag. A small jewelry box invited attention. He flipped it open. Her wedding band and engagement ring, big rock glittering, greeted his eyes. Her wallet was in the purse also. Chase looked back over the seat at Porter.

"This is getting weirder."

Porter looked at the rings and then at Chase. "I don't figure any of this. Where did she get grabbed?" His forehead furrowed. Chase sensed a great insight coming from his partner. "She was having an affair.

Using school as a cover. That's why the rings are in here. That's why the good doctor offed her."

Chase pointed at the texts and notebooks. "Good cover. She even took notes." Still, Chase thought, it was an interesting possibility, especially coming from Porter, family man extraordinaire.

His partner frowned. "Well, then, where was she? How'd she get from CU to where we found her? Someone had to have taken her. Most likely the killer."

Or she had taken herself by some means other than the car, Chase speculated. It was about three miles from the campus to the Mount Sanitas Open Space. Chase very much doubted she'd walked at night. If her car was clean, that meant someone else's car or truck.

They went through the rest of the BMW without much luck. She'd simply parked it, locked it with a key, not the one on her key ring and walked away last night. Or the killer had parked it, taken a spare key and left all her stuff. Besides the rings, the purse contained sixty in cash and several credit cards in the wallet.

Porter slammed the doors shut and stared at the car. "This is going to get worse," he pronounced. He glanced at the sun setting over the Flatirons. "Quitting time. I promised Mary I'd be home in time for dinner." He looked over at Chase. "Where you headed? To see Sylvie?"

"I suppose."

"Be careful."

Chase nodded, wondering about the warning.

Porter headed for his car, but paused and looked over his shoulder. "You did the right thing in Wyoming."

* * * * * * * * * * * *

Chase drove north, up Broadway to the edge of town, stopping just before hitting Open Space. The Silver Satyr was about as classy as a place can get for a strip joint outside of a big city. Originally, the building had housed a steak place called the Cleaver and Ale. The new owner had kept the London Pub exterior, but added a neon outline of a woman. She was in profile, hands on hips, head bent back, impossibly pert breasts pointing skyward. The beveled glass windows had been blacked out. It was the only strip club in town and its existence wasn't really acknowledged by the city council. They'd tried to shut it down when it opened a year and a half ago, but the owner, Nicholas Tai, was also a lawyer and he snowed them under with so much paper they'd reluctantly backed off for the time being.

Chase sort of respected Tai for his stand. His theory, eloquently expressed in a letter to the city council reprinted in the Daily Camera, was that if the citizens of Boulder didn't want a strip club, then people wouldn't come in and he'd be out of business in a couple of months. Since that hadn't happened, Tai felt it was the will of the people that the club remain open. That was a tough pill for the city council to swallow and they solved it by ignoring it for the time being and moving on to the more important issues like voting to make Boulder a 'nuclear weapon free zone' and protecting the habitats of prairie dogs from developers.

There was a hand-painted sign offering the daily luncheon special: all you can eat for $7.99. Also on special: twelve succulent women. Pay the cover and a guy could satisfy all the basic male needs in one chair. This early it was mostly empty. Another ten minutes before the dancers started up again for the evening.

Chase ordered a beer from a waitress wearing a short skirt and bikini top and settled in the cheap imitation leather seat, mulling over what he'd learned today. Not much. They could get lucky in the next few days and forensics or pathology would come up with some startling information that would crack the case wide open. Right.

Tai nodded at Chase from his stool at the bar. Tai was a short man, about five foot seven, with a slight build. But he exuded a strong presence, an American-Japanese version of Bruce Lee.

Chase nodded back as he considered the case. He knew Rachel Stevens' murder had probably been on all the 5 o'clock news reports in Denver. The media people in Denver just loved it when something went wrong in the liberal bastion of Boulder. Unless a prairie dog colony was destroyed in the interim, it would be page one in the Camera tomorrow morning.

Chase figured the case was going to cause quite a stir. Her type wasn't supposed to get whacked on the fair streets or fair Open Space. This wasn't an acceptable death for a pretty doctor's wife from Pine Brook Hills. If she had fallen down those circular stairs at her house or gotten breast cancer things would be fine. But Rachel Stevens had represented living the right life, and if someone like that could wind up dead in the wild flowers, no one was safe; or so the thinking would go.

Chase considered that Porter's theory held possibilities: she was trying to have an affair at school and it had gone to crap in a big way. Some people got very emotional about stuff like that and occasionally they snapped. Chase had heard about things like that. The doctor was weird; Chase agreed with Porter on that.

The only other possibility Chase could see right now was that she had just been dumb and unlucky. Chase could almost picture her walking over to a dark van late at night to give someone directions. She was probably like Donnelly, always thinking the best until the shit started piling up around their ankles or in this case their neck. Rachel Stevens had probably never met a really bad person until the night she died.

Chase was draining the last of his first beer when he noticed the music had changed tempo. Looking over to the small stage, he could see the figure of a woman sliding seductively through the curtain that hung at the back of the stage. He ordered another draft and sat back to watch.

She was dressed in a short black leather skirt and a black bustier. She had a whip draped over one shoulder. A thin black leather collar was around her neck. The dancer was good in Chase's somewhat biased opinion. Smart enough to know that the art of stripping was more mental than physical. Her body was perfect for what she did. She had found a niche and perfected it.

The few people in the room came to attention as the cloth fell from her body with choreographed perfection. Chase was beginning to lean forward a little himself, willing the flesh into view. Her red hair was cut in bangs in the front and hung straight down to her shoulders on the sides and back.

To Chase, her face was different. The mouth a little too wide, the nose a little too sharp, but it all fit together to make her very interesting looking in a distinctive way. Most of the patrons were not focusing on her face or hair though, as she removed her corset. Her breasts were perfect, or at least Chase thought so: slightly more than a handful topped with hard nipples. Her hips flared out sensuously to a rear that was firm and full. She certainly knew how to work the music as she got down to her thong. That was the limit. They did have laws in Boulder.

But it was her black eyes that drew the men in the room in. They emitted something, dark and dangerous and tempting. Inviting, but with a flash that said: here there be danger. Of course, the whip she expertly snapped toward the audience also reinforced that warning.

And of course, there was always those who didn't catch obvious warnings and Darwinism hadn't yet taken care of. A burly man seated right next to the stage jerked back as the dancer cracked the tip of the whip less than a foot in front of his face as he leered at her.

"Fucking cunt," he yelled, loud enough to be heard throughout the room.

Chase was moving, and out of the corner of his eye, he could see Tai was also. The owner got there about two seconds before Chase did and that was all it took. Tai grabbed the back of the man's neck, squeezing, and he gasped like a hooked fish. The man sitting next to him jumped to his feet and pulled back his arm to throw a punch.

Chase grabbed the man's forearm, leveraged it with his other hand on the guy's elbow and the man went to his knees, the pain controlling him.

The music was still playing loudly, but the club was perfectly still. Tai leaned close to the man he held and whispered: "She's a lady and don't ever use that word again." Then he headed toward the door, the man firmly in his grasp.

Chase lifted his quarry up and marched him behind the other. Tai shoved the burly man out the front door and Chase did the same with his. Tai looked at Chase, nodded, then headed back in.

As Chase re-entered the club he noted that the dancer was back in her routine as if nothing had happened. When the music ended, she gathered her skirt and corset and slipped on a robe, tucking the whip into a deep pocket. Instead of going backstage, she moved out into the club. As she passed the other patrons their eyes turned to follow her so that by the time she made it over to Chase there was an audience. She stood close enough for Chase to smell her, a combination of perfume, hairspray and exertion. "Hi, Chase. I didn't expect to see you tonight."

Chase leaned back in his chair. "I needed to see you."

Sylvie tugged on the belt for her robe. "Did you like what you saw?"

"I always like it."

"You liked it earlier today?"

"Did you?"

41

Her tongue ran across her lips as she smiled. "Most certainly." Sylvie pulled out a chair and sat down. "Is something up? No pun intended."

"I was just thinking about you."

Sylvie gave him a look he couldn't decipher. "What were you thinking, Chase?"

"I think you have a pretty good idea, Sylvie." He leaned back in the seat. "Got an interesting case this morning."

Sylvie gestured around the bar. "I wish we could talk about it, but I've got to work. We'll talk about it tomorrow. My turn."

Sylvie went backstage. Chase saw that Tai was looking over. He knew Chase was a cop and he knew Sylvie was involved with him. Tai didn't mind having a cop in the place so he tolerated Sylvie talking to Chase occasionally in between acts.

Tai came over. "What's happening, Chase?"

"Not much," he replied. "What's new with you?"

"City council is trying to pass another bill that would make me illegal," Tai said.

"Assholes," Chase said. If the city council would spend as much time and money on the drug problem on the Hill as they did trying to shut Tai down, they'd have the scuzzes cleared out in two days. But naked women apparently were a much bigger issue with them.

Tai shrugged. "I don't mind much. I feel for the city attorney having to sweep up after them all the time. They only support the law here in town when it fits their personal agenda."

Tai was looking at Chase intently and Chase wondered what he wanted.

"How you and Sylvie doing?" Tai finally asked.

"Fine."

"She's a good person, Chase."

"I know that."

"I don't want to see her hurt."

"Hey, Tai, I'm not going to hurt her."

"She hasn't been too happy lately," he said.

"Mine and Sylvie's relationship is our business," he said, a little more harshly than he'd intended.

Tai leaned forward. "No, Chase, it's my business too. Sylvie's my friend."

"Your friend?" Chase said. "She strips for you, Tai. How can she be your friend?"

"She works for me," Tai said, "but she's still my friend. She makes more money here than she could anywhere else in Boulder with her background. She doesn't strip for me. She strips for the jerks, like the assholes we kicked out, who sit in the seats here."

Chase could tell Tai was a little pissed. He was a black belt in several forms of martial arts, which he kept current in, and for a moment, Chase thought he might reach across the table and try to give him the Vulcan death grip. It would be an interesting confrontation, Chase thought, but he knew Sylvie would not be happy.

"Hey." Chase held up his hands. "I'm sorry I got a little angry. I'm a bit stressed out is all. Things are going all right between Sylvie and I."

"She's different," Tai said. He looked into Chase's eyes. "That makes you different. I don't know if that's a good thing or a bad thing." He stood. "I just wanted to let you know that I worry about her."

"All right. You've let me know." Tai walked away and Chase made his way out, a little perplexed by the incident.

****

Chase drove home. He only made one stop on the way, at a convenience store, for Cheetoos and beer. Chase made his way inside, ignoring Astral, and sidestepping the heavy bag. It was dark and empty in his small apartment. The light on the answering machine was flickering. He popped the first beer, put the rest in the fridge, then hit the play button.

"Matt, it's Porter. You have Rachel Stevens' professors at CU tomorrow. Find out what you can about her whereabouts the night of the murder. You've got Professor A. Silver at ten and a Professor T. Gavin at ten-thirty. Then meet me at the hospital for a re-interview with the husband at eleven-thirty in his office."

Chase scribbled the information down. The machine beeped and a second message played.

"Chase. It's me. I think I've been pretty patient. But I need you to sign the paperwork. Bye."

The machine beeped twice. Chase looked at the manila folder on top of the refrigerator. Anne had sent the final divorce papers via overnight FedEx.

Three months ago.

Chase grabbed the beers and turned on the small television to drive away the emptiness. He sat on the make-shift bed, a couple of ragged pillows propped behind his back, and drank out of the can, the rest of the six-pack resting on a footlocker next to the mattress. He paid little attention to the show on the TV, but the murmuring sound of voices was comforting and chased away the demons of an empty night.

After a couple of beers, he grabbed his shirt off the floor and pulled out his father's picture and his mother's letter. Chase unfolded the single piece of paper:

My Dearest Horace.

We are both at war, but I fear I am losing mine. The cancer has spread too quickly.

Fate has dealt you a final card from the father you never knew and the man I hardly knew. Don't be like your father. Don't be too brave. Come back from the war.

I know we haven't spoken in a long time. I know you don't want to hear this. I blame myself for that. But maybe someday you'll think better about me. I hope you will.

Sometimes there are broken people. Like me. Like you. I was trying to do the right thing for you. Now I know I did wrong by giving you your father's legacy. The Medal of Honor and the Academy appointment that came with it and all afterward. But maybe it isn't too late.

Even broken people should get another chance.

Be a good man.

With my dying love,

Your Mother.

PS: In my will, there's a house. An old house. But it's a good house in a good place. It will be yours. It's the house we spent the summers in on Hilton Head in the Low Country. It's from an old friend. He's a good man. You won't understand now and will think the wrong thing because you tend to think the wrong thing first. It's all I can give you now.

Chase read through, then folded the letter and slid it back into the envelope. He put it, and the photo on top of the footlocker.

Around the fourth beer, he was buzzed. His mother's face kept intruding. And Sylvie's. And another face. He pulled the picture of Rachel Stevens out of his pocket and stared at it in the flickering light from the television. He thought about the murder scene and the wound and was bothered in a way he couldn't figure. This was different than combat, which he understood, even though combat was total chaos once the firing started. Finally, he put the picture away. He lay down and stared up at the ceiling.

Chase started sinking into a 'I fucked up' syndrome regarding Anne. He couldn't put his finger exactly on how he had done that, but he knew there were two sides to the seesaw called marriage and when she'd jumped off her end, she must have had some reasons.

He tried to shift his emotions and get pissed. Anger is a good healer of pain. But he just couldn't sustain it. The funny thing was that he had this feeling that Anne wasn't sitting in her new house, with her new fiancée, feeling guilty or bad, even though she certainly had her share of guilt.

She'd taken up with another officer right after the separation. Maybe before, for all Chase knew. She was ready to pick up the officer's wife life with just the slightest speed bump of the divorce. They were stationed back at Fort Bragg and her new man was on the fast track for higher command, something Anne had bemoaned Chase's lack of enthusiasm in pursuing.

Now she had what she wanted and Chase didn't know what he wanted. He wasn't going to contest the divorce even though she'd served him the initial papers while he was getting shot at in Afghanistan. Bad form, his buddies had said, even as several of them got the same thing. But Chase had known it wasn't the separation that caused her to act, it was the fact he was coming back that had forced her hand.

That he came back on a medevac flight after the initial papers were filed had caused her some discomfort and she'd been a trooper, coming to Walter Reed for a visit and holding off on the final paperwork. But her first visit had also been her last. It was not a place most people could stand, the screams of the wounded echoing through the corridors at all times of the day and night, despite the best efforts of the doctors.

Chase still couldn't sleep and wondered if maybe he needed to finish the six-pack, weighing it against the headache tomorrow.

His mind kept slipping back to the letter. It too had arrived while he was in Afghanistan, via the same re-supply chopper as Anne's initial papers, while he was getting ready to lead his team on a long over-land raid north of Kandahar. By the time, the mission was over and he could make a call via satellite back to the States, his mother had died.

Chase grabbed the last couple of brews, putting one against his leg and opening the other. He tuned in an old movie with the sound still turned low. He tried to stop his brain from working and mindlessly let the tube rule. After the last beer, he gave sleep another try and it worked, although he woke up a few times in the night, feeling the emptiness of the apartment and the mattress.

CHAPTER FIVE

Chase woke to the sound of an incessant beeping. He blinked, shook his head and grabbed the red beeper off the footlocker. He pushed the button on top and read the message:

CALL—HAMMER

Chase grabbed his cell phone and punched in #1 on the speed dial. It buzzed twice, the signal going up to a military satellite and then being relayed.

"Hammer."

"This is Snake-Eater."

"There will be a helicopter at the Boulder Hospital helipad in twenty minutes. Get on it."

The phone went dead. Chase looked at his watch. 03:25.

He spun the numbers on a heavy padlock on a large bolt latching shut a closet door. It clicked open and he reached inside pulling out an army-issue green, metal frame rucksack and a six-foot long duffel bag. One over each shoulder, he ran back out to the Jeep, tossing them in the back seat.

Chase drove the eight blocks to Boulder Memorial Hospital and parked next to the helipad on the west side. He'd used up sixteen of his twenty minutes. Ignoring the looks of an EMT walking by, he stood in the parking lot and stripped off his slacks and shirt, pulling on black fatigue pants and shirt that he took out of the duffel bag. He slipped on a body armor vest, then an equipment harness, strapping a 10mm Glock pistol in a holster around his waist and then a snap around his upper left thigh to keep it from flopping about. He slid a knife into his left boot to back-up the double-edged dagger on the vest.

Nineteen minutes. He could hear the chopper inbound. One thing about Fortin; he was anal about time schedules. Chase popped a handful of mints in his mouth.

The National Guard Huey touched down fifteen seconds before the twenty minutes that Fortin had promised. Chase tossed the duffel and ruck on board and climbed in. He slid the door shut behind him, but the bird didn't take off.

There was only one other person seated in the cargo bay: Fortin. A tall, solidly built man in black fatigues, his background was a bit of a mystery to the members on the team, although the consensus was it most likely covert ops in the CIA or the DEA, one of the alphabet soups, but not military. Fortin had darkly tanned skin and a shock of thick blonde hair that he was prone to run his fingers through as he thought.

He pointed at the seat directly across and Chase took it. He glanced forward and saw the pilot turn and nod and Chase nodded in turn. The pilot had a flight helmet with a bull's eye painted on each side. His name was John Masters and he was on call just like Chase. Masters worked out of Jeffco airport just outside of Boulder and he would give Chase a ring whenever he had to take a maintenance or training flight. Masters had started the bull's-eye motif because that's what he said it felt like flying around Iraq. And if he was hit, he wanted to go fast. Chase thought he did it more as a taunt.

The adrenaline overlapped the alcohol in Chase's system. The sound of the turbine engines, the blades whopping overhead, the smell of JP-4 fuel being burned, the vibration of the helicopter, this was a world removed from the desk he'd been sitting at a few hours earlier. Chase was ready to get back in action.

Fortin pointed at a headset and Chase put it on.

"I don't have much time," Fortin said. "I didn't take a debriefing from you because I was in the field with the rest of the team. Trying to correct your fuck-up."

Chase had been kicked out of the Forward Operating Base two days earlier after getting picked up by chopper and reporting his failure to take the shots. Fortin had called in that order.

"I didn't fuck up."

"You didn't shoot."

Chase stared at Fortin. "I didn't shoot for two reasons."

"I'm waiting."

"One. I would have had to take out the man on the M-60 first. And as far as I know, he hadn't killed a cop. Two. There was another sniper out there. Across from me. Mirroring."

"'Mirroring'?"

"Covering me as I covered the kill zone."

"How do you know this?"

Chase explained the trail and flash of light. Fortin appeared unimpressed. "Bullshit," was his succinct summary.

Chase fought back his anger, wondering why they weren't taking off and heading to the FOB in Wyoming.

"Next time," Fortin said, "if there is a next time—you shoot when I tell you to." Fortin pointed at the door. "Take your gear and get off."

****

Later that morning Chase drove around for ten minutes before he found a parking place. It was unusually hot with the sun blazing down. The CU campus was crowded and alive with that excitement that Chase had missed out on when he went to West Point instead of a real college. For the students at CU, finals were just around the corner and then the freedom of summer. At Hudson High, as the cadets at West Point had lovingly called the Academy, summer had meant military training.

The CU campus was just south of downtown, stretching from Broadway on the "Hill", east to Route 36. The Hill was well known to all the cops in Boulder because it was the hub for the drug trade in town. And Boulder had a lot of drugs. Heroin, marijuana and LSD were the big three.

There wasn't even a space on campus for Chase to use his police sticker on the visor. He was reduced to waiting for someone to leave, which following his ruminations on the drugs, on top of his hangover and the meeting on the helipad, didn't do much for his mood. He checked his watch. It was going to be a close call for his first appointment, Professor A. Silver, Rachel's instructor for her Thursday night course: Life Cycle and Human Development. To Chase, it sounded dull, like there was a formula or a rulebook a person could follow.

The A. turned out to stand for Alice, and she was none too pleased to see Chase, his being a little late and interrupting her academic day. By that time he didn't have much patience either and when she started one of those 'I'm so busy and it's so inconvenient to talk to the police' routines, he had to rein in tight. He gave her a few more minutes as she landed her ivory tower superiority by ignoring him and fussing with papers on her desk.

Chase used the time to check her out. Cold, a real cold woman. She reminded Chase of one of the nuns he'd had in grade school. The one who wore crepe-soled shoes to ensure the smack of the ruler was unexpected and therefore worse.

Professor A. Silver wasn't much help. When he finally got her on task, she told Chase that Rachel Stevens had been a perfect student. Her work was excellent and she had never missed a class. So much for Porter's affair theory so far. The professor couldn't think of anyone whom Rachel had been close to in the class, but she did give Chase a copy of the class-seating chart. After some prodding, she also gave Chase the class directory, saving him some time on the phone numbers. It was a homicide investigation after all; he was forced to remind her.

The next professor was in the same building. Same floor. When Chase knocked on the door to T. Gavin's office, he was prepared for anything. A short, bespectacled man sporting a beard answered.

"Detective Chase, I presume."

He'd stolen Chase's line. "Yes."

"Come in. Come in." He stuck his hand out after shutting the door. "Tim Gavin. Have a seat."

The professor cleared off a chair in front of his desk, throwing Xeroxed magazine articles onto the floor. The office was a jumble of paper and books. Chase hoped the professor's mind was more organized.

Chase sat down and pulled out his notebook, but Gavin beat Chase to the punch again.

"Your partner said on the phone that you wanted to talk about Rachel Stevens." He thumbed through a stack of papers and pulled out a couple of sheets. "Here's her grade sheet and the personal bio she filled out when we started the course."

Chase took a look. Rachel seemed to have been school smart. All A's so far in Gavin's course: The Theory of Psychotherapy. The bio sheet gave Chase some basic background data. Chase was immediately struck by one thing: Rachel didn't list any family on the sheet. In fact, there was very little there other than the fact she had a bachelors in psychology from the University of Nebraska and a post office box number in the school mailroom. Nothing on her personal life at all.

"It's terrible what happened to Rachel. She was a very nice person."

Chase held back a sigh. Porter had told him that people always said that during a murder investigation. Chase figured that when Genghis Khan or Vlad the Impaler had croaked way back when, there had to have been someone standing around saying what a nice guys they'd been. In this case, though, it seemed to apply. He was waiting for the inevitable: "Do you have any idea who could do such a terrible thing?" but it didn't come.

Gavin was leaning back in his seat watching Chase. That made him feel uncomfortable. He also hadn't had a chance to take any initiative so far. Chase had to remind himself that he was dealing with a psychologist here. They were used to controlling meetings.

"Do you have a list of all the students in your Wednesday night class? Preferably one with addresses and phone numbers?"

Another ruffle of papers and another sheet handed to Chase. Gavin was certainly being more cooperative than A. Silver had been.

"Did Rachel Stevens attend class this past Wednesday night?"

"No."

"She didn't show up at all?"

"No."

"Was that unusual?"

"I hadn't really thought about it. Students often cut class."

"Did Rachel often cut?"

"I don't recall."

Chase waited. "Could you check?" He finally asked.

Gavin pulled out a computer sheet and folded it open. He ran his finger down a page. "Let's see. Rachel had been absent, hmm, five times; that's if we include this past Wednesday."

"Could I have those dates please?"

"Certainly. The 29th of January. The 19th of February. The 11th of March. The 1st of April. And this past Wednesday."

There was something about those dates that struck Chase. "Do you have a calendar?"

Gavin looked briefly flustered. Chase had finally asked a question he wasn't prepared for. He opened a few drawers and finally produced a calendar. Chase checked the dates he'd given Chase.

"There's a pattern isn't there?" Gavin observed from across the desk.

"Every third Wednesday. Maybe she had some other commitment."

Gavin nodded. "Most likely. You're a very observant man about details aren't you detective?"

Chase answered, while he tried to figure if there was anything else he needed here or that Porter would want to know. "I try to be. Was there anyone in the class that Mrs. Stevens was particularly close to or talked with?"

Gavin frowned as he thought. "No. Not really. Hard to say, truthfully."

"Do you have a seating chart for your class?"

"Yes."

"Could I have it?"

He pulled out another piece of paper.

Chase accepted it without comment.

Gavin was stroking his beard. "You know it's interesting that you say 'Mrs. Stevens.' I never knew Rachel was married. In fact she never even hinted at it."

"She didn't wear her wedding band or engagement ring to class?"

"No. How did you know that?"

Chase didn't like being asked questions. "Did she say anything about her life outside of school?"

Gavin frowned as he thought. "Not really, now that I think about it. It's funny because I had this impression of her, but now it appears I was all wrong."

"What kind of impression?"

Gavin looked slightly embarrassed. Chase figured it was hard for a psychologist to admit they didn't really know someone. "Well, it's odd, she never really said anything concrete but she acted in a way that made you think things."

Chase wished this guy would get a bit more specific. "Think what things?"

"Well, first off that she wasn't married. It wasn't just not wearing her rings. She didn't act married. Most people, especially women, act a certain way when they're married. They are no longer individuals, but half of a twosome and even when they are by themselves you can tell that there is someone out there with power over their lives that they are constantly filtering their thoughts and actions through."

Chase hadn't observed Anne doing much filtering during their marriage. Of course, he'd been deployed eighty percent of the time so he might have missed some things. "What other impressions did you have of her?"

"She was smart and determined. I pictured her as a divorced woman working as a secretary or something like that during the day and knocking out this degree at night to improve her lot in life. Did you know that she only had one more semester, her internship this summer, and then she'd have her degree?"

"No." Chase wondered why an upscale housewife from Pine Brook Hills would do all the work for this degree. Bored, probably. Chase realized this professor certainly had noticed a lot more about Rachel Stevens than A. Silver had. It was interesting that he'd noted she wasn't wearing any rings, but couldn't recollect that she'd missed class. Chase knew one thing about his gender; men noticed women like Rachel Stevens. They kept track of her on their testosterone radar on the naive off chance that she might rip off her clothes and threw herself into their arms just like on one of those late night Showtime soft-core porn flicks.

Chase knew he had to check out Gavin. After all, he'd been in the right place at the right time and he knew the victim. "What time did you let your class out on Wednesday?"

"Right at ten."

"What did you do after class?"

Gavin blinked. "I talked with a student about her thesis for about ten or fifteen minutes and then went home to my wife."

"Could I have the name of the student you talked to?"

"Patricia Albright." Gavin gave a short laugh. "Does this line of questioning mean I'm a suspect in a murder investigation?"

Chase wanted to say 'you and the rest of the male population of Boulder and Denver', but he held it in. "No. I just have to get all these little facts. Sometimes when you put enough of them together you come up with a totally different picture." *Sounded good,* Chase thought. He vaguely remembered hearing something like it on a Law & Order episode.

Gavin suddenly leaned forward. "I'm interested in something Detective Chase. Which is more important to you when you work a case? The facts or the personalities involved?"

53

Gavin wasn't sure what the doctor was getting at and he really didn't have the time. "Thanks for your help, Professor Gavin. If I need anything else I'll give you a call."

Gavin was graceful about the lack of answer and saw Chase out of his office. The question Chase needed an answer to was where had Rachel Stevens been when she wasn't in class on Wednesday nights.

* * * * * * * * * * * * *

Chase hoped his next stop might yield a partial answer. Doctor Jeffrey Stevens had his office in a modern building adjacent to the Boulder Community Hospital on Broadway, right across from Moe's Bagels, which Chase viewed as convenient.

Porter was waiting in the parking lot. "How'd CU go?"

Chase briefed his partner on both professors. Porter focused in right away on the cycle of absences. "She might have been up to something."

"Maybe," Chase allowed.

"Let's see what the husband has to say," Porter said, leading the way into the building.

As the secretary ushered them into the doctor's office, Chase's first thought was why was the doctor working only two days after his wife's death? Chase's second was where did he find such a good-looking secretary? She looked like a swimsuit model, lush body and vacuous eyes. Show, not substance, was Chase's take on her.

The doctor still looked ragged. Chase hoped he didn't have any surgery scheduled later in the day. He waved the detectives into seats and slumped behind his desk.

"I'm not really up to working, but I couldn't just shut everything down so quickly. I have no partners so there's no one to pick up the slack and cover for me."

He'd answered Chase's first unasked question right off. Chase didn't know if that was good or bad. Chase didn't think he'd take on the second. His focus was on the portrait hanging behind the doctor. Rachel Stevens had been a beautiful woman. But it was her eyes that drew his attention. The photographer had been good and caught something; a darkness and a depth in them that reached out to Chase. There was substance there.

Apparently, he was the only one affected as Porter pulled out his notepad. "There are some things I need to clear up that might help us in this case."

Stevens sighed and leaned back in his chair. "Go ahead."

Porter asked some background stuff about Rachel's life in Pine Brook Hills and at home to get things started. Then he narrowed in. "What time did Rachel leave Wednesday night to go to school?"

Stevens shrugged. "I assume around six. I wasn't there. I didn't get home until almost eight."

Porter continued. "Did Rachel ever talk about anyone from school? Any of her classmates or her teachers?"

"No."

Chase wondered if the two of them had ever really talked given his own experience with marriage.

"Why was she in school?" Porter asked.

Stevens seemed puzzled. "To get her masters."

"But for what?" Porter pressed. "Was she going to get a job?"

"Well, I'm not sure," Stevens said. "Rachel said she wanted to go back a couple of years ago and it seemed like a good idea."

"Why'd she go to night school and not during the day?" Porter said.

"I assume because she had too many social obligations during the day. You know, garden club, museum guild, things like that."

Actually, Chase really didn't know and he had a feeling Porter didn't either. Chase had no idea what Pine Brook Hills housewives filled their days with.

Porter glanced down at his notepad. "Did you have any indication that Rachel might not have gone to class this past Wednesday night?"

Stevens looked confused. "What do you mean?"

Porter spoke evenly. "I mean was there any place else she could have been going?"

"Not that I know of. You found her car at school didn't you?"

"Yes," Porter said. "It's just that she wasn't in class that night."

"Maybe she was attacked before she got to class."

Porter glanced at Chase and gave a slight nod.

Chase spoke up. "Can you remember if she missed any other classes on Wednesday night? Maybe a meeting she had to attend or something?"

Stevens shook his head vigorously. "No. She never missed a class. Rachel was very dedicated about getting her degree. School was very important to her."

Chase pressed. "Can you think of any place that she might have been going to or anyone else that she might have been seeing on Wednesday evenings?"

"No." Despite being tired Stevens was no fool. "Are you suggesting that Rachel wasn't going to class on Wednesday nights?"

"According to her professor," Chase said, "she was absent four nights since the semester started, five including this past one."

Stevens frowned. "But I don't understand. Where was she? As far as I can remember she left the house every single night she had class."

Porter jumped in. "I know this is difficult, Doctor Stevens, but we have to check out every possibility. Is there the slightest suspicion in your mind that your wife might have been having an affair?"

Stevens blinked, looked angry for a second and then slumped back in his chair. "No."

Most people would have amplified that a little, Chase thought. "Are you sure?" he asked, earning a sharp glance from Porter.

"I'm sure, Detective." There was an edge to his voice that told Chase the doctor wasn't going to give too many more answers today.

Porter cleared his throat. "Did you and your wife have sex the night she was killed?"

"You mean before she left for school?"

"Yes."

"No. I told you I didn't get home until eight." Stevens paused as it sunk in. "Are you saying she was raped?"

Porter backpedaled a bit. "No, that's not what I'm saying. All we know is that she had sex sometime that afternoon or evening. We aren't sure whether it was consensual or not."

Doctor Stevens' already fragile world had suffered another blow. Porter pressed the doctor with more questions, but got nothing new. They finally departed, leaving Stevens in his office. Chase had a feeling the doctor was about to cry as they shut the door.

The secretary was eyeing the detectives warily as they walked out. She was indeed all image, Chase thought. Young and with a compact body underneath her tight dress. The type of woman that made construction workers drop their lunch boxes when she sauntered by. Chase wondered if Stevens had a thing with her. Maybe that was why he didn't get home until eight at night. Chase also wondered how Rachel Stevens had felt knowing her husband had this woman hanging around all day. Chase couldn't see why anyone would trade Rachel for the secretary, but he'd watched a few of those late night Showtime flicks and men could be incredibly stupid when their genitals were involved if there was only a small percentage of truth in them.

Porter's initial questions had gotten them a name from the doctor. Rachel's best friend.

"Can I use your phone?" Chase asked.

The secretary, Lisa Plunkett, the nameplate on the desk proclaimed, pointed. "Use line two please."

"Do you have a phone book?" Chase asked.

She slid that across. The doctor was still in his office. Chase could tell Lisa was probably wondering what they had done to him as she didn't exactly have a poker face. There were twenty-three Watkins listed, Chase saw. Luckily, both names were listed: Peter and Linda. How cute, Chase thought. Peter was also listed as the manager of Country Classic Motors in Denver. That explained their living in Pine Brook Hills.

The person who answered had a Hispanic accent. "Watkins residence."

"May I speak with Mrs. Watkins, please? This is Detective Chase, Boulder Police."

"One moment, sir."

Porter was chatting with the secretary while Chase was on the line. Chase had already noted she didn't have a ring on her left hand, but she did have some expensive looking jewelry dangling here and there. Pretty good on a secretary's pay.

"This is Mrs. Watkins." The voice also had an accent, but Chase couldn't quite place it.

"Mrs. Watkins, this is Detective Chase from the Boulder Police. I'm investigating the death of Mrs. Rachel Stevens and I need to stop by and talk to you sometime today."

"Today's a rather bad day." There was a pause, which Chase let ride. He heard her sigh as she realized he wasn't going to let her squirm out. "How about one-thirty at the Boulder country club? By the tennis courts."

Not what Chase had in mind but he'd take it. "I'll see you there at one-thirty." He hung up and nodded toward the door.

As soon as they were outside, he looked at Porter. "It doesn't seem like Rachel's death has devastated the woman her husband claims is her best friend. She wants to meet us at the Boulder Country Club by the tennis courts at one-thirty."

Porter raised an eyebrow. "Well, women usually confide in their best friends. If Rachel had been having an affair, the odds are good that Linda Watkins will know about it. Even if it wasn't an affair, Watkins should have a good idea where Rachel had spent those missing evenings."

Chase checked his watch. It was lunchtime. "I'm supposed to meet Sylvie for lunch."

Porter smiled. "Lunch. Right. Tell you what. You do lunch with Sylvie, and then take the interview at the country club with Watkins. I want to check Doctor Stevens' background and finances. I'll see you back at the office later."

"Trusting me to do more interviews on my own?"

"It's the country club," Porter said. "Just don't shoot anyone."

CHAPTER SIX

Chase walked up the stairs to the third floor trying to put aside all that had happened since his red beeper went off early in the morning. Sylvie answered the door in her terry cloth robe. That was a good sign.

She pulled Chase into the apartment with both hands and then wrapped him in a tight embrace. He looked around over her shoulder at the apartment and noticed once more how neat her place was compared to his. There was lots of wicker and plants. The colors were bright and the windows, curtains wide open this time, were big and clean, ensuring plenty of light. Made his apartment look like the dungeon it was.

She didn't say anything, guiding him over to a large stuffed chair that faced the windows and pushing him down into it. She knelt in front of him, spreading his legs as her hands slid up his thighs.

He was already hard by the time her hands reached his cock.

She unbuckled and unzipped his pants. Her hand slid inside his shorts and he shivered as he felt the contact of her skin. She leaned forward and kissed the bulge, then grabbed pants and shorts at the hips and pulled as Chase lifted himself slightly out of the chair. She shoved both garments around his ankles, kneeling on top of them now, pinning him in place.

One hand cradled his balls while she shoved his chest with the other, pushing him back deeply into the chair. Then that hand slid down, over his stomach, curling around his cock as her tongue worked up from the base. She pulled him into her mouth.

She worked the one hand deliberately slightly out of synch with her mouth while she extended two fingers from the hands caressing his balls and pressed between his legs. Chase gasped. He could feel all the tension of the last few days shifting from frustration to sexual urgency.

He looked down.

She was looking up at him, lips tight around his cock, still working it.

He locked into her gaze.

Her eyes never wavered even as she continued, several distinct movements, any one of which by itself might have sent him over the edge.

He came and she didn't stop, working him as he spasmmed, continuing until he stopped shuddering. She slowed to a halt as he did, unwrapping her hand. She kept her mouth on his cock, perfectly still, still locked into his eyes, for almost a minute.

Then she slowly lifted her head.

She smiled. "You're such a bad boy." She stood, leaned over and kissed him.

Chase got to his feet, pulling his shorts and pants up. He was trying to get his breathing back under control.

Sylvie turned for the kitchen. She glanced over her shoulder on the way. "How's it going, Chase?"

"Not bad." He still felt a little shaky, but the tension was gone. For a little while at least.

"I read in the paper that you're working that CU murder."

"It's a weird one." He checked out the stove as he followed her into the kitchen. Nothing cooking.

"There's cold cuts in the fridge." Sylvie went to the sink and washed her hands. Then she started slicing up a loaf of French bread. "I figured we'd have subs."

"Sounds good. Donnelly's already sweating bullets. He always does any time a case makes the news."

"The papers are hinting about some sort of ritualistic killing."

That's one thing Chase hated about the media. If they didn't have, anything they made it up and quoted some 'unnamed source.' "Nothing ritualistic about getting your throat cut. The one thing the press hasn't gotten a hold of is that the coroner found semen in her vagina." Chase unwrapped the meats and cheeses.

Sylvie stopped cutting and looked at Chase. "She was raped?"

He peeled a slice of ham off. "I don't know."

"How can you not know?"

"Last I checked, women can get semen in the vagina by means other than rape."

"No shit, Sherlock."

He ignored the comment. "There's no sign of a struggle so we don't know if it was rape."

Sylvie put the subs Chase had made on plates and carried both over to the couch. She curled up on one end while he laid claim to the middle.

"Any ideas?"

"About what?" Chase was peering at the part in her robe over his sub.

Sylvie rolled her eyes. "The case."

"No. I don't know. Some. We have to kind of sort it out. This is my first murder case," he reminded her. Chase shrugged. "Donnelly thinks some punk off the street did it and she was just a random choice."

"What does Porter think?"

"Porter thinks that the woman, Rachel Stevens was her name by the way, was having an affair and was screwing the wrong guy and her husband found out and didn't take it too well."

"Do *you* think he did?"

"Nope. But Porter's going to check him out hard anyway. And he's got the experience."

"Why does Porter think she was having an affair?"

Chase went through all the stuff about the cut classes and what had been found in the car. Sylvie listened without comment. She sat still for a few minutes while he caught up and began finishing off his sandwich.

Finally, she rendered her verdict. "Sounds to me like she may have been having an affair and Porter might be right." Sylvie caught him off guard with her next comment. "Why'd you come to the club yesterday, Chase?"

"I don't know," he said, sandwich halfway to his mouth. "Rough day at work like I told you."

"Did it ever occur to you that being there at the start of the evening could make it a rough night for me? You're not yourself when you're there. You send off a strange vibe. I could have handled that idiot, but it turned into a cluster-fuck."

Why was she getting so irritable all of a sudden? Chase wondered. Which reminded him of Tai's confrontation afterward. "What's with Tai anyway?"

"What do you mean?"

"He came over to me last night and wanted to know how we were doing," Chase said.

"Tai's my friend," she said. "He's concerned."

"Why's he concerned?" Chase asked. "You say something to him that I should know?"

"No, Chase. He's concerned because he's my friend. That's the way friends are." She changed the subject. "Where are you headed now? Back to the office?"

"No, the Boulder Country Club."

"Moving up in the world?"

"Doubtful."

****

The country club was in Gun barrel, a subdivision along Diagonal Highway, opposite the big IBM plant. Gun barrel was halfway between Boulder and Longmont. The houses that surrounded the golf course were expensive. Chase figured they were for the rich who didn't want to drive up to Pine Brook Hills in the mountains. Since Gun barrel was northeast of Boulder, it also had the advantage of a better view of the foothills and the mountains behind them. Longs Peak dominated the western horizon, rising over fourteen thousand feet.

Driving through the streets of Gun barrel to the country club put a new slant on Chase's lunch with Sylvie. The houses were older mansions nestled on their half-acre of prime real estate. Chase guessed that all these people had been urologists in the sixties. The Stevens were obviously new money: they'd had to build their own mansion, although from the looks of things the basic style of wealth never changes.

Chase doubted if any of the women safely ensconced in these houses were as exciting as Sylvie, and that made him feel a little better about his own situation. Of course, that thought was followed quickly by the one reminding him that their husbands probably had ample opportunity and resources to find excitement elsewhere. That's why they invented golfing trips, or so he had been told.

The valet looked Chase over and started to ask him one of those membership questions. Kind of like he shouldn't be using asphalt time if he hadn't paid the freight. Chase just didn't understand rich people. It was almost like they went out of their way to pile even more rules on themselves. Then he got an idea; maybe they needed to pay extra for worthless rules because they so regularly ignored the ones that counted. Chase pulled his badge and tossed the guy the keys.

The place was full of what Chase considered poodle women. They only looked great because someone else was brushing their hair and painting their toenails. Sleek and expensive looking, but drop one on a desert island long enough for the cosmetics to wear off and there's bad news coming.

They were all noticing Chase, that was for sure, and just as he was beginning to feel like a manly man, he discerned that the looks they were shooting him were closer to the ones reserved for plumbers and such. He was also beginning to realize why Porter had let him do this on his own—his partner was not dumb.

A waiter pointed Mrs. Watkins out to Chase. She was sitting alone at a shaded table by the courts. Her face was hidden by a huge pair of sunglasses that probably cost more than his watch. She was tall and slim. Chase guess she poured a lot of time and energy into herself. She reminded him of the cons who went to prison and, not having anything better to do, fell headlong into a body building narcissism.

The blond had been expertly applied to the brown hair, which was pulled back from her face giving her a more youthful appearance. Her hands were the only part that gave her away. They were the hands of a woman who had been potty trained during Kennedy's term. Chase didn't understood why cosmetic surgeons didn't focus more on simple things like that, instead of trying to overhaul someone's whole face. Rachel must have had a good fifteen or twenty years on her in the youthful direction. Chase wondered how that affected their relationship.

Chase took the seat she offered him and waited while she told some guy in a white coat to get him an iced tea. He would have preferred a beer, but hell, he had an image too. She looked him over for a while and Chase could tell she was pleased. It kind of gave him the creeps. He guess she figured a detective was supposed to look less fit. Once she had apparently decided his presence wasn't too distracting, he went to work. He explained why he was there and waited.

She finally had the decency to pull the shades away from her eyes. They were deep brown. "I'm somewhat surprised that you would come to see me, detective."

No, I love hanging around the leisurely idle, Chase thought to himself. "Why?"

"For one reason, I'm surprised that Jeffrey would give you my name, and most importantly, I was not Rachel's best friend." She took a sip of her drink and watched Chase swirl the ice in his.

He couldn't decide which statement intrigued him more, she was pretty adamant about both. "Did he give me the wrong name?"

She shook her head. "I'm just saying I didn't consider myself Rachel's best friend. At most, I would say we were good acquaintances. We saw each other at some of the same places, we played some tennis, sometimes golf; but there were usually other people there. They knew her as well as I."

Chase was a little puzzled. "So you don't consider yourself a friend she could have confided in?"

She shot Chase a no-shit look. "That's exactly what I'm saying. Rachel Stevens and I never spoke privately about anything."

Chase shifted in his seat, giving his body the chance to squirm so his brain wouldn't since the sun was hitting him dead on. He noticed some man at the poolside bar watching them. Big guy, thick white hair combed straight back, wearing wrap-around shades. "Do you know who her best friend was?"

Linda Watkins let loose a sarcastic little laugh. "What makes you so sure she had a best friend? And even if she did, what are you hoping to find out? Look around detective. Do any of these women look like the type to confide their innermost secrets to another woman? What do you think a shrink is for?"

Score one for the tennis queen, Chase thought. Properly chastised, he had to admit to himself that it would probably be tough to find someone giving and caring enough to listen in this crowd. "Thank you for setting me straight, Mrs. Watkins. How about you just tell me what you do know about Rachel Stevens."

She started to sputter that what she knew wouldn't be of help. With his best Joe Friday voice, Chase told her to let him be the judge of that.

Finally figuring out that he wasn't leaving until he got something, no matter how small, out of her, Linda Watkins thought for a little bit, playing with her glass and watching the courts, but Chase sensed she was also making sure the guy at the bar was still there. Chase spent the time trying to figure out her accent. English wasn't her first language

64

that he could tell, having traveled to a lot of places around the globe. He sensed a European finishing school, but before that, he had no idea. Finally, she turned back to him.

"Rachel was different. She didn't seem to fit in with everyone, but then she didn't seem to care. People can tell when you're not very interested in them and that's the way it was with Rachel. She wasn't interested in the women at the club. I always felt she was putting in time whenever she was at a meeting or a luncheon."

Chase was watching the guy at the bar. He was more than interested in the two of them. And he had that look, which Chase recognized. Former military or police.

Linda Watkins continued. "If I give her the benefit of the doubt, which I suppose I should since she met with such a dreadful end, I would say she was smart, much smarter than the rest of the women here. The fact that she was going to school meant to me that she wasn't satisfied with the unexamined life. If I had to describe her, it would be as a woman who always wanted more. Maybe she found it."

Chase was a little surprised at that last statement. "You knew she was going to school. Did she tell you that?"

"Everybody knew that. It was quite a topic when she first went. Made the others look bad, you know. Rachel was quite a threat to some women. She had courage, not something many women have a tendency to admire in each other. At least not around here."

"So you would say Rachel wasn't happy with her current life?"

"My dear, show me someone who's happy with their life and I'll show you someone too dumb to realize there's more. Wanting something, more is a fact of human nature. The lucky ones just know what that something is and go for it. The rest live lives of quiet desperation as someone quotable once said."

She stretched her arms over her head showing Chase a sliver of tanned midriff. He wondered if Sylvie was going to hold up this well. He looked for a moment too long and got the feeling Linda was storing that for future reference and decided it was time to go. "One last thing. How would you describe her relationship with her husband?"

She dropped her arms and started to laugh, "Darling, you are just too cute. Her relationship with Jeffrey was just like everybody else's: profitable. Now why don't you be a good boy, and go back to the real world where people do bad things for bad reasons."

Chase didn't like being dismissed. "Do you think Rachel might have been having an affair?"

Linda put her sunglasses back on. "I just told you she was smart. So that means she would have been discreet." Linda pursed her lips. "I'm going to stick my neck out and say Rachel didn't seem like she needed an affair. Like I said, she had a mind of her own and I bet she would have considered an affair emotional garbage. She might have had some sort of plan, but I don't think it was centered around a man. It was centered around herself."

Chase longed for people who knew the meaning of yes and no. "Do you have any idea what this plan might have been?"

"Really, Detective!" Linda stood up and collected her racquet. "What Rachel Stevens did or didn't do, or whatever her plan was, I have no earthly idea. She did play a mean game of tennis, though. I will miss that."

Chase was tired. This well had been pumped dry and he was tired of the abuse. Rachel Stevens was becoming more of an enigma and he'd hated those ever since one of his army commanders had used it years ago on one of his efficiency reports.

"Who's the guy?" Chase abruptly asked.

"'The guy'?" Watkins blinked at him.

"The man at the pool bar who's been watching us."

"My husband," Watkins said. "Now, are we done?"

Chase's departure was swift, but he knew it was going to take a while for the irritation of the afternoon to wash away.

****

It felt comfortable to get back to the office at least. Everybody there was miserable, but at least they had good reason: they had to work for a living.

Chase had a few hours to kill before the end of the day. Porter wasn't in. There was one of those post-it's on the desk from his partner. He was out nosing around. Porter never stayed at his desk if he could help it. He figured if he poked his nose in enough crannies that sooner or later he'd find something. From what Chase had seen so far and by reputation, Porter had a good track record.

Chase checked his cell phone, even though he knew it hadn't received a call. There'd been no news from Fortin regarding the situation in Wyoming. Chase didn't know where he stood with the Team. And he didn't know what to do about it. So he focused on his job here for the time being.

Chase got organized. Contrary to what he'd seen in the movies or on TV, he'd learned that being a detective required a lot of organizational skills. That's one trait of Rachel's that he respected. Chase spent the next thirty minutes labeling manila folders and filing away all the little pieces of paper the case had accumulated so far along with all his notes. He put the folders in separate pockets inside a large accordion envelope. On the front, he used a big black magic marker to label the whole thing: Rachel.

Porter liked to joke that the accordion envelopes were Chase's books. He'd call this one The Book of Rachel. Porter joked about it, but he also thought the books were a good idea: every detective had to have a system and he supported Chase doing it his own way. Porter had his little notepads and his brain and his years of experience.

Chase stared at the Book of Rachel on his desk, letting his thoughts swirl for a while, reading the headings on the file folders. He pulled out the one-labeled Gavin-CU.

Rachel had sat in the first row, left side. Chase checked out the names on either side of Rachel. Sue Pollis and Jim York. He cross-referenced with the class roster and punched in Sue Pollis's number.

No answer.

He tried York's next. A machine. He left his name and office number and requested a call back.

Just for the hell of it, Chase called four other members of the class; the next closest four to Rachel on the seating chart. One more machine on which he left the same message, two no answers and one answer.

The student was most uninformative. She hadn't even known that someone in her class had been murdered.

He shoved the folder back in the book. Chase called Hanson's office to see if the final autopsy report was completed. He was told it would be done Monday. Another good reason not to work weekends. No one else did.

Chase called forensics. Right now, they had zip on the murder scene. No prints, no tire tracks, no nothing. Their report would also be done Monday. Right.

It had been a frustrating day. Chase was looking forward to spending tomorrow afternoon with Sylvie before she went to work. She'd told Chase to meet her at Chautauqua Park at noon.

Chase pulled out the folder marked Silver-CU and the Gavin one again. He cross-referenced the list of students. Three were the same, including Rachel Stevens. Chase called the other two: Susie Lynch and JoBeth Sullivan.

Susie answered on the first ring.

"Hello?"

"Ms. Lynch this is Detective Chase. I'm with Boulder Police. I need to ask you some questions regarding a classmate of yours at CU: Mrs. Rachel Stevens."

"Poor Rachel. It was terrible seeing that about her on the news yesterday. It's getting so you can't feel safe anywhere anymore."

So what else was new? Chase thought. Boulder was ten times safer than New York yet that didn't matter to those who lived here. "Yes, Ma'am. You took two classes with Rachel didn't you?"

Chase went through the routine. He wasn't sure what he was looking for. Rachel Stevens was turning into more and more of a puzzle. Nobody knew her. Not even her husband. Susie Lynch certainly didn't. The fact that Rachel had been a good student had already been impressed upon Chase.

Susie Lynch couldn't really give Chase anything worthwhile. She also hadn't known Rachel was married. Her impression had been that Rachel worked the day shift in a hospital. She couldn't quite say how she had gotten that idea. She couldn't give Chase names of anyone that might have had more than a normal interest in Rachel. A waste of ten minutes.

JoBeth Sullivan wasn't home. Where the hell was everyone at 5:00 on a Friday? Chase wondered. Well, he knew where he was going to be. It was Miller time. Just as he grabbed his coat, the phone rang. He debated answering or leaving.

"Major Cases. Chase."

"Detective Chase, this is Jim York returning your call."

A cooperative citizen. Chase sat down and took out his pencil. "Mister York, I have some questions concerning a classmate of yours at CU. Rachel Stevens. Did you know her?"

"She was in my Wednesday evening class. She sat next to me. But I really didn't know her." Join the crowd, Chase thought. "She seemed like a very nice person."

Seemed. "What do you do for a living, Mister York?"

"I'm a mailman." Another poor slob working for the federal government, Chase thought.

"How well did you know Mrs. Stevens?"

"I didn't know her at all except to say hi. Well, you know, we did talk a couple of times during break."

"Did you talk to her at all this past Wednesday night?"

"She wasn't in class Wednesday night."

"Was she absent a lot?"

"I didn't pay that much attention to it."

"You just said you knew she wasn't in class this past Wednesday."

The voice on the other end was a little abrupt. "Well, detective, that might have something to do with her being killed and it being all over the news the next day." So much for seemed.

"Did you know where Mrs. Stevens was on those nights where she was absent from class?"

"No."

"Did you ever notice anyone else in the class that she talked to?"

"Not really. I mean I really can't remember. It's been a long semester."

"Did you know she was married?"

"I never really thought about it."

"What do you think she did for a living?"

"I'm sorry I can't be of more help, but I'm working full time and taking nine credits this semester and I really can't take the time to try and figure out all my fellow students."

Chase wasn't in the mood for a sob story and it was late and it was Friday. TGIF and all that. "Well, thank you for returning the call, Mister York. If you can think of anything that might help in the investigation, please give me a call."

"I'll do that."

Chase hung up. Definitely time for a cold one. The phone rang again. He looked at the machine long and hard through six rings and then picked it up. It was Porter. He should have known better than to call after five on a Friday, but he had good news. Or at least he thought it was good news. For Chase it just muddied an already murky picture.

"I found her clothes."

"Where?"

"Inside a dumpster at the car wash on Canyon."

"What's the condition?"

"Clean. No tears or cuts. They were taken off. Not torn off. I'm going to drop them at the lab on the way home."

"OK. Sounds good. Anything other than clothes?"

"That's the interesting thing. I found a remote opener for the BMW in a pocket in the dress."

Great. Chase didn't have the brain energy after dealing with the Linda Watkins of the world to figure out what the significance of that might be. At least they now knew how the doors had been locked.

"Anything else?"

"Some cash."

"How much?"

"Six dollars and change."

"What about the location?"

"Nothing. Someone could have pulled up and just tossed them out the window. The top on the dumpster was open. You have anything new?"

"Not really. Talked to her supposed best friend at the country club this afternoon. Smart move not coming with me."

"Why don't you meet me at the Wagon Wheel and we'll talk about it over a cold one?"

Chase stared at the phone. That offer was the most surprising thing that had happened today. "What about Mary and the kids?"

"She's taking them to the movies. Harry Potter Six or some crap. I can live without that."

"Sounds good. I'll see you there in about twenty minutes."

CHAPTER SEVEN

The Wagon Wheel was a quasi-dive. Once upon a time, it had been a country and western bar, but that hadn't panned out. Now a bunch of cops sat at a bar with a big set of horns looming over it. Occasionally some yo-ho's with cowboy hats would wander in and punch up some songs on the jukebox. But mostly the cops had it to themselves. It did a brisk business in well brands.

It was a good place to go because all different jurisdictions were represented. Besides Boulder City cops, there were Boulder County sheriffs, along with Broomfield, Longmont and Lafayette PD. There were even some Denver cops who lived in this neck of the woods. And some State Troopers. Chase didn't feel like such a weird duck sitting among all these different guys, although they all knew he was a Fed, and because of that there was always a certain distance.

Chase waved at the few people he recognized and grabbed a stool at the end of the bar. The bartender got Chase a draft without asking. The TV was on and the second installment of the evening news would be up shortly and Chase wanted to see what the media had to say about the case. He was on his third swallow before Porter came in. He stopped at a table of robbery detectives and chatted for a few moments before finally arriving.

"Sylvie working tonight?"

Chase waved at the bartender for another draft. "Yeah, but I'm meeting her tomorrow at Chautauqua Park."

"Why don't you two come over tomorrow for a barbecue? Mary's potato salad is getting better. I got her to cut back on the celery seed."

Chase shook his head. "Sylvie's got to go to work early on Saturday evenings and we won't have much time."

"Sounds like you have your afternoon already planned."

Chase nodded. "We don't get much time together between our two jobs and we have to make the most of it."

"That's the nice thing about having someone to come home to at night. You get more time together."

Chase laughed. "Like you and Mary have a lot of time alone together with three kids screaming around you."

"That's why they invented videos." Porter took a deep drink. "So what's going on over at the Boulder Country Club? I haven't been there in a while."

"Shit. You've never been there. Lots of rich women lolling around. This woman, Linda Watkins, was supposed to be our victim's best friend according to Doctor Stevens. I got the impression she didn't know her at all. Hell, I'm getting the impression no one knew who she was. The people at CU didn't even know she was married."

"She never wore her rings to class?"

"Nope."

"At least we know the night she was killed, that it wasn't so unusual." Porter gave Chase some of what he had found out that afternoon. "I think Stevens probably had a thing going with his secretary, but he was in surgery 'til almost seven that evening and then he went home. The people at the hospital and the maid back that up.

"They had no outstanding debts other than the house mortgage which is paid up to date. His reported income was over two million last year according to the IRS. I've got some more checking to do on him next week."

"What about insurance on Rachel?"

"Two hundred and fifty thousand. I don't think he needed the insurance money, but if there was a hint of divorce and he wanted the secretary instead of his wife—then it makes some sense. Rich guys don't want to go fifty-fifty with no fault divorce."

"I suppose," Chase said, wondering for a moment about his own pending divorce, realizing that other than the furniture, there wasn't much of a pie to split fifty-fifty. "What about a drug habit or gambling?"

"Nothing I could find."

Chase filled Porter in on the rest of his conversation with Linda Watkins. By the time he was done, it was Porter's turn to buy.

He paid and then was silent for a little while. Chase figured his partner was mulling over the case. It turned out he was thinking something over, but it had nothing to do with Rachel Stevens.

Porter fiddled with his mug and then looked at Chase. "How have you been doing, Chase?"

"What? What do you mean how have I been doing? I'm doing fine."

Porter seemed nervous. "I'm a little worried about you."

This Chase didn't need, but he didn't say anything because Porter was his partner and he'd heard that was important to cops. "Yeah. About what?"

Porter spread his hands. "Where to start? The job. Your divorce. Your mother. Wyoming. Sylvie."

Chase gritted his teeth and Porter saw it, but plunged on. "I don't know, Chase. You've been ragged lately. I don't mean to get into your personal stuff, but you seem a little out of it. I understand getting served a divorce and your mother dying while you were overseas was hard. I don't know what your relationship with your mother was, but you carry the letter around everywhere and you talked one time about that house she left you in South Carolina. Then you got wounded in Afghanistan after all that crap. I probably shouldn't be saying anything at all. And I don't understand what happened. So I'll butt out on that, OK?"

Chase couldn't explain himself to Porter because he didn't know what was wrong. He wanted to tell Porter that he couldn't understand. He'd never been to war. Chase had. Three times. Twice to Afghanistan and once to Iraq in between. Porter had never held men dying in his arms. Watched bodies blown apart. Been so close to someone you kill that you could smell their breath, see their teeth, feel their last gasp on your skin. Chase just couldn't come back here to the normal world and sort it all out like it was some TV show to be discussed at the water-cooler. He just knew there were bad things in his head and for Chase the effect was cumulative. He didn't say that though because Porter was possibly a friend, and Chase didn't have enough of those to just let one go.

"I'm doing OK," Chase said. "I admit I've felt better about life in general, but I'm holding up." He tried redirecting things. "Don't you ever miss it? Making it big in the music business and all? Don't you ever feel like you were trapped or in the wrong place?"

Porter answered Chase's question. "Yeah, I did miss it, until I realized there wasn't a hell of a lot to miss. I wasn't that good, Chase. I was better than a lot, but I just didn't have that special thing that makes it all possible. Took me a while to accept, but I finally did.

"My life now is good and I'm happy because I've accepted it. I know my limits so you might say I've fulfilled all my expectations. To me the worst thing in the world is to go after something that's not in your cards. I understand now that I probably wouldn't have been happy making it big as you put it because that's not the key to being happy. That's an outside thing, Chase." Porter stuck a finger in his own chest. "Happy's in here."

Chase wasn't sure he agreed. It seemed that he was lowering his own expectations every day, but it wasn't getting him anywhere. It appeared to him the less he wanted, the less he was getting, and he certainly wasn't very happy no matter where it was located. "Things will get back to normal pretty soon."

"I don't think you have any idea what normal is," Porter said. He held up a hand. "And I don't mean that in a bad way, Chase. You've had a hard road."

To that, Chase had no reply, the words bouncing around in his brain like so many broken marbles, scratching and irritating, but real.

Porter leaned forward. "Hey. I want to be a cop. I want to catch the bad guys. Some guys like carrying the badge and gun, makes up for something they're missing. I don't see it that way for me. I was lost, playing in all the dives here and in Denver when I met Mary. No clue what I wanted, but I didn't want the music bad enough. Then Mary told me—" Porter glanced around, making sure no one was listening. "She told me she'd been assaulted while she was at CU as an undergrad and that the cops blew it off when she reported it, saying they got calls like that all the time from girls at the university."

Porter's nodded. "It just clicked with me. I knew what I wanted to do. I wanted to be someone who didn't blow something like that off. Who went after the bad guys. I've never looked back on that decision and questioned it."

"I'm sorry," Chase said.

"It was a bad thing," Porter said, "but we've moved on. Doesn't mean she doesn't remember or we don't talk about it once in a while, but we deal with it. We were talking the other night and we're worried about you. You don't talk to anyone, it looks like, not even Sylvie."

Chase shifted uneasily. "I'm not into talking."

"Apparently." Porter leaned back. "Mary and I miss having you around. The kids are wondering what happened to you. Sylvie seems to be important to you and we'd like to get to know her."

Chase was beginning to regret Porter's invitation for a drink. "Like I said, Sylvie works a lot, and odd hours too, so she's usually sleeping around the time you're pulling the burgers off the grill. Plus you told me early on you didn't like me going to that club and she's part of it."

Porter's face tightened. "I don't give a rat's ass about Sylvie stripping. But Tai's shady."

"How do you know?"

"I've been a cop for a while." Porter shook his head. "Forget about that. You really like Sylvie, don't you?"

"Well, yeah."

"How long you two been going together now? Two, three months?"

"About that. Ever since the Peterson case. The kid with the busted jaw outside the club."

"You two have any plans?" Porter continued.

Chase looked at Porter over the rim of his mug. "Plans for what?"

"I don't know." He shrugged. "I just can't figure this out. You've seemed happy and unhappy at the same time over the past couple months and I've been trying to figure out why."

"Sylvie's a good person. We have a good thing."

"Thing? What's a good thing, Chase?"

"We enjoy being together, yet we don't have all the crap that most people try to put on a relationship. No commitments. No plans. We just treat each other good."

Porter frowned. "That doesn't work, Chase."

"It seems to be working for me."

"How about for Sylvie?"

"She hasn't complained. She seems happy." Chase was tired of being interrogated by his partner. "What about Mary? Is she happy?"

Porter smiled, as if he had expected Chase's turn-around. "Yes. She's happy. It's not perfect for her, but we talk about it when either of us get out of whack. Sometimes we scream and yell about it and get it out of our system, but we always make up."

"You've had time—" Chase began, but just then a burly, short man stomped up to the table.

"You're the Fed," he said, glaring at Chase with blood-shot eyes.

Porter leaned forward between them. "Detective Chase, meet Deputy Squires, Larimer County."

Chase nodded. "Nice to meet you, Deputy Squires. Can I buy you a drink?"

"Fuck you," Squires snapped. "I've heard all about you. Badass, fucking Green Beret, Delta Force, counter-terrorist man but your high-speed team let those assholes who murdered my friend get away. Some say you could have nailed the cocksucker cop-killer who did it. Everyone around here thinks you walk on water cause you were in the 'Stan and Iraq. But I was in Iraq. Other guys here too with their reserve units. You aren't so fucking special, Chase."

"I don't think I am. How about that drink?" Chase noted the tattoo on Squires arm. "Semper Fi. The guys I saw in the Corps were the best—"

"Don't fucking Semper Fi me, asshole."

Porter stood and put a hand on Squires' arm. "Listen. Maybe—" Squires slapped Porter's hand off.

"Don't touch me."

Chase could see everyone in the bar was watching. He also could see that Squires was drunk and angry past the point of no return. Chase stood and faced Squires, looking down into the angry man's face. Squires' nostril's flared liked an angry bulldog, the veins and muscles in his neck standing out, the bulging biceps in his arms pulsing down through his forearms to his clenched fists as he squared up. Steroids and alcohol. A big mix.

Chase smiled as he leaned closer toward Squires and lowered his voice so only the Larimer County Deputy could hear. "I did have a shot. You wanted me to kill four men in cold blood? Would you do that?"

Squires blinked.

Before he could respond, Chase reached out and put his left hand on Squire's right shoulder, pinching the nerve, and freezing that arm, stepped in tight, and jabbed with his left hand into the sheriff's gut, just below his sternum. The instant result was a projectile vomit of alcohol and Squire's last meal all over Chase's chest.

There was a collective groan in the bar, not at all, what they had expected and hoped to see. Chase put his arm around the deputy's shoulder. Porter went to the other side and together they escorted him out of the bar.

"Over here," Chase said, seeing an old ice cooler. He sat on it, the groaning deputy still leaning on him.

Porter backed off. "You ok?" he asked Chase, Squires head lolling on his shoulder.

"I'm fine. You need to get home. We'll get together some other time."

Porter leaned in close, ignoring the stench. "Hey Chase. I know you don't have many buddies on the force. You need anything; you can count on me. Sorry if I stepped out of line tonight."

Chase had had a team sergeant like Porter in Afghanistan. Chase felt a hand clutching his guts inside as he remembered Jimmy Keegan. He could only nod at Porter and murmur "Thanks."

Porter looked at the deputy. "You sure you'll be all right?"

"I'm sure."

Porter disappeared into the darkness.

Chase turned toward the drunken and sick deputy. "Who'd you lose over there, Marine?"

* * * * * * * * * * * * *

Astral began barking as soon as Chase opened the back gate. He ignored the little dog and meandered over to his garden.

Nothing showing as far as he could tell in the starlight.

Chase was headed for the basement door when the upstairs deck light went on. He paused as Louise appeared at the railing.

"Horace?"

"It's me." He could just make out her silhouette against the light. "Sorry to have woken you up."

"I was awake. Focusing."

"On?" Chase moved toward his door.

"You."

Chase paused, peering up. He was tired, covered in vomit and not too thrilled after listening to Squires for over an hour. "Am I in focus?"

Louise came down the stairs and Astral scampered over to her. "You look terrible, Horace."

"Rough night," he acknowledged.

Despite his condition, Louise put her hands on his shoulders and peered into his eyes. "You're opening up."

"I am?"

Louise smiled. "Yes.

If this is what it meant to be open, Chase wasn't too sure, he liked it.

Louise removed her hands and stepped back. "Why are you growing a garden?"

Chase stared at her. "I don't know."

"Do you always grow a garden wherever you live?"

Chase shook his head. "I've never lived anywhere long enough to grow one. The army always kept me on the go."

"But as a child—"

Chase half-turned for his door. "Never lived long enough in one place to grow one then either. My mother's—job—kept us on the move."

"That must have been hard," Louise said. "I didn't mean to pry. I was just wondering since you check it very time you come in the yard. I hope you don't mind, but I put some fertilizer down earlier today."

"Thanks." Chase paused. "I had a lot of library cards," he said, surprised that one thing came to the forefront of his brain. "First thing we'd do when we hit a new town was find the library and both get cards. That's how I learned. By the time I went off to the Academy I probably had over two hundred library cards."

Louise stepped closer and put her hand back on his shoulder. "Oh, Horace."

"I've got to go," Horace said. "Thanks for helping with the garden."

CHAPTER EIGHT

Chase was hot, thirsty, hung-over, tired and hungry by the time he got to Chautauqua Park the next day. He was wishing Sylvie had agreed to meet at her place. Sylvie was sitting on the steps of the concert hall reading a paperback when Chase walked up. She was wearing a short black dress and sandals. She looked great.

The park was located at the base of the Flatirons, which were Boulder's most notable landmark. A series of rock faces angled up at about seventy degrees, the Flatirons were named for the long-ago device used to iron pants. The park was a mixture of grasslands and forested slopes below the rock walls. Wildflowers were sprouting and Chase wondered why his garden hadn't yet shown any green.

Sylvie put the book down and smiled when she saw him. "How'd last night go?"

"All right."

"The Wagon Wheel," she said. "A step up from the Silver Satyr."

"Not really. Might be a step down. Met Porter there."

"How'd that go?"

Chase hesitated.

"He's worried about you," Sylvie pushed.

Chase nodded.

"Hell, Horace, I'm worried about you too."

Chase closed his eyes. This weekend was going rapidly downhill. First Porter last night at the Wagon Wheel, Louise in the yard, and now Sylvie. And she was calling him by his first name, which she had never done before. He couldn't even remember telling her it. He sighed and leaned back against the wood stairs.

Sylvie's hand was on his thigh and she squeezed. "Chase, don't start feeling sorry for yourself."

He opened his eyes. Sylvie was smiling.

"What do you want to do?" Chase asked.

Sylvie stood. "Let's walk over to the rock garden."

79

Chase would have preferred going to her apartment. His second choice was food. The rock garden didn't rate at all. But he meandered over there with her and sat on a bench close to a bunch of rocks arranged in what he assumed was supposed to an artistic pattern.

"So what's new with you, Chase?"

He figured they'd beat the Wagon Wheel to death. Wyoming was off limits. He scanned the files in his brain for something she might find interesting. "I went to the Boulder Country Club yesterday." It seemed like forever since he'd sat next to the tennis courts and talked to Linda Watkins.

Sylvie raised her eyebrows. "Moving up in society?"

"No. I had to do an interview."

"The case you got this week? Rachel Stevens?"

"Yeah."

"How'd you end up at the country club?"

"It was the only time this woman could find to see me."

"What woman?"

"I was told she was Rachel's best friend."

"Who told you that?"

"Her husband."

"I wonder what a husband considers a best friend."

Chase shrugged. "Beats me. This woman acted like she hardly knew Rachel. But she did have an interesting view on life."

Sylvie perked up. "So what does a woman at the Boulder Country Club think about life?"

"I got the feeling she equated marriage with the stock market."

"What do you mean the stock market?"

"You know. The sort who thinks love should be a lucrative endeavor."

"What's wrong with that, Chase? Sounds like she's kind of smart to me."

Chase stared at her. "What do you mean smart?"

"Most women barter their body for security. Some women just have more to bargain with. At least she's not a hypocrite, Chase."

Chase blinked. "I'm not a hypocrite."

"Oh, aren't we a bit defensive today?" Sylvie stood. "I didn't say you were. I said at least this woman you saw yesterday wasn't a hypocrite."

Chase stood too. "Is that what you're doing? Bartering your body for security?"

"Sometimes, Chase, you are so obtuse."

That was up there with enigma in Chase's vocabulary of irritating words.

He followed as she walked out of the rock garden. He caught up with her and they headed toward his Jeep. He was trying to think of something to say when she took the initiative. "I said most women, Chase. Not all. I like to think that I'm one of the lucky ones that finally figured this all out."

"Finally figured all what out? What are you talking about?"

"The big trap. Marriage."

"Wait a second, Sylvie. Where do you get off saying marriage is a trap for women? The woman I talked to yesterday didn't look too miserable."

They'd reached Chase's Jeep. Sylvie looked over the roll bar at him. "Let's go to the New York Deli for lunch."

They got in. As Chase pulled out, Sylvie put her sunglasses back on. "So what did this woman say about Rachel?"

Chase snorted. "Same as everyone else. Wonderful person. Good student. Fine upstanding citizen. I get the feeling no one knew her."

"Maybe she didn't want anyone to know her."

"Porter says we'll have to go back to her husband. We caught him at a bad time last visit."

"What makes you think he's going to know anything more than anyone else?"

"I see your point. He didn't know who her best friend was. He didn't even know where she was every third Wednesday."

"What do you mean every third Wednesday?"

"She was absent from class every third Wednesday all semester. Sounds like she was up to something. Maybe Porter has something there with his theory about her having an affair." It was the only thing that fit. Chase had mulled it over, anything to avoid fixating on Wyoming.

"I don't know, Chase. I've been thinking about it a bit since yesterday. An affair by its nature is usually sort of random. People are acting off of emotions, not logic. Very hard to plan like that and stick to it."

Chase diverted his attention from the road briefly. "So now you're an expert on affairs as well as marriages."

Sylvie laughed.

Chase thought about it. "You may have a point though. The woman yesterday didn't think Rachel was having an affair."

"Did you ask her why?"

"She went off on some line about Rachel not needing to."

"You mean she thought Rachel was confident."

Chase saw a large cardboard box on the side of the road and abruptly swerved away from it, tires squealing, the horn from the car he cut off blaring.

"Geez, Chase," Sylvie said.

"Sorry. What were you saying?"

"Sounds like Rachel Stevens didn't need to have an affair."

"Why can't it just mean that her husband was a good lay?"

"Chase, I'm surprised. You're getting sex and love and need all confused. All I'm trying to say is it sounds like she didn't need to trade sex for love. Maybe she loved herself. Or maybe she was more important to herself and she didn't need a man to tell her that."

This was getting too bizarre even for Chase. Rachel Stevens was in the morgue as they spoke. He didn't need to understand Rachel's psyche. He needed to find her killer. Especially now, because he didn't know what Fortin was going to do, but one half of those who controlled Chase's professional life were certainly not very happy with him; he definitely needed to keep the other half happy.

Chase had to park three blocks away from Pearl Street in the municipal lot. They strolled over to Pearl Street. About twenty-five years ago, the city had blocked off a section of Pearl, between 11th and 15th. Put brick down where there had been tar, planted trees and flowers, and the Pearl Street Mall had been born. It was full of restaurants, art galleries and bookstores. With the weather, turning nicer it was full of people this Saturday afternoon. There were a lot of young 'drifters' wandering around, panhandling—the Rainbow People, Porter had explained to Chase. Most other places they'd be considered bums in Chase's opinion.

The New York Deli had good, basic food. In the TV show Mork & Mindy, the floors above the New York Deli had been where the two title characters supposedly lived. Chase considered that to be pretty historic.

Luckily, there wasn't much of a wait. They got a table on the mall and sat on the same side. While sipping his beer, Chase slid his right hand under the table and caressed Sylvie's bare thigh.

While his hand was one place, his mind was another. "If she wasn't having an affair, what was she doing every third Wednesday? I've got to figure out where she met her killer. The parking lot at CU? Somewhere else? It all goes back to this every third Wednesday thing. She deceived her husband on that. She had to have had a reason."

"Why does it have to be a bad reason?"

"What else could it have been?"

Sylvie pondered that until the food arrived. "OK. Nothing else comes to mind. The question is who was she having the affair with, if she was having one?" Sylvie eyes widened. "Someone in her class."

"What?" Chase muttered around his pastrami on rye.

"It was someone in her class. They skipped every third class to be together."

It would be easy enough to check, Chase thought. He'd have to go back to CU on Monday.

Chase looked up at a man who put his hat upside down on a bench opposite the two of them, then climbed up on it and then stood perfectly still, hands pointing in opposite directions. Great a mime. Except this, one was more a statue then a mime. Chase had thought he'd seen it all. He was ready to go for his gun.

Sylvie's mind had moved on. "What are you going to do tonight, Chase?"

Sylvie had just hit on the really bad aspect of dating a stripper. He spent most of his nights alone. "I don't know. I have nothing planned. You put in an awful lot of hours in that joint."

"It's money, Chase."

He couldn't argue with that. He wasn't sure where all that money went and he had never felt it would be polite to ask. "Beats standing on a bench."

Sylvie looked at the quasi-mime who hadn't moved a muscle in the last couple of minutes. "Everybody's got some angle."

"Can I stay at your place till you get off?"

Sylvie gave Chase a sly smile. "I get the impression you want to go there right after lunch."

"That wouldn't be bad. I'm real tired, Sylvie."

Chase thought about telling her all about his conversation with Porter last night, but he was afraid to bring it up. He was indeed disturbed by it. He was beginning to realize that he hadn't been doing much thinking about anything outside of work in a long time. Everything was sort of drifting along. He was even starting to worry that his work was going the same way. After Porter had left, he'd spent an hour listening to Squires cry into his vomit about the members of his squad who'd died or been maimed in Fallujah, before getting the deputy a cab. Then Louise had been acting all weird. He'd been happy to get inside and take a hot shower, trying to wash the vomit and the past twenty-four hours away.

He wanted to talk with Sylvie about what he had done, or more appropriately, not done—the other night in Wyoming. But the bad guys were still on the loose in Wyoming, he didn't know what Fortin was going to do about his inaction, and he hadn't figured out himself how he felt.

Sylvie appeared to be done. "You ready?"

Chase paid the check and they headed for her apartment.

CHAPTER NINE

Chase kept seeing the head of the bearded man in his scope, the reticules centered. Most people have never experienced that feeling. The power of life and death in the crook of a finger. Chase had known the feeling and he'd exercised it in the past, seeing the results of that little twitch of muscle. A metal-jacketed, 7.62 millimeter round hitting flesh, passing through skin without the slightest disturbance, striking bone, splintering it, ripping into the delicate material underneath, spitting blood, brain and flesh out the exit wound. The body instantly dropping like a stone to the ground.

Then he saw Jimmy Keegan. Covered in blood, reaching up toward Chase, his mouth moving, but there was no sound.

Chase woke in a sweat, Sylvie sleeping beside him. He didn't move, focusing on gaining control of his body.

He'd always been drawn to stories about death. He'd made a study of it because it was an integral part of the professions he'd chosen, but now he remembered what he'd told Louise last night about libraries—even as a child he'd been drawn the subject. Probably because his father had died violently before he was born. Even the way he had died had resonated over Chase's life with his father's posthumous Medal of Honor being Chase's ticket to an automatic appointment to the Military Academy.

Chase had read once about a French scientist in the early nineteenth century. The man had been caught up in the Revolution and sentenced to die, so he decided to make a scientific experiment of his own death. He had a comrade wait close to the guillotine and when his severed head rolled into the basket the scientist blinked continuously until he no longer could. The comrade recorded eleven blinks from the head. A long time for the brain to be alive after being cut from the body. Long enough to lie in the basket and know that the body was no longer attached. That death was just a few blinks away.

One thing that Chase always wondered about when he remembered that story was how long those blinks were to the brain inside the severed head. Chase knew time sense could change, especially under stress. When he used to jump-master, hanging out of a C-130 plane approaching a drop zone at a hundred and forty miles and hour, wind ripping into his face, the last ten seconds from the command "Stand in the door" to "Go" took a hell of a lot longer to Chase than ten seconds. Seemed like a minute or two. How long did eleven blinks last knowing the final call was coming?

Chase stared up at the ceiling, no longer able to avoid having his mind go to dangerous places. It was all about death. When he cut to the core, that was it, the final hand to be played. Everything else was just a prelude. Death and taxes someone had said, but hell, the damn Patriots didn't pay taxes so the latter could be avoided. But not the former.

He peeled the covers away and carefully stood, not wanting to wake Sylvie. He padded over to the sliding doors that led to her balcony and silently opened the doors. He went outside and sat, feeling the early morning chill. The first rays of the sun had just begun to come in over the Plains to the west, touching the top of the Flatirons. Boulder was a beautiful place, but the beauty couldn't dispel his morbid thoughts this morning.

Chase had to wonder if he'd held back from shooting the bearded man and the rest of the Patriots because that's what would have had to follow, because he was afraid of being shot in return? He knew that's what Fortin and the other guys on the team thought. But Chase didn't think, didn't feel that----

"Chase?" Sylvie's eyes were blinking in the early morning light, her short hair tousled.

"Hey, babe."

She had a thick robe on and a blanket in her arms. She threw it over him and sat down next to him. "Chase? What's wrong?"

He shook his head. He was so tired. He couldn't speak. Not because Fortin had ordered him not to. It was more than that. He just couldn't speak. Chase leaned his head into Sylvie's chest. She wrapped her arms around him. He realized he was acting a bit like Squires had last night. At least he hadn't puked on her.

"Chase?" Sylvie's voice was worried.

Chase shook his head. She pressed Chase against her body, tighter and tighter.

"It's OK, Chase. It's OK."

Women. They have that thing that everything could be OK just by saying it was so. Chase knew things weren't OK.

CHAPTER TEN

Chase was on his third cup of coffee by the time Porter dragged into the squad room on Monday morning. Chase picked on him a little bit by informing his partner that since he had spent all Sunday in bed, he felt extremely rested.

Chase know that was cruel and a lie, but he also knew that Porter with his house full of kids had probably spent all of his off time mowing, trimming, raking and grilling. When he went to bed, it was to sleep. But Chase was in a bad mood.

Porter was holding a hand full of reports, meaning that he had had the smarts to round up all the paperwork before coming up stairs. He tossed them down one by one: the coroner's report, forensics on the car and clothes, phone messages and witness interviews. The last was slim enough to make a detective cry. In exchange, Chase handed him one of the jelly donuts that he had picked up on the way in.

"How was your time with Sylvie?" Porter asked.

"All right."

Porter nodded and gave Chase a look he couldn't interpret.

Chase tapped the folder in his hand. "We need to figure out who whacked our housewife from Pine Brook Hills." To make a point, Chase carefully wiped the jelly from his fingers and opened the coroner's report with a flourish.

"Since when are you running this case?" Porter asked. But he followed suit with forensics and for a while, neither said anything as they tried to put the technical information together.

Chase read that Hanson had narrowed the time of death to around ten-thirty, give or take a half hour. From the blood pooling, he estimated that she was dumped within ten to fifteen minutes of her death. There was more on the semen. A lot more than Chase wanted and he knew anyone else wanted. From the initial DNA typing there seemed to be evidence that she had traces of at least four different typed ejaculates in her vaginal cavity. Just great. It looked like Donnelly was right. A sex crime. An unfortunate victim of a gang rape.

They'd grabbed her and when they were done, one of them had killed her.

Chase looked over at Porter expectantly; maybe there was something in the lab report from the car. The sullen look in his partner's eyes told Chase that his optimism was for naught. Porter quickly filled Chase in on what he had. Basically nothing. The car had no unexpected prints.

There were a few carpet fibers from the body. Industrial type material, rust colored. If they ever got a suspect, they could check their home or vehicle for a match but it was nothing that could be traced to a manufacturer and then a buyer. Of course, she could also have picked up the fibers at school, at home, or anywhere in between.

There was nothing significant around or in the trashcan at the car wash. Porter decided that some Martians had dropped her body over the park and then hit the dumpster on the way out to get rid of her clothes. Chase pointed out that the DNA typing on the semen was human. Neither laughed at the weak attempts at humor.

Chase showed Porter the paragraph in the coroner's report on the contents of Rachel's vagina. His partner frowned as his eyes moved down the page. "What's chlorhexidine gluconate?"

Chase looked over Porter's shoulder. "Damned if I know. Probably some sort of medicine. You know women."

Porter read the rest of the report very slowly. "Four? What the fuck?" He slammed the report down on the desk.

Chase said nothing, letting his partner cogitate.

"The doctor could have hired some guys—" Porter began, but then he shook his head. "Nah. That would be stupid."

Porter worked his way through the rest of it while Chase looked at forensics. Porter was right. Nothing there that was useful, other than the fibers. The only prints on the car were Rachel's and her husband's. The remote opener found in her clothes only had her prints on it.

After a half hour, they had both read almost all of it. They put their feet up on their desks and sipped coffee, collecting their thoughts. Finally, Porter looked at Chase. "You tell the lieutenant."

"Tell him what?"

"That we got a random. That he was right. A sex killing."

"Why do I tell him?"

"You seemed so gung-ho earlier," Porter said.

89

"What about the money and the car opener?" Chase asked. "Why didn't they take that?"

"Hell, they were raping her. They were all probably high on something. We can't expect them to be thinking too damn straight. We aren't dealing with geniuses here. Maybe she had other money on her that they did find."

"I don't like it." Chase wasn't sure why he said that because he knew that Porter was probably right, but something in his gut said it was all wrong. The pieces didn't fit. "Where did she get picked up from?"

"Most likely the parking lot at CU. The punks probably had a van or big car and were cruising around, looking for some young coed to pick up. Instead, they got a housewife from Pine Brook Hills. They didn't care. They didn't exactly look at her resume beyond the fact the she was female and good looking." Porter stood. "Don't worry. I'll brief the LT. Then I'm going to hit the streets. Check the Hill first and see if any of the druggies or Rainbow people are talking. You stay here and go through the phone messages." Porter patted Chase on the back as he prepared to leave. "Hang in there." He paused and Chase could see the question forming, then, with a brief shake of his head, Porter left the squad room without asking.

Chase breathe a sigh of relief and gathered in the last folder. The only one they hadn't gone through yet. This one contained all the call-ins.

Every large case that made the news seemed to inspire a whole wave of people who felt they had something to contribute. And they all looked up the number for the desk downstairs and called. And the poor duty sergeant had to listen and be polite and copy everything down. Ninety-nine percent was garbage. But it was because of that one percent that he did his job, which meant reading every one of the memos and following up on anything remotely interesting.

There were nineteen call-ins so far. Actually, kind of low for a high profile case, but Chase figured the fact that the victim was from Pine Brook Hills and had been snatched at CU helped a bit. Not as many crazies in either of those places.

No confessions, which was a little surprising. Porter had told him that there was usually there was at least one nut-cake who called to confess. Those people had to be checked out. Not just on the remote chance they might actually be the murderer, but primarily because if they caught who they thought was the real murderer, a savvy defense lawyer would dig and find out that someone had called the police to confess and the cops hadn't even bothered to go talk to him or her. Looked bad in front of the jury.

There were two psychics claiming they could help out. Chase recognized one of them. She called on every case that made the papers. He was glad Louise wasn't one of those calling.

The seventh slip caught his eye. A woman, Beth Wilson, left a message Sunday afternoon saying she saw something from her dorm room on campus on the night of the murder. It was probably nothing, but his pulse picked up a little as he dialed the number the duty sergeant had logged in. Chase didn't expect anyone to be there, but the phone was answered on the second ring.

"Hello?"

"Is this Beth Wilson?"

"Yes."

"This is Detective Chase, Boulder Police. In reference to your phone call about seeing something last Wednesday night that might be connected to a case I'm working."

"I was wondering if anyone would return my call. It probably wasn't anything, but the news did say that woman was killed on Wednesday night and she probably had been kidnapped from this parking lot here outside my dorm. So I just thought I'd report what I saw."

"What exactly did you see?"

"It was a little after ten. I was studying for finals and I happened to look out the window and I saw someone get out of a cab."

"Could you see the person well? Well enough to recognize if it was a man or a woman?"

"Not really. I'm up on the fourth floor you know. And it was dark. I just thought that you might be able to find the cab driver. I know it's not much, but the news did ask for anyone to report anything they might have seen."

She was right, Chase thought. It wasn't much. But it did open two doors. One was the cab driver who was in the parking lot where Rachel's car had been just before she was killed. The other was whoever had gotten out of the cab. Slim chances, but ones Chase would have to check.

Chase questioned Beth Wilson a while longer, but she didn't have much more. She had just seen the cab and someone get out. She had noted that the person headed across the lot in the direction of the library. Beth had a big economics test the next day and had returned her attention to studying.

Chase hung up. He looked through the rest of the messages and they weren't even worth the time. He closed the folder. Chase found the picture Jeffrey Stevens had given them and stared at it a while. His attention was too focused because when he looked up Donnelly was watching Chase with a mild, worried frown. "Do you think she's going to send you a message from beyond the grave and tell you who did it?"

Chase hadn't even realized the LT was around and it bothered him to be caught in the act of looking at Rachel's picture.

"I just received a call from Agent Fortin," Donnelly said.

Chase waited through the pause. He didn't know how much Fortin had told Donnelly and despite his limited experience, he had interrogated enough suspects to know better than fill in the gap with an explanation that might tell Donnelly more than he already knew.

"I was called the other night to say you were working full-time on a CT mission involving that deputy who was killed."

Again the pause. Donnelly couldn't have gotten a confession from one of the phone-in's, he was so bad at it. Chase was staring at a point just to the left of the lieutenant's head, another technique learned as a plebe at West Point.

"Then Fortin called this morning to inform me that you were off the CT assignment and back with us full-time."

Chase nodded. "Then I'll proceed with the Stevens' investigation."

"Did something happen?" Donnelly asked, finally giving up his feeble fishing attempt. "They still haven't caught those guys yet."

"They didn't need me," Chase said. "Anything else, lieutenant?"

"No."

Chase left the office. The foreplay was beginning. Fortin was going to screw Chase, but he was starting slow. The fact that they hadn't caught the Patriots yet meant he had other priorities right now and Chase was just a sideshow.

Chase waited until Donnelly was gone, then went back to the squad room. He called around to the various cab companies. He found the one that had dropped off someone at the right place and time-- the driver would be on duty that evening. He arranged for a meeting.

Then he dialed another number at the Jefferson County airport.

"Masters. You call, we haul."

"Hey, bud, it's Chase."

"Fuck," Masters said. "You sure pissed off the boss."

"How come you aren't in Wyoming?"

"They're using the state police chopper on stand-by," Masters said. "And they wanted me back here, in place, you know, in case fucking Al-Qaeda decides to take out the Pepsi Center or something. Plus, you know, I got a real civilian job."

"What have you heard?" Chase asked.

"Fortin thinks you fucked up. Of course, what he thinks isn't necessarily what everyone else thinks. You were the man on the ground. Your call."

"And the Patriots?"

"No one's seen anything and Fortin doesn't want a blood bath by going in. So the State Police have roadblocks up—fat lot of good that will do them—and the rest of the team is sitting around jacking off. You're better off back in Boulder."

"Anyone have an idea why those Patriots were here in Colorado? Why they killed the cop?"

"Nope." There was a short pause. "But if you want to know more about them, you might want to talk to Thorne."

"Colonel Thorne? Merck Magazine?" Chase remembered the article he hadn't had time to read.

"Yeah. He's a tough old son-of-a-bitch, but a straight-shooter."

"All right."

"Hey, bud, you need anything, give me a call."

"Thanks."

Chase hung up and left the office.

****

Chase drove his Jeep east on Arapaho listening to Warren Zevon sing about *Lawyers, Guns, and Money*. Past Scott Carpenter Park, named after one of Boulder's favorite sons, until he reached an industrial area. He cruised around several buildings to a bland, nondescript, cinder-block two-story structure. A small sign on the door indicated it was home to Merck Enterprises.

He pressed the buzzer.

"Yes?" A voice crackled out of the speaker above the buzzer.

"I need to see Colonel Thorne."

"And you are?"

"Horace Chase."

"Wait."

Like he was going to do something else. A minute passed, then the door clicked open. Chase stepped into a small foyer. Another door at the end, another buzzer. A video camera watched Chase walk the ten feet to the next door. It opened with a click. A middle-aged woman sat behind a receptionist's area.

"Colonel Thorne will see you now--" she inclined her head to the right, at a set of large wooden doors. Chase walked over, swung them open and froze as a pair of pit bulls snapped and growled at him at the end of their chains, bolted to opposite sides of the doors.

"They're harmless," the man behind the desk informed Chase. "Unless you piss me off."

"I'm not here to piss you off." Chase still hadn't crossed the threshold of the doors and his eyes were on the dogs. He could now see that the leashes allowed about a three-foot gap directly in the center.

"Come on in. Sit down, detective."

Chase walked between the snapping teeth, knowing he'd lost points already and that was what the dogs were for. The man behind the desk wanted to control any meeting in his office and this was like a big executive in New York having a view of Central Park in the window behind him, except a lot less subtle.

Thorne was a short, fireplug of a man, seated in a black leather chair. His face was weathered, his hair totally gray and shorn into a crew cut. The walls of the office were completely covered with plaques and photographs. The ultimate 'Look At What I've Done And The Places I've Been And The People I Know' display.

It worked. Just the glance Chase had on the way to the chair in front of the desk impressed the hell out of him. Chase recognized plaques from Special Operations units all over the world-- Israeli Commandos, German GSG9, Norwegian Yaegers, Thai paratroopers, Canadian 1st Parachute Regiment, British SAS, just about every top-

94

notch unit there was. Chase had a similar, albeit fewer, bunch that he kept in a trunk in the same closet as his CT gear.

The two pit bulls sat as Chase did, tongues hanging, breathing hard, their beady little eyeballs on him. Above Thorne's head was a framed guidon-- 10th Special Forces Group (Airborne). A green flag with yellow crossed arrows. It was the last unit Thorne had commanded before retiring and beginning his new career. Thorne published Merck Magazine and several handgun magazines. Chase had always though it quite bizarre that Merck was published in Boulder, the bastion of left wing liberalism in Colorado, but Thorne had been in Boulder longer than most of the left-wingers, when only 10,00 kids went to CU, not the current 70,000.

"You're a FLI," Thorne said. "Does that make me a pile of shit since you're buzzing around here?"

"No, sir." It figured he knew who Chase was.

Chase read Merck. Those who didn't dismiss it too easily, as ignorant people tended to do. Merck was the only magazine of its kind-- dedicated to covering Special Operations the world over. The articles were written by guys who went there and saw first-hand what was going on in most of the world's hot spots. It was right wing for sure, but smart right wing, and the people who ran the magazine weren't what Chase called "wanna-be's". Particularly Thorne. The wall and what Chase knew of him from the Special Operations old-boy network said he was the real deal.

"Then what do you want?"

"I need information on the Patriots."

No sense beating around the bush. Thorne had a column in the front of each issue where he discussed whatever was grating his ass that month-- sort of like Jon Stewart's rants on TV, but with a lot different subject matter and a different perspective. And sometimes more realistic because Thorne actually got out of that chair and went where the bullets were flying to take a look. Chase knew Thorne was card-carrying NRA, and held many other beliefs of the right, but Chase also knew he wasn't one of those New World Order people who thought the UN was training a secret army to take over the United States. Thorne had been around enough crap-holes in the world to love the United States more than most. And he'd bled for the country.

Thorne stared at him. "You were in Tenth Group, weren't you?"

Chase nodded. He'd been there long after Thorne retired, but he'd heard stories about the colonel.

"Afghanistan?"

Chase nodded again.

"You were on ODA zero-five-five during the invasion," Thorne said. "We did an article on your extraction."

Chase had read the article. The reporter had interviewed one of the other guys who'd been with Chase and the Nightstalker crew that had picked them up. Just reading about it had given Chase the chills as it pulled him back to that long night.

"And then you were in Delta, weren't you?"

Chase shrugged. "I can't discuss that."

Thorne laughed. "Part of Delta's Task Force Eleven in the 'Stan for a second time, weren't you?"

"I can't discuss that."

"That's the only reason I let you in," Thorne said, ignoring Chase's denials. "Because of what you did, not what you're doing. I don't like the FLI program. We've got the federal government down our throats enough; we don't need you guys in the local police station."

For the second time in an hour, Chase remained quiet.

Thorne leaned back in his chair. "But I don't agree with the Patriots' methods either. And I don't agree with the Federal government's response either."

"It's people," Chase said. "People can go too far trying to accomplish their goals no matter who they work for or what they believe. Like killing a cop."

"You sure it was the Patriot's? The Patriot who that Blazer was registered to has been in jail for over a year now, serving a six-year term for tax evasion. Your buddies in the FBI found it abandoned."

"How do you know that?"

Thorne laughed. "CNN reported it two hours ago. They say Saddam watched CNN throughout the war. Best intelligence he could get. Sometimes we're our own worst enemies."

"Sometimes," Chase agreed.

"Maybe it's the CIA setting the Patriots up."

"The CIA killing a cop?"

Thorne shrugged. "Or the UN. ATF. Any of the alphabet soups. Maybe something went wrong. Who knows? You'd be surprised at some of the stuff that's really going on."

"It was the Patriots," Chase said. "I saw them just south and east of the Medicine Bow Mountains."

"You *saw* them? And they're still alive and you're still alive?" Thorne considered that. He shrugged. "Yeah, it was probably them. You know the CIA has been pretty interested in the Patriots."

Chase thought that odd given it was a domestic group, not the CIA's area of operations. "They're the FBI's case."

"The CIA and FBI don't like each other much," Thorne noted.

"Why were the Patriots in Colorado?"

"What do you know of the militia movement?" Thorne didn't wait for an answer. "It's not one group. There's a whole bunch of different organizations out there. Some of them hate each other worse than they hate the federal government. Some say the Klan is a militia group. The resurrected Black Panthers too. Can't see those two groups sitting in the same meeting hall, can you?"

"People have tried to consolidate the groups. Some for good reasons, some for not-so-good reasons. Any time you get organizations like that, they're subject to being corrupted by outside influences, especially if those outside forces have their shit together better than those on the inside."

Chase knew all that but he waited.

"The Patriots have splintered ever since the invasion of Iraq," Thorne finally said.

"Meaning?"

"There's a strong, radical cell among them that believes they were betrayed by the government. Sent to fight a war in Iraq to line the pockets of chicken-shits in Washington who got deferments for Vietnam and hide behind the flag. You know Cheney got five deferments during Vietnam—says he quote 'had better things to do' end fucking quote? Tell that to the kids screaming in Walter Reed with no fucking legs."

Chase said nothing. He'd heard those screams. And he knew about Halliburton. Seen the contractors in Iraq. Seen the pipeline in Afghanistan.

Thorne wasn't done. "Wolfowitz got deferments. Ashcroft had seven. Rove. All the fuckers who pushed for the Iraq war with lies. But they can wave the flag and make a speech. Send others to do the dying while they make the money."

"And this cell?"

97

"You think I'm pissed about it?" Thorne asked. "Most of them were wounded. All lost buddies over there. Careers in the military trashed." He tapped the side of his head. "PTSD. Some of those guys did two, three tours like you did."

"So what are they doing now?"

"The same thing the fuckers who sent them did. Looking out for number one."

Chase frowned. "How?"

Thorne shrugged. "However they can." He leaned back in his chair. "Your father was in Special Forces, wasn't he? Bill Chase?"

"You knew my father?" Chase reached in his pocket and pulled out the black and white photo. He handed it to Thorne.

The old man looked at the photo of the young man wearing a green beret and nodded, almost to himself. "Yeah, I knew him. He was awarded the CMH." He handed the picture back. "That was other reason I let you in."

"Tell me about my father."

"Now's not the time to get into that."

Chase started to object, then remembered the real reason he was here, although the way Thorne phrased it seemed odd. "All right. Some other time then."

Thorne let out a deep breath, then spoke. "Do you know Arty Rivers?"

"I've never met him," Chase said, confused at the abrupt switch, "but I've heard of him."

Rivers was another legend in the Special Operations community, an old warrior dating back to Vietnam who'd stayed in Special Forces for over three decades.

"Arty Rivers is interested in the Patriots too," Thorne said. "Might be affiliated with them."

"What does affiliated mean?" Chase asked.

"Mean's he's either too chicken-shit or too smart to put his ass on the line yet. You figure which."

Given that Rivers had won a Distinguished Service Cross in Vietnam, spent over thirty-five years on active duty in infantry and Special Forces, Chase was sure it was the latter.

Thorne pulled a thick cigar out of an ornately carved box. He didn't offer Chase one. He clipped off the end with an expert snip, then fired it up. "Let me tell you something about Arty Rivers. I knew him way back when you were still in diapers. We were young bucks, in the Highlands, working with the Montagnards. That was my first and only tour in Nam. He'd done a tour enlisted in the 101st prior to that as a tunnel rat so he had combat experience before coming to Special Forces. He started out enlisted, worked his way up through the ranks. The village Arty's team was working was about fifteen clicks from where I was."

Thorne puffed out a large cloud of smoke and chuckled. "You wouldn't believe it. We were arming those people with World War Two vintage M-1 carbines. But a lot of the warriors still wanted to use their crossbows. And we weren't sure who they wanted to fight more-- the VC or the South Vietnamese government. It was a pretty touchy situation."

Chase knew some of that history of Special Forces in Vietnam. The Montagnards were a hill tribe, and Special Forces' A-Teams had been sent in to train them to defend themselves. The big problem, as Thorne had just noted, was that the South Vietnamese government viewed the Montagnards to be as much of a danger to their regime as the VC.

Thorne walked over to the wall and pointed with his cigar. Chase got up and joined him. A black and white photograph-- a half-dozen white men in tiger stripe fatigues towering over smiling dark skinned men. Some of the Montagnards were indeed armed with crossbows. Chase looked closer. One of the men was Thorne with a full head of dark hair and a large, mustache. A Swedish K submachinegun was tucked under one arm, the other hand was resting on the native to his left's shoulder.

"That's Rivers," Thorne tapped the photo, indicating a tall, thin man with a wide smile standing next to Thorne.

Thorne pulled back his right sleeve. He had a bronze bracelet on the wrist. Chase had seen the like before on old, retired SF veterans. They'd been given by Montagnards to those they'd welcomed into their tribe as honorary members.

"They were good people," Thorne continued. "Innocent and naive about the world outside of their hills, but damn good fighters when someone threatened them. They didn't give a shit about the VC. Hell, the South Vietnamese tried to wipe them out every chance they had. They fought because we asked them to. Because we became part of them, like Special Forces is supposed to do. Not like the bullshit recons you guys were pulling in the Gulf the first time around."

Chase didn't say anything because he was right. The primary mission of Special Forces was to be a force multiplier, teachers who trained others to fight for themselves. In the First Gulf War, they'd sent two battalions from the 5th Special Forces Group among the Kuwaiti refugees to train them to fight for their own country, but it had not been a very successful effort. Not because the 5th Group guys didn't do their job, but because the Kuwaitis would rather let the Americans do the fighting for them. As the South Vietnamese had eventually done also. And the Iraqis were doing now. And the Afghanis.

Thorne went back to his chair. "Art's team had just finished a MEDCAP to a nearby, smaller village about five clicks from his base camp, hoping to get them into the fold. You know, the usual. Fixing minor injuries and infections, dental work, inoculations. Improving the village well, teaching sanitation. Spreading good will and helping the people.

"The night after his team left, the VC came into that village." Thorne turned slightly in his seat. His eyes were staring at the wall, not at any particular spot, but seeing memories. "Every person that had been inoculated-- man, woman, child-- had the arm that received the shot cut off. Those who had dental work-- every single tooth was smashed out of their mouth. Everything Rivers' team medics had done was undone and then made ten times worse. The VC dumped the bodies of those they killed outright-- the headman and his entire family-- into the well, contaminating it. Needless to say, those that survived didn't sign up for our civil defense program.

"We didn't quit though. And we were still able to recruit from other villages. Then, after years in the Highlands, we were ordered to pull out. To abandon the Montagnards. Because the President in Saigon was worried more about their potential for revolt than beating the VC and NVA. We were ordered not only to pull out, but to get back all the weapons we'd given them. Leave them defenseless between the VC and the South Vietnamese army, both of whom wanted to slaughter them.

"Damn near had a revolt in the Special Forces. You don't know what that was like. We'd lived and bled with these people for years, and because some politician in Washington wanted to appease those fat, corrupt pigs in Saigon, we abandoned them. Most of us left the weapons. The Group Commander's career was trashed over it, but he considered it a small price to pay.

"Hell, Chase, a lot of us would have volunteered to stay with our Yards'. But orders were orders and we were young enough to think obeying orders was more important than anything else." He was twisting the cigar in his hand, end over end. "I send twenty percent of my profits from Merck to an organization in North Carolina that brings Montagnards to the States and gets them jobs and a new life. They might be second or third generation but we owe those people and it's the honorable thing to do."

Thorne puffed on his cigar. Chase could still hear the pit bulls heavy breathing behind him, probably hoping their owner would feed the visitor to them.

Thorne finally spoke again. "Rivers last tour was in Afghanistan. He stayed in way too long. Should have got out when I did, or at least when he had his twenty. Even his thirty. He kept thinking he could do the right thing in the face of all the evidence to the contrary. Afghanistan did him in."

Chase wasn't sure why Thorne was telling him this. "Why does Rivers support the Patriots? Is he with that splinter cell?"

Thorne's eyes refocused. "Maybe it's not so much that he supports them. Maybe he's using them or after them for his own goals."

"And what would those be?"

"I wouldn't presume to speak for the man. I knew him a long time ago, but I don't think I know him anymore."

"He served and bled for our country," Chase said. "I can't see him associated with cop killers. Is he in Wyoming? Can you put me in contact with him?"

"The Patriots, that splinter cell, killed the cop, not him. Maybe it's that he loves our country, but he hates our government. Maybe he's angrier than I am. Maybe he's braver than I am." Thorne abruptly stood. "I have an editorial meeting. You know the way out."

CHAPTER ELEVEN

The pickup truck in front of Chase had no taillights. He had to just guess by the guy's head movements if he was going to change lanes and estimate if and when he was going to brake. Traffic was heavy for this time of the evening and Chase's mood was going from bad to the 'I want to kill a small living thing' mode. After leaving Thorne's office, he had his afternoon wasted at the courthouse waiting to be called to testify on an earlier case. The lawyers had dicked around, sniveling about piddly stuff and he'd never gotten on the stand. What a waste. He did manage to confirm that CNN had reported the truck being found, the authorities had 'closed off' the Medicine Bow Mountain area, as if they could really bottle those guys up, Chase thought, and beyond that nothing much was going on in Wyoming.

There was a quirky twist that was news to Chase. CNN had uncovered the reason the Deputy pulled the Blazer over. Someone had called 911 from a payphone in Boulder to report a red Blazer driving erratically on Route 287. The deputy had probably figured he was dealing with a DUI. The story told Chase either the deputy or the Patriots had been set up, most likely the latter.

Chase pulled into the garage of the A-1 cab company and parked. He was hoping somebody would come out of the little office and tell him to move his Jeep just so he could jump in their stuff, but no one did. Chase took a few deep breaths to compose himself and then got out of the Jeep.

The dispatcher was a little old lady who spoke very slowly. "Can I help you?"

Chase flipped his badge. "Detective Chase. Boulder PD." She was the first person he'd met on this case so far who seemed impressed by that. That made him feel a bit better.

"What can I do for you, detective?"

"I called earlier and talked to a Mister Jackson about a run one of your cabs did last week on Wednesday night. He said he'd have the driver down here at eight to talk to me." Chase looked pointedly at the clock on the wall. The big hand had about a fraction of an inch before hitting the big twelve.

The woman blinked and then reached down to sort through a bunch of notes on her desk. "Well, Mister Jackson left about thirty minutes ago and he didn't say anything to me." She pulled small slip of paper out. "Oh-my-gosh! I'm terribly sorry, officer. Here it is right here. It's my fault. I should have looked through this earlier. I was supposed to call Terry in. I'm real sorry."

She was looking at Chase with big old eyes that he expected to see tears pouring out of any second. He felt his anger drain away. "That's OK, Ma'am. If you could just call the driver in now, I can wait."

She got on the radio and called Terry's cab, ordering the driver to report in. Chase grabbed a newspaper and accepted the cup of coffee she offered. He knew she felt better when he took it even though the coffee was terrible.

He waited fifteen minutes. Terry was a petite, dark haired woman who appeared to be around thirty. She wasn't happy about being called in. Chase guessed she got paid by the mile and not by the hour.

"What's up?"

The old lady pointed at Chase. "Mister Jackson wants you to talk to the detective there."

Terry gave Chase an appraising look. Chase stood and offered his hand. "Detective Chase. Boulder PD."

She took the hand and then a seat. "What's up, Detective Chase, Boulder PD?"

Chase sat across from her. "I'm investigating a murder that occurred Wednesday night. We think the victim was abducted from the CU campus around ten or slightly after. I got a tip that a cab was in the vicinity of the victim's car around that time and I did some checking. Your supervisor says you logged in a drop-off at CU around that time."

She didn't have to think long about it. "Yeah. I dropped someone off Wednesday night at CU."

Chase wondered why she remembered it so easily. "Do you recollect anything about the person you dropped off?"

She nodded. "Yeah. A woman. In her thirties. Real classy. Dark hair. She was kind of neat."

Chase rummaged through his notebook and pulled out Rachel's picture. "Was this the woman?"

"Yep."

"What time did you drop her off?"

"Hold on." Terry got up and went over the file cabinets that lined one wall. She rummaged through and then came back with a folder. "All right. Let's see. OK. Pick up at nine-forty-three. Drop off at ten-oh-eight."

"Where did you pick her up at?"

She checked the log. "Broomfield. Hemlock and 2nd Avenue."

Broomfield was along Route 36, the major link between Boulder and Denver. It was more a suburb of Denver than anything else. "Do you know what she was doing there?"

Terry shook her head. "She was standing on the corner. I don't exactly remember what was there."

"When you dropped her off did you see where she went?"

"Nope. I had another call near Pearl Street."

"Did you see anyone hanging around or people in a car? Anything?"

"Not that I remember."

"Did she have anything with her? A book bag or purse?"

"She had a bag—like a large workout bag. Black."

They hadn't found that with the clothes. Chase went back to her original statement. "You said she was a neat lady. What was neat about her?"

"She talked to me. I can't remember exactly what all we talked about, but she had her shit together. I remember she did tell me that she thought it was pretty cool that I was driving a cab and that I wasn't married." Terry paused. "She the dead woman I read about?"

"Yeah."

"Fuck." Terry seemed genuinely sorry. More than Chase could say about Patsy Watkins.

Chase pumped Terry for every drop of information, but there wasn't much more. She was probably the last friendly person Rachel had seen, Chase thought. At least she thought well of her.

He got Terry to rummage through the files. What they found was interesting. Every Wednesday night that Rachel had missed class, she had used an A-1 cab to pick her up in the parking lot at CU at around six-forty-five and drive her to the same corner in Broomfield. She was picked up a little more than three hours later.

Chase knew where his next stop would be. He thanked Terry and gave her his card in case she remembered anything else. She offered to buy Chase a beer after she got off. He tactfully declined, telling her that he would be working most of the night.

****

Chase drove Foothills Parkway south until it linked up with 36. He took that toward Denver and got off at the first Broomfield exit. Hemlock and 2nd was only about five minutes from there.

It was a residential neighborhood. Upper middle class. Older homes for this area, which had a lot of new development. What had Rachel been doing here? Where had she gone for three hours? What had been in the black gym bag? Chase walked around, several blocks in each direction. A few local grocery stores. Had Rachel bought something in one of the stores and that was what had been in the bag? An elementary school. A Catholic church that was locked up. Chase guessed criminals didn't respect God.

In a sad sort of way, finding out where Rachel had been all those evenings still didn't matter. She'd gotten out of that cab at ten-oh-eight at CU alive. She'd been dead around ten-thirty, maybe plus a half hour. Someone had gotten her between the cab and her car.

Chase drove back to Boulder and into the lot where they'd found her car. He located the spot Terry had dropped Rachel off at from her description and then went through his notes and located where the BMW had been parked. A couple of hundred feet across asphalt. What had happened to Rachel Stevens during that walk?

Then he noticed something else. The library was not on line with a walk direct from the cab drop-off spot to BMW. The three made a triangle. Where had Rachel been heading if not her car? The library to do some research?

Everyone had said she was smart. Real smart. But that didn't mean she had a lot of common sense. She might have been sucked in too close to an open door on a car or van. Then hit on the back of the head. Dragged inside. They raped her. Most likely in the vehicle. Someone cut her throat. They drove to the park and dumped the naked body. They remembered the clothes on the way out and threw them in the garbage can at the car wash. But the bag hadn't been with the clothes.

It all sounded very logical. Chase drove from the lot to where it all had started that first day. It took Chase nine minutes. With the cover of night, he could see why the killers had used this spot to dump her. It was quiet out here. No houses. There was only the one road in and one out and you could see headlights coming either way for warning.

Chase got out of his Jeep and sat on the hood. It was a clear, cool night. He could see the stars clearly overhead. A slight breeze was blowing from the mountains. In the moonlight, the rocks and meadows looked beautiful. He wondered where along that nine-minute drive Rachel Stevens had died.

It was logical, but it was wrong. There were still a few pieces that didn't fit. Donnelly would want Chase and Porter to jam them in whether they did or not. Chase knew that wasn't Porter's style. His partner needed to be sure before he brought a case in to the DA. They have the electric chair in Colorado for murder one and Porter would never want to have the slightest doubt when it came to the possibility of someone getting fried; not that a jury in Boulder would sentence someone to fry. Now Colorado Springs-- anywhere else in Colorado for that matter, except maybe Aspen and Vail-- the jury would want to string a killer up themselves.

The timing bugged Chase. If four scuzzes had snatched Rachel at ten after ten for a good time, they sure had been quick about it. Even going with the far side of Hanson's estimate of time of death that left them only fifty-two minutes to snatch her, rape her, and kill her.

Chase remembered that Hanson had also said that she had stood up sometime after having had sex. That didn't fit either. Unless they were in a van or some sort of truck. Or they'd let her out here and then killed her.

Shit. Hanson couldn't guarantee she was raped. Chase trusted the Doc. If he doubted rape, then Chase doubted it too. And a jury would doubt it too, because that's the way Hanson would testify unless he found something to change his mind. Which meant Porter wouldn't go for it either.

The gym bag and the misdirection in the parking lot also bothered Chase although it was possible his witness in the dorm had been mistaken about the latter detail.

Chase took a deep breath and looked about. He remembered the strange feeling he had the first morning he'd been here. The lack of tracks to the body. The way her throat had been cut.

Screw Donnelly and the media. Chase made his decision. Porter could handle the street angle. Chase was going to have to backtrack a little and take a long hard look at who Rachel Stevens had been and find out what the hell she had been doing that night for two hours and forty-five minutes. The first step was to go back tomorrow morning and see Doc Hanson. Chase headed for his apartment.

* * * * * * * * * * * *

Chase was a block away from home when his beeper went off. His black one. He pulled over and checked the small LED screen. The code was for an immediate Boulder SWAT Team alert. It gave an address. North Boulder.

As he squealed the tires pulling a U-turn, he wondered if it was a drill. They had them every once in a while. His second thought was to wonder if it was a set-up. If Fortin would be waiting there for him. Damn, he was getting paranoid.

Chase cocked his head and heard sirens. All heading in the same direction he was, paralleling his route over on Broadway while he shot up 9th. This was no drill.

The large black van that was both SWAT headquarters and held the team's special gear was pulling up next to two black and whites as Chase arrived. The cops from those two were behind their cars, shotguns pointed at a large house on the other side of the street. It was backed against Open Space, which meant there was nothing man-made behind it as the land rose up to the foothills.

Chase scuttled out of his Jeep, careful not to expose himself to the house, and got over to the van. The shift sergeant was present, as it was his duty to get the van to the alert site from the station. He had it parked front toward the house and slid between the seats, opening the back doors. Chase joined him.

"What do you have?" Chase asked as he pulled his vest off the wall and slipped it on.

"Shots fired. Neighbors called it in."

"And?" Chase pulled his keys out and unlocked the weapons bin. He grabbed an MP-5 sub-machinegun.

"That's it so far."

Another SWAT member raced up. Doug Pederson, a detective. He was a good man, but in Chase's opinion, Boulder SWAT was about as good as army MPs when it came to door busting. Pederson slipped his vest on and grabbed another MP-5. Chase longed for a set of night

107

vision goggles. That way he could get the power cut, then move up on the house in the dark-- odds were whoever had fired off rounds inside didn't have NVGs and Chase would have the advantage.

Of course, they didn't have NVGs in the van. Chase supposed he should be grateful Boulder had sprung for the MP-5s. The idiot who let the contract had allowed the salesman to talk him into buying the flashlight that clipped onto the bottom of the barrel-- a poor man's way of seeing in the dark. Chase wasn't a big fan of walking around with a light on his gun-- sort of like saying, *hey, here I am and please shoot me!*

"How many shots?" Chase asked the shift sergeant.

"A couple, then a burst of automatic weapon firing."

Shit, why hadn't he told me that in the first place? Chase bit his tongue to keep from saying anything. New ballgame. More black and whites were arriving. Hell, the entire evening shift was showing up.

"Any of the neighbors say who lives there?"

"A young couple and their baby."

Chase was getting ready to hit the shift sergeant-- he didn't have a clue how pissed Chase was. All that good West Point training kept it bottled deep inside because it would only screw up this already fucked up situation.

"Move those other cars out of here," Chase ordered the shift sergeant. "Clear the houses on either side through the garage doors-- they should be covered there. Then clear every house across the street through the back doors." Chase knew there were probably idiots looking out their windows, just waiting to catch a stray round in the head. "Then shut the street down. No one but SWAT members come through. Got it?"

The shift sergeant nodded, happy to have marching orders. He scurried off to do as he'd been told. Chase looked at Pederson, who appeared none too happy. As far as Chase knew, no one other than Chase on the SWAT team had ever fired shots for real-- real being when someone was shooting back.

Chase reached out and stopped Pederson as he was pulling an MP-5 out of the bin. "I need you on the long gun."

That cheered him up a bit. It meant Chase wasn't going to ask him to bust open the front door. Of course, Chase didn't plan on doing that himself either. There were eight men on the SWAT team and as the seconds ticked away, Chase began to wonder where the hell the rest of them were.

It was decision time. The police book said wait until the entire team was on station, then proceed cautiously. But someone probably had been hit by those bullets and could still be alive but bleeding out. And there was a baby. And Chase had been trained differently in the 'killing house' at Fort Bragg: hit fast and hard. It wasn't correct police procedure, but correct police procedure could get people killed in unusual situations like this as Columbine and Virginia Tech had demonstrated.

Chase lay down in the street and edged his head around the van's back tire. The house was set into an incline as the Open Space behind it rose to a ridgeline. Garage doors on first floor, stairs to the front door on the right of the garage going up to the second level. Small balcony on the front of the top floor. No lights on. Nothing moving in the windows.

Another SWAT man arrived and geared up. Three of eight. Pederson was on the other side of the van, rifle pointed at the house. The two black and whites were still parked caddie corner, their former occupants waiting with shotguns trained. At the range they were from the house, Chase knew those shotguns were worthless.

"Joe," Chase nodded at the newest arrival. He nodded in return, continuing to gear up.

The shift lieutenant should have been here by now, Chase knew. This was his call until someone higher ranking arrived. Where the hell was everyone?

"Hey!" Pederson hissed from his position. "Front door!"

Chase got back on his belly and looked. The door was opening very slowly. One of the idiot patrol car officers trained his spotlight on the door, blinding the person coming out. Chase almost yelled for him to turn the light off, then he saw the figure in the door. A woman. She had a short skirt on and was naked from the waist up. Her chest and stomach were covered with blood. A gun was in her hand, but like an afterthought, as if she wasn't even aware it was there any more. She took a step out, onto the small landing, and then collapsed almost in slow motion, to her knees, then doing a face plant onto the steps. The gun tumbled down a few more steps before coming to a halt.

Chase knew she was dead. He'd seen people die and she was dead as the proverbial doornail. But he also knew he was the only one watching who was sure of that. Everyone else was on edge, anxious to do something, but waiting on orders. And there might a baby. Of course, there was someone else with a gun in there. Unless she'd shot herself a couple of times in the chest. Right.

The shift sergeant came running up. "What are we going to do?"

"Joe. Doug."

Both of them stared at Chase expectantly. Yeah, in normal time, the Boulder PD looked at Chase like dog shit as a cop, but they knew his background and right now, both of them wanted Chase to solve this problem. To take charge.

"Here's the plan." It took Chase thirty seconds to outline, and that was speaking slowly. He'd always given plans in the simplest language and spoken carefully, looking men in the eyes to make sure he saw a spark of understanding. Given it took only thirty seconds meant it wasn't much of a plan. But as his first team sergeant in Special Forces used to say, even a shitty plan was better than having Rommel stick it up your ass on the drop zone. Chase had never been quite sure what he'd meant by that.

"Got it?"

Both men nodded, Joe less enthusiastically as he was going to be the more exposed of the two. Like Chase gave a damn. His ass was going to be the one on the line literally and legally.

Chase turned to the other person in the back of the van. "Got it?"

The shift sergeant nodded, then ran back to the black and whites to update the patrolmen there.

"Let's go."

Pederson took his place at the back of the van with the sniper rifle.

Chase put his hand on Joe's shoulder, letting his finger slide above the armored collar. He could feel the man's pulse racing, but not out of control. "You ready?"

Joe nodded.

"On three. One. Two. Three."

The two broke from the back of the van, running all out for the front of the house. Chase's head was tucked down and they were both leaning forward, as if going into a fierce wind. Chase remembered reading Killer Angels and that was how Shaara had described the Confederate Troops as they approached Cemetery Ridge during

Picket's charge-- hunched forward, anticipating the bullet. It's bizarre the things that go through a person's head in three seconds of running.

They reached the garage doors. Joe pulled a flash-bang grenade off his vest and held it tight. Chase moved to the right where the molding cornered underneath the drainpipe. He slung the MP-5 over his shoulder, then grabbed both sides of the molding, around the corner.

Chase began to climb, feeling naked as he went up. Anyone inside the house would have to stick their head out a window to see Chase, so that wasn't too bad, but he didn't exactly trust all the people behind him, who were supposed to be on his side. If someone with a gun stuck, his head out there were three possibilities, two of them bad. One that Pederson would shoot the bad guy and that would be that. Two that Pederson would miss and the bad guy would shoot Chase. Three, that either one or two happened but some other idiot with a shotgun or pistol would plug away, miss the bad guy and hit Chase. Chase should have told the shift sergeant to have his men lower their weapons. Too late now. It's the details that get you killed, Chase had been told time and time again in his various assignments and training.

But no one stuck their head out, so no one had to shoot. Chase reached the top of the house, his arms quivering with exhaustion. The roof had a thirty-degree slope, not a problem, and he quickly moved to the peak until he was over the bay doors that opened onto the third floor porch. Which should lead into the master bedroom. Regardless, he was on top and the one rule that had been beaten into Chase during close quarters battle training, CQB as the army called it, was the optimum way to proceed was to clear from the top. Military guys like the high ground any way they can get it.

Chase crouched on the edge of the roof and looked down. The balcony wasn't as big as he had thought. Maybe it was the perspective, because if he missed it, there was a hell of a fall to the driveway. Joe was looking up at Chase, the grenade still in his hand. Chase nodded, hoping Joe could see the movement, while Chase unslung the MP-5, holding it in his left hand.

With his other hand, Joe smashed the small square window in the garage door, pulled the pin, then tossed the grenade in the garage. Chase had three seconds. He waited one and a half, then jumped. He hit and his right knee, the one he'd hurt on a jump years ago, buckled. He ignored the pain and pushed forward, smashing through the glass.

111

The flash-bang went off in the garage, the sound echoing loudly through the house at exactly the same time Chase went through the glass. He was on his feet moving, sweeping the room with his eyes, the muzzle of the MP-5 following wherever he looked.

It was the master bedroom but no one was in it. Chase limped to the door, bleeding from a half-dozen cuts on his exposed skin. He 'pied' into the hallway, taking the door in sections, weapon extended, until he was completely in the hall.

There was a noise coming from the other end. As Chase took a step forward, he tried to place it. He moved down the hallway, his finger ready over the trigger. As he got closer, he recognized the sound. Someone trying to breath and not doing a good job at it, struggling for air because they had a hole in one of their lungs; what the medics called a sucking chest wound. Chase had heard this exact sound before and he paused, then shook his head, getting rid of that memory.

The door at the end of the hallway was partly open. Chase could see a blood trail leading from it to the stairs. Chase looked over the railing. The blood went down as far as he could see. The wife's. She'd made it to the front door, dying all the way.

Chase tucked the stock of the MP-5 tight into his shoulder. The sound was coming from beyond the partially open door on this floor. He could see a small section of wall, dimly lit by a low-level glow, perhaps a night-light. The wallpaper was Winnie the Pooh and the rest of the cast of characters.

Chase stood perfectly still. The hoarse breathing was the only sound he could hear other than the thud of his own heart. He slowed his breathing and focused all his consciousness into his senses and the weapon in his hand.

Chase hit the door fast and low. He didn't do any of those bullshit rolls like actors did in movies. Just skidded to a halt in a squat, presenting as small a target as possible, weapon tight to his shoulder and his sight picture square on, dead center between the eyes of the man lying half-upright against the wall next to the crib.

Chase's finger tightened on the trigger, then paused. The man had a gun in his hand, but it was on his lap, not aimed at Chase. He wasn't even looking at Chase. He was looking at the crib.

Chase didn't want to, he shouldn't have-- bad procedure-- but he looked too. He felt something slam into his chest and he rocked back on his heels. Not a bullet, but pain and shock, as if someone had just swung a sledgehammer and hit Chase. The tiny body in the crib was nothing but dead flesh and splattered blood.

Chase looked back at the man on the floor. His shirt was soaked in blood and ripped open to his waist in the front. Chase could see an entry wound in the man's upper right chest, the bubbling froth of pink where air was desperately being sucked in, and blood and air came out with each exhale.

"Kill me."

Chase looked into the man's eyes.

"Kill me," he repeated.

Chase was amazed he could even speak given his wound.

"My fault." He leaned ever so slightly toward the crib. "Kill me."

"Anyone else in the house?"

The man shook his head. Chase kept the MP-5 trained on him and with his right hand keyed the radio handset clipped to the upper part of his vest. "Pederson. Over."

"Here!" The radio crackled, before Pederson remembered proper procedure. "Over."

"Come in. I think the rest of the house is clear, but I wouldn't bet your life on it. I've got the husband and--" Chase paused-- "baby here. Third floor, rear bedroom. We need paramedics. Move! Now! Out."

"Kill me."

He was like a bad tape recording. He began to lift the gun.

"Don't do that." Chase let go of the radio and put both hands on the MP-5.

The man's hand was shaking.

Chase heard the front door get busted in.

The man pointed the gun at Chase. The muzzle was wavering, but it was in the general direction of Chase's head. He knew that because the opening at the end of the barrel was growing larger. "Put it down!"

Chase heard boots on the stairs.

The man's finger curled around the trigger. Chase saw the look in the man's eyes. Chase had seen that before too.

Chase fired, the round hitting the man just three inches to the left of the other hole, and an inch up. Straight through the heart. The man died without blinking.

CHAPTER TWELVE

Chase stood in the police chief's office. It reminded Chase of going around to upperclassmen's rooms as a plebe at West Point. They'd had a ritual called the 'magical mystery tour'. Some upperclassmen would play the Beatle's song loudly on his stereo to drown out the screaming, then plebes would get sent from room to room, not knowing what to expect with each new door. Some upperclassmen would flame you, others would be doing homework and barely acknowledge your presence, making you stand at attention in a corner until the song started again and it was time to move to a new room.

This looked like a flaming to Chase. The chief was behind his desk, flanked by the mayor and DA. They were sitting, Chase was standing. Nobody had said 'Hey, Chase, how's it hanging?' when he'd walked in. Nobody looked happy.

Chase had told his story for the fifth time and they had a copy of the report he'd typed up in the wee hours. He made sure his knees weren't locked so he wouldn't cut off the flow of blood to his lower legs and keel over. Just like he used to during parades on the Plain at the Academy. It occurred to Chase that he was reverting, going back to all the places he'd said he'd never go to again.

"So the suspect didn't fire at you?" District Attorney Wheeler asked.

Chase turned his gaze toward the DA. Wheeler was of medium height, with gray hair that was little too long in Chase's opinion for someone who worked for the people. His face was permanently flushed, a result of too many business lunches and after-work cocktails. Wheeler had a reputation for being afraid to tackle any hard cases. Porter had told Chase that he couldn't remember the last time Wheeler had set foot inside a courtroom to actually try a case. The DA's office plea-bargained everything they could. That was winning in their opinion.

Chase kept tight rein on his voice as he answered Wheeler. "Perhaps I should have waited until the suspect shot me in the head."

"And he asked you to kill him, right?" The chief was supposedly a different story. He was post-Ramsey, post-Karr, and he was smart. At least that was what the Daily Camera said. Chase had never spoken to him before. The Chief spent his time playing politics in the minefield of Boulder's hierarchy. Chase had never seen him in the squad room.

"I put that in report because that's what happened. He felt bad about killing his kid."

The chief looked inside a file folder, then up at Chase. "His gun didn't fire the bullet that killed his baby."

Chase locked into the chief's eyes. "Then he was torn up about his wife having shot the baby while trying to shoot him."

"The gun the wife carried out the door didn't kill the baby either," the chief informed Chase. "And the first round that hit the man you killed-- Barnes was his name, Tim Barnes-- wasn't fired from the wife's gun. We haven't recovered that gun. It wasn't in the house."

Chase felt a flash of anger as he realized he'd been ambushed.

The chief was watching Chase. "You thought a husband-wife domestic fight? Baby shot accidentally?"

Chase nodded.

"You were wrong."

"I made the right decisions on the scene," Chase said.

"That will be for the review board to decide," the chief said.

"Why weren't you there?" Chase asked. A red flush ascended from the chief's collar and across his hatchet-like face. "We were on scene for almost ten minutes before we went in," Chase continued before the chief could say anything. "The shift sergeant was there, but not the shift lieutenant. Don't you think that's curious? Sir?" Chase added, his tone on the last word indicating what he thought of the chief. "Don't you think the review board ought to consider the entire situation, sir?"

"It's your actions that—" the chief began, but Chase cut him off.

"I work for two bosses," Chase said. "You can put me before your review board, but my other boss is going to be very interested in the timing of events last night. Very interested. They know how a competent police force should react in that type of situation."

If looks could kill, Chase would have been incinerated on the spot. Chase didn't know how much, if anything, they knew about

Wyoming and how his far 'other' boss would be willing to let him hang out to dry, but life is a poker game. Sometimes you call the bluff and you play the hand.

"And if he isn't that interested, the media will be," Chase threw the last gauntlet on the table. When you have nothing to lose, you have nothing to lose.

The chief exchanged glances with the DA and the mayor. "You're dismissed," was his way of ending the interview.

Chase walked out.

****

Chase didn't get over to see Hanson until very late in the morning. It wasn't only the meeting in city hall. There was paperwork to be filled out. Detectives never fill out forms on TV as far as Chase had ever seen, but he not only had to fill out his but Porter's too. It was part of the deal they had. Porter was still out pounding the streets. He hadn't even come into the office this morning. He was smart enough to know that if he did it would be hours before he got out again. Chase had to wonder if his partner didn't come in because he was afraid of fallout from the shooting from the night before. He didn't think so, but things were beginning to get hairy.

Porter's paperwork wasn't too bad this time, but Chase had enough forms to fill out about the previous evening on top of his original report, that he wondered how anything got done. After finally achieving that satisfied feeling of having, an empty in-box, no matter how briefly it lasted, Chase got the hell out of there. He still hadn't heard from the chief or Donnelly so it seemed as if his bluff was holding.

A cold front was moving through Colorado and Chase had to turn on the heat in the Jeep. It was a fifty-minute drive to Denver and Hanson's office. The coroner was seated at his desk looking through a thick book and making notes.

Chase took a seat and waited. The coroner wasn't being rude. He was just working. Finally, Hanson closed the book. "Found something intelligent to ask?"

"A couple of things. First. Rachel Stevens. The woman from last week?"

He nodded.

"You said it wasn't rape even though you found the semen. How sure are you?"

Hanson steepled his fingers together and looked at Chase for a few seconds before replying. "I can't guarantee it, but I would not be willing to testify that it was rape based on the physical evidence."

"But couldn't she have been threatened into having sex? Wouldn't that have kept her from getting torn up?"

"You're forgetting something, Detective Chase. Even if she'd wanted to, the men who supposedly raped her wouldn't have worried too much about not hurting her. They killed her after all."

Chase checked his notebook. "What's chlorhexidine gluconate?"

Hanson gave a ghost of a smile. "I should have known better than to use big words with cops. Finding that was another reason, I don't think she was raped. I've never heard of a rapist who used KY jelly in the commission of his crime."

Another piece of the puzzle that didn't fit. Chase felt much better about his decision last night. If Rachel hadn't been raped, and robbery had already been tentatively ruled out, then all they had was that she'd been killed. In a way, they had been using the rape as the motive for the killing. If they took the rape away then why was she killed?

It could have been a random killing, but she was taken out of that parking lot. It almost made Chase think someone was waiting for her specifically. He could have been wrong. But the theory of four men snatching her, raping her (with KY jelly), then killing her and making the drive to the park all inside of an hour had a lot of holes in it too in his opinion. The wound and the lack of tracks near the body also bothered him. A lot.

Chase felt the need for an objective opinion. He told Hanson about the cab and the timing and all the other little pieces that made it a confused picture.

Hanson summed it all up from his perspective. "I don't deal in motives. I deal in physical evidence. She had sex, Detective Chase. Unprotected sex. With four different men. She stood sometime after having sex. Then she was killed by one man. The others might have been there, but it was probably only one set of hands that made the wound on her throat. Those are the facts that I have."

"There's another thing," Chase said.

"Yes?"

"The baby from last night. And the parents."

Hanson grimaced. For the first time Chase saw an emotion cross Hanson's face. "I don't like doing autopsies on babies. Especially those that die because of violence." He shook his head. "It's—" he searched for words. "It's looking into the soul of the devil. It's profane."

"I was told the bullets that killed the baby and wounded the father weren't fired by the wife's gun."

"All three were shot by the same weapon-- barring your fatal shot into the father--" Hanson amended. "Seven point six two millimeter by thirty-nine."

"Soviet AK-47."

Hanson nodded. "Most likely, although some other Russian weapons fire the same round. The SKS was the first rifle that used that size round, but I agree it's most likely an AK-47."

Chase let that sink in. AK's were pretty common, even in America. In fact, he knew it was the most widely manufactured gun in the history of mankind. But the neighbor had told the shift sergeant that she heard automatic firing. That meant an AK illegally modified to fire on automatic. Chase knew an AK like that was used just a couple of days ago.

Could the Patriots have been involved? Someone had gone into that house, shot both the husband and wife, the baby, then been gone by the time the cops got there. It would have been easy to escape. Out the back door, into the Open Space and freedom.

Were the Barnes hooked in to the Patriots? But they had gone back to Wyoming and the local authorities and Feds had that place sown up tight so they couldn't have come back, could they? Chase had no doubt though, that the Patriots could circumvent any sort of 'blockade' that was in place with their four-wheel drive vehicles as they knew the terrain and all the trails in the area. The same way the Taliban could cross the Pakistan-Afghan border with ease. Or had someone been with the Barnes that night and that same person set the Patriots up to be picked up and that person was still in Boulder? A lot of questions with not much to start on.

And Chase knew that he couldn't count on whomever the chief had assigned to the case to have a snowball's chance in hell of catching whoever had done this or connecting two dots, never mind the half-dozen this situation seemed to call for.

"You all right?" Hanson asked.

"No. I'm not."

"Detective Chase--"

Chase looked up. "Yes?"

"Even if EMT got to him, Tim Barnes would have been dead in ten minutes. Your shot just saved him some misery and pain."

"Yeah, I'm a regular angel of mercy. Tell the chief that."

Hanson looked at the door, then at Chase. "There's something else. Actually a couple of other things that are strange."

"What?"

He pulled a file folder from his out-box. He opened it and slid a couple of photos across to Chase. "They'd been tied up. The parents. Check out the ligature marks on their wrists and ankles. A smooth, thin, nylon cord."

That didn't make any sense. "Like 550 cord?" 550 cord was a bunch of strings wrapped inside a green nylon outer-shell that was used extensively in the military. It was the same cord used on the risers for parachutes.

Hanson nodded. "I would say that fits the marks."

Chase didn't have time to dwell on it as Hanson continued.

"And the baby--" Hanson shook his head at a loss for words. Chase knew what was coming was bad. Hanson passed Chase another photo. Chase stared at it without comprehension. It was a close-up of pink, jagged flesh. Chase wasn't sure whose body or what part of the body he was looking at. He'd never seen anything like it.

"Someone did something to the baby's mouth. That's the interior. I'd have to say somebody used a hand-held dental drill to cut into its gums, into the base where its teeth were forming."

Chase dropped the photo on the table. "Why?"

"To hurt it," Hanson said.

"Why?" It was the only thing Chase could say in the face of his shock.

Hanson shrugged. "That's getting to motive again, detective. I can only give you the physical evidence."

Chase tried to think. The Barnes had been tied up and someone had drilled into their baby's mouth. To make them talk? But whoever it was had untied them. Then shot them. Or shot them and they got untied after the intruder left? Trina Barnes made it to the front door and died of her wounds. Tim Barnes stayed with the kid. She'd been half-undressed. Nothing fit.

"Was Trina Barnes raped?"

119

"No evidence of that."

Even in war, Chase had never seen a baby that had been tortured. Died of neglect-- yes. Abused-- yes. But nothing like this. He felt a chill pass through his body. Chase thanked the Doc for his time and left. It was a long drive back to Boulder and he used it to try to get his composure back.

****

Chase pulled up to the hangar and parked off to the side. He could see Masters sitting on top of the Huey, a cowling off one of the engines, his hands buried inside the machine. Jefferson County Airport sat on a high plateau between Denver and Boulder and the foothills, white-capped peaks behind them, loomed a dozen miles to the west.

Chase got out of the Jeep and walked over to the chopper.

"What's the good word?" Masters called out from his perch.

"No good news," Chase said.

Masters shook his head. "Man, you are one grim motherfucker." He got up and climbed down a ladder on the side of the bird.

"If you'd just seen what I did, you'd be pretty grim too."

"I heard about last night," Masters said, leading him into a cluttered office on the side of the hangar and pouring them both a cup of coffee.

"You didn't hear all of it." Chase quickly relayed to Masters what Henson had just told him.

When he was done, Masters put the mug of coffee he'd been cradling in his hands onto his desk. "You're talking about evil."

Chase frowned. "What do you mean?"

"Pure fucking evil," Masters said. "You and I both seen some bad shit in combat. But torture a baby? That's evil. That's someone who's operating on an entirely different level. A fucking sociopath."

Another psychobabble term, Chase thought, but he knew what it meant and it fit. "Same kind of evil that would rape a woman and garrote her?"

"Could be, but it seems like a different sort of act." Masters shrugged. "How the fuck do I know. I'm just a pilot. You're the cop."

"Yeah, right."

"Hey." Masters leaned forward in his chair. "You *are* a cop, Chase. You carry a fucking badge."

120

"Should I have killed those men in Wyoming?"

Masters didn't seem surprised at the abrupt question. "It was your call. No one can answer that but you. I know Fortin's probably got his boot knee deep in your ass, but he's gotta respect that."

"Think he's going to?"

"No."

Chase nodded. "That's what I thought." He took a sip of the coffee. Masters sat quietly, letting the silence play out.

Finally Chase spoke. "You know Colonel Rivers?"

"Heard of him," Masters said. "Why?"

"I heard he might be messing around with the Patriots."

"You run that by Fortin?"

"Fortin ran me over, I'm not about to disturb any more shit."

The phone rang. Masters picked it up. "You call, we haul." He listened, checked his watch, then said bye. "Got a job, Chase." He headed for the hanger. "You need anything, give me a call."

* * * * * * * * * * * * *

Chase had a lunch date with Sylvie. He thought about calling to cancel, in no mood for either sex or food, but he figured she's prepared something and didn't want to be rude.

When he entered the apartment, he could smell food cooking. Sylvie came out of her bedroom, dressed in the same outfit she'd worn on stage the previous evening, including the whip. She gave Chase a wicked smile, which slowly faded as she sensed his mood.

"You all right?"

Chase shook his head. "No."

Sylvie turned around and went back into the bedroom, reappearing a few seconds later wearing her thick white robe. She came over and gave him a hug.

"Smells good," Chase said.

"Me or the food?"

"Both."

"Thanks." She went into the kitchen turned up the heat. "Put some plates out."

Sylvie didn't cook fancy stuff, but it was good basic food. Today it was some sort of noodles with Sylvie's homemade sauce. Chase tried to eat but he didn't have much appetite. He also noticed Sylvie wasn't

121

eating. She was just sitting there watching him. He put the down the utensils. "What?"

"I heard about what happened last night. I thought I could get your mind off it."

"I appreciate the thought. I'm dealing with it."

"I don't understand you, sometimes," Sylvie said. "You seem to need me at times and other times you don't. You killed a man last night, Chase. Yet--" she ran out of words and shrugged.

"The coroner says the man I shot would have been dead in ten minutes anyway," Chase said. "I guess you might say I did him a favor."

"A favor?"

"Hey--" Chase put his hands on the table, perhaps a bit too hard but he was tired. "He begged me to shoot him. I had another shot I could have taken the--" Chase caught himself. "Listen, Sylvie, I appreciate your interest in my work but can we talk about something else?" Chase picked up his fork and forced a smile. But his fork paused halfway to his mouth and he realized he couldn't eat. He thought of the baby's mouth and knew he could never say anything about that to her.

Sylvie put down her fork. "This woman's death is really getting to you isn't it?"

Chase felt on safer ground discussing Rachel's case because everything else made even less sense. "It's the whole thing, Sylvie. Something doesn't fit, and I can't seem to figure out what it is."

Chase told Sylvie everything he had learned in the last day and a half about the case. It took a while, but she was right; this case was definitely affecting him, like an irritating itch deep inside a wound that wasn't healing.

Sylvie was sipping the coffee she had brewed during the course of his monologue, and paying very rapt attention. After he finished and asked her what she thought, she continued to stare silently at Chase.

Finally, he couldn't take it anymore. "Are you upset? Why aren't you saying anything?"

She put down the mug and stood up. At first Chase thought, she was leaving the room, but she began clearing the table. "Chase, tell me about Rachel."

He started to rehash the facts of the murder, but she cut him off.

"I know all the stuff about her death."

This time Chase interrupted, "You don't know who killed her."

She put the dishes down and motioned for Chase to follow. She perched in the big wicker rocker that seemed to be her favorite spot; aside from the bed. Chase took that as a sign that she just wanted to get comfortable, and made his own spot amid the dozen pillows on the bed. He lay on his back and stared at the ceiling. She had a nice mattress with a down comforter and it felt so good, he was afraid he might just fall asleep.

"You're right, Chase. I don't know who killed her, but neither do you. And I have to admit that although I find it interesting to speculate on who killed Rachel Stevens, what I'm really interested in is who was this woman? Her life is as much a mystery as her death. I want to know about her life. Who she was."

Chase rubbed his eyes with both hands and tried to stifle his yawn. "Sylvie, I know you want to get at the psychological core of this, but right now I'm still at the basic shit level. What I need to find out is where she was while she skipped class. But even if I find that out, I still won't know who killed her. I need to know what she was doing so I can go some place with this." Chase turned his head and looked at her.

Sylvie nodded. "My point exactly, except I think you're going about it backwards. You want to know what she did, but unless you ask everyone in that neighborhood in Broomfield where she was during those hours you're never going to know.

"Hell, she could have been sitting in a closet chilling out every third Wednesday night, unseen by human eyes. I'm just trying to tell you that you need to know who Rachel Stevens was. When you understand her as a person and, more importantly, as a woman, you might be able to sit down and figure out where she would go.

"Think about it Chase: here's a woman with a husband, lots of social obligations and a very demanding academic career. Time was the most valuable asset she had. There has to be a very good reason why she spent three hours every three weeks so mysteriously. Especially if she took it out of her school time, which her husband says was important to her."

Chase nodded in Sylvie's direction to let her know he understood. What he wanted at that moment was to hide in a closet himself and think about everything. Maybe that's what Rachel had needed: to just get away for a while. But he had started all this and Sylvie wasn't going to give up that easy. She asked Chase if anyone else had been absent the night Rachel was killed. When Sylvie first brought this up at the

New York Deli, Chase had thought it was a good question. But other events had set Sylvie's idea on the backburner.

Chase told Sylvie that finding out who Rachel had been with was still critical, but as she had just said, he needed to look at Rachel's life differently to understand where she had been that Wednesday.

"Chase, quit focusing on where she was, what she was doing, and with whom. Put your attention on the part of the puzzle that will give you the answer. Why was Rachel Stevens' hiding a part of her life?"

Then she looked at Chase very calmly and asked something he should have thought of a long time ago. "Did she go some place every third Wednesday for three hours *before* she entered the program at the University of Colorado?"

Chase had gotten so used to thinking of Rachel's class as a ruse that it had never occurred to him to wonder if the secret extended any further back.

Chase made another mental note to talk to Doctor Stevens as soon as possible. If Rachel had only started disappearing in the last year and a half, then Sylvie was right about the CU connection. But Chase had a feeling that even if Sylvie were right, there was still something very wrong.

CHAPTER THIRTEEN

Chase had called on his cell phone and found out the doctor would be in his office at three. He then checked in with Porter on his street crusade, arranging to meet him downtown. His partner was in his element, stalking downtown and hitting all the out-of-the-way places scumbags hung out. He hadn't found squat, but he was happy. He felt something would break soon. Chase met his partner and filled him in on what he had learned from Hanson about Stevens and a little bit about the direction he was headed in.

They were standing outside of Custard's Last Stand, a hot dog joint on Broadway. Porter was wolfing down something dripping with all the trimmings that Chase was trying not to look at as it made his stomach rumble.

"You're showing a lot of good initiative," Porter said. "I agree with Hanson. I don't think this murder was about a rape. And I still think the husband was involved."

Chase didn't want to disagree with Porter. "Could be," he said. "I just need to know more about Rachel."

Porter paused with the over-loaded hot dog halfway to his mouth. "'Rachel'?"

"Mrs. Stevens."

"You sure you don't have too much going on?" Porter asked. "I haven't seen you since last night, but that must have been a hell of thing."

Chase shrugged. "It was pretty much over by the time we got there."

"You killed someone Chase."

"He was already dying. I just hastened it."

"I suppose that's a way of looking at it, but the word is your ass is in a sling."

"I don't know what the hell went down in that house before we went in," Chase said. "No one does."

"But a baby." Porter shook his head. "Jesus."

Chase knew better than to share the information from Hanson about the baby with Porter. His partner would go crazy with it.

Chase waited, knowing he had to follow his partner's lead on the case. Porter finished the hot dog. "There's something going on in this town, Chase." Porter began walking toward the Broadway Bridge over Boulder Creek.

"What do you mean?"

Porter glanced at him. "Don't act stupid. First the shooting of that deputy with the call originating from here. Then the murder of Mrs. Stevens. Then last night. I don't see any connection at all between the three. But something fucking weird is going on. Maybe it's the weather. Maybe it's just the town. Maybe it's just a bad spirit."

Chase was startled by the last one as it echoed the feeling he'd had in Wyoming and at Rachel's crime scene.

Porter came to a halt on the bridge, looking down at the torrent of water from the spring thaw. "What do you think?"

"I don't know," Chase said. "I don't see any connection either." Except a slight one between the Barnes and the Patriots with the type of round, but that was very slight and he saw no reason to mention that to Porter. "I'm not really a cop, Ben. You know that. I'm doing the best I can. Hell, I'm going back to Doctor Stevens because Sylvie suggested it."

Porter nodded. "It takes a woman to know a woman. I've got no problem with it, Chase. I was a little worried when they assigned me to partner with you. But you're doing all right. I'm worried now about you as a person."

"I'm all right."

"You like being a cop?"

Chase blinked. "What?"

"You like being a cop?" Porter repeated.

"I like helping people."

Porter nodded. "Yeah. Me too. But you have—" he paused, searching for words—"a wicked edge to you. I don't know how else to say it. What you did last night. I couldn't do that. No one else in this department could do it."

"Someone has to do it."

"Yeah," Porter agreed. "But do you *want* to do it?"

"It's the job," Chase said.

"But you choose the job." Porter seemed to be searching for words. "Being a cop isn't being a soldier. In the army you followed orders. Here you follow the law."

"Same thing."

"No." Porter shook his head. "Donnelly might be an asshole, but he doesn't decide what right or wrong is or what the law is. Same with the chief and the DA. They decide policy, but not law."

Chase was trying to follow where Porter was going. "My commanders in the army didn't decide who we went to war against."

Porter sighed. "I don't know what exactly I'm trying to say, Chase. But there's a line and I feel like it's getting blurry. I believe in the law. It only fails when the people who are responsible for enforcing it fail." He slapped Chase on the back. "Let's figure out who killed Mrs. Stevens. All right?"

Chase nodded. He felt a chasm opening between his partner and himself and he didn't have the energy to bridge it and he wasn't even sure what the chasm was. "That's the idea."

* * * * * * * * * * *

Lisa Plunkett gave Chase a tentative smile when he came in the door. She was nicely dressed in an outfit that definitely showed off her figure. She ushered Chase straight into Doctor Stevens' office. He was looking better. Rachel had been buried yesterday and maybe that had helped. Chase caught the look Lisa gave him as she closed the door and Chase had little doubt that when the doctor came out of his bereavement, he'd find someone waiting in the wings. According to Porter she was already on stage with him.

Chase didn't know why he was being so suspicious of every little look, but the doctor, despite an airtight alibi, was high on Porter's list of possibilities and he trusted his partner. A person could hire some bozo from Denver to whack someone for a couple of hundred bucks. Stevens had more than a couple of hundred. Maybe he really had known that his wife was up to some funny stuff every third Wednesday and he had known what it was.

Chase questioned the doctor hard, much harder than Porter had before. Chase was pushing not only for background on Rachel, but to see if he squirmed any. Chase rode out the doctor's irritation with the questioning. He probed the doctor first about himself, checking out his alibi and his marriage with Rachel. He knew he wasn't being tactful, but he figured that was why Porter had let him come here alone. Porter envisioned himself the velvet glove of questioning while Chase was the blunt object.

Chase hadn't caught Stevens on anything after fifteen minutes of questioning so he switched over to Rachel. As far as Stevens could recollect she hadn't been gone on any sort of schedule, third Wednesday or not, prior to going to school.

"Why'd she go to school then?"

Stevens must have been doing some remembering on his own because he could dredge up more now. "About two and a half, maybe three years ago, she started acting restless. She never really talked about it, but I could tell she wasn't happy. Rachel was a very intelligent, complex woman. I tried to understand, but as you can see my work takes most of the hours in my day."

He was looking over Chase's head as if what he was saying was written up there on the wall. "It's funny, but now I think she was the happiest when we were first married and times were hard. I was still a resident and we didn't have a dime. She was working as a receptionist for an optician, keeping us afloat. Then, when my practice was new and she was helping out here in the office, it took all her time just to keep everything running here and at home."

His eyes slid down and met Chase's. "I've been thinking about this a lot, detective, and I believe that Rachel had a hard time coping with her life once things got easier for her on the outside and she didn't have to work here or even at home."

It didn't sound like such an exciting life to Chase either, waiting around a house that had a full-time maid, for some husband who had such a good-looking secretary to come home. Stevens was starting to stare off into lala land again, and Chase was afraid he was losing him. His next words confirmed that.

"Did I tell you how Rachel and I met?"

Chase assured him he hadn't and checked his watch, hoping he wasn't missing something. Porter had probably tripped over the killers somewhere and was in the middle of a raging gun battle while Chase was here getting Stevens' version of love story.

"I was in the residency program at the university medical school and Rachel was a junior in the psych program. I was working in the clinic the day she came in. She was beautiful, I mean really beautiful." Looking at the picture over his shoulder Chase couldn't argue with that.

"But that wasn't the thing that struck me most. She was so strong and determined, as if she had this plan worked out to the smallest detail. She was the first coed who came in there and treated me like just another human being. Another equal. That was so refreshing after all my previous experiences with women looking at me as a prospective meal ticket. I think I fell in love with her that day."

Chase stared at Stevens without comment. The doctor went on without being prompted.

"She had come to the clinic for a diaphragm. Pretty funny right? My future wife coming to see me for birth control? The weird thing was that when I examined her, she was still a virgin. I asked her about that because it's difficult to fit a diaphragm for a woman who isn't sexually active. She gave me a matter-of-fact look and said of course she was a virgin, she didn't have any contraception yet. I was pretty impressed with that. You know, I saw so many pregnant students lamenting their fate that it really struck me how bright and efficient Rachel was."

Chase asked how soon had they gotten married. Stevens looked a little surprised that Chase had broken into his memories.

"It took me two months just to get a date with her," he said. "I pursued her for that entire time. It was hard with my schedule and hers. She was taking a heavy load and doing very well. She was less inclined than I to marry, but I guess I was persistent. Who wouldn't have been? She was smart, pretty, everything I was looking for. On top of that she was the most sexually responsive woman I had ever been with."

This last remark caught Chase off guard, and if Stevens felt it was out of place he didn't show it.

"Detective, you don't know how much thought I've put into this. What makes it so damn frustrating is the fact that if Rachel and I had ever talked about this, maybe she would be alive. But I was selfish; my time was valuable and we always spoke of Rachel's needs in the vaguest of terms."

What the hell was he talking about? Chase wondered. What needs? He hated to interrupt, but this was not in his area of expertise. And what had the doctor meant by her still being alive if they had talked and her being so sexual? "Do you think she was having an affair?"

The doctor's eyes narrowed and he gave Chase a look usually reserved for something smeared on the bottom of a shoe. Not a good question apparently from his perspective, but it seemed logical from Chase's.

"I know this is difficult for you, Detective Chase, but not every unhappy woman is looking for sex."

Chase tried to remember what Linda Watkins had said when he asked her the same question. She had said something about Rachel not being centered on a man, but rather being centered on herself. But Chase would have to think about it later because the good doctor had more to say.

"Rachel was different. She had a very strong idea of what she wanted. Her image of herself was constantly at odds with what society intended. For the most part she could handle that pressure. The only time she let another human being influence her actions was when she married me. Her youth, combined with my insistence, caused her to conform."

He shook his head. "Hell, it scares me now to think why I wanted her so much. I have the horrible notion that I did her an injustice. Her virginity meant a lot to me, and I suppose at that time I was such an egoist that I believed she felt the same."

For a moment there, Chase thought that if he just let Stevens talk long enough he would confess. In a way, Chase realized, Stevens was confessing. Even if Jeffrey Stevens hadn't slit Rachel's throat, he was smart enough to realize that she wouldn't have been in that parking lot at CU last Wednesday night if he hadn't wanted her so badly so many years ago.

Suddenly Chase realized that he was experiencing that most dreadful of human conditions: understanding another human being when it was too damn late to do anything about it. If Rachel had just run off, Stevens could have gone to her with his new awareness and maybe hashed it out, but he had screwed himself with the silent sort of indifference that pervades most relationships and there was no going back, or forward. Chase felt a little sorry for Lisa Plunkett. She would be playing second fiddle to a dead woman for a long time.

Chase checked his watch. He still had to see Gavin and this discussion was depressing him. Stevens finally broke the silence. "I gave her the only thing I could: freedom. That was the reason she married me. I never tried to tame her; to make her fit a mold that wasn't hers. Didn't even push her about children. But ultimately I let her down, because I left her to fend for herself. She just seemed so strong and capable, never threatened by anyone. It never occurred to me to worry about her."

Chase noticed that tears were streaming down Stevens face.

"What hurts the worst is knowing that the freedom wasn't something I gave her out of love and respect. I just didn't have time to mess with who she was as a person. A nice epithet isn't it?"

There wasn't a thing Chase could say. He still didn't have a clue where Rachel spent her last hours, but he was beginning to see her a little better.

Chase's time was getting short. Stevens didn't pay too much attention as Chase arranged to leave. Chase didn't even think he heard. Little Lisa was surprised with Chase's fast exit, but seemed glad to be rid of him all the same. She slid in the office as Chase let himself out.

Chase sat in the Jeep for a few minutes and made notes about the conversation. He had an idea that he had heard something important. He just didn't know what it was.

Chase leaned back against the headrest. *Who the hell were you Rachel Stevens?* Chase's next question was more personal. *Why do I care so much?* The answer came just as quickly-- because it was all he could do now. Chase didn't know how much longer he was going to last in Boulder or with the FLI program. But he wanted to close this case out before the hammer came down.

If Chase hadn't had an appointment with Gavin, he probably would have skipped going back to CU. It didn't seem important to check the attendance sheets now. Chase was pretty convinced that whatever Rachel was up to it wasn't an affair.

Thankfully it was late enough in the afternoon to find a decent parking space on the campus. Chase retraced his steps and made it just in time to the psychologist's cramped office. He was hunched over his computer keyboard and he didn't pay much attention at first. Chase looked at the professor's screen trying to see what he was typing, but only spotted a bunch of big words. Chase was surprised to see an open beer sitting on the desk.

Gavin turned. "You look the worse for wear detective. The case is proving to be most complicated, I presume."

No shit, Chase thought. The doctor didn't know about the previous night-- it had been in the news, but Chase's name had been kept out of it. "It's a difficult case. It seems nobody knew Rachel Stevens, so you shouldn't worry that she fooled you too."

Gavin gave Chase a slight grin. "I never said she fooled me. As a matter of fact, I think the woman who was my student was the real Rachel Stevens, and that person I knew quite well. Obviously her other life was the ruse."

What a self-centered asshole, Chase thought. "How about we skip the linguistic technicalities and cut straight to the chase? Tell me about the woman you had in class." And make it fast, Chase thought. He wasn't in the mood for a lot of psychobabble.

Gavin picked up the beer and took a sip. "Would you like one, detective?" He nodded toward a small fridge underneath a bookcase.

"I'm on duty."

"Right."

"I'll take one." Chase realized that the professor seemed a little drunk. Porter had said always treat potential witnesses like your best friend, not the enemy, a concept Chase had had a hard time swallowing.

Gavin opened the fridge and took out a can. He tossed it to Chase. "You finally answered the question I asked during your previous visit."

"What question was that?" Chase popped the top and waited.

Gavin seemed a little hurt that his question wasn't sitting in Chase's frontal lobe, anxiously awaiting this conversation. "I wanted to know which was more important in a case, the facts or the personalities."

"Oh yeah, I remember. So what's the answer?"

Gavin put down his beer and crossed his arms. Chase had had Psych 101 at West Point: Gavin's body language said he was closing himself off. "It's perfectly obvious. You're interested foremost in the facts, right?"

This guy wanted Chase to coax it out of him, and Chase just didn't have the patience for that. "Tell me about her." Chase was surprised at the coldness in his voice and evidently so was Gavin. So much for Porter's advice, Chase thought.

Gavin's tone let Chase know he'd pushed him too far. But Chase didn't care. Who did these people think they were? Chase thought. So far everyone he'd talked to about Rachel had given him a whole bunch of goobly-gook. No wonder she had some secret life; she spent too much time around egocentric assholes.

Gavin slid something across the desk. "Here, detective. I found these a couple of days ago. I've also included the copies of the attendance roster for that class as you requested."

Chase looked at the folder. "What is this?"

"Some assignments Rachel turned in while she was in my class. You seem to have reached the point where her personality has become important to your case. I think these papers will tell you more than I could."

Now Chase knew why the good doctor was acting more confident about supposedly knowing Rachel when he hadn't even known she was married on the last visit.

"I've been reading the newspapers," Gavin said.

"Good for you."

Gavin tilted the beer can up and drained it. He tossed it in a trashcan and rolled his chair over to the small fridge and pulled out another beer. He looked and Chase questionably.

Chase shook his head. He'd barely sipped the one he had.

"Tragic about that couple and the baby dying last night."

Chase stared at the shrink.

"I would assume you were involved in that?"

Chase didn't react.

Gavin nodded, as if he'd confirmed something. "You can detach, can't you?"

"'Detach'?"

"Emotionally," Gavin said. He took a drink of his beer. "I can feel it coming off you. Dissociative behavior. It's a form of protection from psychological trauma. Repressed memories and—"

"I remember everything I do," Chase said, cutting off the on-the-fly diagnosis. He put the almost full beer down on Gavin's desk. "Thank you for your time." Chase took the papers and left.

Chase's nasty side hoped he found something that pointed to Gavin as a suspect, but a person could look at him and tell he wasn't strong enough to strangle his dick. Besides, the student had backed up his story when Porter had questioned her. Gavin had been tied up until 10:15 that night at the University and then home right off campus by 10:35 according to his wife. Not even enough time if he was very fast. And there was still the question of the other three guys who'd been in on the gang-bang.

In the Jeep, Chase did a quick check of the attendance roster. There was no other student in Gavin's class who had missed all the same days Rachel had, never mind four of them. Of course there were numerous other classes at CU on Wednesday's at the same time and she might have been seeing someone from one of them, but right now Chase didn't have the time or resources to go off on that tangent. If Rachel had a lover it was just as likely he worked a day job and didn't have any commitments at night.

****

Porter was at his desk when Chase entered the major cases squad room, which was unusual. Chase collapsed into his chair, throwing the files onto the desk. "What's new?"

Porter ran a hand through his sparse hair, finishing with a reassuring pat of his ponytail. "Got some more info on Doc Stevens."

"What?"

"I talked to enough people over there at the doctor's building to confirm that the Doc and his secretary were having an affair. Seems like several of the doctors have that sort of thing going with their secretaries or nurses. Big old Peyton Place."

That wasn't too surprising. Chase realized he'd asked about the wrong person having an affair when he'd questioned him. "You think he might have hired someone to kill her?"

Porter was non-committal. "Don't know. He's got motive and money. But that doesn't help explain the semen."

"Maybe Stevens hired one punk and the bozo brought friends along for the fun?"

"That puts me back where I was before. On the street busting ass, trying to make one squeal."

"Great. Got anything there?"

"Nothing specific."

Chase could tell something was on his partner's mind. "What was unspecific that you got?"

"Someone's been shaking down dealers," Porter said.

"Ripping them off?"

Porter shook his head. "No. Asking questions. Sounds almost like a cop. Trying to find who their supplier was." Porter squinted. "Chase?"

Chase thought if he heard his name with that tone one more time he'd have to pull out his 10mm and shoot somebody. "Yes?"

"How did it go this morning with the chief?"

"He wanted to know why I didn't let Barnes shoot me first. If Barnes had done that, then it would have been fine with the chief for me to off him. I think. I don't know. Maybe not. The chief still might have been a tad disappointed and upset with my police procedure."

"The chief's a dick. A brown-noser."

Chase shrugged.

Porter stood, reading the mood and ready to go home. "You need to talk, Chase, I'm here for you."

"I know."

Another great day at work done. Chase checked his messages and headed out.

****

Waiting for Chase in the parking lot was Fortin. He was standing next to a black van with tinted glass and waved Chase over as he slid open the side door. He was dressed in an expensive grey suit Chase had never seen before. Chase couldn't even see the bulge for his gun. Fortin didn't say hello. He just stared at Chase like he was a minor irritant.

Chase climbed in the back and took a seat, while Fortin got in, shut the door and sat across from him. Another man was seated behind the wheel. He didn't turn his head.

"How's Wyoming?" Chase decided to beat Fortin to the punch.

"We've got the Patriots locked up tight," Fortin said. "No thanks to you," he added.

"Screw you." Chase tried to keep the anger out of his voice. "You ever kill someone in cold blood?"

"I've--" Fortin began.

"Bullshit." Chase stayed on the offensive. "Am I fired?"

"Not yet."

"Then what do you want?"

"To tell you to do your job," Fortin said. "Again." He was trying to keep his cool, but his face was flushed with anger. "You have your assignment with the Boulder PD. Do what you're ordered. Don't stick your nose where it doesn't belong."

"What--" Chase began but Fortin cut him off.

135

"I'll pull the rug out from under you so fast your eyeballs will spin. You can kiss your retirement good-bye. You can kiss your job good-bye, and you screw with me again, you can kiss everything good-bye."

"You really scare me."

Fortin's eyes went dead and Chase immediately realized he had underestimated his boss. He wasn't just some flake. Chase had seen that look at the classified holding pens at the airstrip in Kandahar where the CIA hard-cases worked over the detainees that weren't on any roster.

"You're CIA," Chase said.

Fortin didn't say anything, as he continued to stare at Chase with his dead eyes. It was as much a confirmation as anything.

"Is there something specific I'm supposed to stop doing?" Chase asked. "How can I stop whatever it is if--"

"Don't do anything other than what you are specifically told by either me or your Boulder PD bosses," Fortin said. "Is that clear?"

Fortin was already out of the chair, opening the door. Fortin wasn't even looking at him for an acknowledgment. He just assumed he had one. That bothered Chase more than anything else as he climbed out. Fortin slid the door shut.

Chase stood on the sidewalk, staring at the rear of the van as it drove away. Whatever Fortin's intent had been, Chase knew only one thing: he was more than angry now, he was pissed.

CHAPTER FOURTEEN

Chase took a booth by the dark-tinted, front window of the Silver Satyr. It was only 5:30 and the evening crowd was just beginning to dribble in. He had barely enough light to read the papers Doctor Gavin had given him. Sylvie was backstage in the dressing room and he figured he'd just read until she showed up out front.

But he had trouble focusing. He kept replaying the scene inside the van again and again. His sense of duty had restrained him, he realized, even though he knew he had done the right thing and that Fortin was wrong. He should have—Chase paused in his thoughts when Tai walked up and sat down across from him.

Tai leaned back in his chair. "Hey, heard about last night. Pretty bad."

Chase stared at the owner, knowing his name hadn't been in the papers. But it seemed like everyone just assumed he'd been there.

Tai saw the look. "Chase, I know things." He tapped the side of his head. "Boulder acts so prim and proper it makes me want to puke. The dark side, and there is one, a lot of it comes through here. And I listen."

"And what do you hear?"

"I hear you offed that guy who killed his baby."

Chase didn't say anything. Tai was half-right and Chase couldn't confirm the other half and disabuse him of what he had wrong.

"I knew Tim Barnes," Tai added as he signaled for one of his girls to bring some beers.

"How?"

"A name. A face."

"Do better than that."

"You're my guest here," Tai said it low key, but Chase read the message underneath. For the first time Chase wondered if this club staying open had more than just legal briefs behind it and how right

Porter might be about Tai. Everyone had some dirt somewhere in their past or present and that could be pretty strong leverage.

Chase decided to take a chance. Sylvie had said Tai was a stand-up guy and Chase trusted her instincts. "I killed him, Tai, but someone was there before me. Someone shot him, his wife and the kid."

The waitress came over with two beers, then left. Tai took a deep drink, and then turned to Chase. "He didn't kill his family?"

Chase shook his head.

Tai tapped a finger against his lips. "That's interesting."

Chase forced himself to keep quiet. If Tai was going to tell him something, he would. Chase had already let out more than he should have.

"The Barnes were into money." Tai laughed without any humor. "Hell, everyone's into money, aren't they? It's the American way. Just most try to do it the American dream way. You know. Work hard. Save. Send the kids to college. Then there's the others. Who want a short cut. Who want it now."

Chase waited as Tai waved at two men who walked in.

"It wasn't so much the husband, Tim. He was dumb as a tree stump. His wife-- Trina. What a bitch. She wanted to work here, but when she found out I didn't allow tricking with the customers, she got pissed at me. She couldn't make enough dancing, she said. What kind of titty-bar was I running she wanted to know? Stormed out."

Chase thought of the woman collapsing on the steps of the house. Her baby.

Tai gave the same hard laugh. "Hell, I got the city council saying I go too far and others saying I don't go far enough. Can't please anybody." He seemed to realize Chase was still there. "Trina would do anything or anybody for a buck. And she'd make Tim do whatever she wanted. It wasn't just that he was pussy-whipped; he thought he loved her. I mean she was pretty, he was ugly and she married him. What more could a guy like him ask for? He didn't realize he'd be paying for it all his life-- and probably die because of it."

"What were they into most recently?"

"Drugs."

"Dealing?"

Tai nodded. "Somewhere in the supply chain. They sold not to users on the street, but higher-end dealers. Add it up and they did some heavy weight."

"Who was their supplier?"

Tai shrugged. "Don't know."

"Could they have been hooked up with the Patriots?"

"The militia guys in Wyoming?"

Chase nodded. The club was filling up, men getting off work, looking for a little fun before going home to either nothing or someone not as exciting as what they saw here, or so they thought.

"Where would the Patriots get drugs, Chase?" Tai asked,

Before Chase could answer, the bartender was waving, holding a phone in his hand. "I'll ask around," Tai said as he got up.

"Thanks."

He walked to the bar and Chase picked up the papers Gavin had given him. The top piece of paper was labeled: TELL ME ABOUT YOU. Chase loved psychologists. They were so subtle. Rachel had answered the questions in a very neat print.

NAME: RACHEL STEVENS

MY HOME TOWN IS: NORTH PLATTE, NE.

THE THING I LIKE MOST ABOUT THE UNIVERSITY OF COLORADO SO FAR IS: THE FREEDOM.

THE BIGGEST PROBLEM I'M HAVING RIGHT NOW IS: JUGGLING MY SCHEDULE SO I CAN COMPLETE SCHOOL.

I CAME TO CU BECAUSE: WHAT A PERSON CAN BE, THEY MUST BE.

MY FAVORITE HOBBIES ARE: READING, THINKING.

THE NUMBER ONE THING I HOPE TO GET FROM THIS PROGRAM IS: A CAREER.

WHAT OTHER QUESTIONS SHOULD I HAVE ASKED YOU: WHY CAN'T YOU BE CONTENT LIKE MOST OF YOUR PEERS?

WHAT ELSE WOULD YOU LIKE TO TELL ME ABOUT YOURSELF: DEEP DOWN I'M SECRETLY PLEASED THAT I'M NOT CONTENT LIKE MOST OF MY PEERS.

Chase thought the last one was pretty weird. Her husband was right. She had been very goal oriented. Chase looked up. Tai was off the phone and looking back at Chase. When they made eye contact, Tai turned back to the bar and Chase turned back to the papers.

The next sheet was THE NEED AUCTION BID CARD. It looked like typical crap psych teachers pull out on those class days when they forget to prepare their lecture. The number one priority bid on Rachel's list was for: 'Complete self-confidence with a positive outlook on life.' Interestingly, her lowest priority was: 'A magnificent, servant-maintained mansion.'

Chase thought that was typical. It's easy to low prioritize things a person already had. Rachel Stevens had had the freedom to think all these great thoughts. People like Chase were too concerned about making it through each day.

There were several more surveys and papers. The interesting point that Chase noted was that Rachel had never once revealed her true life outside of school. There was no mention of husband, Pine Brook Hills, the Boulder Country Club or garden club. Gavin was wrong. Reading these papers had given him an idea of a fictional Rachel. She hadn't been truthful in her answers.

Sylvie was first dancer. She always was. They usually had a lineup of five or six women. That meant about ten minutes dancing with forty off in between working the floor for half of that. Sounds easy but it wasn't. Chase didn't watch as he continued to peruse the papers, but his mind was wandering.

In the beginning Chase hadn't give much thought to Sylvie being a stripper. Now he was thinking about it more and liking it less. Chase forgot about Rachel and thought about the woman in his life. He guess he thinking about it a little too hard, because he didn't notice Sylvie was finished until she slid into the booth next to him.

She gave his arm a squeeze and he looked at her. "Why do you strip, Sylvie?"

If it's possible to be angry and pleased at the same time, Sylvie achieved it. "The proverbial nice girl question. I was wondering when you were going to ask it. Three months is definitely a record; most men ask on the first date."

Chase tried to keep jealousy to a minimum in his life because it's such a worthless emotion. He didn't always succeed.

Sylvie crossed her arms and stared at him. "Why do you kill people?"

Chase felt the emotion drain out of him. "It's my job."

"You choose the jobs," Sylvie said. "You choose West Point, Special Forces, Delta Force and this job, right?" Before he could say anything she went on. "Is that what you came for Chase? To ask me why I expose myself to a bunch of jerks, who are mentally fucking me while I watch? Why do you think I do it?" She held her hand up.

"Never mind, don't answer that. I do it for money. I get a lot of money to show what's only special when it's free. My body means the same thing to me as my mind. If I were an accountant, I'd be charging someone by the hour for my knowledge of the tax code. Instead I'm looking at the bottom line. I can get a CPA when I'm forty, but I'll only have these tits for a few years. It's economic feasibility, Chase. You use the perishables first."

"You really believe that?"

Sylvie leaned back in the booth and regarded Chase with a sad smile. "That line usually works. It usually impresses the hell out of people. That some dumb stripper could talk like that.

"You're getting more perceptive, Chase. OK, the real reason is my ex-husband actually was an accountant who preferred snorting coke and gambling to crunching numbers. By the time I figured it out, we were hopelessly in debt and he was in jail. You wouldn't believe the high price of a legal defense nowadays."

Chase didn't hide his surprise very well. "You were married? Why didn't you ever tell me that?"

"You never asked."

"That's not something you wait around with. That's something you tell."

"Do you care?"

Chase opened his mouth to answer, then stopped as he tried to gather his thoughts. Finally he replied: "Sylvie, I'm sorry. I had no right to question you the way I did. It's just that I had a weird day today and I really needed to talk to you."

She softened a bit. "What do you need to talk about?"

Chase told her about his conversation with Doctor Stevens. It took about five minutes, but he figured he covered everything. Then he pushed the papers over to her. "Read these."

She was a fast reader. When she was done she looked at Chase. "What do you think?"

"I don't think she was having an affair." Chase went over the discrepancies to that theory. That left him with the basic question that evidently meant everything in this case. What the hell had Rachel Stevens been doing every third Wednesday night?

Sylvie was most interested in the fact that Rachel had pretended to be single at school. She was just starting to say something when a new song came on.

Sylvie got up. "Gotta work the floor, then do the stage."

Chase waited out Sylvie's routine wondering about why he had never really asked her about her past. She had never given any indication that she had once been married. Chase didn't even know how old she was. That was a question he'd thought you were never supposed to ask a woman and Sylvie had never volunteered the information. Chase guessed she was in her late twenties, but he realized he might have to bump that up a couple of years. She wasn't like most of her fellow dancers who had the advantage of a great body in its physical prime-- Sylvie worked out hard to stay in shape that he did know.

It was still early, but there were more men crowded around the stage. Chase had never really thought about how much Sylvie made, but he had seen her count her take at her place every so often and there were a lot of bills and they were rarely ones.

That brought Chase to another thing he'd never thought about. What did she do with all that money? He not only didn't know her past, he didn't know her future. If he'd been in a cartoon, a light bulb would have come on above his head as he had a moment's inspiration: he had been treating Sylvie the same way Doctor Stevens had treated his wife. Just drifting along without thinking.

By the time Sylvie got back to the booth Chase was feeling kind inspired. He had decided to adjust his attitude toward her and listen more. Her first words derailed that.

"I know what she was doing for those three hours."

"When did you figure this out?"

Sylvie gave Chase a look usually reserved for idiots. "Chase, it doesn't require much brain power to take your clothes off or talk to these guys."

If she wanted to discuss Rachel, Chase would listen. "All right. Tell me your brainstorm. Then I'll tell you mine."

"She was hooking."

"What?"

"Hooking, Chase. You know, prostitution or illegal solicitation as you cops call it."

"But why?"

"The money."

Chase sounded like a bad recording. "But why? She had plenty of money."

"Wrong, Chase. Her husband had plenty of money."

"Well, damn, Sylvie. I'm sure he gave her some."

"That's just it Chase. She needed money that he didn't know about."

Chase's first thought, probably prompted by Sylvie's revelation about her own life, was that Rachel had needed money for drugs, but that came to an abrupt halt as he remembered Hanson's autopsy. Rachel had been clean.

"OK. Maybe she needed money, but isn't hooking a little drastic? I'm sure Rachel could have found an easier way to get money."

"She had pride, Chase."

Chase was lost. "She had pride? So she became a hooker? What kind of pride is that?"

"She wanted it to be her money."

"Why didn't she just get a job?" But Chase was thinking. About his mother and money. She'd had pride too, but she'd done whatever it took to make money. Pride can come in many different guises, Chase knew.

"She was working toward a career, Chase. Not just a job. She was in a Catch-22. She couldn't make the money she needed in order to have the career to make the money she needed."

"But that's my whole point. What did she need the money for?"

"So she could leave."

Chase sorted the facts from this new perspective. It scared him how well they all fit: she'd had sex with four men; the KY jelly; the cab ride so no one would recognize the car; no ID on her so no one would know who she was. The gym bag could have held clothes or whatever she needed to turn tricks. Then he had a disconnect and Sylvie must have seen it.

"What's the matter?"

"The money."

"What?"

"We found six dollars on her. If she'd been hooking wouldn't she have had more than that on her?"

"She was robbed."

"Then why didn't they take the six dollars?"

Sylvie laughed. "Chase, in three hours she could have made over four or five thousand dollars. Once the killer had that, would he care about the change from her cab fare?"

143

"Four or five thousand dollars? Are you kidding? They turn tricks for twenty-five bucks in Denver."

Sylvie shook her head. "Rachel Stevens was from Pine Brook Hills. She was beautiful, intelligent, and from what you've told me she had unsafe sex. Basically, Chase, she could name her own price and be selective about her clientele."

"If she was so smart why was she having unsafe sex?"

"Considering the type of men she was probably with, she wasn't taking that big of a risk. Not too many IV drug users will put out five hundred to a thousand dollars to get laid. They'd prefer to shoot the money in their arm. I don't think she would've had to worry about gay men for her clients.

"Sometimes, Chase, you get to the point where you're willing to take a gamble for the payoff. Maybe Rachel was at that point. There're plenty of people meeting in bars here in Boulder and around the country every night and having unsafe sex. At least Rachel was smart enough to make some money off it. Check with her gynecologist."

"What?"

"She probably had a standing appointment." Sylvie frowned. "But she wouldn't go to her regular doctor. If she was careful she wouldn't even use anyone in Boulder. She probably went to Denver."

Chase remembered the phone numbers with no names in Rachel's address book. He mentally logged that in as something he needed to check again.

Sylvie wasn't done. "Her biggest worry must have been that she'd run into some husband from Boulder who knew her, but even then it wasn't like he'd want to expose her. Like I said, she must have been very selective with her clients, which also would have helped on the disease angle too."

Chase wasn't convinced, but it was sounding plausible. Especially if Rachel had known about her husband and Miss Plunkett. "Can a housewife just become a call girl?"

"It's not like you have to have a lot of skills, Chase. Mainly you just have to have a good body and a willingness to use it. There are cathouses and escort services all over Denver a woman can contact and get work one night a week. Or in this case once every three weeks. Or she could advertise on-line."

Chase remembered her husband had said something about Rachel and sex. He would have to look it up. He wondered how Sylvie knew all this, but that was a question where Chase wasn't willing to accept some of the possible answers, so he didn't ask it.

At first the idea had sounded far-fetched, but Sylvie, and the evidence he had, made it more convincing. Chase knew where he had to go now.

When Chase walked out of the club he could see two guys sitting on the hood of his Jeep. One was tall, black, and had shaved his head. The other was medium height, white, and looked like a weightlifter with broad shoulders under his windbreaker. The bulky muscles spoke of heavy steroid use and his forehead had Cro-Magnon man stamped all over it. They slid off the hood as Chase approached.

"You been asking questions." This was from the weightlifter. Chase was amazed he could even speak. The black guy was just watching, moving a couple steps away from his partner, flanking Chase.

"It's my job," Chase replied. "What's your's?"

Chase caught the blur of movement to his left and reacted instinctively, sweeping his left arm out in a middle block, catching the black guy's turn kick on the bone of his forearm, but that was a lot better than his head where it had been directed. The arm stung as the guy pulled the leg back.

Chase backed up and drew his gun. He aimed at the black guy. He figured by the time Mister Muscles got all that weight moving, he could have changed his aim and drilled him with half the clip.

The black guy smiled. "Come on, man. A little test. Man to man. I won't hurt you too bad."

"Screw man to man," Chase replied. "You just assaulted a police officer."

"You green beanies are pussies," the black guy continued. "Wear fucking girl scout hats. Did you sell cookies door to door, too? We used eat you guys for breakfast in the SEALs."

SEALs were the Navy's Special Operations people. The black guy had that competent, shit-together, look that most special ops people Chase had served with had.

"And now what do you eat?" Chase asked.

The black guy shuffled his feet, hands loose. "Let's party."

"Don't think so," Chase said, seeing no upside.

The ex-SEAL laughed again. "You think we didn't know you were armed? You think we weren't prepared? You got a rifle pointing at you right now, and you got five seconds to put the gun down." He smiled revealing a row of perfectly straight teeth. The navy must have had better dentists than the army hacks Chase had gone to.

"One."

Chase had never enjoyed gambling. He figured any form of bet was controlled by someone other than him, therefore the odds were against him.

"Two."

This guy had no reason to bluff. There were plenty of places a man with a rifle could hide around here.

"Three. Look at your chest."

Chase glanced down and saw the small red dot indicating a laser site was aimed at him. He lowered the gun before the guy could do four and slid it back into his holster.

"Very smart." And then the SEAL came at Chase in flurry of snap kicks toward his midsection, which Chase blocked with his hands and forearms, while backing up, knowing this was just a prelude.

Then came a feint snap-kick, flowing into a reverse back-fist as the SEAL spun, arm extended toward Chase's head.

Except Chase has seen the move coming in the slightest shift in the SEAL's eyes and he ducked, grabbed the wrist as it went over his head with one hand and the SEAL's elbow with the other, and he levered up on the elbow and down on the wrist.

The crunch of the joint giving way in the wrong direction echoed across the parking lot.

Chase had to give the man credit—he didn't scream. A hiss of pain escaped the SEAL's lips and he froze, his arm still in Chase's grip.

"Your buddy going to shoot?" Chase asked, shifting so that the man's body was between him and the direction the red dot had come from.

"No." The word came thought teeth clenched in pain. "We just wanted to talk."

"That's why you came at me?" Chase asked. "What do you want?"

"For you to stop asking questions," the ex-SEAL informed Chase.

"About what?" Chase could see Muscles trying to follow the conversation with a furrowed look on his brow, trying to think if he should charge. He must have been heavily coached even to ask that first question, mainly to distract Chase and give his buddy a chance to kick his head off.

"You're not that stupid are you?"

"I seem to be lately," Chase said. "I've got a lot going on in my life right now and you need to be more specific."

"Just stop asking questions."

Chase had the feeling the guy actually didn't know what he was supposed to stop digging into. "And if I don't?"

"You can't beat us," the ex-SEAL said.

"Just did. Still got your arm and I can make the surgery much worse if I twist. Who's us?"

The SEAL shook his head, the security light reflecting off the shaved ebony skin. "See, you're asking questions again."

Chase let go of the man's arm and drew his Glock, pressing it under his jaw, still keeping the body between him and the unseen gunman, even though he knew the human shield wasn't adequate. The SEAL cradled his damaged arm with his good one.

"Truce," the SEAL said. And now Chase could see the small receiver in the man's ear. Someone was talking to him. "You let us walk, we let you walk. He's got you in his sights. And if it comes to it, he'll shoot right through me to get you."

"This isn't over," Chase said.

"It is right now," the SEAL said. With that he turned and walked away, Muscles following.

Chase sat down on the hood of his Jeep and watched them until they turned the corner and disappeared. He could have called a black and white to grab them for threatening and assaulting a police officer but he didn't. They were like the green scum on the top of a pond. He needed to know what was in the dark waters and he didn't think those two had the answers he wanted.

First the CIA. Now this.

Unless they were two of the four who had killed Rachel, the questions they were referring to were the ones Chase had asked about the Patriots and/or the Barnes. There were only three people who Chase had posed such questions to: Tai, Masters and Colonel Thorne. The latter was the most likely to have ties to the Patriots, but it didn't sit right that he'd send a couple of thugs to threaten Chase. Then again, he did run a magazine called Merck. He could have answered one of his own classifieds to hire these guys.

Tai was a possibility considering this was right outside his club. Chase had no doubt now that he dealt in information. He'd given Chase some and gotten some from Chase. Who knows who else he talked to.

On top of who had sent these bozos, Chase had to consider who had called in the CIA. And if these bozos were part of the Clowns In Action.

Chase got in his Jeep and drove away, not bothered by the traffic as usual, but deep in thought.

CHAPTER FIFTEEN

Chase drove from the Silver Satyr back to Police headquarters. There were two things he wanted to do before calling it a night.

Chase dug through his folders until he found Rachel's address book. He flipped the pages looking for doctors. By checking the phone book against her notations he found a local gynecologist. She had him listed under D. Chase copied the name and number onto his notepad. Then he listed out all the numbers in the book that had some sort of code next to them. There were three. All with 303 area codes meaning they were local. Chase used the reverse directory to look them up.

The first, labeled CC, was the Boulder Country Club. The second labeled F was a floral shop. Chase hit pay dirt on the third: CB. Although it had a 303 area code, the next three digits weren't listed in the Boulder Directory.

Chase expanded his search and eventually found it in the Denver Directory: Doctor Carl Bednarick, Physician and Surgeon, MD, Gynecology. Sylvie had called this one perfectly.

Chase left his desk and went down to the first floor to Boulder's small vice and drugs division. At almost ten at night, most of the desks were empty as the occupants were out on the street doing their thing. Vice and drugs worked nights when business was good.

Chase scanned the few occupied desks looking for a friendly face. He spotted one in the far corner. It wasn't a friendly one, but it was a known one. Buck Rudolph looked like a typical redneck. And he was. He didn't just hate minorities, he hated everyone, except cops, equally. To him you were either a cop or you were scum. He was from somewhere in Alabama and Chase had no clue how he'd ended up here in Colorado.

Rudolph had busted more than his share of all strata of society as they partook in the various sins that laws classify as no-no's; because of that he'd learned that it didn't matter if someone wore a three piece suit or a cut-off t-shirt. To him everyone was just as dirty inside.

Chase could tell Rudolph was watching him approach from across the room. He was only about five foot seven and weighed no more than a hundred and forty pounds. He had scraggly black hair and a pinched face. He'd have looked good in a pair of jeans with no shoes up in the hills of his home state playing a banjo. Chase had worked with him in the past once and after the case they'd gotten drunk together. Chase didn't care for his personality, but he was good at his job and it paid to cultivate efficient friends. They'd exchanged favors as vice and major cases crossed paths more often than not.

"What brings you down here, Chase? Bored with the high speed cases and want to wallow in the pig trough?"

Chase rolled over a chair. "I got a body."

"What else is new?" Rudolph let loose a long line of tobacco juice into the empty coffee can on his desk. "You guys get dead bodies. We get bodies too, except ours are alive and yours are dead. So did one of my live ones become one of your dead ones? The only body I know of is recently is that Stevens' woman. And the one you shot. And his family."

"This body screwed four men in less than three hours just before she was killed." Chase filled him in on the facts without adding Sylvie's idea. "What do you think?"

Rudolph gave Chase a tobacco-stained smile. "What do you mean what do I think? You're the major case detective. I'm not smart enough to figure out who-done-its."

Chase shook his head. "About the victim."

"What about her?"

Chase hated it when someone played stupid. It was Rudolph's right to bait Chase though. He'd come down here. "What do you think she was doing before she got killed? Could she have been hooking?"

Rudolph spit into the can again. "She might have been. We get some of those. Usually though, these suburban housewives work the lounges of the nice hotels in Denver. We get some that work our nicer hotels too. They drive their mini-vans on in, sit around the bar and go upstairs with some out of town businessman. They get pretty good money, but I think a lot of them do it mostly for the thrill. Then you got all those who advertise in the paper saying they give full body massages. Hell, we even got a couple of them escort services here in town. And don't even get me started on the crap you can find on-line.

"Honestly, Chase, we don't mess with them too much. They aren't hurting anyone. I like to think that they help the tourism industry of Boulder." He cackled bitterly.

Chase told him about the cab ride to Broomfield every third Wednesday.

Buck rubbed the stubble of his beard. "There ain't nothing I know of at that location you said the cabbie dropped her off at. At least off the top of my head. There may be a high-class house or something that's been set up recently there. Maybe she had an apartment she rented that she free-lanced out of."

Chase doubted that last bit. That would put quite a bit of overhead on an operation that apparently only ran one night every three weeks. On the other hand, maybe Rachel borrowed a house or apartment at that time from a friend.

"Could you check on it for me?"

"Check on which? The body or the location?"

"Both." Chase passed him the basic info on Rachel Stevens and a copy of her picture. Chase very much doubted that Rachel had ever gotten picked up for soliciting, but it paid to play the long shots. There was something else Chase wanted to bounce off him.

"You know the family that was killed the other night?"

"I can read, Chase," he said sarcastically. "And I got ears. The word is you did good."

Coming from Buck that was a compliment and it meant the grapevine from SWAT was positive. "Did you know the Barnes were dealing?"

"Both had been picked up a couple of times. Pled down and never had to serve time. They were lucky we never caught them with the major weight they moved. I arrested Trina once. Real bitch. Offered me use of her body if I let her go, then when I didn't-- use her body or let her go-- cursed me out better than a sailor. I learned a couple of new phrases."

"Why didn't you bust her on the bribery?"

"Right. My word against her's. The DA is real good at taking cases like that to court."

"So the killings could have been drug-motivated."

"This isn't your case, last I heard."

"I'm involved. I was the one on the scene and I killed Tim Barnes. Could there be a connection between the Barnes and the Patriots?"

Buck frowned. He looked at the door, then back at Chase. "I talked to Gotleib."

The Barnes were Gotleib's case. He was nearing retirement and not the brightest light on the street. That told Chase the DA and Chief didn't want any more dirt uncovered. "And?"

"They pulled the phone records at the Barnes' house. Monday, just before the shots were fired, they made a call to a local hotel. Whoever was registered there also paid cash, bullshit name."

"What are they doing about it?"

Buck snorted. "Nothing. Last thing Donnelly or the Chief wants is more trouble. If the Barnes' deaths are tied to the Patriots somehow, they'd prefer to let it go since that's out of our jurisdiction and the Barnes are dead. You know everyone in the DA's office is scared shitless of fucking up once more."

Chase thought of Hanson describing what had happened to the Barnes and their baby. Chase had several pieces but none of them fit.

"Who supplied the Barnes?"

"Don't know. We've been trying to go up that chain for a long time with no luck. Someone's bringing major weight into town and we have no clue who it is. It could be the Patriots, but how they're distributing it, we have no idea."

"How could the Patriots be getting it?" Chase asked.

"Through Canada. We're so busy stopping illegal immigrants coming up from Mexico, it's an easy stroll across the Canadian border, especially for guys trained like the Patriots to move cross-country. Not much border patrol on the north. And the Canadians aren't as tight as the US letting stuff into their country."

"So you've been shaking down dealers, trying to find their suppliers and the link to the Patriots?"

"We're always shaking down dealers when we can, but we haven't done anything special lately. The thing I don't see is the Patriots distributing that kind of weight here. We're missing something."

"Who did the Barnes supply?"

"Several local dealers."

"Could one of them have tried ripping the Barnes off and it got out of hand?"

"Doubtful. Pretty much everyone who deals on that level is also a user. You don't kill your supplier."

Chase felt like he was in a deep pool of molasses, slowly pushing his way around, while the answers were way over his head and out of reach.

"Thanks, Buck. I'll be upstairs for the night."

Chase slowly walked to his office. Before he'd talked to Rudolph, he'd already decided to spend the night. It was only a ten-minute drive home but he didn't feel like going there and crawling into the cave. Donnelly had a couch in his office. He certainly never stayed late enough to use it.

Chase stopped at his desk to check on something else. The SEAL had been good but he shouldn't have boasted. He reminded Chase of some of his old buddies from Special Forces who wore gold rings with the SF crest engraved on the surface. They had to let people know somehow that they had served.

Navy SEALs had two Naval Special Warfare Groups (NSWG), each roughly the equivalent of an Army Special Forces Group. NSWG1 was based at Coronado, California and the other at Little Creek, Virginia, each Group having two SEAL Teams. There was also SEAL Team Six, which, like the Army's DELTA Force was focused on counter-terrorism. Sounded like a lot, but all in all, Special Operations was a small community.

Chase sent some emails to buddies still on active duty at Special Operations Command at Fort Bragg, asking to them check on any ex-SEALs fitting the description.

Then he went to the Merck Magazine home page and found the article on the Patriots. It told him little more than he already knew. Then Chase checked the magazine for anything involving Rivers. He wasn't surprised to see an article from the previous year. Chase checked the synopsis-- it had nothing to do with Rivers' affiliation with the Patriots, but was focused on Special Operations work in Afghanistan. Chase almost clicked on the back button when he paused.

He scrolled down and began reading. The gist of the article was that Rivers had been in command of a Joint Special Operations-Drug Enforcement Task Force in Afghanistan, sent there to help train local anti-drug forces. Just two years ago Rivers had been relieved of command and sent packing back to the States and forced to retire. The author of the article claimed that Rivers had been relieved because his work had gotten too close to CIA-backed narco-guerrillas in Kazakhstan. The old CIA-pushing drugs story. There was no substantiation of the claim. Just rumors. Chase thought of the cold look that had come into Fortin's eyes earlier in the day.

Drugs. That was the connection to the Barnes. Were the Barnes getting supplied by the CIA? Was that why the CIA was involved? Was that why they wanted him to stop asking questions? How did Rivers figure into all this?

The door swung open and Buck Rudolph slouched in. Chase turned off the computer. "What's up?"

"I checked around, Chase. No word of any high-class house of ill repute in that neighborhood. I showed the picture around. No make on Rachel Stevens, even using an alias. If she was hooking she was very good or very lucky or both." He tossed the copy of the picture on the desk. "Anything else you need?"

"Nope. Thanks, Buck. I owe you one."

He yawned. "Uh-huh. Take it easy."

Back to Rachel. If Chase were in Rachel's position would he have started hooking? But that was Chase's problem was it? Chase didn't know what Rachel's position was in her life.

Chase took everything he knew about her, all that people had said, and tried to build a complete person, not a piece of paper, out of them. Then he slid into the skin of that person. It took a while, filing away the rough edges, making it fit. It was a weird experience.

When he was done he had a realization: Sylvie was close to the target, but she missed in one essential area. Chase glanced at the clock on the wall. He'd been at this for almost five hours. It was almost three in the morning. Sylvie ought to have just gotten home. Chase punched in her number.

She was irritated. "What do you want, Chase? My feet hurt and all that cigarette smoke gives me a headache."

"I've been thinking about things."

"Great. We'll talk about it at lunch tomorrow. I'm beat."

"I just want to run something by you about the case right now. We can talk about us tomorrow."

Sylvie's voice sounded more lively. "What do you mean 'talk about us'?"

"I said tomorrow. Right now I want you to listen. You said Rachel was probably hooking. I've been thinking about that. Thinking that if I were Rachel I probably wouldn't do that."

"Then how did she screw four guys, Chase?"

"She liked sex, Sylvie. If I could screw four women in three hours-" Sylvie snorted "-yeah, well, if I was a woman and didn't have to get it up-- and I could have sex with four different people in an evening without any emotional garbage involved, I think I might do it." Chase flipped through his notepad. "Her husband said she was the most sexually responsive woman he'd ever been with. I mean, who says a woman can't just like sex and do it?"

Her answer was succinct and to the point. "Society." Sylvie was apparently totally awake now. "Chase, you're amazing me. You actually seem to be thinking. Are you sure you haven't hit your head or taken some drugs?"

"Two Tylenol, Sylvie, for my headache. What do you think about what I just said?"

"I think it's fine except for one problem. Besides the fact that society would trash her if she got found out, that is. Where'd she find four guys she felt reasonably safe about having sex with? You said she was smart and--" There was a pause. "I know where."

Chase waited.

Sylvie's voice was excited. "She went to a swinger's club."

"I thought those things went out with the advent of AIDS and the end of free love."

"I've heard there's a couple of swingers clubs that operate around Denver. As a matter of fact, the whole swinging thing is coming back."

"Do you know where they are?"

"If I answered yes to that, Chase, wouldn't it bother you? Remember you telling me how women always ask questions they only want to hear one answer to?"

Chase laughed. "All right. Point made. But have you heard where these clubs are?"

"No. But you could probably go to an adult book store and get a magazine or newspaper that would give you a phone number to call to find out."

"I'll do that. I'm sorry I called so late. I'll let you go so you can get some sleep."

"OK. And Chase?

"Yeah?"

"Tomorrow I want you to tell me exactly how you came up with this idea. Goodnight."

She hung up before Chase could say anything else. If he was right about Rachel there was a perfectly good explanation. She did it because she wanted to and she could.

CHAPTER SIXTEEN

With only three hours sleep Chase was irritated when Donnelly turned on the overhead in his office, the light jerking Chase out of a deep slumber.

"What are you doing in here?"

Chase covered his eyes and tried to get oriented. His mouth was dry and his head hurt. He swallowed a few times and tried to get some saliva flowing. He felt hung-over, yet he hadn't had anything to drink last night other than several pots of coffee.

Chase swung his feet off the lieutenant's couch and planted them on the floor before lifting his upper body off the imitation leather. He opened his eyes and Donnelly was still standing there, hands on hips staring at him. So it wasn't a bad dream. That oriented Chase. He looked over his shoulder at the clock on the wall. Seven forty-five.

"I was tracking some leads down and it got too late to go home," Chase croaked.

Donnelly seemed undecided whether to applaud the dedication to duty or bitch about Chase's sleeping in his office, so he took another approach. "What have you got on the Stevens' case?"

Chase certainly wasn't going to give him the swingers' club theory. Donnelly would be all over that with both feet. Then, if he believed it had possibilities, he'd want to come down on it like a sledgehammer. That would be a mistake. Chase also wasn't going to get into the hooker angle either. Donnelly would never believe a housewife from Pine Brook Hills capable of such a thing. Chase wondered how the LT would feel knowing about Jeffrey Stevens and his secretary.

"Just going through my book. Nothing startling. Trying to put it all in perspective." Chase was never worth a dang in the morning without his workout and then two cups of caffeine.

Donnelly had assumed his favorite position, seated behind his desk, looking pontifically across the polished wood surface. "Detective Chase, we've got to solve this one. The chief is very upset. The chancellor at CU is applying quite a bit of pressure on the mayor's office and it's flowing this way. This isn't reflecting very well on any of us."

Chase was gratified to see there was such a tremendous interest in justice being served. "Things are clearing up a little bit, lieutenant. I think we might have something by the end of the week." It was the most positive thing Chase could think of and he was following Porter's example.

Donnelly didn't buy it. "Do you need more manpower? I can bring the second team in. They've been floundering around with their case for almost three weeks without any results. I think we can close that file and use the manpower more efficiently."

Chase knew the team mentioned was working a drive-by beating where a sixteen-year-old Rainbow person had gotten his head bashed in and then was thrown in the creek. He'd been in the wrong place at the wrong time. Chase knew in Donnelly's, hell in everyone else's that 'mattered,' opinion, that case was nowhere near as important as Rachel Stevens'.

Chase really didn't need another brain mucking things up. He was doing a good enough job of that by himself. Besides, he felt good about this swingers' club angle and he could check it by himself. "No thanks, lieutenant. I think Porter and I have everything under control."

Donnelly was tapping a pencil against a mug. He looked much less confident than Chase felt. "All right. Let me know right away, though, if you need help."

"Yes, sir."

Chase exited before the lieutenant could think of anything else. Chase was anxious to start out on this latest path of investigation. He flipped through the file of Rachel's phone calls that forensics had run. There were even copies of Rachel's flower orders. She had bought a lot of flowers. There was a delivery to one Lisa Plunkett, obviously a birthday from the message on the order. Evidently Rachel handled things like that for her husband. He guessed Lisa ordered the flowers for Rachel's birthday. So much for the personal touch. Had Rachel known about Lisa? Had Jeffrey known about Rachel's Wednesday night activities, whatever they were? The water was getting real dirty in this case.

Chase contacted Doctor Bednarick's office. Rachel had a standing appointment with Bednarick every six weeks.

There was something else very interesting in the folder. A twelve-digit number that obviously wasn't a phone number. A bank account that had been traced by Porter to Third Federal. In her name only. For Chase that made Sylvie's hooking angle that much more likely. There was $42,000 in the account.

Shit, Chase thought to himself. She'd only had several Wednesday's. That was a hell of a lot of money to make in just a couple of nights. Even Heidi Fleiss hadn't made that much in a few nights, had she, Chase wondered? He'd have to check on her husband to see if he had known about the account or where she had gotten the money.

It was after eight and Porter hadn't shown up yet. Chase checked the paper for anything new on Wyoming or the Barnes since he wasn't getting anything through official channels. The Patriot's land in the Medicine Bow Mountains was 'quarantined' according to a spokesperson. In a desire to avoid further bloodshed, the woman went on to say, the authorities were prepared to starve the Patriots out.

Chase almost laughed out loud hearing that. He was willing to bet a month's pay the Patriots had more food stockpiled than the local supermarket, plus they could live off the land practically forever.

The local report on the Barnes took the party line that police were still investigating and no information was being released. The paper couldn't even report if it was the result of a family dispute or an outside intruder.

Chase folded the paper and tossed it in the recycle bin, then headed out. He walked the eight blocks down to 15th Street. Boulder didn't have a red light district. He'd looked in the phone book for adult bookstores and the only one listed was on 15th. The ad in the Yellow Pages said it was open twenty-four hours a day.

'Adult World' had a blacked out-front window and a very small sign. The street had a few people on it, hustling to get to work. Chase walked in the front door.

He was immediately greeted by a large rack portraying X-rated videos. An old man was seated behind the high counter watching a small TV. He looked at Chase briefly, figured he was over eighteen and went back to watching Jerry Springer.

Other than the clerk, the place appeared empty. Besides racks of videos, there were magazines catering to every possible interest: Sort of a name the fetish, they had the book.

Chase moved in a clockwise direction. He was three quarters of the ways around the room when he found what he had come for. He picked the two most appropriately named magazines: The Swinger's Express and Denver Contacts. On the back of the latter was an ad for a swinger's club in Denver: The Denver Social Club.

Chase took them, walked over to the counter and laid them down. The old man didn't even look up, just rang them up and took the money. He put them in a brown paper bag.

Chase walked briskly back to the office, ready to look over his booty. That plan went out the window though when he got there. Porter was sitting at Chase's desk with a big shit-eating grin on his face.

Porter stared at Chase, waiting for him to ask the inevitable. Chase sat on the corner of his desk and stared back solemnly for a little while. Porter wiggled his eyebrows at Chase and smirked.

Chase finally broke down. "All right. You win. What have you got?"

Porter shoved a computer printout at Chase. He looked at it. Eight license plate numbers were listed. All had the same three letters to start with: SRW. They all also had the same first two numbers on the three number set: 37. They only differed on the last number.

"You got a partial on what?"

"The van that was parked near the body drop site at ten-thirty on the night of the murder."

Bingo, Chase thought. Jackpot. Turn on the flashing red light. Give the man a cigar. "You got a witness?"

The smirk lost some of its luster. "Sort of. A call in."

"From who?"

The smirk disappeared. "Anonymous."

"Give me the story from the beginning."

Porter scratched his belly through his shirt. "It's the essence of good police work, Chase. I just wanted to double-check. Be thorough. Cover all loose ends. Leave no stone unturned. Sift through--"

"All right. All right. I get the picture."

Porter dropped the act. "I just picked up the new call ins at the front desk while you were out. The caller said he was driving down Sunshine. He—and the sergeant who took the call noted it was a male voice-- happened to notice a light colored panel van parked there, partially on the road, right at the trailhead." Porter put his feet up on

160

Chase's desk. "Could you get me a cup of coffee, Detective Chase? Talking is making my throat dry."

As Chase went over to the machine he wondered if he rubbed Porter's nose in it as much when he came up with the big break in a case. Of course, Chase thought, he'd never really come up with a big break on case.

Porter took a sip and smacked his lips. "Where was I? Oh, yes. The reason the caller says he noticed this van was because it was partially parked on the road and he almost hit it. So he noted the license plate and wrote what he remembered down. Unfortunately he only got the first five digits in his headlights as he drove by."

"Did the caller spot anybody?"

"No. Just the van." Porter passed over a piece of paper and Chase read the official report. Porter must have typed it up while Chase was nosing around in an adult bookstore. Porter only typed up really important and good reports. The crap he left for Chase to do.

Porter pointed at the computer printout. "I had DMV run the first five with the ten possible last numbers. There are eight plates issued. Look at the third one down."

Chase scanned the paper. SRW-374 was registered to a Joseph Hatcher, 310 Gray Street. The vehicle was a 1987 white Econoline van. None of the other seven was a van.

Porter got up and crooked a finger. "Come here." Chase followed him across the room to where a street map of Boulder was tacked up. He pointed. "Check out where Gray Street is."

Less than a half mile from where they'd found Rachel Stevens.

"Did you talk to the lieutenant yet?"

Porter's good mood dissipated slightly. "No. I figured we'd do it together. I want to get a warrant and go grab this guy. At least go through the van and his place. You know the lieutenant. He's scared of warrants."

Chase shook his head. "He wants to close this case. He'll go for it."

****

Chase should have trusted Porter's feelings and also thought more clearly.

Donnelly didn't go for it. He may have wanted to close the case, but not so badly that he'd risk being wrong with the DA. Donnelly told them that they were full of baloney to think about running out and arresting some guy who just happened to have a van, which just happened to have this particular number. He didn't seem to be impressed about where Hatcher lived either. Nor was he too happy about an anonymous tipster. Not enough facts to establish probable cause to get a warrant issued, he said. The fact that he was right when they stopped and thought about it was doubly irritating. Behind all that, of course, was the fact that even trying to get a warrant would have involved more people than Donnelly was inclined to call and later admit to that he was wrong if the search bombed. The specter of John Karr was going to hang over Boulder for a very long time, along with the ghost of Jon Benet.

Donnelly told Chase and Porter to pull a couple of people to keep an eye on Hatcher and nose around. "He could have a solid alibi, so let's check it out a little before we drag anybody into this and possibly put our butts in a sling. You get me probable cause and I'll get the warrant."

Porter and Chase trudged out, their enthusiasm having ebbed with Donnelly's words. Porter left to arrange the surveillance on Hatcher, and Chase started checking him out through the computer.

Chase spent the rest of the morning working the Hatcher angle. Swingers, adult bookstores, hooking and Stevens' affair he quickly forgot about. Along with Wyoming and the Patriots.

He was so absorbed that he didn't even notice Sylvie standing by his desk until she cleared her throat. He should have known something was up because all work in the squad room had ceased. She had become the focus of everyone's attention, but if it bothered her, she was kind enough not to show it.

She did look wonderful, though, Chase thought, her hair was pulled back by a headband and it gave her face a youthful, innocent quality. She was wearing a dress, which looked great because of what was in it. Chase took a moment to bask in the hormonal glow of his coworkers' envy. After the crappy days he'd been having it felt good.

"You look like shit, Chase."

He rubbed the stubble on his face, looked down at his slept-in clothing and had to agree. "I didn't go home last night. We had a break in the case."

"That's nice. I came to take you to lunch as we agreed. A picnic. Up in the mountains." She reached forward and slid a concerned hand across his forehead. "You look a little worse for wear. We don't have to do anything if you don't want to." Chase's headache seemed to have disappeared with her touch.

Chase assured her that with a clean shirt and a shave with an electric razor he wouldn't embarrass her too much. She looked a little less sure than he would have liked.

As he started to leave to get cleaned up, he remembered the magazines. He went back to his desk and reached deep into the drawer where they were stashed. He tossed them to Sylvie and told her she might find them amusing. She took one look at the naked couple on the cover and shoved them into her oversized leather bag.

Chase thought he looked OK when they hit the outside. It was a nice day and he had the top down on the Jeep. Chase pulled out and drove over to Mapleton and then up Sunshine, past the site where they'd found Rachel's body and headed west, into the mountains. They drove uphill, following the twists and turns until Chase turned off onto a barely visible dirt trail, pushing through some brush and following the old mule trail up a ridgeline. He glanced over at Sylvie. She smiled at they negotiated the narrow trail further into the forest.

Chase was watching the trail and spotted an opening to the left. He pulled into it and stopped the Jeep. They were looking west, down Sunshine Canyon, toward Boulder and the Great Plains.

Sylvie slithered between the seats to the rear of the Jeep, where there was no rear seat. She stood, hands on the sound bar.

"Turn the mirrors," she ordered.

Chase adjusted both large side mirrors so that Sylvie could see herself in them.

Sylvie leaned forward. Chase climbed in the cargo bay, behind her. He slid his hands down her body. Over her breasts, to her hips, to her thighs. He reached the hem of her dress slowly lifted it. She wore nothing underneath. He reached around and felt between her legs. She moaned and he stroked her. She pressed her ass back against him as he continued.

After several minutes, she hoarsely whispered, "Now."

Chase unzipped his pants. He slid his cock between her legs and she reached down with one hand guiding him into her. He gasped as he

163

felt her moist warmness. He put his hands on her hips, pulling her back toward him.

Sylvie put both hands back on the sound bar. "Don't move," she ordered.

Chase froze in place and removed his hands as Sylvie shoved herself back tight against him, then pulled forward. Chase could tell she was watching herself in the mirrors, alternating looking right and left ever so slightly.

He looked past her, down the canyon toward the crime scene even as Sylvie increased her speed, slamming back into him, rocking him, causing him to grab the roll bar to hold on.

Chase realized someone would have had excellent coverage of the crime scene from up here. It's where he would have gone to have surveillance on it. He remembered his feeling the morning he and Porter had been down there.

His thoughts were interrupted as Sylvie suddenly straightened and turned. "What the fuck are you doing?"

Chase was startled. "What?"

She stared him. Chase grabbed his pants, zipped, and buckled up.

"Where was your mind?" Sylvie asked. "You weren't here. I could feel it."

"I'm sorry," Chase said. He nodded toward the canyon. "I was--" He stopped, not sure what to say.

Sylvie looked in that direction. "Is that where she was killed?"

"That's where her body was found. We don't know where she was killed."

"Why'd you take me here? Of all places?"

Chase blinked. "I don't know." He searched for a reason. "When I was out there, the first morning. When we found her body. I had a feeling that someone was watching from up here."

"So you figured you'd take care of me and do your job at the same time?" Sylvie didn't wait for an answer. She climbed between the seats and sat down. Chase took the hint and got in the driver's seat. He started the engine and backed them out of the opening, onto the trail. He drove back to Boulder and pulled up in front of Sylvie's apartment building, not a word spoken between them the entire trip.

Sylvie seemed to have calmed down during the drive. She turned to Chase when he cut the engine, pulling one of the magazines out of her bag and putting it on the console between them. A black and white photo of a young couple, naked of course, was on the cover. They were standing and the woman had the man's penis in her hand. Very subtle. He had a tattoo on his arm. Surprisingly, she was quite pretty. Sylvie opened to the first page.

The entire page was filled with disclaimers, warnings and a welcome letter from the publisher. Chase liked the endorsement for safe sex. Nice touch.

"Chase, what do you think of these people?" She quickly flipped through, giving Chase a few seconds on each page. There were numerous ads with about every third one having a black and white photo. Chase was amazed at the variety of people who would put an ad in such a magazine. He was even more amazed at the people who allowed their faces to be shown. There were quite a few weird looking folks. There was one woman who had a full-page spread of her in action with both men and women. She didn't appear to be practicing safe sex to Chase.

"I don't know, Sylvie." Chase turned the pages back to an ad for the Swing Club, Denver Chapter. It listed a bunch of parties for the year, one a month, at an unnamed local hotel. There was a number to call for more information. It was strange to think that a phone call was all that stood between the normal monogamous life style most people pretended to live and this. Of course, Chase had to wonder, what was normal? Was what he had done in Afghanistan and Iraq, been normal? He knew what he did with Sylvie would not be considered normal by most people.

Sylvie turned the page and pointed at a few pictures. "Do you think there's something wrong with these people?"

Chase grew wary. He sensed a Sylvie logic trap. "No," He said. "Maybe they're just different."

Sylvie rewarded Chase with a smile. He'd escaped that pit.

"Good answer. I don't think I could do this with relative strangers, but some of the girls at the club understand it. I dance for the money. You know that, right, Chase?"

He nodded.

"Some of the girls dance because they really like it. I mean they get off on it. Taking their clothes off. The audience. The power they feel they have over the men sitting there. Some of them are really angry at men. Most of them actually. Plus, they're into the money. A few are really into the sex scene where they control the entire thing. That's how

I knew about swinger's clubs. One of the girls, let's call her Melanie, goes to them."

Chase started to wonder which one of Sylvie's co-workers was Melanie. "Why does she go?"

"For the sex and the atmosphere."

"But she could get sex pretty much anywhere she wanted to." Any of the dancers at the Silver Satyr could have damn near any man she wanted.

"Don't forget, I said atmosphere. Think about it Chase. They have social organizations for just about anything you can think of. If a woman loves to garden she joins a garden club so she can spend time around other people who feel the same way. The other people in that club have a level of expertise and understanding that she couldn't get just talking to anyone about flowers."

Chase thought he understood what Sylvie was saying. "Or people who are gourmets meet to have really fancy meals and spend their time talking about twenty ways to make gravy?"

Sylvie looked very pleased. Chase felt like the dog bringing back the Frisbee. "That's a much better analogy, Chase. Not everybody gardens, but everybody eats and most everybody has sex. My friend Melanie goes for the sex. She doesn't want to put up with the bullshit most people associate with sex. The emotional baggage."

Sylvie paused, lost in thought for a few seconds. "You know, I never really spent that much time thinking about it, but imagine going someplace where there aren't any games being played. You go to a nightclub and it's a damn meat market for a woman. I bet more women than men go to swingers clubs."

"I don't believe that." Chase hadn't met that many women really into sex. Most had treated it like a battlefield or had engaged in sex for many other reasons having nothing to do with the physical act. They had a goal that sex was only a path to.

Sylvie was adamant. "Men can go to a regular nightclub, pick some woman up, take her home, fuck her and then dump her. A woman can't do that. She can try, but the odds are greatly stacked against her. She does it too many times and then she gets a reputation. Think about it, Chase. Is there any equivalent of the word slut for men? Men are studs. Women are sluts."

Chase wasn't surprised at Sylvie's renewed anger. He knew it wasn't all directed at him, but still it was intense. "Hey. Are you all right?"

Sylvie jabbed a finger in his chest. "Let me tell you something about your dead woman, Chase. From everything you've told me I would say she was trying for it all. She wanted to get a degree, start a career, get a life.

"She liked sex. You said her husband told you that. The only way-- other than her husband who probably had three-quarters of his mind back in the office when he was screwing her or thinking of his bimbo secretary-- she could get sex relatively safely was to go to one of these clubs.

"And hell, Chase, sex with her husband wasn't very safe, was it? He was screwing Lisa Plunkett behind her back and who knows what Lisa Plunkett was doing that Doctor Stevens didn't know about." She tapped the magazine. "At least these people are honest. You can't say that about anybody else you've met in this case."

Chase rolled that around his brain. Except Rachel got killed right after one evening at whatever swinger's club she went to. If she went. How safe was that?

Was Hatcher tied into the swinging scene? Was there a connection there? Maybe the surveillance would pick something up. Even better, maybe they might get something incriminating if Donnelly would allow the goddamn warrant and let them toss his place or the van.

Sylvie abruptly changed the subject. "Last night you said you wanted to talk about us. What about?"

All of his great revelations at three in the morning seemed kind of stupid now. "I don't know, Sylvie. I just had some thoughts."

"What thoughts?"

"You know. About men and women and how they interact."

"Yes? And?"

Chase looked at his watch. "Listen, I really can't get into it right now. I've got to get back to work."

The edge in Sylvie's voice was cold. "You could call me at three in the morning to talk about your case, but you can't give me ten minutes worth of conversation today?" Sylvie opened the Jeep door and got out.

She walked into the building. Chase thought about following and apologizing, but he was tired of being the catcher's mitt in the great shit-ball game of life. He closed his eyes for a minute and tried to refocus his mind. He couldn't handle all this turmoil in his life. One thing at a time.

As he started the Jeep up, he noted the date display on the radio. Today was Wednesday. Tonight was one week since Rachel had died. They had a suspect. Chase wanted to close it. Then he could concentrate on other things.

CHAPTER SEVENTEEN

With Porter supervising the surveillance of Hatcher at CU, Chase went back to the computer screen and finished off that search. Nothing new or startling. Then he sat at his desk and pulled out the Book of Rachel, trying to fit the new suspect in.

Chase's earlier enthusiasm for Porter's lead dimmed. It was a shaky path from anonymous tip, partial license plate and a vehicle description, to having Hatcher cutting Rachel Stevens' throat.

Sylvie had had a point. He had to get back to Rachel. Chase had to see if there was a connection between her and Joseph Hatcher. Chase had to-- the phone interrupted his litany of "had to's."

"Detective Chase. Major Cases."

"Chase, do you have a current AIDS test?"

He figured that was Sylvie's way of saying hello. Chase was surprised to hear from her after the way she had left after their 'picnic'. "What does current mean? I've got the one you made me get when we first started going together. That's about two and a half months old." He thought for a second. "Why? Are you worried, because I haven't--"

Sylvie cut him off. "I think I found the club Rachel Stevens went to. It's only three blocks from the corner you told me the cab dropped her off and picked her up at."

Chase digested that for a second. "What do I need the AIDS test for?"

"To get in. We're going tonight. They want one current within the month for new members, but I think I can at least get us in the door with the ones we have."

"Why?"

"So you can learn who Rachel Stevens was and so you can find out where she really was the night she was killed."

"How did you find this place?"

"I looked through these magazines you bought and called all the numbers that were listed for clubs. I think this is the one Rachel went to, not only because of the location and timing, but because they require an AIDS test to even get in. It's for couples and select female singles only. It's called the North Denver Social Club. They meet on Wednesday and Saturday evenings."

Chase thought about it. His first concern was whether going there with Sylvie would screw up the case. Taking a girlfriend to a swingers club was not exactly routine police procedure. As far as he knew about police procedure and he couldn't recall this situation being covered in the short course he'd had. On the other hand, Chase knew he'd get laughed out of the office if he went to Donnelly with this. If he could establish that Rachel was at the North Denver Social Club the night she was killed, that would open up several new lines of investigation and also might close out some of the loose ends that might have nothing to do with the case.

"Are you there, Chase?"

"Yeah. I'm here. I thought you had to work tonight?"

"I told Tai I needed the night off."

"Why do you want to go to this place, Sylvie?"

"I'm interested. I want to see what it's like. I want to see what Rachel Stevens was doing."

"All right. What time do you want to meet?"

"Pick me up at seven. And dress nicely, Chase."

"As if I don't--" he was speaking into a dead phone.

It was now almost three. Chase decided to get the hell away from the office. The encounters with Fortin and the guys in the parking lot at the Silver Satyr were nagging at Chase, urging him to try to figure out what the hell was going on. At the same time his common sense was telling him to do exactly as they had advised. He also knew his anger was going to over-rule his common sense.

He grabbed his stuff and headed out. He drove to the CU campus.

****

Porter was over by Folsom Field where the Colorado Buffaloes played. He was in his car in a parking lot outside the stadium. Chase got in and sat down next to Porter. "Where's the man?"

"Painting seats in the stadium. Gotleib is keeping an eye on him."

Chase had seen Hatcher's DMV picture. "What do you think?"

Porter pursed his lips. "Well . . . I tell you, it's kind of hard to figure. He looks bad. Mean. But so do the other guys in there working minimum wage. He doesn't have killer stamped on his forehead."

Looking mean wasn't a crime. "What about the night of the murder? You do any checking?"

Porter nodded. "I talked to the supervisor. Told him to keep it under wraps. Hatcher got off at four that afternoon. Showed up for work at seven the next morning. He says Hatcher's a good worker. Always on time. Doesn't appear to drink or do drugs during work. He also works days so he wasn't here when Rachel was coming to class. At least not working."

The timing meant Mister Hatcher was going to have to cover for where he was at the time of Rachel's death. "This looks like a waste of manpower," Chase said.

Porter shrugged. "It's the best lead we have. I've been waiting for you to go look for the van. We picked him up on surveillance here at work. The van should be in one of the lots around the campus. There are specific areas set aside for university workers. I want to look through the window and check if there's a carpet on the floor inside."

"Can I see Hatcher first?" Chase asked.

"Sure." Porter led Chase through one of the tunnels into the stadium. He spotted Gotleib, poorly disguised as a worker, wandering around the playing field. Porter pointed. "He's there."

Chase looked, staying as far back out of sight as he could. Five men wearing coveralls were painting bleachers. It looked like a long, boring job. He spotted Hatcher right away, about a hundred feet in front of them.

Porter was right. He looked mean. He'd grown a beard since the license photo. He was about six foot and lean. His dark hair was in tangles and Chase was willing to bet he drank most of his pay.

Chase wished he could see his eyes up close. Some killers had a certain look in their eyes. Chase knew that sounded stupid to people outside the world of violence and he couldn't go into a court with it, but the ones who killed out of dumb meanness had it. He'd seen it in Iraq and Afghanistan. Guys who fired when they shouldn't have. The type who'd kill a person if they cut them off in traffic, or said something bad about their girl in a bar, or blasted civilians at a check point if they didn't stop soon enough.

171

Bob Mayer

Chase's glance had done little but let him know what Hatcher now looked like. The fact that Donnelly had shifted Gotleib to work on this case told Chase that the Barnes investigation was getting deep-sixed.

Porter and Chase went back out to the car and started cruising the lots after calling campus security to find out which ones it would likely be in. At least finding a van wouldn't be that difficult. It took fifteen minutes.

SRW 374. The body of the vehicle had seen some better days. The white paint could use a good washing. Chase couldn't imagine Rachel walking over to this vehicle late at night in the CU parking lot unless she was a lot stupider than the A's she had been getting. Of course, he knew there were school smarts, there were street smarts and the two didn't necessarily add up.

Chase wondered if Hatcher had been a member of the swingers club. Maybe he had even had sex with Rachel and then followed her from the club. Chase didn't know. Even if she didn't have street smarts he couldn't imagine Rachel willingly having sex with Hatcher, her being really into sex notwithstanding. Besides, Sylvie had said they only let single women in, not men.

Porter told Chase to keep an eye out, just in case Hatcher got off early. The van had no windows except in the front and two small panels in the back. The two in the back were tinted.

Porter went over and peered in the side windows, then came back. "He's got a blanket hung behind the front seats so I couldn't see the rear."

"That's strange."

Porter shrugged. "Not enough to get a warrant." They got back in the car and Porter drove Chase back to his Jeep.

"What's the plan?" Chase asked

Porter sighed. "We keep an eye on him. You got any ideas?"

Chase trusted Porter. Besides there was always the slim possibility that they might trail Hatcher to the same club he was at this evening. That could be awkward.

"I think I know where Rachel was the night she was killed. I'm going with Sylvie to check it out tonight."

Porter's gray eyebrows arched. "With Sylvie?"

Chase told his partner the story and where he was going. When Chase was done Porter just looked at Chase for a minute as he mulled it

172

over. "It sort of fits. I never even thought of something like that. What are you going to do when you get there? Show Mrs. Stevens' picture around?"

Good question. "I don't know. I'll play it by ear."

"Why is Sylvie going?"

"She wants to. And it will be easier for me to get in with her."

Porter grinned. "You going to do anything?"

"What do you mean?"

He winked. "You know. It is a swingers club after all. I'm sure Sylvie will be the hit of the party."

Porter and Chase had worked together for four months but this was the most he had ever pissed Chase off. Through his anger Chase realized his partner's comment was just an echo of the way he had talked about Sylvie for the past several months. He'd treated her as a good deal. An object.

Chase opened the door. "I'll see you tomorrow."

Porter reached over and grabbed his arm. "Hey, Chase. I'm sorry. I didn't mean that. It was stupid."

Chase nodded. "I know. It's more my fault. Take care."

Chase shut the door and went over to his Jeep. He tried to shake off his irritation, realizing it truly was more with himself than with Porter. He was getting worn down with bad feelings.

There were only two things Chase knew that he was doing that he hadn't been told to. One was checking on the Patriots and Colonel Rivers. The other was checking on the Barnes. And what he had learned so far indicated the two might be connected. So how did the third leg of this triangle-- the CIA-- fit in? Thorne had hinted at that.

Chase needed more information-- exactly what Fortin had told Chase not to seek.

CHAPTER EIGHTEEN

The North Denver Social Club met in a large three-story house, nestled in the midst of a middle class community. There was nothing on the outside to suggest it was anything other than a home. If Sylvie hadn't had the address, Chase would have questioned going up and knocking on the door. As she had said, it was only three blocks from where Rachel had caught her cab.

Chase sensed someone watching them through the peephole. Then the door swung open and they were ushered in. The doorman was a middle-aged man, slightly balding, with a smile on his face.

"Good evening. I'm Andrew." He looked at Sylvie. "You must be the young lady I talked to on the phone today."

Sylvie smiled and offered her hand. "Yes. I'm Sylvie and this is Chase."

Chase was looking about. The inside was much different than the outside suggested. Someone had gutted the main floor, making it into one large room. A rectangular bar sat in the front half. The rear half held a dance floor with tables scattered about it, and booths around the wall. A large screen TV was set up there also. There were about fifteen, maybe twenty people spread about the place, but it was hard to pick up details about them. The place was dimly lit and cigarette smoke hung in the air. That alone would have canceled the place in Boulder.

"Do you have your tests?"

Sylvie pulled the copies of the AIDS tests out. The man frowned. "These are too old. We require current within one month."

Chase let Sylvie do the talking.

"I know. We went this afternoon and had our blood drawn for current ones, but the results won't be in for a week. We just want to look around tonight. We won't do anything with anyone. We're as concerned as you are about safe sex."

Andrew looked us both over. Chase knew he liked what he saw, especially Sylvie. She was dressed to kill, looking very sharp in a nice dress with a thigh high cut on one leg. Chase didn't think he was looking too bad either, but he wasn't sure he wanted the guy to let them in because he liked the way he looked.

"All right. You can stay. But you mustn't have sexual contact with any of our members. It will be forty dollars for this evening. If you come back with current tests we'll sign you up as members and that fee will be one thousand dollars for a year's membership."

A thousand bucks. Chase doubted Hatcher could come up with that. Hell, Rachel hadn't been making money when she came here-- if she came-- she'd been giving it away. So where'd the money in the account come from?

Andrew turned as a woman came up. She appeared to be in her mid-thirties. Short blond hair, slim figure. She was wearing a very short black leather skirt and a halter-top through which Chase could clearly see her nipples.

"This is my wife, Lauren." He introduced Chase and Sylvie and explained to her about the AIDS test.

Lauren nodded. "It's all right. Let me show you about and explain our rules."

Chase had to admit to himself that he was surprised. He had half-expected some sort of dive, run by questionable characters. The place wasn't exactly high class on the inside like the Stevens' house, but it was better than his basement cave.

Lauren led them along the first floor. "The bar is BYOB. We don't have a liquor license. You bring in whatever you want and give it to the bartender. She'll serve you only what you brought."

Chase did a double take at the girl behind the bar. She was a blond, who didn't happen to be wearing a top. She was slightly overweight, but it looked nice on her. She smiled at them.

Lauren stopped at the edge of the small dance floor. "We have our own DJ. We all gather here on the main floor until eight. Then we open the up and down stairs. No screwing on the main floor. You can have oral sex or use your hands however you like, but you can only have intercourse on the other floors."

The last was said so matter-of-factly that Sylvie and Chase just stood there and nodded. Chase felt like he was in a sort of erotic twilight zone.

"No drugs," Lauren said. "Not even pot. We run a clean place and we don't want any trouble with the police. You want to smoke some pot, you can go outside and down the street to the park and take your chances. But you do any in here and you're out. You get caught doing it outside, you don't tell them that you are members."

She pointed out the bathrooms and then led the two of them upstairs. The foyer looked like a locker room, which it was. "When you come up you can put your clothes in a locker. We have never had any trouble with stealing, but you can bring your own lock if you like."

She pointed out the bathroom next to the foyer. It had been remodeled with a large tiled shower room with three heads.

The rest of the level consisted of rooms with mattresses covering the floor in each. She stopped in one room where there was a strange device that looked like it belonged in a gym or a doctor's office.

"What's that?" Sylvie asked.

The woman hopped up on a bicycle seat and put her legs up on the two stanchions that came out. She gestured down at a padded platform between her legs. "One of you sits there and the other person sits where I am. Makes it very convenient for oral sex don't you think?"

Her tiny skirt had ridden up to her waist and Chase could see that she was wearing just a small g-string. She didn't seem in the slightest bit embarrassed. Sylvie turned to Chase and smiled. "We'll have to try this sometime. Almost as good as a Jeep sound bar."

Great, Chase thought. Slam the only thing he was proud of.

He was trying to remember his original reason for coming here as the hostess led them down through the main floor and into the basement. It was one big room half covered with mattresses. The two walls flanking the mattresses were lined with mirrors.

"This is where it gets pretty wild sometimes," Lauren informed them. Chase could imagine. It looked like they could fit twenty or thirty people on that floor.

She led them back upstairs. "Like Andrew told you. No sex with any of our members until you get more current tests and can join, but you two can do whatever you want with each other tonight.

"We do ask though, that you not be voyeurs. It's all right to watch anything here on the main floor, but don't go up or downstairs just to stand there and watch others without their permission. Everyone here has the right to say no to anything, even someone just watching.

"Naturally, there are no photos allowed and anyone you meet in here you leave in here. What I mean is that we value everyone's privacy. If you see someone out in the world that you only know through the club, then you act as if you don't know them.

"We don't like pushy people here," Lauren added. "If you have any problems with anyone please let Andrew or I know. We have three other new couples here tonight. Usually a good fifth of the people in here on any given night are newcomers who just want to check it out. Do you have any questions?"

Chase and Sylvie shook their heads. The DJ was playing some rock and roll at a level where one could carry on a conversation and still have the brain function. Sylvie went to the bar and got them two plastic cups of soda. "What do you think?"

Chase looked about slowly. "It's different than I thought it would be."

"What do you mean?"

"It's not a dive. The people aren't low-lifes."

Sylvie smiled. "You always expect the worst don't you?"

"It's my job." Chase peered over her shoulder to make sure he was really seeing what he thought he was seeing. A woman was seated, facing out on a stool, leaning back on the bar, while another woman was kneeling in front of her, head buried between her legs.

"This is different."

"Why, Chase?"

He gestured. "Look at that."

Sylvie glanced over her shoulder. "So? Isn't the Silver Satyr weird? There I take my clothes off so men can pay money and watch. Here at least people seem to be meeting on some sort of equal basis. Remember, Lauren said the one right you do have here is to say no. Nobody here is paying to see someone else take their clothes off."

Chase tried to regain focus. "Do you think Rachel would have come here?"

"What do you think?"

Slowly, Chase nodded. "Maybe. It fits. I think she would have felt reasonably secure here. I just have to figure out how to find out if she had been here. I don't want to spook anyone."

"Why don't you just ask Andrew or Lauren?"

Chase drew his attention away from the two women. "Because it occurs to me that if they require an AIDS test to get in here, then they must have had one from Rachel with her name on it. If that was so, then they knew she came here.

"Rachel's name was all over the papers last week. If she spent the last evening of her life here, then why didn't anybody come forward and say so? If they didn't just because they're so concerned about their privacy then I have some questions about the type of people we're dealing with. There's a big leap from protecting privacy to murder. They could have called us confidentially."

Sylvie didn't have an answer to that.

Chase looked over the other people. He could vaguely see people in booths doing things to each other. As far as he could tell, Hatcher wasn't here. Besides, he really couldn't imagine Hatcher being allowed in.

He and Sylvie were approached several times by couples who introduced themselves and sat down and talked for a little bit. No last names, no questions about what they did for a living, just some chitchat. No "Hey, do you want to fuck?" questions either.

They were asked by one couple if they wanted to go upstairs with them. Sylvie explained about the AIDS test thing. The man said he appreciated her honesty and they moved on. This was getting stranger by the minute, Chase thought.

At eight, people started gravitating toward the stairs. There seemed to be about thirty people here now; more women than men which fit with Sylvie's theory. Chase was still uncertain how to proceed. Before he left, he needed to know if Rachel had been here last week.

Chase got up to go the bathroom. "Are you going to be all right?"

Sylvie looked at Chase. "I think I'm safer sitting here than I am dancing at the Silver Satyr."

Chase made his way past the tables. He glanced in a booth as he went by and froze. Two women were seated there tight together. One looked to be in her early twenties and her dress top was pulled down, exposing pert little breasts. The other woman was older and had an arm around the younger girl's shoulders, casually playing with the nipple of her right breast. The older woman was Linda Watkins.

CHAPTER NINETEEN

Linda Watkins was one cool woman. Her hand never left the young woman's breast as Chase slid into the bench opposite them.

"Detective Chase, what a pleasure to see you."

Chase didn't say anything for a long minute and just eyeballed her. She finally told the young woman to get a drink as she had to talk privately. That had not been the primary purpose of Chase's quiet. Mainly, he was trying to rein in his anger.

"Well, detective what brings you here?" Her voice was coated with a husky sensuality that hadn't been there the last time he'd talked to her. He wanted to lean over and slap the superior bitch look off her perfectly made-up face.

"What the hell do you think brings me here?"

She was cool; she also wasn't dumb. "Why are you so tense? Should I be fearing for my health at this moment?" She picked up her drink, which was empty, and absentmindedly tried to take a sip.

Chase leaned forward. "Why don't we talk about what you're doing here and maybe we'll have a few minutes left to talk about unimportant things, like obstruction of justice for one. Or maybe withholding evidence." He knew he was being a prick, not a good interview technique, but he just couldn't hold it in.

Chase watched a worried frown flit its way across her features before she could stop it. He had to admit he liked it. "I don't understand what you're talking about Detective Chase."

"I think you do understand, Mrs. Watkins. Tell me everything about Rachel. We can do this now or I can haul you down to the station and we'll do it there. Makes no difference to me."

"I don't understand why you're being so threatening. I haven't done anything. You can't just talk to me like I'm some common criminal."

"I don't think you're common. You're probably one of the most uncommon women I've ever met. I don't care what you're doing here, but I care very much if Rachel was here the night she was killed. Seems

179

to me you said you hardly knew her. I feel like I've been jerked around. I don't like that feeling, do you understand me?"

She was playing with the little straw that had come with her drink. "I'm starting to understand you very well. You think this club had something to do with Rachel's death."

A genius, Chase thought. "Wouldn't you? If Rachel came here I'd say that puts an entirely new slant on things."

Linda's manner rebounded. "You're so pathetic. For a minute there, when I first saw you, I thought you would be different. The fact that you got this far in your investigation made me think that you understood something about Rachel, and therefore something about this place. But you're not different. You're small-minded, but don't feel too bad. You have lots of company."

Chase saw what she was trying to do and he decided to cut her off at the knees. "Don't mess with me. You're too old and I'm too tired. I don't gave a rat's ass what you think about me. I want to know who killed Rachel Stevens and if I have to drag you through the mud to get that, you better be ready to suck some dirt."

The girl came back with some drinks. Linda took hers and waved the girl off. Chase turned to check on Sylvie. She was talking to some big guy with his back to them. Chase didn't feel too threatened as Sylvie could take care of herself. He sat back to let Linda spill her guts or rip them out of her, if he had to.

"Rachel and I weren't really good friends. We just had a few things in common. It didn't take me long to figure that out. I like to think I'm a good judge of character.

"Her going back to school was part of it. I had been coming here for a year or so and other places like this before that. Rachel was intrigued and she was smart enough to handle this. She was extremely discreet. She would have never let this interfere with her life.

"This place was safe; that's why I didn't tell you about it. It was a part of her life that I believed should remain her secret. I didn't think her husband needed to go through that sort of disclosure either."

She leaned forward. "I do know one thing and that is that she was very much alive when she left here last Wednesday. She usually left right around the time I got here. If I thought there was anything to be gained by telling you about this place, I would have. But most people don't understand. I don't think you do. When I said she wasn't like other women at the tennis courts you didn't seem to understand. She, or should I say I; we need more."

Chase interrupted her. "Yeah, I know. You're like people in a gourmet club. You want to talk to people who know how to make gravy."

She stared at Chase for a moment. "What does that mean?"

"Forget it. You talk and let me decide what makes sense."

Chase was getting a little tired of people who needed more out of life. It looked to him like it was just another way to end up dead. It pissed Chase off that Linda Watkins had taken it upon her shoulders to decide what was important in his murder case and what wasn't. To save time going around in circles about the higher plane of sexuality that she was obviously trying to explain to Chase, the lug headed cop, he told her about the theory of being really into sex as a woman. He asked if that was what she was getting at.

"That is putting it in somewhat simplistic terms, but I can tell you have the general idea."

Chase looked her straight in the eye. "So basically Rachel liked to fuck, and I don't really know or really care what you yourself like to do."

In the second it took for those words to wound, Chase thought he saw the person that Linda hid behind a mask of bravado. She appeared to be a lonely, scared woman trying to survive in a society that had no place for her. He truly saw for the first time why women came here. So they would never have to listen to a man say what he had just said to Linda Watkins.

Linda put a pretty effective end to Chase's deep ruminations. "You are a piece of shit, detective. Why don't you go ahead and drag my good name through the mud. What do you think? That you're going to ruin my life? That my marriage is going to go up in a blaze of innuendoes and incriminations?"

She pointed. "I notice you keep looking at that lovely thing in the corner that you came in with. Is she your girlfriend? I personally think it's kind of interesting that she's having such a deep conversation with my husband."

Chase looked and when the man turned, he recognized the guy from the country club. "What's he doing here?"

Linda gave Chase a very smug look. "I'll put it in words you can understand. He likes to make gravy."

181

It was time to readjust, Chase thought. Right now his priority was to get Linda to tell him what had happened the previous Wednesday. "You may not believe this, but I'm sorry. I had no right to talk to you that way. You have to understand that all this is very new to me, and I guess I'm letting some old prejudices die hard."

Some of the anger appeared to go out of her and she sat back. "I like a man who will even contemplate the fact that he doesn't know everything. You're seeing something you don't understand and you're at least fighting that very normal human compulsion to slam something that frightens you."

"This doesn't frighten me."

She leaned forward. "Oh, but it does. It frightens you very much. And that's the reason you don't understand it. Not the other way around. If you were 'into sex' as you call it, this house and everyone in it would appeal to you because of the honesty and acceptance that prevails here. But you're not. Sex is love for you. It's filling an emotional need, not a physical one. It's a need you have, not a want."

"I'd disagree," Chase said, thinking about what he had with Sylvie, "but this isn't about me."

She continued as if he hadn't spoken. "You find all of this threatening, and you should. You have society on your side, Detective Chase. But suppose society is wrong? What would happen to your world if women grew tired of their perpetual unequal status?"

They both turned at a new voice. "That's a very interesting question, Chase. What do you have to say?" Chase hadn't noticed Sylvie come to the booth. She was getting good at sneaking up on him.

Chase didn't know how much she had heard. "Would someone please tell me about Rachel Stevens? I'm not interesting in solving the world's male-female problems. I'm tired of trying to figure out Rachel's psyche, or anyone else's for that matter." Chase jabbed a finger across the table. "We can save the philosophy for later. I need to know what happened the night Rachel died."

Linda tapped a long fingernail on the tabletop. "Just the facts, right?" Chase nodded. "The night Rachel was killed, I got here earlier than I usually do. My husband was on a business trip and I hate being alone in that big house. Rachel was already upstairs. She usually went there right away. I guess she thought she only had three hours every few weeks and she was going to make the best of it.

"There were four men around her, along with their wives standing in the shadows. Rachel preferred sex with men in long-standing marriages. It makes sense in today's world wouldn't you say? They were acting out one of her fantasies. When it was over, they all said good-bye to her. I only spoke to her briefly, but she seemed very happy. She did say she was almost done with the semester and anticipated getting A's again.

"None of the men she had sex with left for several more hours. At least not before one in the morning, so I guess that's why I decided that whatever happened to Rachel, it had nothing to do with this place. People do get killed, detective; people who aren't swingers."

Chase tried to understand how someone as obviously intelligent as she was could be so stupid. "How did you know none of those men left?"

"Because I had sex with them. Sort of act two after Rachel." She gave Chase a wicked smile. "Your first sight of me in this booth made you think something about me didn't it? See how easily you make suppositions?"

Chase had walked into both those comments. But she seemed to get off on it so he let it slide. "I think I understand why you chose to hide this from me, but do you see how wrong it was? I've spent a week trying to find out where Rachel was the night she died. That may be the week that cost me the chance to find out who killed her."

Chase leaned across the table. "And something you don't seem to be very concerned about. What if she were killed by someone who knows about this place? How safe does that leave you?"

Linda was obstinate. "It wasn't someone from here. Rachel had been coming here for just under a year. No one who knew her on the outside, except my husband and I, was aware she came here. No one in the club, except us again, knew who she was on the outside. That cab ride was her insulation."

"Almost a year?" Chase repeated. "She was coming here even before she went to school?"

Linda nodded. "Old Jeffrey was too caught up in his work and that pretty little secretary of his to have noticed. Oh," she said, seeing the look on Chase's face, "Rachel knew about Miss Plunkett. It was just another reason for her to be here."

"Another justification, you mean," Sylvie said.

Linda shrugged.

Sylvie threw some logic in. "Rachel had to use her name on the AIDS test. Andrew and Lauren knew who she was."

Linda shook her head. "We're not stupid. We got our tests through the same doctor in Denver. We took the tests and whited-out our real names and inserted false ones and Xeroxed them. Everyone here knows me as Lori. Rachel was known as Nora."

"Nice literary references," Chase said. Seeing her surprise, he amplified. "My mother was into the classics. What about Rachel's husband? Could he have found out about this?"

"He could have, but, as I said, I don't think it's likely. Even if he did, he loved Rachel very much in his own way despite what he was doing himself. He wouldn't have killed her over this. She didn't hide this from Jeffrey because she was afraid of what he would do. She hid it because she was afraid of what he would think."

Not very good logic in Chase's opinion. Some men he knew might kill their wives for doing what Rachel did. Or at least contemplate killing them. But Doctor Stevens had a solid alibi and if he had known about this club and Rachel, Chase would have picked something up when he had questioned him. Of course there was also the factor of Lisa Plunkett. While Rachel was here, Jeffrey was with her. Which was worse? Chase wondered.

Linda wasn't done. "If you're going to think that way, then I suppose my husband might be a suspect also. But he can prove he was at his business meeting out of town the night in question.

"For that matter, I suppose I might be a suspect except for the fact that at the time Rachel died I was rolling around on the floor with four men upstairs. Two of them are here right now. Would you like to confirm my story?"

Chase knew Rachel a whole lot better, but he was still at ground zero as far as the case went.

"What was in the bag?"

Linda seemed startled. "What bag?"

"The gym bag Rachel had."

Linda shook her head. "I don't know. I didn't see any bag."

Chase had had enough of Linda/Lori for one sitting. He nudged Sylvie so he could get out of the booth.

"I'll be back in touch."

"Have a good time, Detective Chase."

He and Sylvie went back to their table. The lights were even dimmer and it looked like some woman was giving a man a blowjob in the booth adjacent to them. Two naked women were slow-dancing out on the center of the floor. Chase looked at Sylvie. "All right. I've found out where she was for those three hours. But that doesn't seem to help too much."

Sylvie had apparently been doing her own thinking. "I disagree with what Linda said. I think this place had something to do with Rachel's death. For Linda it cuts too close to home to even think that Rachel could have died because she came here. Both because she was the one who introduced Rachel to this place and also because she's still here. Maybe someone was blackmailing Rachel. Or maybe Rachel was blackmailing someone she recognized here. Who knows?"

Great. That did Chase a lot of good. At the moment he would have given anything to have Joseph Hatcher walk in the door. He'd have drawn down on him and arrested him on the spot.

"What now, Chase?" Sylvie asked.

Chase had all the pieces. He just couldn't figure out a way to put them together. He'd listened to many differing philosophies and he wasn't sure he agreed with any of them.

"Let's go," he said, taking Sylvie's hand.

CHAPTER TWENTY

They were both quiet as they drove back from the club. Chase was lost in thought about the case, trying to see what he had missed. Aside from the fact that he still had no idea who killed Rachel and why, he felt good that he'd at least solved part of the mystery.

Sylvie's voice, when it came out of the darkness of the Jeep, startled Chase. "What did you think about the club?"

That was a good question. Chase didn't know how to explain what he felt, but he could tell she wanted to hear something. "It was very interesting. I'm glad I went. It satisfied some curiosity. I don't know."

"Try."

So much for squirming out of that one with a shotgun blast of vague answers. "I guess it made me feel excited and nervous at the same time."

Sylvie started popping the questions fast. "Which did you feel more: excited or nervous?" She was beginning to tap her fingernails on the hard surface of her purse. It was very irritating.

They were getting close to his place and his speed was picking up. He had a feeling that if they didn't get out of the confines of the Jeep soon, she was going to be at his throat. He might be emotionally obtuse, but he could sense seething in a woman. He wondered if she was remembering the 'picnic'.

"I don't know what you want me to say Sylvie. You seem to be upset and I don't know why."

"What makes you think I'm upset?"

Boy, Chase thought, was she upset. He pulled into the alley that ran behind the house and told her they could continue this over a cold brew in his lovely abode. Sylvie didn't say anything, which was another portent of a coming storm. She got out of the Jeep and led the way to his back door. Astral was in the yard as usual and gave a quick yap to let them know they'd been spotted, then she went back to sleep.

CHASING THE GHOST

Chase went to the fridge. He grabbed two brews. He even got Sylvie a chilled mug from the freezer. He knew she liked to have one and he always kept one in there special for her even though she'd rarely come over. He hoped that would give him a nickel or two in the bank and maybe cool her off.

They went into the bedroom as it was the only place where both of them could sit. Sylvie tossed Merck magazine off the mattress and sat down. She moved the empty cans from the footlocker and put her beer down.

"Chase, you live like a college kid. Got an ash tray?"

"Use the empty beer can there. It's the newest wave in ash trays." Chase felt they were even so far. It could still go either way. He was hoping that Sylvie would call a truce as she normally did. Maybe they could end up at her place. They'd never spent the night here; the lack of a decent bed or pretty much any other decent furniture precluded that.

Sylvie lit a cigarette. "All right. We're here. We've got our beers. Why did you say you were nervous in the club?"

"I don't know. I just felt funny." Chase sat on the edge of the footlocker. It was old and the black was liberally sprinkled with dings and dents. He'd been issued it as a plebe at West Point and his name, (CHASE, H.) and social security number was stenciled on the top, the letters and numbers almost faded out with time. It had traveled a lot of places.

"You need to talk to me, Chase. I want to know how you felt."

Sylvie was staring at him hard. He knew something had changed between them today, but he'd spent too much time thinking about Rachel and the damn case and being threatened by the CIA and two thugs that it had passed relatively unnoticed until now. He needed to get his act together real fast or something was going to go bad between them. Before he could figure it out, it went bad.

"What do you think of Rachel, now that you know where she spent those Wednesday evenings?"

"I don't feel like talking about Rachel right now. She's dead. She's my work."

Sylvie cut in. "What am I, Chase? You had me earlier today and took me for a picnic that was really about your work. You're the one who mixed things up."

He sensed he was on the edge of a razor, getting ready to lose a ball whichever way he went. "What do you want to be, Sylvie? You sit

187

there and ask me questions all the time. How about you talk and give some answers to your own questions? I'm tired of having to guess."

"You've got a good point there, Chase, because you're not a very good guesser." Sylvie sighed. "Just a little while ago, I asked you what you thought of Rachel now that you knew the truth about her. I would say that you think less of her now."

"Well, yeah."

"I guess then that my stripping doesn't thrill you either."

A dim light went on in Chase's brain. It was time to lay some cards on the table. "To be honest, no, it doesn't."

"It's been three months. You could have said something sooner."

"What could I have said? It's your business."

"I would have at least known your true feelings. It doesn't mean I would have quit my job, but at least I would know then that I could trust you. That you would tell me what you feel. You think by not telling me what you felt you were protecting me. It's not your job to protect me in that way, Chase. I can take care of myself. What I want from the people in my life is honesty and trust and I can't trust you."

"I'm just like that club to you, aren't I, Chase? I make you excited and nervous at the same time. Ultimately you don't think much of me. You thought a lot of Rachel because you only saw her on the outside. Pine Brook Hills and the Boulder Country Club. It's the same thing with your mother."

"Don't talk about my mother."

"I might as well since you don't, but it hangs over your head like a black cloud everywhere you go. You carry that letter in your pocket everywhere you go. So it's got to be important to you in some way. But it's also a secret. What you and I do together, that's a secret too. For you. I don't care if people know. I get on stage and take my clothes off, and you pin on a badge and act so righteous."

Sylvie leaned forward. "Don't you see, Chase? This doesn't have anything to do with sex or stripping or swingers clubs. It has to do with perception and reality and tolerance. Since you never tried to see who I really was, you treated me as you saw me on the surface and that wasn't that great other than my body and the sex. I've been trying for the last month to open up to you, but you can't open up to someone who doesn't want to come in and who won't open himself up in turn.

"You didn't start to think less of Rachel until she started to become more like me on the surface. That hurts, Chase."

Chase simply stood there. Sylvie kept going, which was good because Chase knew whatever he said, it was going to make things worse.

"The real problem with Rachel is that she wanted more. That's what all those people in that club wanted tonight. More." Sylvie shook her head. "They're full of shit with their AIDS test. That's no guarantee someone didn't pick it up this morning and hasn't developed the antibodies yet. You have to wait at least six months to be sure. Plus there are other nasty bugs other there besides AIDS that can screw you up.

"You know, Chase, even though I made you get an AIDS test, I took a chance with you having unprotected sex as early as I did. I trusted you. You didn't even ask me what protection I was using. Didn't even occur to you, did it?

"Those people at the club are looking for something more and that makes them unhappy with their own lives. And that's exactly the way you've been the last couple of months. You want more and that makes me feel pretty crappy because I'm sitting here in front of you and I can't give you any more than what you already have from me. If that's not good enough, then I have to start thinking of me."

Chase closed his eyes. He could understand some of what she was saying, but he couldn't do anything about it.

Chase heard Sylvie move and opened his eyes. She came over and sat on the edge of the footlocker, pulling Chase down next to her. She put a hand on his shoulder. "Don't look so sad, Chase. It didn't cost you too much to figure this one out. Not sixteen—well, twenty if you count West Point—years. You still have a lot of time left."

Chase put his arms around her waist and hugged her. "Can we start over?"

"I don't think so. Not right now. Because we both have a problem. I think you finally understand what I've been saying, but it hasn't truly sunk in yet." She tapped Chase on the head, then his chest, as she said: "You understand with your brain, Chase, but it takes time to get to your heart, if it ever does. Until it does, we'd just be pretending."

Chase sensed Sylvie was right, but that didn't make it feel any better. This was the third serious choice of his life. He was just beginning to realize that somehow he had managed to screw them all up.

Sylvie headed for the door.

"I'll drive you home."

Sylvie held up her hand. "No. I'll walk."

"It's dark and--"

"I'll walk." The back door slid shut behind her. Then the back gate shut with a thud.

Chase waited half a minute, long enough for her to make it to the corner of the alley, then edged his way out the door. He followed Sylvie without her knowing he was there. It felt good to be moving in the dark-- the only good feeling he'd had all day.

Chase waited down the street from her building as she went in. When the light in her apartment went on, he headed home deep in thought. He cut due north, passing Pine until he hit the alley between it and Mapleton, then he turned west toward the mountains and his house. He liked walking along the Farmer's Canal. With the Spring thaw, it was bubbling with water.

Less than fifty feet from his back gate, Chase paused. Only his eyeballs moved in small arcs trying to pick up whatever it was that had alerted him. When he'd come on active duty, the last of the Vietnam veterans still populated the senior officer and enlisted ranks of Special Forces. One of them, his first team sergeant, Dave Riley, had taught Chase a very important lesson about sixth sense. He'd told Chase to trust any feeling of danger or misgiving he ever had, regardless if he could find a source for it. Right now, the hairs on the back of Chase's neck were standing straight out, but he couldn't see anything unusual in the dark shadows in the alley. All he could hear was the water in the Canal going by. A slight breeze picked up now and then, lightly flowing over his exposed skin.

He still didn't move. Then he finally noticed something. The light on the back porch was out. Chase was sure it had been on when he left. The bulb could have burnt out. While he was trailing Sylvie home. Right.

Someone was out there in the darkness. Chase could sense the presence, a blacker hole in the shadows.

Another thing his senses had noticed but his mind had been slow on finally registered-- Astral hadn't made a noise.

Chase finally moved, sliding his left hand inside his jacket and retrieving the Glock 10mm. He felt exposed and vulnerable, but if whoever was out there had wanted to shoot him at a distance, the final curtain would have been pulled minutes ago.

Chase very slowly knelt down, weapon ready. Then he lay down, feeling the dirt under him. There was the slightest noise-- cloth rustling about forty-five feet down the alley, slightly past the back gate. Chase aimed in that direction and waited. A tiny glint, the distant streetlight reflecting off metal. Chase's finger curled around the trigger. It could have been a garbage can or debris. It also could have been a gun or knife.

The seconds ticked into minutes. Chase didn't move and was faced with the uncertainty of whether whoever was out there was moving. Either coming toward Chase, which would be bad, or moving away, which wasn't good but not as bad.

Or being still just like he was, waiting for Chase to screw up and move first.

Or maybe there was no one out there. The cloth could have been the breeze on a rag. The metal a piece of garbage. The light bulb could have actually burnt out. Light bulbs did burn out every so often. The presence he'd thought he felt might have been just that-- a fabrication of his severely over-taxed and tired mind.

A car rolled up eighth. Chase shut his eyes to avoid having what night vision he did have from being damaged by even the periphery of the car's headlights as it passed the end of the alley.

It was chilly, the warmth of the sun long gone, the cold air blowing in from the Rockies. Chase had dressed for the swinger's club, not a standoff in an alley. He was dead tired, not having had more than a handful of hours of sleep in the past week. His fun meter was definitely pegged out.

Chase didn't move.

He estimated he had been lying down for over thirty minutes. He blinked, trying to clear the haze that exhaustion was scrolling across his eyes. He scanned the dark in short arcs, concentrating off-center of his focus, where the night vision was slightly better. There was a bush next to the gate. Two trees opposite the gate, overhanging the Canal.

Another car went by.

Forty-five minutes. He was cold through and through, his skin, his muscles, his bones all telling his mind that he needed to go inside and get warm. Only fifty feet away was a hot shower.

Chase blinked his eyes open. Scrunched his face to stay awake. He'd seen men on winter warfare training curl up into little balls in the snow and fall asleep, willing to freeze to death than face the difficulties of staying awake when exhausted. He'd eaten instant coffee straight from the small pouch in field rations to stay awake. Whatever it took.

An hour at least, although he didn't dare move to check his watch. The gun felt heavy in his left hand. It had to be close to freezing.

There was no one out there.

Chase wasn't even sure he could move. As he began to flex the muscles in his legs, someone stood up from behind the bush. A man, slinking back down the alley toward eighth.

Chase brought the Glock up to aim.

His answer was a muzzle flash. The subsonic round from the man's silenced gun hit just above Chase and to the left, a solid thunk into the plank of the wood fence. Chase rolled right as the muzzle flashed again. He didn't know where that round went or how many more times the man fired as Chase rolled over the edge of the dirt road, onto the ledge of stones on the edge of the canal and into the freezing water.

He surfaced, muzzle of the Glock leading the way but there was nothing there. Chase sprinted down the Canal through the waist high water, not caring about stealth any more until he reached where it went under Ninth Street.

Whoever had shot at him was gone.

Chase climbed up onto the alley road and slowly walked back home. He opened the back gate and froze.

Astral's severed head was on the ground just inside the gate. The small hand ax Chase used to split firewood for Louise lay next to her. Her long collie ears dangled over the torn flesh of her neck. Chase sank to his knees; wet, tired, and dirty, cradling the head in his lap.

CHAPTER TWENTY-ONE

Chase could tell that Porter picked up on his mood as soon as he slumped down at his desk. His partner had been sitting there sipping on coffee and trying to appear inconspicuous.

"I'm afraid to ask what happened last night at that club, especially considering the way you look."

Chase didn't want to talk about the swingers club or his personal life. He didn't want to talk about anything. He had about an hour of sleep under his belt.

He'd checked the alley for shell casings and found nothing. That meant the intruder had used a silenced revolver. He knew he should have gone to Louise and told her about Astral. He should have called in the duty lieutenant and reported what happened. But he didn't give a shit about should-have any more.

Chase had found the rest of Astral's body under a bush near the fence. He buried it and the head in the yard, on the edge of his garden. The light bulb above the porch had been unscrewed. He didn't think the house had been broken into. The head might have been a message and he'd just come down the alley before the intruder could get away. Or whoever it was had been waiting for Chase to get closer to insure the job was done right. A silenced revolver with sub-sonic rounds was inaccurate above twenty feet or so.

"Chase?" Porter had his hand on Chase's shoulder.

Chase shook his head. He'd knelt for a while holding Astral's head, the water dripping off his clothes making mud in the dirt under his knees, then slowly freezing. When he'd finally staggered to his feet, he'd broken the ice that had frozen his pants to the ground. He was tired, but simmering underneath was anger. He held on to that feeling.

Chase tried to think of something to say. "Nothing much at the old swingers club other than seeing Linda Watkins there."

"Linda Watkins of tennis court fame?"

"None other."

"Well, that's certainly interesting." Porter didn't seem very interested in it. He was still staring at Chase hard.

Chase sat down at his desk. He let go of the coffee mug and pressed his fingers together in front of his face while he spoke to Porter. The pressure helped him focus. "Yes and no. Yes, because now we know where Rachel Stevens spent her last evening and why the coroner found four different DNA types on the sperm inside her. No,

193

because I don't have any leads out of the club to CU or the park where we found the body. There's no immediate connection to her death."

Chase slowly went through the events of the previous evening with his partner. It reminded him of the debriefing after they brought him out of the induced coma in the hospital in Germany. When he was done, Porter just sat and looked at Chase for a while. Then he surprised Chase. "What happened between you and Sylvie?"

"What?"

Porter leaned forward and lowered his voice so it wouldn't be heard at any of the other desks in the office. "Something's wrong, Chase, and it just isn't this case. I'm not the smartest guy in the world, but even I can figure out that if it isn't the case then it must be something else. Now, I know it isn't my business to get involved in your personal life, but I think you need to talk to someone."

Chase wouldn't have known where to begin. Getting shot at last night? Burying Astral's severed head and body? Fortin threatening him? Two unknown thugs threatening him? His wife divorcing him? His mother dying while he was deployed and her strange letter?

"Sylvie and I broke up." To Chase that sounded real stupid. Like he was in high school, she was the head cheerleader, and he was the star quarterback. They were a long way from those days.

"She didn't like going there with you?"

"No. That wasn't it." So Chase took twenty minutes of the taxpayers' time to explain his personal problem to my partner.

When he was done, Porter got up, went over to the machine, got them both fresh coffees and came back. Chase took that as a sign that his partner was really concerned. Porter handed him a coffee. "It's what I said to you the other night, Chase. You got to figure out where you're at and who you are and be satisfied with it."

"Yeah. I know."

Porter leaned forward. "How come you never brought Sylvie over to meet Mary and the kids?"

"I know you've invited us, but I really didn't think Mary would want to meet her."

Porter got angry then which surprised Chase. "Don't give me this shit, Chase. You're the one with the problem with Sylvie. Not Mary and not me."

"I don't have a problem with her. I'm the one dating her." Was, Chase thought as soon as the words left his mouth.

194

"You're not dating her, Chase. You don't ever take her anywhere. She's part of your life like a six-pack of beer and a bag of chips." Porter shook his head and went back over to the coffee machine.

Chase realized that even Porter saw it. No matter what arguments Chase used, it came back to the point Sylvie had made last night. He did think less of her because of what she did for a living, same as he had his mother. The problem was that he felt less about himself by affiliation and that was wrong.

Chase didn't think he could talk about this with Porter. Basically, he didn't want to admit how attracted and repelled he was about her stripping. Not the physical aspect, but the strength it had taken for her to do it when she'd hit her own bottom. That took more guts than he'd displayed. And it was his problem now, not hers.

Plus there was the aspect of his childhood and his mother and the father he'd never met, but who had loomed over his entire life. A lot of Freudian shit even Porter wouldn't want to touch. Porter had politely left Chase to his thoughts, and he must have figured he'd pushed as hard as he could, because he changed the subject completely. "So, you didn't get any tie in with Hatcher last night at that club?"

Chase snapped back to attention. It was time to focus on Rachel. He wanted very much to find her killer. A person shouldn't get killed just because they wanted more and went about it in the wrong way. Or in what society said was the wrong way.

Also, Chase didn't want to deal with whoever had killed his neighbor's dog quite yet. He figured it had to be one of two groups-- Fortin or Baldie and Muscles, and he was still trying to track the latter down.

"No. I don't think Hatcher was ever there. What did surveillance get last night on him?"

Porter poked at a single piece of paper on his desk. "Nothing. Left work. Stopped at a Minute Mart, a video store and went home. Didn't leave all night. I need to get over to CU soon to relieve Jameson. What are you going to do?"

Chase grabbed the Book of Rachel. "I'm going to start over."

"What do you mean?"

"I'm going to go through everything I've got in the book. Now that I know who Rachel Stevens was and what she was doing that night, I need to put everything I have in perspective."

Porter shrugged. He preferred the street. Chase preferred his file folders. "All right. Have a good time. You know where I'll be."

Before Chase did anything else, though, he picked up the phone. He dialed Louise's number.

"Visions," she answered the name of her psychic group.

"Louise, its Chase."

There was a moment of silence. "You've seen Astral haven't you?" Her voice was sharp, not the usual flighty discourse he was used to from her.

"Yes, she--"

"She's dead, isn't she?"

"I'm sorry, Louise."

"I told you to be careful, Chase."

"I'm sorry."

"Are you going to catch who did it?"

Chase wondered how much she knew. He decided to start being honest. "I don't know, Louise. I don't know exactly what's going on."

"Chase, you have to open your eyes and see all that surrounds you."

"I will," Chase promised.

"The universe is a strange place. There are connections, forces beyond what is apparent."

"I know."

"And Chase?" Her voice changed once more. Now it was quivering and sad, as if she was going to start crying at any second.

"Yes?"

"Did she suffer?"

"No."

"You're not good at lying even though you think you are. We'll mourn, and then we'll go to the pound. You and I. You need a dog too. I have a friend who works there. She'll find us someone special."

Chase apologized once more and hung up. He left his desk and went to the briefing room, shutting the noise of the office out. He pulled all the folders out and laid them on the table. Then he went to the blackboard and started diagramming, like he used to in Isolation before going on a mission.

In the center, he put Rachel Stevens. Around her, he put all the people who had a role in her life and all the places. Under each, he summarized what that person had said about her. Under each place, he put the way she had acted. Then under her name, he put the way he thought she truly had been.

Then he sat at the table and stared at it for a long time. There were several common threads. The two places that stood out were CU and the North Denver Social Club. The two people who had known her best at each place were Gavin and Linda Watkins.

They'd both agreed on one thing: Rachel Stevens had been smart and determined. Now Chase could add in the factor that she'd wanted more out of life.

Chase stared at the line between the two places for a long time. Something was wrong there. That was a contradiction. No. Not a contradiction, but an anomaly. One took away from the other. By going to the swingers club, Rachel had cut class. Yet Linda Watkins, and her professors, had said Rachel was going to get A's in both her courses. How does a person get an A when they missed one third of their classes? Was there more going on between Rachel and Gavin than appeared on the surface?

It was a long shot. Chase grabbed the phone and called Gavin's office. The professor was out. Chase ended up talking to some graduate student. He got to the point quickly.

"How many A's does Professor Gavin give out in his classes?"

There was a choking noise, which Chase guessed might have been a laugh. "Few and far between. He's one of the hardest graders in the department."

"What do you think the chances are of someone who misses a third of his classes getting an A?"

The student laughed again. "Impossible. Gavin doesn't even use the text. Everything on his tests comes from his class lectures. If you don't have good notes, you're sunk."

Chase thanked the student and hung up. He left the briefing room and went down to the evidence holding area. The clerk got Chase the box with Rachel's stuff. He pulled out her notebook, signed for it, and took it back upstairs.

Chase flipped it open. Rachel's handwriting was very neat and precise. The contents were a model of efficiency. She had everything blocked out with headings highlighted and key points starred. Chase continued turning the pages until he got to the first date she had missed class that semester: the 29th of January.

There were notes there, but they were typed and Xeroxed. Chase checked the other dates. Someone had taken the time to type up the class notes. The same person had given Rachel the notes for all the classes she'd missed up to the night she'd died. Chase stared at those notes for a minute. There was only one way he could find out who had given those to her. He'd have to go to CU.

But before he left, he did one more thing. He got out all the information he had on the Patriots and on Art Rivers. He printed out the article from Merck Magazine and tucked all the information into a new book he was beginning. He labeled this one the Book of Patriots and locked it in his lower right drawer, the one he used his own personal padlock on, not trusting the lock built into the drawer.

****

Driving to CU during the noon lunch rush wasn't relaxing. Contemplating what he was going to say to Gavin wasn't relaxing either. There was something going on, something Chase had missed. Maybe Gavin had given Rachel Stevens those notes. They were meticulously typed, probably computer printed. What if he had known Rachel a lot better than he let on, Chase wondered? And then there was that off the wall question about personalities the first time Chase had questioned him. Of course, maybe she had just asked Gavin for notes and he'd given them to her as a good teacher? Chase had the feeling he was grasping for straws.

Most of the staff had split for lunch. Chase parked, gathered the notebook and made for Gavin's office. He had seemed distant and put out when Chase had arranged for another interview. No doubt, he wondered why Chase kept returning.

Chase was right about Gavin's attitude. The professor was in another world; he seemed to be bothered about something. And he was drinking again. A couple of empty beer cans were on his desk.

Chase started talking about Rachel's grades, but the professor wasn't listening. Chase noticed Gavin had some documents on his desk in front of him. Chase tried to peer around the jumble of papers, but he wasn't very subtle.

Gavin picked them up. "Are you wondering about these, detective?"

Chase told him he was.

Gavin laughed. Not a pleasant sound. It was more of a sarcastic grunt. "My wife just had me served with divorce papers. In class, as a matter of fact. Very apropos. I didn't know she had it in her. I do believe that things would be different if I had even had the slightest inkling she was so clever. You know what she said?" He didn't wait for a guess; Chase wouldn't have given one anyway. "She said we didn't communicate. She said all I was interested in was lecturing. I suppose the old adage is true. If you can't do something teach it instead."

Chase let Gavin ramble on a few minutes while he casually opened Rachel's notebook to the mysterious typed pages. He was no expert, but he could see right away that they didn't match the pages in the bin on top of Gavin's printer.

Chase was so busy checking that out that he didn't hear Gavin until he repeated himself. "I said. Have you ever been married detective?"

"Yeah, I was married."

"Since you use the past tense, I assume you have some experience with divorce?"

"Yes. It sucks."

"Indeed it does." Gavin checked his watch. "What else did you come for? I'm sure it was more than to talk about my divorce."

Chase showed him the notes. "I got these out of Rachel Stevens' notebook. These pages are from the nights she missed. I'm presuming Rachel got these from someone in the class. I was hoping we could compare them to some of your other papers and figure out whom."

Gavin gave them a cursory glance. "Pretty much all students have laser printers although fonts vary."

"Do you have some papers from that class I can compare it to?"

"They might not have come from that particular class. Students have a little black market going on class notes. She could have purchased them from someone who took the same class a previous semester."

At West Point that would have been an honor violation, Chase thought. "I'd just like to check that class for now, if you don't mind."

"Why is it so important who gave her the notes?"

Chase hated it when people asked him why. "Do you have a folder from that class?"

Gavin glanced over his shoulder at a stack of folders. "Yes, but--"

"The papers, please, doctor."

Gavin frowned, thought for a moment, then grabbed a folder off the shelf. He reluctantly handed it over. He was right, Chase noted; all of the papers were done by a laser printer, but the font matched exactly on only one set: Jim York. The name rang a bell, a loud bell. It was the guy who had returned Chase's call, the guy who had sat next to Rachel in Gavin's class. But most importantly, it was the guy who said he never noticed if she were absent or not. Yet had given her the notes for those classes she'd missed.

"Find something?" Gavin asked. He seemed more in the present now.

"No," Chase replied handing him the folder back, tired of answering other people's questions when they gave him so much crap answering his.

"How is the case going?" he asked as Chase stood to leave.

"It's going," Chase said. He was anxious to follow up this new angle. York had held back and Chase's antenna always went on alert when people lied. Chase left Gavin to his drunken woes and headed to his Jeep.

****

By the time, Chase made it to the squad room he was breathing hard from the climb up the stairs. He realized he needed to stop smoking and go back to running the trails, but it just seemed like too much effort.

Porter wasn't around, but Chase knew he had some time. He went back to the attendance sheets for that class. Rachel's absences were the most notable. He finally found it. Three weeks before she was killed, Jim York hadn't been in class either. Chase looked forward. Damn. York had been present the night she died. Why wasn't anything ever simple? Chase thought about it for a second. That didn't rule him out though. He might have been waiting in that parking lot after class. They'd ruled out Gavin, but not the students in the class.

Chase looked up York's name in the roster and checked his address and phone number. Chase was writing all that down when Porter finally walked in.

"Nothing with Hatcher. I'm beginning to think we could watch this guy forever and get zippo." He sat down with a sigh and loosened his tie. "Anything new on your end? I tried calling earlier, but they said you were out."

Chase brought Porter up to date about the notes and Jim York. "I've got his address here. I think we should pay Mister York a call and check out his story."

Porter looked at what Chase had written. Porter started to smile and the energy level in the squad room went up a few notches. "You're not going to believe this. Look."

He reached over to the pile that pertained to Hatcher. Sorting through, he found the computer printout of the license numbers. He trailed his finger down until he reached Rogers, Arnold D. 3267 Church Street. Then with his other hand, he pointed. *Jim York, 3269 Church Street.*

"I was going over these this morning. I started to get a feeling Hatcher wasn't the one. This can't just be coincidence." Porter looked at Chase expectantly.

Chase scratched his head. "What about Arnold Rogers? It says here he drives a '74 Buick. It *could* be just coincidence he lives next door to York." Even as Chase said it, he didn't believe it. But after the enthusiasm for Hatcher, he was trying to temper things as much as possible.

Before Porter could answer, Chase knew what his partner was going to say. It was so absurd, but he knew it was true. This was Colorado after all. It cost a lot of money to register cars here. Jim York, to save on registration, was driving around with his neighbor's plates. Or maybe not just to save a few bucks. Maybe he was driving around with his neighbor's plates to throw the cops off. Rogers may have a '74 Buick, but Chase was willing to bet that Jim York drove a white Econoline van.

Before Chase could say another word, Porter said something about vehicle registration and to hold on as he grabbed the phone.

Chase waited by going through the notes of his call with York. There was no rush. York had said he worked for the post office and since he went to night classes, it was reasonable to presume he was at work now.

Chase tried to remember how York had sounded when they spoke. Very polite. Not too informative. But he had returned the call promptly. He had been the only one. He had also known Rachel was dead before Chase had said anything, although it had been on the news by then. Chase tried to think if he should have figured something out sooner, if there was something he had missed.

Hell, Chase cut himself some slack. How could he have figured anything out? There had been nothing there until he'd noticed the notes and then he'd been so distracted by all the other stuff: the semen, the swingers club, Linda Watkins, Wyoming, the Barnes, Fortin, and all the other bullshit that had floated around this case and his life. Chase still didn't have a clue why Jim York might have wanted to do in Rachel Stevens, but at least they had a trail that looked better than hanging around the CU campus.

Chase found the address book that her husband had given him. Chase had sorted out the numbers with no names. He could account for those. He flipped to the Y's, no Jim York. Then he had an inspiration, *think like Rachel,* and he started to flip through the book looking for York's number. He found it under the P's. She had listed him as Jim's Printing and that explained why it hadn't been checked it out. She had probably called York with questions about the lectures she had missed. Chase wondered what else they had talked about.

Before Chase could berate himself for not cross-referencing all the numbers in Rachel's book with the class rosters, Porter was back. He waved the paper with a flourish. "Jim York, 3267 Church Street, drives a white Econoline van. Let's go check it out."

* * * * * * * * * * * *

Arnold Rogers turned out to be seventy-two years old. He still kept the Buick in his garage waiting for the day those young punks at the licensing department would realize he was still capable of driving and renew his license.

He didn't know if the car had its plates or not. He hadn't been to the garage out back in over a year. But if Jim York had the plates, then that was fine with him. Jim offered to take him places, not like his good for nothing children who didn't give a damn and were just waiting for him to drop dead so they could sweep through like vultures. He said he'd even signed the car over to York so his kids wouldn't get it.

Chase and Porter listened to him ramble on about ungrateful kids until it was polite to leave. They assured Rogers that he was in no trouble and that went for York as well. Chase was worried that he might call York at work, but Rogers didn't seem too concerned. Plus,

York shouldn't get too jumpy from someone checking on the registration. Unless there was something else, he needed to be worried about. They went out back and looked in the garage. The car not only didn't have plates, but it was covered in dust and all four tires were flat. It wasn't going anywhere for a while.

No one had been home next door when they entered Roger's house and it was still empty as they trudged back to the unmarked car and moved it a few houses away. Now it was time to just sit and wait. Porter pulled a couple of candy bars out of his pocket. They were mushy, but not bad. Chase didn't say anything and neither did Porter. When the van finally pulled up, Chase checked the plate. It was Rogers. York hadn't switched back to his own, which Chase thought was a little odd. Of course, York had probably figured no one had taken down the number.

Chase looked at Porter and he still didn't say anything. It was time to just do it.

CHAPTER TWENTY-TWO

Jim York was not what Chase had expected when he opened the door. Chase was prepared for some dark, sinister type. Some guy with big hands. Instead, Chase was half-right. York was big, just over six feet and he filled out his postman's uniform with solid bulk. But meeting him, Chase felt like he was looking into the face of a poet. One of those pale faces with light liquid eyes and lips that belonged on a woman. His round gold-rimmed glasses were perched on a nose that was thin to the point of sharp. Add to that, the unruly mass of straw colored hair that was thinning on top and the sensitive soul appearance was complete.

"Are you Jim York?" Porter asked.

He nodded, eyes flickering between the two.

"I'm Detective Porter from Boulder Police and this is Detective Chase. He spoke to you on the phone last week and we have a couple more questions. Since my partner and I were in the neighborhood we thought it would be a good time."

York's voice was deeper than one usually allotted to such a soft looking face. But Chase did remember it from the phone conversation. "How did you know where I lived?"

Good question, Chase thought. He had discussed with Porter how they wanted to do this while they were waiting in the car. They'd settled on not making him suspicious from the start. So much for that idea, Chase thought.

Porter stepped up. "Mister York you know you don't have to answer any of our questions and just to be sure that you understand that, I'm going to read you your rights."

When Porter was finished, York was really beginning to vibrate. With great effort, he steepled his fingers and placed them under his nose as if contemplating what to do next. "I was just making some coffee. Would you care to join me?"

Chase exchanged a puzzled look with his partner. But Chase followed him out of the foyer though the living room toward the kitchen all the same, with Porter flanking. The living room was neat and tidy, everything in its place. Chase noticed what appeared to be a makeshift altar at the end of the room. It looked like a couple of tall stereo speakers pushed together with a white sheet draped over the top. Chase could just see the rim of the speaker fronts on the bottom before the shag carpet started. There were candles and a large Bible on the altar.

A vivid portrait of the Crucifixion hung on the wall above. Someone had carefully lettered the words: "HE DIED FOR OUR SINS" above the edge of the frame. There were also statues. Chase recognized the Virgin Mary, some of the others he wasn't too sure about, but he assumed they were saints. They were all gathered around the Bible. As Chase got closer, he noticed that someone had blacked out the eyes on all the statues.

Porter nodded his head in the direction of the shrine in case Chase had suffered total sensory failure and missed it. Porter mouthed the word "nut" behind York's back.

Chase noted some photos on the top of the altar and halted as he saw that they were of Rachel Stevens. There was one of her getting out of her car in the CU lot. Another one was of her walking across campus. Another of her sitting in the cafeteria. It was obvious she hadn't known she was being photographed. Chase nodded back at Porter, keeping one eye on York who was in the kitchen. Porter looked at the photos and his face tightened.

Chase checked out the Bible. The print was large and he could see it was opened to Deuteronomy. All that curse upon thee stuff. *That's not good*, Chase thought. He wondered if they should bust York now before he went off with a butcher knife. He decided to follow Porter's lead, but loosened his gun in its holster any way. He went into the kitchen.

York poured the coffee in silence, but Chase noticed a tremble in his hands as he set the mugs on the table. It seemed odd to Chase to be sitting in this comfortable kitchen with the late afternoon sun streaming through the window knowing that this gentle looking man had probably killed Rachel Stevens.

Chase was putting the coffee to his lips with his off-gun hand when York spoke. His words were startling enough for Chase to spill some of the scalding liquid.

"I didn't kill her, you know."

Porter took it in stride and reminded York that he didn't have to talk. York didn't seem to pay much attention to what Porter was saying. He was busily cleaning up the spilled coffee, wiping it carefully with a sponge so as not to leave any on the floor.

"This stuff is so hard to get up once it dries on the linoleum." He said it apologetically, as if trying not to bother anyone with this little quirk.

Porter met Chase's eyes over York's bent head and mouthed the word "loon."

"No shit," Chase mouthed back. He took his gun out and held it ready under the table.

Finished with the clean up, York sat down across the table and took a few sips of coffee. Chase knew Porter was thinking the same thing though: York could clam up at any moment. They had to be very careful about this. If York wanted to talk about how he didn't kill someone as a normal occurrence, they would follow suit.

Porter started. "Detective Chase and I have learned a lot about Rachel Stevens in the last week."

Chase picked up the cue. "She was certainly an intelligent woman. Her grades were outstanding."

Porter nodded, agreeing with what Chase had just said and added that it was pretty remarkable that she could make such good grades when she cut class so much.

York perked up at that statement and Chase could tell he wanted to say something. After a few seconds, he decided to help him. "Rachel would have never gotten an A in Professor Gavin's class without your help, would she, Jim?"

York leaned back in his chair, lifted his glasses from his face and set them carefully on the table. He used both hands to rub his eyes. When he spoke, his voice was tinged with fear. "I know she…" he searched for words, "wasn't what she appeared. I know I shouldn't have taken those photos. But she was so nice to me. I was afraid you would come. I've almost been waiting for this. But I didn't kill her. I swear."

Porter nodded as if agreeing. "Why don't we start from the time you first met Rachel? I think it would be a good idea if we taped this. That way there won't be any questions about what was said. And we can make sure everyone really understands your side of things. That's very important since you say you want to establish your innocence. The

206

more we know, the easier we can clear you off the list of suspects. Is that OK with you, Jim?"

York was agreeable to the taping, so Porter pulled out his pocket recorder. He held it close to his mouth and spoke the date, time, his, Chase's name and the purpose of the tape. Porter led off by repeating the Miranda to York and then getting his approval of the taping for the record. He double-checked to make sure York didn't want a lawyer and York said no thank you.

York's lips seemed to tremble for a moment and Chase thought he was going to cry. York struggled and pulled himself together.

"When did you initially meet Rachel?" Porter asked.

York swallowed hard, and then spoke. "I first met Rachel Stevens last summer. We were in a class together. I noticed her the first night because she was late. There were no seats left so she had to sit near the door. There were some folding chairs against the wall. She just set her stuff on the floor, opened one up and sat down. No hesitation. She had an air about her. Something." York shook his head, as if he still hadn't figured it out, and then continued.

"Later, on the break, she just walked right up to me and asked what she had missed. You know, if the professor had said anything important. I showed her my notebook and she asked me if she could borrow it. Right then she went to the library and Xeroxed it. Later she started asking for my notes for the nights she was absent.

"She missed class every so often. At first, I didn't think about it, but then I saw her in the parking lot one night after class when she'd asked me to take notes for her. That's when I began to suspect that she was up to something. She was there at school, but she wasn't going to class. I wondered where she was and what she was doing?"

"When did you take the pictures of her?" Porter asked.

York looked down. "Different times."

"Before or after you saw her that time in the parking lot?"

There was a long silence. "Both."

"You've got more than the ones on that table?"

York nodded.

"How many more?" Porter asked.

With a sigh, York got up and walked over to one of cabinets under the counter. He pulled out a photo album and put it on the table. With his free hand, Chase opened it and flipped through. There had to be at least a hundred pictures of Rachel Stevens. Chase paused on one page. "You followed her to her house?"

"I didn't follow her there," York said, with a slight tinge of indignation. "I work in the post office. I looked up her address. I went there when they weren't around—they'd put a stop-hold on their mail for a week over Christmas."

"Why did you go to her house?" Porter asked.

"I just wanted to see where she lived."

Porter had his eyes on York. "Did you know where she was going when she cut class?"

York glanced up, then back down. "I waited again at the parking lot a few weeks ago. She showed up five minutes after class started and waited in the lot, and then got into a cab when it came. I followed her. I saw the house she went in to. The next day at work, I did some checking on the address. I found out what went on in that place."

"So she was using you while she went there," Porter said.

York's head twitched in a nod. "Yes. I prayed for her. God was worried for her too."

"God talks to you?" Chase asked it before he could think, and Porter shot him a look.

"The Lord answers prayers," York said.

Porter leaned forward. "Did God tell you to kill Rachel Stevens?"

"I swear, I never touched her," York said. "I didn't kill her."

"What did you do after class last Wednesday?" Porter asked.

"I came home."

"Were you in the parking lot waiting for her?" Porter pressed.

A nerve ticked on York's face. "I..." he fell silent.

"You were waiting for her." Porter made it a statement. "Why?"

"I wasn't waiting for her," York said. "I came home. I never saw her that night. I swear."

Porter stood up and pulled out his handcuffs. "Come on, we have to go now."

Chase also stood his gun at the ready. York acted surprised and for the first time fear came into his eyes. "But why? Why? I didn't do anything!"

"We'll let others decide that," Porter said, snapping the cuffs on him.

For a brief moment as the left the house, Chase dwelt on Rachel, and what he had learned about her. She had paid a heavy price to live her life by her own rules.

CHAPTER TWENTY-THREE

They say time heals, but Chase wasn't sure he bought off on that as he crawled out of bed the next morning and headed into the yard to work out. Donnelly was happy about the Stevens case when they brought York in. Porter was like the dog that got the bone, and then buried it. Sylvie still wasn't talking to Chase. York already had a court-appointed lawyer who was claiming his client, while innocent, was a nut job. Not those exact words, of course, with God speaking to him and he already had a shrink coming in this morning to examine York to see if he was capable of standing trial.

And Chase thought everyone was wrong, himself included.

Nevertheless, with York's arrest, the Book of Rachel was closed and the DA had a copy of everything. There'd been a meeting last night at the courthouse with the DA's reps, the chief, Donnelly and even Doctor Stevens had shown up for a little while. There had been lots of people patting each other on the back.

Chase and Porter had discovered little more about what had really happened. They had the partial license, the photos and the stalking.

But no confession or murder weapon.

Chase's private little Book of Patriots was still locked in his lower drawer. Chase had no positive ID on the ex-SEAL who had accosted him. The Patriots were still hidden in the Medicine Bow Mountains of Wyoming. The authorities still thought they had all the roads in and out blocked off. That standoff continued, fading further and further back in the pages of the newspaper as the days went by.

The attack in the Barnes' house was still an open case, but getting less priority as the couple's drug history came to light. As Buck had predicted, the phone call to the local hotel had gone nowhere.

Chase had yet to hear from Fortin again, about what had happened in Wyoming. The rest of the team was still in Wyoming, as the stand-by force in case the Patriots decided to break out, and Chase hadn't been called in to work with the CT team again. He had a feeling the wheels of federal bureaucracy were slowly turning and eventually he would be ground under.

Chase's shooting of Tim Barnes was to go before a review board. Catching York had made Chase look good for the moment, and he had a feeling the chief was burying the paperwork until his name was out of the paper as one of the two detectives who caught a suspected murderer. That happened so rarely in Boulder that he and Porter were sort of heroes for the moment.

Chase hit his watch and began pound on the heavy bag with his feet and hands. It felt good, a simple routine that pushed away all the confusion in his life for the moment. He was near the end when he saw someone out of the corner of his eye. Chase stopped as Louise came down the stairs, two mugs in her hand.

"You'll catch your death out here, dressed like that," Louise said, offering one of the mugs.

Chase accepted it and took a sip, all the while eyeing Louise, expecting her to say something about Astral. It was tea, warm and soothing.

"Horace," Louise began, but then stopped.

Chase waited, steam rising off both his body and the mug in his hands.

"Were you named after the Roman poet?"

Chase was surprised. "Yes."

Louise nodded as if that confirmed something, but abruptly changed the topic. "I saw in the paper that you caught the killer of that woman yesterday."

"Alleged killer," Chase said.

"You don't think he did it?"

"I don't know," Chase said.

Louise frowned. "Horace. Uncertainty doesn't suit you." She looked over at his garden. "You buried Astral there, didn't you?"

"Yes. On the southern edge."

"You didn't want me to see her."

Chase simply nodded.

"Does this murder have anything to do with what happened to her?"

"I don't," Chase began, but then nodded. "I think there's a chance it does." *Although how,* Chase had no idea.

"And this man you arrested. Did he kill Astral?"

Chase thought of York and knew he had not done the standoff in the alley the other night. "No."

"So." Louise said it in a way that got through to Chase.

"I don't think he killed the woman either," Chase said.

"Do you have an idea who did?" Louise asked.

"Not yet."

Louise patted him on the arm. "It's chilly. You need go inside. But trust your instincts, Horace. I believe you have good ones."

****

His instincts led him to Jefferson County Airport. Chase knocked on the old wooden door and walked into Masters' office. His friend was seated behind his desk, staring out the window at the Rockies.

"Bad weather coming," Masters said, nodding his head toward the mountains. "Thunderstorms."

"I saw Fortin again," Chase said. "Or more appropriately, he saw me."

Masters turned from the mountains to look at Chase. "Do tell."

Chase succinctly told Masters of the confrontation in the black van.

"Strange times indeed," was Masters comment when he was done. "So what exactly triggered him to say this to you?"

"The only thing I can think of is the computer search I did in the office regarding the Patriots."

"Carnivore," Masters said.

Chase sat down. "What?"

"It's a program the FBI uses on the Internet. I'm sure the other alphabet soups have it too. It's a sniffer program. Monitors all Internet traffic from targeted computers. It's like a fucking wiretap on your computer. Originally called Omnivore, then Carnivore, and now technically called by the much nicer DCS1000. It can be programmed to search for any number of key words or phrases."

"Fuck," Chase said.

Masters nodded toward the dusty computer in the corner of his office. "I use that for ordering parts and that's it. Any electronic signal, and I mean any, can be picked up by the government."

"We *are* the government," Chase pointed out.

"Not *that* part of the government," Masters said. "That's the black world."

"And Fortin is black ops?"

Masters shrugged. "He's never said where the fuck he comes from, but I'm figuring CIA or NSA. Technically the FLI program falls under the FBI, but if Fortin is a Fed, then I'm a fucking Girl Scout."

"Fuck," Chase muttered.

"You're getting repetitive," Masters said. "Listen. I know some people. In the dark world. Let me ask a few questions, very discreetly."

"You sure you want to stick your neck out?"

"I'm just asking questions."

"I was just running a Google search," Chase pointed out.

"I'll be careful," Masters said, but he paused. "Are you sure you want to stick your head into this hole? Because it might be full of nasty rattlesnakes."

"I can be pretty nasty myself," Chase said.

Masters smiled. "Amen to that."

* * * * * * * * * * *

Chase and Porter took off at six and went to the Wagon Wheel ostensibly to celebrate breaking the case, although Chase didn't feel much like partying. They settled in at the end of the bar and ordered the first round.

Porter held up his mug. "At least we got the killer."

"You really think York is guilty?" Chase asked, and he saw the smile fade from his partner's face.

"Damn, Chase." Porter put his mug down on the table. "You couldn't give me a couple of days of happiness?"

"The defense's shrink told the DA's office today that York has an atypical psychosis, whatever the fuck that is."

"Fucking lawyers," Porter said. "Fucking shrinks. Fuck 'em all."

Chase looked at his partner. "We don't have a murder weapon and we don't have any solid physical evidence linking York to the crime scene."

"We have the photos and the fact he was obsessed," Porter threw back. "We have the license plate. He admitted he went to her house."

"Partial license plate from an anonymous source," Chase pointed out. "I might not be a real cop, but even I think that's kind of flimsy."

Porter took a deep chug of beer. "All right, smart-ass. If York isn't—"

Chase held up a hand as his phone buzzed. He pulled it out. "Yes?"

"Hey, bud, its Masters. I got someone you should talk to. He's DEA, on the edge, kind of in the dark. He's flying through Denver tomorrow. He'll meet you in between switching flights. Name's Cardena. Ask him about Colonel Rivers." Masters gave him the flight number and location for the meeting, and then hung up. Chase had wanted to know about Fortin, not Rivers. He frowned at this twist, remembering his conversation with Thorne.

"You were saying?" Chase asked his partner.

Porter shook his head. "Nothing."

They sat for a long time, lost in their own thoughts. "She's a good woman no matter what she does." After four brews, Chase's words were getting slurry.

Porter shot Chase a questioning look and Chase realized his partner thought he was still talking about Rachel Stevens. "No, no. I mean Sylvie. She really is a good woman."

Porter slammed his mug down on the bar. "Shit, you don't have to tell me that, Chase. I don't know her that well, but if the last couple of days are any indication, she's a lot better than what you have now."

"I don't have anything now."

Porter nodded in drunken affirmation. "That's what I mean: you don't have anything. Don't you think there must be something special about Sylvie if you turn into a world-class bum when she leaves you?"

Chase gathered a little indignation, hard to do when the room was spinning faster than the CD in the jukebox. "Sylvie didn't leave me. We mutually decided to part."

Porter tried to grin and sip at the same time. The trickle of beer that escaped from the corner of his mouth had almost made it through the meandering roll of flesh on his neck before it was wiped away. "Does that mean she's a bum now too?"

Chase hadn't thought about that and for the first time he did. Porter had a point. Sylvie was probably doing pretty well. Her problem had been him. When she realized Chase wasn't going to get his act together, she had solved her problem. Chase was sure she missed him a little; he hoped maybe, but not enough to backtrack. He missed her a lot. First, it was just the sex. Then it was the talking. Now it was just her.

Porter was right, Chase knew. He was a big walking wound and he didn't know how to heal himself. Instead, he was picking at his scab until it became terminal. Shit, he thought. *Life sucks then you die.* That was a bad thought because his mind did a one-eighty and he was back to thinking about Rachel. "She was a person who just wanted more. She didn't deserve what she got."

Porter looked more confused than drunk and Chase realized that he had once again got his partner mixed up over Rachel and Sylvie, so he amplified his comment.

"I wonder how much Rachel's lifestyle is going to affect the way the system handles Jim York? I got the feeling at the meeting with the DA last night that there wasn't a whole lot of sympathy for her there. And the way they treated Doctor Stevens wasn't much better. Sort of the old 'you should have kept a better leash on your wife' thing."

Chase tried to remember what Jeffrey Stevens had said that first time Chase talked to him in his office. Something about giving Rachel enough freedom to get hurt. That was the impression Chase got from the men who knew about this case. Somewhere in the back of their mind, they found fault with a man who couldn't control his wife any better. The fact that Doctor Stevens hadn't known what she was up to didn't seem to affect the lowly opinion many held for Rachel's cuckolded husband.

Of course, most didn't know about Lisa Plunkett. Chase wondered how much that had factored with Rachel making the decision to go back to school and to accept Linda Watkins' offer to go to the swingers club. That had been stupid on Rachel's part. Something that Chase didn't completely understand given all the other things she was doing in her life, especially how well and how hard she was working at school. *Why did she jeopardize all that to go have sex with strangers?* Chase wondered. It didn't make much sense. He guessed Sylvie's sex addiction theory might account for that. However, he shied away from contemplating the subject too heavily. Chase also had no doubt the defense would dig and find out about Lisa Plunkett and offer that as motive for Dr. Stevens to have arranged his wife's murder in some manner. Anything to muddy the water and grasp for reasonable doubt. It was going to be a mess in Chase's limited legal experience.

The other thing that still really bugged Chase was that they still hadn't been able to figure out the money in Rachel's bank account. He guessed it was her bankroll to get her out the door after she graduated, but they didn't know how she'd gotten the money. Jeffrey Stevens had been surprised when they'd shown him the account and professed ignorance. It was a loose end and Chase didn't like it.

The next logical step in Chase's drunken thinking was how would he have reacted if Rachel had been his wife and he had discovered her secret life. He'd already put himself in Rachel's position and sort of understood why she'd done what she did. For the first time Chase put himself in Jeffrey Stevens' position and tried to crawl around a little bit.

Chase tapped Porter on the shoulder. "What if Jeffrey Stevens had known about Rachel's swinging before she died? Maybe even known about her bank account and that she was planning on leaving him?"

Porter wasn't too surprised by Chase's line of thinking. "Then I guess Jim York did him a favor."

"Maybe he loved her anyway?" That's what Linda Watkins had said. But could Chase trust anything Linda said?

"Would you have loved her Chase? Knowing what she did? Besides, he was porking Lisa at the office. It was all a big pile of shit with everyone only giving a damn about what they wanted and themselves." Chase had rarely seen Porter so worked up. "She wanted more; he wanted more. Everyone wants more. Fuck 'em all," he slurred.

"I don't think I want more," Chase said, unsure of why that thought occurred to him.

Porter calmed down a bit. "Hell, Chase, then why couldn't you be happy with anything you had? What about Sylvie? Wasn't she good enough for you to work a bit on keeping her? Most guys would be more than happy to have Sylvie in their life." He held up a hand. "And I'm not talking about sex, either there bud."

Chase had done a lot of thinking the past couple of days about what had happened between him and Sylvie. "Sure I made mistakes, but she should have stuck with me. She had her share of mistakes in the relationship too. She should have opened up to me more. I wanted to hang in there."

"Did you open up to her?"

"What?"

216

"Chase, you haven't even really talked to me about what happened in Wyoming—you told me sort of what happened, but not how you felt about what happened-- and I'm your partner and that was work and you haven't said word one about how you felt about it. Did you tell Sylvie what happened in Wyoming?"

"I was ordered to--"

"Which was more important? Your job or her? You got pissed because she didn't tell you she was married, but you didn't tell her about Wyoming. What's the status of your divorce, by the way? You didn't tell her about what happened in the Barnes' house, did you? I know for damn sure there's shit you aren't telling me. I see you making those phone calls and locking those files in your desk. Who the fuck just called you now on the fucking high-speed phone of yours? I'm sitting right fucking here and you don't say anything." When Porter was on a roll, he couldn't be stopped.

"What the fuck happened in Afghanistan? What's going on with your mother? That fucking letter you keep reading all the time? The one you keep in your breast pocket? You're dying on the inside, Chase, because you've got all this black crud stuffed in there and you can't handle it yourself. It's fucking poison."

That was the longest speech Chase had ever heard Porter make. It was doubly remarkable considering their current state of inebriation.

Porter leaned his head close and Chase felt his beer-drenched breath wash over him. "You need to get your act together, Chase. You're losing it. You're boozing it up too much. You're all alone." He slid a thick arm over Chase's shoulders. "Get it together partner."

Chase realized that when someone he was drinking with was telling him that he was drinking too much and that he needed to get my act together, then he was bellying out on the bottom.

CHAPTER TWENTY-FOUR

Once more Chase had beaten the alarm, even though little gremlins were running around his skull drilling for intelligent life. He cracked an eye and tried to focus on the ceiling. The cracks were familiar so he knew he was in his basement hovel but he could barely remember getting here. He tried to recall his last conscious thought of the previous evening. It was something vaguely to do with challenging Porter to either a game of pool or a fight.

Chase sat up slowly, holding onto the mattress while his head did loops. Finally, he managed to gain his feet. Chase peered at his watch, trying to make sense of the numbers. Damn. He had to meet the DEA agent and he only had an hour to get his act together and make it to the airport. He skipped the workout routine and went straight for the shower, popping a couple of Advil on the way.

Louise was outside with a puppy scampering about her feet. "Hi, Horace!"

Chase paused in his rush. The puppy ran over and rubbed its nose on his pants leg. "Who is this?" It was a German Shepherd-mixed-with-something-else-big puppy with short hair, big eyes and a broad chest.

"That's Star," Louise said. She came up; her wrinkled face just inches away. "Horace."

He paused, fumbling for his Jeep keys. "Yes?"

"You're in a bad place again," she said. "You're closed off. I've checked your stars. You have to be open."

"Open," Chase repeated. "Right." He climbed in.

Louise smiled at him as he backed out. "Open, Horace!"

"Open. Got it."

The smile disappeared and he stopped the Jeep, surprised at the seriousness of the look on her face. She leaned down, close to the window. Chase felt a pang, remembering his own mother doing that, a long time ago, when he was driving away from her trailer after graduating West Point, heading for the Infantry Officers Basic Course at Fort Benning. It was the last time he ever saw her. Eighteen years ago. She'd been beautiful, but worn down from life.

"Be careful, Horace Chase."

Chase's reply to her was just as serious, all bantering gone. "I will, Louise. I promise."

She suddenly smiled. "Star's got brothers and sisters. Their mother is still in the pound. She's German Shepherd and Chow mix and we're not sure about the father but very good breeding. Very calm. You need calm. I have a friend who works there. You can get one of the puppies. I asked her to keep one hidden for you."

"I'll think about it."

"Don't think too long. She won't be able to hide the puppy forever."

Chase headed for the airport. They called it Denver International, but it was about twenty miles northeast of the city itself, in the middle of the Plains. As he drove along the perfectly straight road that was 104th Street, he could see the tower twenty miles away on the horizon. As he got closer, the white peaked ceiling of the terminal began to appear. The roofs were supposed to represent the white-capped Rockies, but to Chase they always looked more like big circus tents.

Chase parked and made his way into the terminal. The agent had a layover between flights. He had arranged to meet Chase at the sports bar in Concourse B. Chase flashed his badge and cut through security. He was a little early when he slid into a booth with a good view of the entrance.

The DEA guy showed up exactly on time. He walked like a man who had a lot of enemies, his eyes shifting constantly. Chase stood as the agent entered the bar and he looked Chase over for a few seconds before coming to the booth.

"Horace Chase." He held out his hand.

"Let me see you badge," the agent demanded, instead of offering his own hand.

Chase flipped his wallet open for him. He checked the badge number, then Chase's Federal ID card. Chase knew he must have run the number and then he finally seemed satisfied. He nodded. "Rico Cardena," he introduced himself.

He was dark-skinned, short and wiry. His hair was prematurely gray and his eyes had that tired, haunted look Chase had seen in covert operators who'd stayed on when they should have retired five years ago. A nerve on the left side of his face twitched as he ordered a cup of coffee from the waitress.

"I've got to catch a flight in eighty-four minutes," he said.

"I know." That was some pretty exact timing. Reminded Chase of Fortin.

"What do you want? Your friend wasn't very specific on the phone."

"Do you know Agent Fortin in the F.L.I. program here?"

"No."

"Did you know Colonel Arty Rivers in Afghanistan?"

Cardena's eyelids drooped down, giving his face a hooded look. "Colonel Rivers was the coordinator for Central Command for military forces operating along the Northern Border from May 2003 through June 2005."

"On counter-drug operations," Chase amplified.

"On all military operations," Cardena said. "But the majority of what they did was counter-drug stuff. Mostly training local forces to fight the drug war."

"Rivers was relieved of command," Chase noted.

Cardena nodded. "Yeah, he was."

"Why?"

"Because he tried doing his job."

Chase waited out Cardena, wanting more. Chase stirred some sugar into his coffee.

The DEA man sighed. "Why do you want to know about Rivers?"

"Because I think he's hooked up with the Patriots now."

"They're in Wyoming," Cardena noted.

"They killed a cop here in Colorado. I think they might have also killed a family in Boulder. Husband, wife and six-month-old baby. The husband and wife were dealers."

"Killing babies." Cardena looked past Chase. He reached into his coat and pulled out a pack of cigarettes. He offered one to Chase who was surprised, knowing the entire airport was non-smoking. Chase shook his head. Cardena shrugged and fired one up. "Drugs are dirty. And anyone who operates around them ends up getting dirty eventually. It can go either way. You can get dirty trying to do the right thing or trying to do the wrong thing."

His eyes came back to Chase, still half-lidded as he smoked. "The money that's involved is out of the realm of reality for most people. I've seen rooms full of money. A new wrinkle is to buy a top of the line plane, maybe a Lear or a Gulfstream, costing millions, and fly it in to the States, the pilot parachutes out with the drugs in bundles and lets the plane crash-- that's how much money is involved. There are customs guys I've arrested who've been bribed with a million dollars cash to look the other way to let one shipment through."

"Rivers was dirty?" Chase was confused. Cardena had said Rivers had been relieved for trying to do his job.

"It's complicated," Cardena said. "Let me tell you what happened. As part of the training, Rivers would send nationals to the School of the Americas. Some were people his office recommended who should go, but a lot were pushed down the military's throat by the country team. You were in Special Forces. You know what that means."

The country team was the state department, the CIA, the NSA, a whole bunch of spooky people hanging around the Embassy. Chase also knew about the School of the Americas. It was a hot topic with peace activists. Located on Fort Benning it trained foreign nationals in military and police techniques and some said torture and illegal interrogation. The American way of spreading democracy.

A waitress came over. "Sir, you can't smoke here."

Cardena slapped his badge down on the table. "Call a cop."

The waitress looked at the badge, confused. She opened her mouth to say something, but then didn't as she met Cardena's eyes. She went away, over to the manager, they whispered, and Chase knew nothing would happen. It wasn't the badge. It was the look in Cardena's eyes. They would wait it out until he left; and hope he'd never came back.

"It's a question of objectives," Cardena said. "Rivers saw his orders in black and white." He shook his head, flicking ash on the floor. "Things aren't black and white, especially not when drugs are involved. The CIA had different goals. The war on terrorism. It's more about leverage, politics, economics. And politics in Afghanistan-- like everywhere else-- means power and money. And power and money in that part of the world equals drugs. It's the number one cash crop. Opium. It's like oil is to the Arabs. Eighty percent of the world's opium supply comes from Afghanistan. And production has been rising steadily since we went in there. One thing the Taliban did do was crush the opium warlords in the name of Islam. Now that we're in charge, in the name of democracy, they're flourishing again."

"Is that by chance or plan?" Chase asked.

"Good question. We estimate the street value of the last harvest was 176 billion dollars, US. When you consider that Ford, GM and Chrysler combine for 75 billion, you get an idea of what's involved."

Cardena's voice was low and steady. Like he was on the stand testifying about a case that he'd investigated long ago and no longer had any feelings about. Chase really felt like asking him for a smoke. More, he wanted to order a beer. And he noticed that Cardena has sidestepped his question.

"I worked with Rivers for a while in the 'Stan. There was a man named Vladislav. From Russia. I don't know if that's his first name or last name. It's the only name he goes by. Former Soviet Spetsnatz."

Chase knew that was the Soviet form of Special Forces, but he was confused about the abrupt switch in topics.

Cardena continued. "Vladislav decided he'd rather be rich than in a military that was deteriorating. Went into the Russian mafia as an enforcer. Worked his way up. He became notorious for his torture techniques." Cardena gave a wan smile. "Vladislav liked violent movies. Especially American movies, because we make the best. Scarface was one of his favorites. He always carried an M-203, just like Pacino at the end. But his all time favorite was Marathon Man. Watched it over and over. Thought the dental drill scene was the greatest thing he ever saw. Bought his own hand drills and other dental gear and brought it with him to Afghanistan. Carried it around in a little black bag, just like a doctor."

Chase felt his skin go cold. He remembered Hanson's words about the Barnes' baby.

Cardena continued. "I saw him work with the drill a couple of years ago. I don't think he cared about the information he extracted--" Cardena grimaced at his poor choice of words.

Chase blinked. "You saw? But—"

"Oh, Vladislav was an opportunist. When we invaded Afghanistan, he saw an excellent opportunity. The Taliban were a pain in the ass as far as the opium market. Islamic law and all that. So Vladislav worked it perfectly. He offered his services to the Agency, the CIA," he clarified, "which of course, had nothing in place in the

'Stan, right after nine-eleven. They paid him, and paid him well. Even sent him to the School of the Americas for a little special training. More importantly to Vladislav, they promised to turn a blind eye to his drug operations. A pact with the devil."

Cardena put out the cigarette and took another sip of coffee, before continuing. "He was doing the job I saw under contract to the CIA. He liked doing it. The CIA rep took me with him when he got the information he wanted. Left the suspect with Vladislav. Guess he tortured him to death after we left."

Cardena beckoned at the waitress for a refill. She immediately came over and did it silently, then quickly retreated. Cardena looked tired, but Chase had the feeling he always looked that way. Chase needed more. He needed to know how Vladislav ended up in Boulder. He needed to pull all this together-- the Barnes, the CIA, the Patriots, Colonel Rivers. "How was Vladislav connected to Rivers?"

Cardena lit another cigarette. "There was an aid program designed to help farmers switch from drug crops to other cash crops. Kind of like asking the Arabs to invest in solar power. But Rivers saluted and did as ordered in support of that program. He sent his Special Forces MEDCAP teams to help the villagers out."

Chase forgot about his coffee as the second chill of the morning passed over him.

"Just so happened one of the SF medical teams stumbled across a big opium shipment in transit in a village from Afghanistan to Kazakhstan, where it would get cross-loaded onto a plane and end up, of course, in various forms, in the States. The mules the opium was loaded on were in the village, the guards taking a break.

"They began shooting as soon as the Americans walked in-- hard to say which side was more surprised, but there was no doubt who was better trained. The Special Forces team wiped out the guards. After opening packages, they called us-- the DEA-- in. We found four thousand kilos of opium there. Depending on market value you're talking somewhere around forty-five million dollars street value worth."

Chase shook his head. That much, loaded on donkey's backs. He'd seen a lot of weird shit in the 'Stan.

Cardena drained his coffee and checked his watch. "The results? Rivers got relieved and all MEDCAP missions canceled. The opium was appropriated by the Afghanistan military under orders of the CIA rep. Most of it was returned to Vladislav, some of it siphoned off by the hands that touched it between. A lot of people got very rich and most of the opium ended up here in the States anyway.

"And the village where the opium was seized…" Cardena paused. "Vladislav led a group of his mercenaries there. They killed every man, woman, child. Over two hundred people. They didn't just kill them. They raped every woman, every girl. They buried some people alive. They hacked many to death. Burned some alive.

"Rivers and I flew in to the village the next morning, just before he was sent out of country. We saw the results. And no one gave a shit. No one reported it. The CIA put a lock-down on everything to do with it." Cardena stood. "That is all I can tell you of Colonel Rivers. I have a plane to catch."

Chase stood. "What happened to Vladislav?"

The nerve on the side of Cardena's face jumped once more. His eyes were moving again, scanning the crowd. "He disappeared from Afghanistan. Rivers made a big stink and even the CIA felt it was best to do a little damage control. Some reporters were sniffing around."

Cardena flicked his cigarette into the coffee and headed out of the lounge. Chase was beside him. "Where is he now?"

Cardena didn't break stride. "Here."

No shit, Chase thought. "Dealing?"

"It's all he knows."

"How did he get here?"

Cardena snorted. "How do you think? The CIA got him out and relocated him. He did a lot of nasty work for them and they rewarded him. Plus, they still use him when they need a dirty job done."

"Is Fortin CIA?"

"Told you I don't know the man, but if he's stopping you from going after Rivers or Vladislav, then, yeah, he'd have to be."

That explained Fortin.

"Does Colonel Rivers know that?"

Cardena smiled for real for the first time. "Yes. I told him three months ago."

That explained Rivers.

Cardena pulled a ticket out of his pocket, walked to an entryway and disappeared.

* * * * * * * * * * *

By the time Chase got to municipal court, he was almost ready for some food. So naturally, for the first time, things were on schedule. Chase was the leadoff witness for the prosecution this morning, so he went on the stand and did his act for an hour while his stomach growled and his head pounded.

Luckily, the defense didn't have much to ask Chase. They had the defendant's prints all over the stolen car, which happened to be found in the defendant's garage. The defense attorney's tactic seemed to be the less said the better. The Assistant DA seemed confident enough with that evidence to pursue the case, which probably meant a plea bargain, was coming soon.

Done, Chase went in search of nourishment. The cafeteria there was lousy, but it was close. He grabbed a bear claw and a cup of coffee. As he was paying, he spotted a familiar face sitting at a table in the corner and made his way over.

"What brings you here, doctor?"

Gavin didn't seem particularly thrilled to see him. "Detective Chase. How have you been?"

"Not too bad," Chase lied. He'd been more depressed than normal, which meant almost suicidal, during the drive back from DIA and while in the courtroom. Cardena's story about what had happened in Afghanistan weighed heavily on his mind. He wasn't sure exactly yet what it meant about Colonel Rivers, but it meant a lot to Chase about the state of mankind.

Chase was not only depressed, but also on edge, because Cardena's information also meant that both Vladislav and Colonel Rivers were probably close by. But battling through the depression and edge, he was also pissed.

He figured one of the two had sent Muscles and Baldie and also one of the two was responsible for cutting Astral's head off and had been waiting to bump him off. To Chase the latter seemed more like Vladislav's work, but how had he known about Chase? The only thing he could think of was his actions at the Barnes' house. Which further confused Chase because it seemed like both Vladislav and Rivers had been at that house before he got there. Vladislav was working on the baby, Rivers shooting everyone. Unless, of course, Vladislav used an AK. He was Russian, after all. But Cardena had said he preferred using an M-203, which was 5.56mm. Or were the two working together? Had

Rivers blown a gasket and decided to sell out? That didn't seem likely but who knew what 35 years in uniform in the shit-holes of the world had done to Rivers.

And then there was Jim York. Despite Porter and the DA's confidence, Chase just didn't see the postman slicing Rachel Stevens' throat with a garrote—or any other weapon for that matter.

To get his mind off his dark and confusing thoughts, Chase pointed at the file Gavin had on the table. "Are you testifying as an expert witness?"

Gavin's bitter laugh caught Chase off guard. "I suppose you could say that. My divorce is final today and we go before the judge to get him to sign it."

That clicked. "Sorry to hear that."

Gavin shrugged. "We don't have any kids so it isn't too bad. We agreed on pretty much everything."

"Yeah, but it's still bad." Chase changed the subject. "We arrested Jim York for Rachel Stevens' murder."

Gavin didn't seem too interested. "I saw it in the paper."

"He says he didn't do it. His appointed lawyer is already talking about a diminished capacity defense. Saying he's a nut job, even while claiming that he's innocent. Covering all the bases."

Gavin was withdrawn, in his own little place of pain. Chase didn't have much sympathy for him after having listened to Cardena. Everything was perspective. Chase was sure every person who had lived in that village in Afghanistan would have given anything to be sitting in this cafeteria right now.

"Do you buy that stuff?" Chase asked. Pieces of last night were coming back to him and he remembered saying something to Porter about Jeffrey Stevens.

"What 'stuff', detective?"

"Diminished capacity making it less wrong, at least that's the way it appears to me, to kill someone?"

"Yes, I do." Gavin stood to go. He wasn't exactly a fount of information or friendliness as he walked out.

Chase finished his meager lunch and headed to the office. He drove absent-mindedly, alternating in his head between trying to remember what he had talked to Porter about at the Wagon Wheel last night and what Cardena had told him at the airport.

Chase turned onto 2d Avenue without really thinking about it. This was the third time in the last couple of days he'd done that. He looked up at Sylvie's apartment as he parked. The shades were drawn and he imagined her cuddled up in her big bed, resting. He'd thought long and hard the about how to approach this. He'd settled on simply letting his actions speak and see how she reacted. He took the copy of the signed divorce settlement, flowers, along with the short note of apology and climbed the stairs to her door. He figured she was sleeping. She might even have someone in there with her, having already buried Chase into her past. He placed the three items at the door and retreated to his Jeep.

As Chase turned into the parking lot for headquarters, he began to have a feeling in the deep recesses of his stomach. He'd had it before. Chase spent the rest of the morning and the early afternoon doing paperwork. At 2:45, he slipped out and headed for CU.

****

Gavin wasn't back yet to his office, which was just as well with Chase. A graduate assistant was sitting in the small anteroom, typing away at the computer and she eyed Chase warily as he pulled out his badge and introduced himself.

"I'd like to see Professor Gavin's papers from his Theory of Psychotherapy course this semester."

Chase could tell she didn't want to give him the papers. The student was torn between the authority of the academic world and the legal. "I just need to look at something that the professor has already shown me," he added. "I won't take anything."

That was all the push she needed and she handed over the file for the class. She watched him as he thumbed through and pulled out York's papers.

York's TELL ME ABOUT YOU yielded little of interest. His answers, unlike Rachel's were typed.

NAME: JAMES YORK
MY HOME TOWN IS: BOULDER, CO
THE THING I LIKE MOST ABOUT THE UNIVERSITY OF COLORADO SO FAR IS: THE CLASSES.

227

THE BIGGEST PROBLEM I'M HAVING RIGHT NOW IS: WORKING FULL TIME AND GOING TO SCHOOL.

I CAME TO CU BECAUSE: I WANT TO HAVE A BETTER JOB.

MY FAVORITE HOBBIES ARE: STUDYING. READING.

THE NUMBER ONE THING I HOPE TO GET FROM THIS PROGRAM IS: A BETTER PAYING JOB.

WHAT OTHER QUESTIONS SHOULD I HAVE ASKED YOU: NONE.

WHAT ELSE WOULD YOU LIKE ME TO TELL ABOUT YOURSELF: NOTHING.

The student looked past Chase and he turned. Gavin was standing there, staring at Chase. He couldn't tell if Gavin was happy about his divorce or not. He didn't look thrilled to see Chase. He had a twelve pack of beer in his hand. The simple man's therapy.

"Not exactly the world's most outgoing personality is he?" Gavin commented as he noted the paper in Chase's hand. The graduate student escaped, shutting the door behind her.

"What did you think when you read this?"

Gavin gave the ghost of a smile. "I thought he was sucking up, especially the part about studying as a hobby."

"He had the career thing in common with Rachel," Chase noted.

"May I ask why you're looking at this?" Gavin put the beer in the fridge, pulling one out. He offered another to Chase, who declined.

"You asked me whether I thought facts or personalities were more important," Chase answered. "A lot of people seem to have decided the facts in this case, but I'm a little interested in the personalities now."

Gavin moved past Chase and sat behind his desk. "Any specific reason?"

"Curiosity."

"Perhaps I should take that back from you and require that you get a court order to read them. Considering the fact that the York case is open, at least that's what the news said last night, I don't think you have a legitimate reason to be here."

"I just told you," Chase said easily, "curiosity. This isn't in an official capacity."

Gavin shook his head. "York was a strange man, but I never really thought he was capable of murder. Obviously, I was wrong."

"Goes to show you can't really judge a book by its cover." Chase felt stupid as soon as he said it.

Gavin shrugged. "I suppose. I certainly had a high attrition rate in that class. Makes me wonder sometimes if this entire semester wasn't cursed in some way. What with my divorce, and Rachel Stevens, and now York."

Chase returned to something the professor had just said. "You mentioned a moment ago that York was a strange man. What did you mean by that?"

Gavin started playing with his can of beer. "Maybe strange isn't the right word. He made me uncomfortable so that's probably why I found him strange. I pride myself on understanding the human psyche and it's not often I allow someone like York to affect me. Of course now I understand why, given that he was just accused of murder."

"Maybe you recognized on some level that he was dangerous."

"I suppose."

"Did you guess he was a nutcase?"

Gavin didn't look very pleased with Chase's terminology. "From what I read in the newspaper, the defense's psychologist is claiming York is an atypical psychotic. That means that he was in the throes of a psychotic episode when he killed Rachel Stevens—if he did kill her, which they're denying. The psychologist is setting this up to try to see if York can avoid standing trial."

"That doesn't make sense. It seems too convenient to me."

Gavin slid effortlessly into a lecture mode. "If Jim York killed Rachel it was because she threatened the very sanity we are speaking of. When he was around her, he became anxious and afraid that she was going to destroy him. He became psychotic when he committed the act of murder, not before.

"Once she was dead and no longer a threat, he lost his anxiety. His psychosis dissipated and he returned to reality. You might say York murdered his way to mental health, if he did murder."

It all sounded like a bunch of bullshit to Chase. "That doesn't do Rachel Stevens much good, does it?"

"I'm afraid not. She might have run into the one man who couldn't allow her to live the way she was. Bad luck really."

Something was pestering Chase. Gavin seemed to think it was all so rational. Maybe that's what bothered Chase. People just didn't go around snuffing everyone that made them anxious. Or else there'd be a lot less people in the world. There were still loose ends to the case.

Chase looked at the papers in his hand. There was another page filled out by York. The paper was THE NEED AUCTION BID CARD. York's number one priority bid was for Guaranteed Lifelong Financial Income.

Chase mentioned it to Gavin. "This doesn't sound too crazy to me," he commented. "You'd think God would have fit in there somewhere up near number one if you've seen the guy's place. I had the impression the two were on a first name basis. This sounds like a very practical man."

Gavin ran his hand through his thinning hair. "You have to understand the nature of that survey. Students rank order their needs and then we correlate their priorities with Maslow's hierarchy of needs.

"That need that York ranked number one is on Maslow's second level: Safety. A person at that level wants security and freedom from anxiety and chaos. That fits in very well with his psychosis."

Chase tried to follow that. "So basically he had a need to get rid of Rachel Stevens because she was a threat in his mind. But now he's in jail. So much for the need for security."

Gavin leaned back in his chair and smiled. "The security need is more a desire for structure and order. I'd say you couldn't get much more structured than prison. York's in the perfect place for him."

The professor had a point, Chase allowed. "You mentioned York maybe murdering his way to sanity." Gavin nodded and Chase continued, groping for words. "But it seems he went out of his way to make Rachel a threat. He had to follow her to the club to find out where she was going. Then he had to check the mail to find out what was going on in that place. He also checked on her life to find out she was married."

"But she entered his life and upset its balance by asking him to take notes for her," Gavin countered.

Chase could tell the professor was tired of this conversation and wanted him out, but that feeling in his stomach was still there. It could have been the result of the jarring airport conversation, but Chase didn't want to let go of Rachel Stevens yet. "Yeah. I suppose. It's just hard for me to understand. I guess I like clear cut motives and this one is too confusing."

"That's probably why you had so much trouble with this case," Gavin observed.

"I had so much trouble with this case not only because I couldn't get a motive, but also because York did a good job killing her—if he did. We were damn lucky to get that partial plate. Without it, we might never have caught him." Chase could tell Gavin was clearly done with the conversation, but Chase didn't care. "Do *you* think York killed Rachel Stevens?"

Gavin put the stapler down and leaned back in his chair. Chase was prepared for some long psychological bullshit answer.

"No."

Chase waited, but Gavin didn't say anything else. "Why not?" Chase finally prompted.

Gavin shrugged. "I just don't see him doing it. I think he was infatuated with her, but not to the point of homicide. I mean, maybe, if he approached her and she rudely rebuffed him, it's possible he could have reacted in a rage, but I just don't see it."

Chase hadn't seen much capability for rage in York, but then again he'd seen some unexpected reactions from people in combat. But the crime just didn't look like something that had been done in a rage. The site was too clean, the wound too neat. The lack of physical evidence indicated--

Something struck Chase then. Something he should have seen weeks ago. He realized it was a combination of sitting there in Gavin's office along with his conversation with Porter the previous night. "What if York wasn't crazy when he killed her, if he did?"

Gavin shook his head. "Psychotic is the proper term."

Chase wasn't sure where he was going, but he was excited in a positive way for the first time in quite a while. "Can you fake an atypical psychosis?"

Gavin blinked and was silent for a few moments. "I suppose you could if you really knew what you were doing. But it would be very, very hard. Almost impossible even for someone who is trained in the field."

Synapses were clicking in Chase's brain. "York was in a master's program in psychology wasn't he? Would he have learned enough to be able to pull it off? To convince his lawyer and the shrink he's seen?"

"No." Gavin seemed sure of it. "In fact, the court psychologists are trained to look for that sort of thing." Gavin took the folder out of Chase's hand. "Now if you don't mind, I have some drowning of sorrow to do."

"Let me ask you something else."

"Really--" Gavin began but Chase waved his hand.

"Not about York or Stevens." Seeing that Gavin was willing to listen, if barely, Chase continued. "Could someone give up all the values they'd maintained for almost sixty years of their life and operate in a cold, calculated manner going against those values?"

Gavin frowned, so Chase amplified his question.

"His lawyer's shrink is saying York acted out of a psychosis-- a temporary one. But could someone have a permanent psychosis? A permanent change from an honorable, ethical, person to someone who would do anything to pursue a goal, no matter what laws were broken, no matter who was killed?"

Gavin rubbed his chin. "I suppose. But whatever caused that change would have to be incredibly dramatic. It's very, very hard for people to change their natures."

Two massacred villages, at the beginning and end of a career, seemed pretty drastic to Chase. He thanked the professor for his time and headed out. He headed back to the office, his mind racing.

****

Chase was on a roll and Porter just listened as he lay out his York-possibly-not-crazy theory.

"He's had graduate level courses in psychological disorders and evaluation. Hell, he's been given all of the tests in the classroom that the damn shrink gave him in jail. And he got A's in all those classes."

Porter looked puzzled. "But if he wasn't suffering from psychosis or acting out of rage why did he kill Rachel?" Porter waved a hand dismissing the whole affair. "Besides it doesn't matter does it? York's been arrested and it's in the DA's hands now."

"If York killed her," Chase said, "he did a really clean job of it for someone in a rage or being a nut job."

"If?"

"I don't think York did it."

"Then who did?"

"I don't know."

"Then stick with the known." Porter sighed. "If he's not crazy he had to have had a real motive. And perhaps it was premeditated for some reason if he did such a good job."

Porter kept bringing it all back to the same issue that had stymied the investigation from the start. Chase bounced it back to him. Hell, he wasn't supposed to be the only one doing all the thinking. "What's the most common motive for premeditated murder?"

"Money in one form or another." Porter's face lit up. "York found out what she what she was doing three weeks before he killed her. What would you-- given that you're not the noble and honest person I know you to be--" he added with just a touch of irony-- "do with that information if you had it?"

"Blackmail." Chase tried realigning all the pieces of the puzzle to fit that angle.

Porter was nodding. "Yeah. That makes sense. Stevens certainly made enough money."

Chase shook his head. "But the whole point would be to keep the information from her husband."

"I'd say both Rachel and the good doctor had plenty of reasons to keep what she was doing quiet."

"But then Stevens would have known what she was doing before she died. And then why would York kill her?"

Porter was getting excited. "Blackmail isn't the only way to get money. What if York killed her because Stevens paid him to do it?"

Chase shook his head. "That's a big jump from crazed killer to paid killer. We never came up with any evidence that indicated Stevens had anything to do with it."

"True, but we never really considered him because we knew he didn't kill her himself. And besides, we didn't have a good motive for him then. That was before we knew about the swingers' club. We've had this all screwed up, getting the information bit by bit."

Porter was pacing back and forth. "All right. Let's add it up. Rachel's lifestyle, the insurance money and Stevens' good-looking secretary. If Doctor Stevens had known what his wife was doing he could have divorced Rachel, but it would have been ugly and he would have lost a hell of a lot of money. Colorado has no fault divorce. This way, not only doesn't he lose, he makes money on her insurance. Even if he paid York just the insurance money, he'd have kept all his money and saved himself a hell of a lot of embarrassment. Plus there was the money Rachel was squirreling away-- Stevens might have known about that too. She might have been stealing from the household account somehow."

Porter looked at Chase. "York probably would have gotten away with the murder if we hadn't had the luck of the partial license number. The crazy stuff had just been his back-up plan that he'd cooked up from stuff he learned in school."

Chase wasn't totally buying it, but there was a logic to what his partner was saying. "All this is just speculation, though. We had—and have-- nothing tying Jeffrey Stevens to Jim York. If there is a connection, I'm sure the two would have buried it very deeply."

Chase could see the stubborn look on his partner's face, so he decided to play along. "All right. Let's say Stevens knew what his wife was doing and let's say he got angry enough to want her dead. What'd he do? Just go to her class and try to find someone willing to kill her?"

Porter shook his head. "No. Go back to the blackmail angle. We know York followed her three weeks before he killed her. We know he used the post office to find out what was going on in the swingers' club. We know he went by the house and took pictures. Suppose York came to Stevens threatening to expose Rachel. Then suppose Stevens turned it around and made him a better offer than blackmail."

"That's a lot of supposing without any hard evidence."

Porter held his hand up. "Stay with me on this. York goes to Stevens and threatens to expose what Rachel is doing. First off, Stevens is going to be surprised-- to say the least-- to find out that Rachel had been going to the swingers' club. Maybe he even agrees to pay off York to keep him quiet.

"But then he sits and thinks about it. Why would he want to be married to Rachel anymore? He's already got Lisa Plunkett well in hand. Why pay York to keep quiet about what Rachel's doing? Maybe Jeffrey even confronts her and she blows him off. Or even brings up divorce, which is going to cost him a lot. I don't know. But say somewhere along in there, Stevens decides to get rid of his problem. His problem isn't York. It's Rachel. So he makes a counterproposal to York. He offers him a lot of money to kill her. It ends the problem and it ends the blackmail at the same time. And Jeffrey certainly is smart enough to know that you can't ever get away from someone blackmailing you. He'd also be getting York out of his life too."

Chase was trying to keep up. "Ok. But I still don't understand the crazy thing."

"If you were York and I was Stevens, we'd both be sitting here worrying about the death penalty if York is caught. If York gets murder one, he has no reason not to drag Stevens in with him. In fact, he'd probably do it to cop a plea and implicate Stevens to stay out of the chair. So they figure out a way to keep York from the chair, if he's caught. At the same time, keep us from digging any deeper into why York killed Rachel. The DA certainly doesn't look ready to. I can just picture those two sons-of-bitches sitting there trying to figure out how to cover their asses and York, with his background in psychology, coming up with the perfect answer."

Porter suddenly stood.

"Where are you going?"

"I need to check something. I'll be back."

While Porter was gone, doubts continued to swirl around in Chase's head. This whole line of reasoning was based on assumptions. But assuming the assumptions were correct-- making himself a double ass, Chase supposed-- he mentally berated himself for not having worked this possibility out while he was investigating the case. He'd dismissed Jeffrey Stevens as a possible suspect much too easily. He went down to the storage area, signed out the Book of Rachel, and brought it back up to his desk. Maybe there was something in there he'd missed.

When Porter came back in, he tossed a copy of a computer printout on Chase's desk and sat down with his own copy. "Those are all the numbers York called in between the night he followed Rachel to the club and the night she died."

It was a short list. "Obviously, York didn't have many friends."

"He called the Stevens' residence three times in that time period."

"So what?" Chase said. "He might as easily have talked to Rachel about the notes he took rather than Doctor Stevens. We need more than the fact that York called the house. If you're right, Stevens will never admit he talked to the man and we can't exactly ask Rachel if she talked to him. And York sure as hell isn't going to talk. If they were in this together, we need to find how they worked out the money."

Porter nodded. "If Stevens paid York to kill Rachel you can be damn sure he didn't give him all the money up front. I bet it was

Bob Mayer

something like half up front and half after the case was dropped. Since we caught York, Stevens is probably holding onto that other half."

Chase considered the situation. "Yeah, but he'll have to pay York soon or else face York turning on him."

Porter's brow was furrowed as he thought about it. "You know, Stevens is in a shit position if that's the case. York is in jail. The only thing Stevens has keeping him quiet is the money he has yet to pay. We need more."

"The money York got paid—if your theory is true, would be a good start," Chase said. "If York had been paid off by Stevens, then what would he have done with the money? He couldn't deposit it in a bank for several reasons. One is that on any deposit over ten thousand dollars the IRS is automatically notified and we checked that out on York yesterday."

Porter nodded. "He could have spread the money, however much it was, out into many smaller accounts, all below ten grand, but then he'd still have a paperwork trail. Let's check York's house again." Porter was anxious to do something, anything other than sit at his desk.

Chase wondered if all this was keeping him from facing what he had learned about Rivers and Vladislav. Nothing had changed in Wyoming, but Chase knew that Rivers was too smart to be trapped like a rat in a cage. He wasn't in Wyoming. Chase had a very strong feeling Rivers was close, very close. And if he was close, there was a good chance Vladislav was close.

But he had to back up his partner. Chase got up and followed Porter out of the squad room.

****

The police tape was still across the front door of York's house. Porter put his hand on the door handle to get out, but Chase stopped him.

"Hold on. Let's think like York for a moment. If he had a bunch of cash he wanted to hide, where would he put it?"

"The uniforms did a pretty good job checking the house, looking for the murder weapon," Porter said. "So—"

Something clicked for Chase. "It's not in York's house."

"Then where is it?"

236

"Follow me." Chase got out of the car and walked up to Arnold Rogers' house. He answered after about ten rings. Chase asked him if he could take a look at his car. The car that would be Jim York's when Rogers died and that never moved out of the garage. Rogers gave Chase a set of keys and he went out to the garage behind the house with Porter following.

The door swung up with a loud protesting of rusted metal. The dark blue Buick had definitely seen better days. Chase opened the trunk while Porter opened the driver's door.

A spare and the jack along with an old rotted blanket made up the contents of the trunk. Chase lifted the spare and checked underneath. The rust had been scraped off the head of a bolt far up in the trunk. He climbed in and checked. Someone had recently worked on all the bolts that held the back seat against the front of the trunk. Chase got out and searched around the garage until he found an old adjustable wrench.

"What do you have?" Porter asked, appearing at the rear of the car.

"Watch."

Chase squatted in the trunk and went to work. All the bolts came off easily. He climbed out and went around to the back seat. With a pull, the back of the seat fell forward. Taped to the steel framework were packets of cash, wrapped in plastic.

"I guess you were right," Chase said.

* * * * * * * * * * * *

Porter looked at the cash on the conference room table and then at Chase. "How much?"

"A quarter million."

Porter whistled. "He didn't get that by savings pennies. What did Rogers say about it?"

"I didn't tell him about the cash. I asked him if anyone had done anything with the car. He didn't know anything. He said the only person who'd been in the garage as far as he knew was Jim York."

Porter picked up a packet. "What now?"

"If this two hundred and fifty grand was York's by legitimate means, it seems logical that he would hire some high speed attorney to represent him instead of going with the public defender that he has. So I think we can safely assume this is ill-gotten gains."

237

Porter tossed the packet back on the table. "I think Stevens paid York this money and it was just bad luck that we even caught the man. I wouldn't be surprised if there might not be another quarter million or so payment awaiting York."

Chase nodded. "That may be true but we still don't have anything solid to nail Stevens with." He pointed at the computer printouts. Not only had there been a blank on York but he'd also come up with zip on Stevens making any significant withdrawals over the past year.

Porter pulled out the background he had dug up on Stevens. "I've got Stevens' annual income at almost two million. That's reported income. Who's to say he hasn't been skimming a lot of his cash income and not reporting it to the IRS?"

Chase considered that. "Yeah. It's possible. Lots of lawyers and doctors do that to save on taxes. But two hundred and fifty grand is a hell of a lot of cash and not have anyone know."

"Maybe someone did know," Porter said. "Who's the one person whose help he would need to skim on his reported income?"

Chase smiled. "Lisa Plunkett."

Porter nodded. "She could have done a number on the office books. What if we hit York up? Tell him we found his cash?"

Chase shook his head. "Wouldn't work. If York's got more money coming to him, he won't talk. He's got nothing to gain and everything to lose by talking."

"I've got an idea," Porter said. "If we can't break York, then we have to break Stevens."

Once he explained the concept of what he wanted to do, the plan seemed to take on a life of its own. Chase caught on very quickly. They worked on the letter together. It was addressed to Stevens from Jim York. Chase typed the entire thing-- York had been anal about typing things and they do have typewriters in the prison library. The postmark wasn't too hard. The county lock-up was in the same zip code.

Chase knew it was risky, so he made a pact with Porter that he would take all the heat it went awry. Porter, after all, had a wife and kid.

For Chase there was only one question: would Stevens fall for it? That he had paid York to kill Rachel, Chase was now accepting as the only explanation, but how nervous was the doctor? So far, Jeffrey Stevens had been a pretty cool customer. Chase almost got sick thinking of the act he had pulled in the DA's office yesterday.

Porter was betting on the fact that a letter from York threatening to expose Stevens' involvement in the murder unless he got even more money right away for his defense would shatter the doctor's cool facade. Chase didn't want to think about what would happen if Stevens blew it off, but he couldn't see that happening.

****

Porter covered for Chase at work while he set up quarters at the First National Bank and waited for Stevens to do something stupid.

The longer Chase sat there, the more he worried. Chase pictured him and Porter hanging out under a bridge somewhere sipping their cocktails from a paper bag if this blew up in their faces. Chase knew he wasn't that far from doing that anyway, but Porter had a family. Chase knew he could cover for his partner so far, but if someone dug, the blast zone might take Porter down.

Chase hadn't told Porter about Fortin, Vladislav, Rivers, and that whole mess, because he figured he didn't want Porter's dog to lose its head or worse. But here Chase was putting Porter's ass on the line, even though it was his partner's idea.

Chase's lack of pursuit after getting the information from Cardena bothered him. Because it meant he also was much smaller. He'd been threatened, shot at, and his landlord's dog killed and here he was sitting in a bank. He was keeping his eyes open for any information concerning Rivers or Vladislav, but he wasn't actively pursuing either because he had nothing more to dig into. Also, he didn't want the CIA to pull the plug on him before he wrapped up the Stevens case once and for all. Chase knew it was rationalization, but it worked for the time being.

Chase was so busy watching the safety deposit room that he didn't even realize someone had come up behind him until the shadow from the front windows fell over him. He turned in his seat and looked up into Donnelly's face.

"What the hell do you think you're doing, Detective Chase?"

Chase was still trying to come up with an answer when Donnelly pulled a piece of paper out of his pocket and shoved it under Chase's nose. It was the letter to Stevens telling him to immediately deposit two hundred and fifty thousand in a specifically numbered safety deposit box at this bank or the writer, Jim York, would inform on him in the matter of the murder of Rachel Stevens.

CHAPTER TWENTY-FIVE

Chase had on his best suit, not a very good one, as he went to the chief's office. The secretary ushered him right in and he took the one open seat, plastic and rigid, all alone in front of the big desk. Donnelly was seated against the wall and shooting Chase dagger looks. The chief was looking through a file folder and let Chase squirm for a few minutes before finally acknowledging his presence.

"What did you think you were doing?" He held up a hand. Chase figured that was what they call a rhetorical question. "I've read Lieutenant Donnelly's report and I just cannot believe an officer in my police force would do such a thing. Don't you think Doctor Stevens has suffered enough with the death of his wife? Do you have a personal vendetta against the man? Do you know that the doctor is seriously considering suing the city?"

Chase wasn't sure which question the chief wanted him to answer so he did the smart thing: he kept his mouth shut. The only good thing to happen since Donnelly had confronted Chase at the bank was that Chase had managed to keep Porter's name out of it. As far as everyone knew, Chase had done this alone.

The chief was still glaring at Chase so he figured the man was waiting for him to say something. "What about the money I found, sir?"

"That's another thing, Detective Chase. What authorization did you have to search that car?"

"I had the owner's permission," Chase replied.

"How did you connect the money with Jim York and Doctor Stevens?"

Good question. That was the whole point of the letter they'd sent to Stevens, but Chase certainly wasn't going to go over that again. He decided that silence was the best he could come up with to that one.

"And where is this money?" the chief asked.

"In the safe at our squad room," Chase said.

241

"You're keeping a quarter million dollars in the safe in your squad room?"

Chase assumed that was another rhetorical question.

"You never officially reported finding this money, did you?"

"No, sir."

"It's not from Doctor Stevens," the chief said.

Chase wanted to know how they knew that, but he figured now wasn't the time to be asking more questions.

The chief snapped the file shut. "I'm not sure what exactly we're going to do about you yet. I have to send this before the ethics review committee." He turned and looked at Donnelly for the first time. "Mister Chase is suspended without pay effective this minute. Now, both of you get out of here."

Chase silently followed Donnelly directly to his office.

The lieutenant held out his hand. "Your badge and gun."

Donnelly had seen too many cop movies. Chase gave Donnelly his Boulder PD badge. He still had his Federal ID and badge. "The gun is my own. I have a license to carry it."

A vein on the side of Donnelly's jaw pulsed. "Give me your gun."

Chase went very still and looked Donnelly in the eyes. "You'll have to take it."

The vein looked ready to exploded, but Donnelly's eyes shifted, checking to see if anyone was witnessing this through the partially open door. "Get out of here."

Despite this Pyrrhic victory, Chase knew he had finally made Donnelly happy. After four months. Chase didn't slam the door on the way out. That would have like pissing into a tidal wave.

Chase went back to what used to be his desk. Porter was sitting across at his, looking at him with concern.

"How'd it go?"

"They're sending it before the Ethics Committee. I'm suspended without pay." Chase laughed bitterly. "They don't even pay me, the dumb shits."

"That's true." Porter was trying to look at the bright side. "I'm sorry. Was I that stupid?"

Chase shook his head. "No. I thought about it all day. There were too many loose ends to the Stevens' case. There was something going on and it wasn't just Rachel going to that club. We can't explain York's money and we can't explain Rachel's money either. There's a whole other level to this thing that we haven't even touched yet."

"So what now?" Porter asked.

Chase looked in the drawers and began pulling out the stuff he owned. "Well, *we're* not going to do anything. I just want to get out of this with my butt intact." Chase unlocked the bottom right drawer and pulled out the Book of Patriots. It felt much heavier than the few pieces of paper filed in it.

"Chase?" Porter was staring at it. "What are you going to do?"

Chase had made a decision while sitting in the commissioner's office. The case of Rachel Stevens might have destroyed his career, but there was something he could still salvage out of the entire affair.

"Something I should have done a long time ago."

****

Chase drove down Second Avenue more out of habit than desire. He could see the shades were drawn on Sylvie's apartment and he was about to turn the corner when he saw someone come out the front door of the building.

Nicholas Tai.

Chase stopped the Jeep, and then backed up, double-parking. Tai saw him and paused, waiting.

"Super-cop," Tai said, as Chase walked up to him.

"Not anymore."

"Fucking up?"

"Are you?"

Tai smiled, but Chase could see his stance as he spread his feet ever so slightly. Chase took a step closer.

"Sylvie's my friend," Tai said.

"That all?"

"No." Both men turned slightly as Sylvie spoke from the open door to the lobby of the apartment building. "No, Chase. He's my boss. And I just fucked him. Too much information. Or not enough?"

"For how long?" Chase asked.

Sylvie looked her watch. "About forty-five minutes."

Chase felt his face tighten.

Sylvie stepped out of the door, between the two men. "I got your note, Chase. And the flowers. And the copy of the signed settlement.

The note was nice. Thank you. Same with the flowers. The settlement—why should I care?"

Before Chase could say anything, he saw her eyes soften and she took a step toward him, putting a hand on his arm. "I'm sorry. But you kept me out of your life, why do you think you have a right to look into mine?"

"I did what I had to do," Chase said.

"So did I," Sylvie said. "You have a secret life. I have one too. But yours could get you killed. That was a little hard to deal with. And you probably never thought of me having to deal with it. Did you?"

Chase looked her in the eyes. "No."

Sylvie nodded. "Thank you for being honest." She looked over her shoulder at Tai. "Could you give us some privacy?"

Tai nodded, but he was staring at Chase. "Sure. See you at the club." He walked away.

"You don't have to go to the club again," Chase said.

Sylvie gave a sad smile. "What? Are you going to take care of me, Horace Chase?" She didn't wait for an answer. "Come upstairs."

Chase followed her. They went into the apartment and to her bedroom. She went to her wicker chair and curled into it. Chase sat on the edge of the bed.

Sylvie placed her hand on her chest. "Chase, you've got a dark place in you right here. I know. I've got one too. I can talk about the money I get for stripping, but there's something else that brought me to the Silver Satyr. At least mine hasn't killed anybody, though."

"Sylvie, I only--"

"Chase, I know you had to do what you had to do. But you've put yourself in positions where you have to do things like Wyoming and the Barnes' house. And before that Afghanistan and Iraq."

"I didn't want--"

"No--" she cut Chase off. "I said I have to dance for the money, Chase, and it was a lie. I have choices and you have choices. We just don't believe we do. Sometimes we take the easier way; sometimes we take the way we were twisted into taking. Our sex was never normal because we weren't normal. Doesn't take a shrink to figure that out."

Chase could see that her face was drawn and he realized she was tired, very tired. And that she had been crying. A lot. "I didn't fuck Tai. I said that to hurt you. I'm sorry. Chase, did you ever wonder why I went out with you in the first place?"

"Well--" he decided to be honest again. "Not really."

"When you came in to question us about that kid who got beat up I could tell something about you. That you gave a damn. You didn't come into the dressing room to get a cheap thrill. Oh, I know that's what you told Porter and maybe even what you told yourself, but you gave a damn, I could tell. You did more than go through the motions. That meant you cared about somebody other than you. Even if they were just a case. That's why we went out the first time."

"Why'd you stay with me?"

"Because you were as broken as me."

Chase took a deep breath.

"What's in that letter from your mother?"

"She wrote to tell me she was dying." *And that I was broken,* Chase thought.

"You didn't go see her, Chase."

"I was at war."

She nodded. "I know. But when you came back from war, did you go where she was buried?"

"They didn't bury her," Chase said. "She was cremated and her ashes spread by boat into the water of the Intracoastal off-shore of the house in South Carolina she mentions in her letter." Chase was surprised to feel tears in his eyes.

"Did you go there?"

Chase couldn't speak. He could only shake his head.

"I'm broken, Chase. I've known it for a long time. The problem is you're more worried about your relationship with me than with your relationship with you, aren't you?"

"I was."

"Do you see how misplaced that is?"

Chase nodded again, sealing his fate.

"You need to start with yourself, not me. You can't give me or anyone else anything until you mend yourself." She stood. She looked down at Chase. "Tell me one thing."

"What?"

"What did your mother do?"

"She was a dancer."

Sylvie smiled. "It's not too late for you, Horace."

And then he left her apartment.

245

CHAPTER TWENTY-SIX

Chase drove east to the warehouse district and parked a slight distance away where he could watch the door. Since he was suspended, he had nothing but time. In a way, by suspending him, the chief had freed him, cutting the chain of duty that held Chase to his Boulder PD desk. He didn't know exactly what he expected, but Merck magazine and Lou Thorne seemed like a good place to start.

Forty-five minutes went by, less time than he had spent on his belly in the alley two weeks previously, when the door swung open and who should walk out but Baldie, the ex-SEAL, his ebony skull gleaming in the sunlight, his arm in a cast.

Chase pulled his Glock out and exited the Jeep. Baldie was walking away from Chase, in no big rush, heading toward a red Camaro, no idea Chase was closing. Baldie must have sensed something at the last second because he started to turn, which only served to jam the barrel of the 10mm pistol into the side of his face, instead of the back of his head.

"Whoa! Take it easy."

Chase quickly backed off, getting four feet between, making it difficult for Baldie to strike before Chase could pull the trigger and have a bullet heading his way. Bullets beat hands or feet every time. A trickle of blood ran down Baldie's cheek where the front sight post of Chase's gun had ripped skin.

He touched the spot, pulled his hand away and stared at the small smear of blood on his fingers. "Damn, man. You messed with the face."

"'The face'? You're lucky you still have a head."

He shook his head. "Hey, you got no issue with me."

Chase raised his eyebrows.

"Really," Baldie insisted. "I wasn't going to hurt you. Just doing what I'm told. You know all about that, right?"

"Doing what who told you?"

"Me."

Chase recognized the voice behind him right away-- Lou Thorne. Chase edged sideways, keeping an eye on Baldie while taking in the old man who was about ten feet away. He had a cigar in his hand and he poked it back toward his building. "Why don't we sit down and chat like civilized people?"

"Was it civilized when you sent this asshole to threaten me?"

Thorne laughed. "Hell, son. He wasn't threatening you. He was sent to motivate you." He nodded at Baldie. "Jimmy, go to lunch. I'll take care of this."

"You fucked my arm up, man," Jimmy said, glaring. "Payback is a medevac."

"Jimmy," Thorne said with a warning in his tone.

"Try payback and it will be the morgue for you," Chase said, holstering his gun. "I'm done fucking around."

* * * * * * * * * * * *

The pit bulls didn't leap at Chase when he entered Thorne's office this time. They just lifted their ugly little heads and growled deep in their throats. Thorne walked behind his desk and Chase took the chair he'd had the only other time he'd been there.

"Motivate me?"

"You're slow, sonny, real slow." Thorne's gravelly voice and Chase's new nickname grated on his nerves. "Expected to see you here a while ago."

"I was busy."

"Yeah, read about it in the papers. Boulder police actually nabbing a killer. Well, alleged killer. Outstanding. Although wasn't Karr an alleged killer?"

His sarcasm wasn't lost on Chase. "Why'd you expect to see me here a while ago?"

"I was impressed you came to talk to me about the Patriots. Most Feds got their head stuck so far up their ass they wouldn't ask for help from anyone, never mind someone like me. I thought I gave you enough to go on the first time you were here, but you didn't do shit with it. So I sent Jimmy and his buddy to shake you up. Figured they'd get your blood flowing. You'd either kick some ass or be a pussy and wimp out."

"By threatening me?"

Thorne shrugged. "It's a technique."

"I've been threatened by professionals."

Thorne frowned. "CIA?"

Chase nodded, not too surprised Thorne had leapt to that conclusion.

Thorne frowned. "Figured they'd come nosing around sooner or later. Fucking spooks aren't exactly what I'd call professionals, though."

"What the hell is going on?"

"I don't really know all of it, but what I do know says it isn't good."

Chase had gotten over his initial anger and settled back in the chair, waiting for Thorne to fill him in.

"Rivers is in town," Thorne began.

"I know."

"He's the one that called the Patriots in to the sheriff's office when they were heading back to Wyoming."

Chase hadn't known that. "So he set that deputy up to get shot."

Thorne shook his head. "No. He set the Patriots up to get caught before they could make it out of Colorado. Both those guys in that Blazer had outstanding warrants. Rivers didn't know that sheriff's office was going to be so incompetent about stopping them and get one of their people killed."

"The best-laid plans--" Chase didn't finish the rest of the sentence, realizing he'd already done one stupid cliché in Gavin's office.

"I imagine he feels bad about the deputy and the troopers wounded in Wyoming."

"You 'imagine'?" Chase asked. "How do you know all this?"

"I talked to him just after he got in town. We met up in the hills."

"Before or after the shooting at the Barnes' house?"

"Before. And that was Vladislav."

Chase shook his head. "I don't think he shot them. I think Rivers did."

Thorne grunted, which meant what, Chase had no idea. He hadn't spoken Neanderthal since leaving the Infantry.

"He shot a baby, for Chrissakes," Chase added.

"If he did, it was an accident." For the first time, Thorne had lost his hard edge.

"Rivers is after Vladislav," Chase summed up what he'd already figured out on his own. The only thing Thorne had added was the connection to the Patriots.

Thorne nodded. "Rivers been after that shit-bag for two years. Tracked him to the States. To Colorado. Then tracked him here to Boulder. Asked me to help pinpoint him. I told him I wasn't going to get into that. To let the law handle it. That's why I tried to get you involved."

"You could have been more direct." Chase felt like he was back investigating Rachel Stevens' murder-- everyone knew better about how things should go. And he knew that Rivers hadn't exactly *tracked* Vladislav here.

"Then you would have known I knew about Rivers," Thorne said. "And you would have gone to your bosses and they would have shut you down. The CIA wanted to shut you down with the little you did do and we both know the Boulder PD would have had a cow if they knew anything about what was going on."

"They did that any way."

"No, they didn't," Thorne said. "You're here now. They didn't stop you."

Chase had to admit Thorne had a point.

"Besides," Thorne said, "if someone has to take down Rivers, it ought to be one our own, not some donut-eating policeman and definitely not the fucking Agency."

Chase took what he had learned and tried to project forward. "Do you know where Rivers is now?"

Thorne shook his head. "He was in some flea-bag motel under an assumed name for a while, and then moved into mountains."

"So the Barnes called him that night. Why?"

Thorne shrugged. "I don't know what happened with the Barnes or any of that crap. I assume Rivers was hitting up dealers, trying to track down Vladislav. The dirt-bag was doing his same old shit, this time right here in the good, old US of A while under the protection of the CIA."

Chase remembered what Buck had guessed at. "And the Patriots are supplying Vladislav?"

"Yeah."

"So Rivers was trying to find Vladislav by tracking the Patriots here."

"Makes sense."

"Do you know where Vladislav is?"

"I'd have served him up to you already if I knew that," Thorne said. "Or taken care of him myself."

"Or given him to Rivers."

Thorne shook his head. "There's been enough blood."

"Oh, yeah, you've been so helpful so far. Pardon me if I forget."

"Hey. I knew about Vladislav long before Rivers did. I got a video from one of my stringers several years ago. Of Vladislav in action in the 'Stan right after the invasion. Was going to do a story on it, then my source decided he preferred to keep living, so we did nothing." Thorne pulled open a drawer and slid a DVD across his desk to Chase.

Chase took it. "You see Rivers, tell him to call me."

Thorne shook his head. "If he killed the Barnes, then he's up for murder. He'll never surrender."

Great, Chase thought. They had a Rambo in the hills. Not a Hollywood wanna-be, but the real thing.

"You have anything else that can help?" Chase asked. "I think I've peaked out my motivation meter."

Thorne put his cigar in the ashtray. For a second all Chase saw was a worn-out, old man. "End this before anyone else gets hurt. When I saw Rivers, I knew he was about done in. Then you showed up and I thought you might be able to bring him in peaceful. But now--" he shook his head. "Rivers has got nothing left. He's seen too much and he can't come back. He isn't on the edge anymore; he's fallen in the pit. The fucking heart of darkness. These civilians don't have a clue. You do."

Chase knew exactly what Thorne was talking about. He'd spent most of the past month right on the edge of that pit himself.

"I'll let you know how it turns out," Chase told Thorne. "That's if I survive."

"You need help, give me a buzz."

"So you can motivate me again?"

****

Chase drove up 9th, toward Chautauqua, the Flatirons ahead. To the right, the sun setting over them. Tourists came to town to the see the view. He barely noted it.

9th ended at Baseline. Chase let gravity take over and turned left, going downhill toward Broadway. He turned left onto Broadway, the third leg of a lost triangle.

On impulse, he turned out of the heavy traffic into a tree-lined lane on the CU Campus, a corridor of tranquility out of the madness of the city. Chase drove to the Psych department building. He needed help and Sylvie was no longer an option.

Chase parked and sat for a few minutes, rolling the pieces around. He pulled out his Satphone and made a call.

"Porter."

"It's Chase. I've got a question for you. What if the money York had didn't come from Doctor Stevens? Where could it have come from?"

"Fuck. I don't know. Someone else who wanted Rachel dead, I guess. But we had no other suspects."

"Remember what you said to me on the bridge over the creek last week?"

There was a short pause. "About Boulder?"

"What if all these things are linked?"

"How?"

"What are the pieces that don't fit?" Chase didn't wait for an answer. "York's money—if it didn't come from Doctor Stevens, where did it come from? Rachel's secret money. Where did it come from? The gym bag the cab driver said Rachel had—we never found it. What was in it?" Chase knew his partner was in the dark about some key pieces—specifically Vladislav, but he wanted to see what Porter's police expertise came up with.

"So she was doing something involving a lot of money," Porter said. "It might have been money in that bag. Maybe York ripped off that money from Rachel?"

"And why would she have that much money?" Chase asked, although he already had his own answer.

"Money laundering. Blackmail. Drugs."

"Thanks," Chase said.

"What are you doing?" Porter asked. "You're suspended, remember?"

"Suspended from the Boulder PD," Chase said. "Not from the Feds. Not from honor. Thanks, Ben."

"Chase?" Porter sounded worried.

"I'm all right. I've just removed my head from my fourth point of contact."

"What?"

"Airborne School," Chase said. "When parachuting, the first point of contact with the ground is your feet, second is your shins, then your thighs, then your ass."

"Oh." There was the static of silence over the Satphone for a few moments. Then Porter spoke again. "Be careful. And if you need back-up, call?"

"I will," Chase said. *But not you,* he thought. His partner had already put too much on the line. "Later." He turned the phone off. And this was way too far in the black for Ben Porter and Boulder Major Cases.

Chase got out of the Jeep and walked into the psych building. It was practically deserted with the down surge for the summer semester. There was no graduate student guarding the approaches to Gavin's office, so he rapped on the door.

"Come in."

The Professor was packing his stuff and looked none too excited to see his visitor. "Detective Chase. What a surprise. What can I do for you?"

"Going on vacation?"

"No. Leaving."

"Where to?"

"I've accepted a position at another university. Seemed like a good time to make some changes. The academic year is done. My papers are to date. My research is dead here. And I don't particularly want to see my wife driving my car around town and pass by the house that used to be mine."

Chase wasn't here to listen to Gavin whine about his divorce. "You got some coffee?"

"Too much partying last night, detective?"

Too much death over a lifetime, Chase thought without answering.

Gavin caught the mood and rustled up two cups.

"Why was Rachel so deceptive?" Chase abruptly asked.

252

Gavin's handed Chase the cup and took a step back. "Can't you just give up on that? Her killer is in jail."

"Yeah, he's in jail, but I'm thinking there's more to this whole thing than came out. And I'm not sure he's the killer."

"What do you mean?" Gavin said, tiredly sinking down into his chair.

"Nobody knew Rachel Stevens and exactly what she was doing. From reading the papers, you know all about the swinger's club and how she hid herself even here at CU, but now I'm uncovering stuff that makes it look like she was involved in something to do with drugs."

"Rachel Stevens?" Gavin's jaw dropped. "What do you mean she was involved with drugs?"

"We found some money in her account. We also found two hundred and fifty grand in cash that York had squirreled away."

Gavin shook his head slowly. "Are you sure drugs were involved? I find that very, very hard to believe."

"Let's just say that I found some information that indicated Rachel might have been a mule. Carrying drugs or cash to someone here on campus. I'm starting to wonder if York also wasn't a dealer, although we uncovered nothing during our investigation of him to show that. Maybe he was working for a dealer."

"Here at the University?"

If he'd had the energy, Chase would have smiled at Gavin's expression of dismay. As if some of the people at CU didn't do some snorting and shooting up. "Yeah, here at the University. I got a good idea who her supplier was, but it doesn't make any sense for the supplier to have bumped her off. I need to find out why York killed Rachel, if he did." Chase made a decision on one of those balls that had been rattling around in his head. "I'm going to go see York tomorrow at the jail."

"But he won't talk, will he?" Gavin cautioned.

"We found his money. That might make him change his religion."

"But how did Rachel get involved in all this?" Gavin wanted to know. "Her husband had no idea?"

"No, but he was being deceptive in his own way."

Chase didn't want to smear Jeffrey and bring up Lisa Plunkett. He longed to deal with people who didn't have all these secrets, but that was the nature of the job. Sometimes Chase wished he worked as one of those guys who mow the grass along the edge of the interstate. Each day they did the same thing but with changing scenery. At the end of the day, they could look over their shoulder and see that they had really accomplished something. Most of the time, particularly now, he felt like he had his finger in a crap filled dike and it was constantly leaking all over him. He'd felt like that in the Army and it had led to his abrupt resignation after being wounded.

The professor derailed Chase's doom-filled train of thought. "Maybe Rachel was being deceptive to all those around her because she couldn't afford to let anyone see the real person inside of her," Gavin observed. "With all that you say she was involved in, in her secret life, I would say she most certainly couldn't let her husband or any of her Pine Brook Hills friends know what she had planned or what she was doing to try to achieve that plan. If she had a plan," Gavin added.

"But why couldn't she just live the life she had?" Chase wanted to know. Hell, he'd seen her house and been out to the country club. It didn't look too bad.

Gavin slipped into lecture mode. "She choose her surface life when she was young. Who knows what her reasons were then?" But even Gavin seemed stumped by the whole thing. "The whole field of psychology tries to figure out why people do what they do and we're as often wrong as often than we are right. Sometimes you just have to accept that there are some bad people in the world."

No shit, Chase thought. Bad people. There was one of them out there who had drilled into a baby's mouth.

"Who else knows about your York faking it, theory?" Gavin asked.

"I just came up with it," Chase said.

Gavin started packing again, which Chase took as a hint that it was time for him to move on. "Thanks for your time, Doc. Good luck at your new job."

"Thanks, Detective. Good luck to you too."

Chase turned for the door, when Gavin's voice stopped him. "You should have left well enough alone."

Chase turned around and looked into the gaping muzzle of a large caliber revolver. His eyes slid from the manhole-sized black hole to the face above.

"Don't move, please," Gavin gestured with the gun, which was the sure sign of an amateur.

"You've got to be shitting me," Chase said.

Gavin edged over to the small refrigerator underneath one of his bookcases. He opened it and pulled out a beer. Gavin rolled it across the floor to Chase's feet.

"Open it."

Chase did as told. "I'm going to hurt you, maybe kill you. I'm in a bad mood."

"Drink."

Chase took a sip.

"No, I mean drink it. All of it." Gavin nodded as Chase shot gunned the beer. "I've got eleven more although we might not have to do all."

Chase felt the cold beer swirl around inside of him. "What are you doing?"

Gavin rolled another beer across. "Can't you see the headline, buried somewhere in the middle of the paper tomorrow or probably the day after since it will take them a while to find you? I can sum the story up in one sentence: Drunken, divorced, suffering PTSD, ex-vet cop in trouble at work, kills self after seeing a shrink at CU. I'll say you came to me for help. You were despondent, suicidal possibly. I told you to go the emergency room for immediate help

"There's a logic to it. I'm sure all your co-workers will say nice things about you at your funeral that they certainly don't mean and would never say to your face."

"Why?"

"Why what?" Gavin asked.

"Why are you doing this?"

"Oh, I think you have an idea now, don't you detective?"

"Pretty much," Chase said.

Gavin gestured at the second beer in Chase's hand. "Let's make a deal. For each beer you drink, you get to ask me a question and I'll answer. It's the least I could do for someone who has been so helpful to me."

What an idiot, Chase thought. "You're another CU connection. A dealer."

Gavin laughed, his eyes sparkling above the revolver's muzzle. *That's not good,* Chase thought. *Crazy eyes.* "That's not too bright asking close-ended questions. The answer is yes. Well, at least one of the pick-ups at CU. I would think you would want to know more, seeing how much this case bothered you. Think real hard before your next question." Another beer rolled across the floor.

Chase popped the top. "You know this isn't my brand. Someone might think that's suspicious

"It's a cheap brand," Gavin replied. "I figure that fits your personality."

"Got me figured out, huh?" Chase asked.

"I could give you a diagnosis based on what I've seen," Gavin said.

"You already did," Chase said. "And you were wrong."

"Was I?"

"You'll find out shortly."

"I've got the gun."

"For now. Why did you pay York to kill Rachel?"

"Ah, good!" Chase realized Gavin was more of a loon than York. He was enjoying this. Like Rachel, he was too naïve to realize he'd ventured into the part of the world that on old maps used to be labeled: *Here there be monsters.*

Gavin continued. "An open-ended question. That's what psychologists are taught to do. Requires the patient to work harder on the answer and gives more information."

Chase looked at the gun, but the muzzle was still centered on his chest. It looked like a .357. Something a Clint Eastwood wanna-be would buy. Chase was sure Gavin would try to get his gun when he was ready to try to do him in. *Fucking amateur.*

"I didn't pay York to kill Rachel and York didn't kill her, or so he told me." Gavin laughed at the surprise on Chase's face. "I had a good business going through my student dealers. Rachel was bringing a big load in every three weeks for me and God knows who else. I was insulated from the supplier. The supplier was insulated from me. Hell, I'm not even sure Rachel knew what she was carrying, although she must have guessed. It was the perfect set-up and Rachel was the key."

"What about the Barnes?"

Gavin shrugged. "I wasn't the only one she supplied. York screwed everything up for all of us who were supplied by Rachel. That bitch should never have asked him to take the damn notes. I would have given her an A if she'd never shown up once. But you know how she was. Or maybe you don't. She really wanted to be a psychologist!"

Gavin didn't seem to believe someone could so stupid. "It doesn't matter.

"Anyway, he learned about the club, but more importantly three weeks before her death he saw her make the drop at the library and he saw me make the pickup. We used one of the lockers on the third floor. We each had a key. He wasn't stupid. He knew she and I were up to something very strange. Maybe, the Barnes had a locker there too. Maybe others. Rachel was the only one who knew how many drops she was supplying and where and how.

"The next time she did it, he was waiting in his van after class when she got back to CU. He snatched her in the parking lot, short-circuiting the drops. She had a bag full of produce with her." Gavin's voice was harsh. "A lot of high quality produce. Just my cut was worth a quarter million before hitting the street, where I could double that. York looked in the bag and saw the goodies. He got her to talk and she told him about the money she had waiting for her after delivery.

"She must have thought that would be that. She probably thought she could just walk away from it all. York says he took the drugs and let her out and that was the last he saw of her." Gavin shook his head. "I had split from the library already of course. My alibi was legit. He looked me up in my office the next day."

It sounded so cold and dispassionate, but for the first time everything was fitting in place for Chase. "Why'd he kill her?"

Gavin frowned. "Is that one of your questions? As I said, he told me he didn't. Actually, I kind of believe him. He said he grabbed the drugs and let her go, figuring she wasn't exactly going to call the cops.

"I think York was obsessed with her. But he was more obsessed with the money he knew he could get for the drugs. The money was important to him. That's why I don't think he killed her. York came to me and I paid him for the drugs. I had people waiting and they weren't the type of people you wanted to keep waiting. Two hundred and fifty thousand in cash. Of course, my link with the supplier was cut with the death of Rachel, but things were screwed up enough as it was and it was time to call it quits anyway. York kept the money and I figured I was safe if Rachel had never told the supplier who I was. Since she'd never told me who the supplier was, that was a reasonable assumption.

"As you could tell today, I've stayed around long enough to close everything out without raising any suspicions." Gavin caught himself.

He grabbed another beer and rolled it to Chase. "That's more than enough of an answer for one question. Next?"

Chase forced half the can down his throat as he thought. "So York's mental stuff is legitimate?"

"No. I helped him make that up."

"What?"

Gavin looked at Chase like an idiot stepchild. "Haven't you figured it out yet, Detective? We worked out the whole scene just in case. Then you kept me pretty much up to date on everything. I called him after you left my office that day on the way to his place and told him to be ready for you, just in case. He wasn't that crazy. Or should I say he wasn't that smart?" He rolled another beer across. Chase wasn't done with the previous one.

Chase had to check. "York didn't tell you who Rachel's supplier was?"

Gavin shrugged. "I didn't ask. I didn't want to know. I don't know if he knew. Doubt it. Obviously, whoever it was never got paid for their product so they were pissed, but only Rachel knew both ends, so with her dead, her supplier was out in the cold. I did get scared when I read about the Barnes getting killed in the paper, but everyone knew they were dealing. The supplier must have known too. I was more careful."

"And today? Why this?"

"I can't let you go to York. I don't think he'll talk, but I can't afford to take a chance on that. My worry is that he *does* know about me. I don't think he killed Rachel, but then again, if he didn't, who did? And there's a good chance he'll try to implicate me, making a deal to save his ass. I can't have that." Gavin waved the gun about, the first time it wasn't centered on Chase's chest. "You just wouldn't let this go would you?

"Not even after you found out that Rachel wasn't the little miss innocent you must have imagined her to be." He squinted at Chase. "I asked you the first time we met what was more important: the facts or the personalities. I know the answer now. You were caught up in the personality you imagined Rachel to be. I was too when I first met her. She was most definitely different."

Chase thought about Vladislav going to the Barnes. Drilling into their baby's mouth, looking for his money for the drugs they never got. He was done with this bullshit.

Gavin continued, still waving the gun about. "I suppose I could tell you how we hooked up on the deal, but that's really not important right now. I think--"

Chase threw the full can with all his might. It hit Gavin in the forehead with a solid thud. Chase was moving as soon as the can left his hand.

Gavin fired on reflex as he staggered back, the gun pointing toward the ceiling, the roar echoing through the room.

Chase grabbed the hand holding the gun and twisted, the sound of the forearm bones breaking filling the silence after the gunshot.

Gavin screamed and Chase didn't give a shit as the gun dropped to the floor. He hit Gavin in the throat with the knife-edge of his other hand, holding back from a fatal strike at the last second. The psychologist dropped to his knees, gasping for breath. Chase grabbed his hair and twisted his head.

"Did you kill Rachel Stevens?"

Gavin tried to speak as Chase pulled out his Glock and shoved the muzzle into the soft part under the professor's jaw. Gavin shook his head, still trying to speak through his damaged throat. A wheeze came out.

"Did York?" Chase put pressure on the gun and Gavin's eyes widened.

Gavin shook his head and tried to speak again. He managed to gasp some words out. "I don't think so."

"I don't think so either," Chase said. Then he rapped Gavin on the side of the head with the gun, and the man keeled over to the floor unconscious.

CHAPTER TWENTY-SEVEN

Chase had had the shift sergeant come and take Gavin into custody. He was supposed to go to the station and fill out forms. but screw them. He was suspended. He'd walked away and uniform cops gathered had parted like the Red Sea.

Fuck it, Chase thought as he walked in the backyard toward his apartment. He was going to stay and fight before he went off into the rising sun. If he did go down the tubes, he was going to make as big a stink as possible. Then he could get a job delivering pizzas or something in South Carolina and check out his mother's legacy.

Chase threw a cup of cold coffee into the microwave, turned on his laptop and slid the DVD into the slot. The microwave dinged as the screen booted up and he grabbed the mug.

The screams came a second before the screen came alive with an image that made even Chase flinch. An Afghan man was tied to a post, naked. A Caucasian soldier in un-marked camouflage fatigues was using a blowtorch on the man's skin, picking skin to seer into blackness and then red. There was a voice off-camera, urging him on, giving directions. Chase's Russian was very rusty, but he could make that much out from the intent in the tone.

Whoever was holding the video camera wasn't very steady on the job. Whether it was from disgust at what he was seeing, or excitement, Chase didn't know. The soldier appeared to be a 'snuffy'. Someone from the lower ranks, being used as a blunt object to torture by the off-camera commander. There was no questioning of the man tied to the stake. This wasn't interrogation, Chase could tell, which meant it had one of two objectives. Either it was a warning designed to scare others from doing whatever the man had done, or the torturers were getting their rocks off. Or from what Chase had seen done in some of the cesspools he'd traveled to in Special Operations-- both.

The screen went blank. Then a new scene. This one inside what appeared to be a one-room schoolhouse. An older woman and a half-dozen young girls in blue skirts and white blouses were cowering in a corner.

Chase hit the fast-forward button, knowing what was coming next. He did it because he didn't want to see the faces of the girls and their teacher as they were raped. It went on for a while, even at fast-forward speed. Chase was beginning to empathize more and more with Colonel Rivers. Chase had known what Cardena was talking about at the airport, but seeing it was a different story. Especially when one of the satisfied soldiers replaced his penis with a bayonet.

Chase turned the DVD off. This wasn't getting him any closer to Vladislav or Rivers. Chase pulled out his hand-cruncher and began squeezing it hard.

He turned the DVD back on. The camera panned over the bodies of the girls and the woman. Some had died easily-- a bullet to the head. Others not so easy. Blades and blunt objects and suffocation had done the work. Chase remembered reading about the killing fields in Cambodia, where to save the price of a bullet; they put plastic bags over victims' heads with their hands tied behind their backs. Some of the girls had died the same way. At one point, there was a close-up of a girl, maybe ten or eleven, with the clear plastic over her head, a man's hand twisting it tight behind her as she kicked mouth open, eyes wide. The hand had a large gold ring on the middle finger. The camera stayed on the girl's face until she died.

Three seconds of black with a sound Chase tried to place.

A drill. A dentist's drill.

A man was tied to a heavy wood chair. Two soldiers had their arms clamped on his head, holding it back, their arms muscles bulging in their attempts to keep it immobile even with the leather strap tight around the man's forehead assisting them.

A man in a black fatigues was leaning over the man's mouth. He was a big man, his hands holding a drill. He turned his head to call over his shoulder and--

Chase dropped his crunch ball and stared at the screen. He knew the man.

CHAPTER TWENTY-SEVEN

Masters' face was pale. He'd already puked his lunch into Chase's sink. That had happened only thirty seconds into the blow-torching opening.

Chase fast-forwarded to Vladislav doing his work, skipping the rape scene. "That's him. New name is Peter Watkins."

Masters washed his mouth out with some water. "The husband of that woman you interviewed at the country club?"

Chase nodded. "Linda Watkins." He paused the screen, freezing his face turned toward the camera.

There was a hand over the edge of the camera, that same large gold ring glittering. Chase forwarded a couple of more frames until he had a clear view of Vladislav's face.

"And he's dealing drugs?" Masters rubbed a palm across his forehead as he thought about it.

"And I have a very good idea how he gets the drugs into the States," Chase said. "The Patriots bring it in via Canada. Right over the border, probably in four-wheel drive vehicles on old mule and jeep trails. They bring it down here to Boulder and probably do a dead drop that Vladislav services.

"Then Vladislav passes some or all of the drugs on to Rachel at the swinger's club, which is a perfect cut out. It was his way of insulating himself from whomever he was dealing to. Rachel Stevens was his cut out. She picked up the stuff from the swingers club. Think about what a great cover that place was. No one admits being there; no one knows the others real names. It's perfect. Vladislav followed me home from the club that night I was there, killed my landlord's dog and took a shot at me.

"Rachel dropped the drugs in the gym bag off at the lockers in the CU library. She probably in turn picked up the cash her next night at school and brought it to the damn country club when she played Linda in tennis. Whoever was getting the drugs had no idea Vladislav was the supplier. He or she could even watch Rachel do the drop and not know."

The pieces were falling in place in Chase's mind faster and faster. "That's why Rivers was hitting up dealers. He was trying to work his way up the supply chain. The only problem is that we taught Vladislav how to use such things as a cut out and a dead drop ourselves. Right here in the States at Fort Benning at the School of the Americas."

Masters pointed at the TV screen. "This guy is bad news. Really bad news. Let someone else deal with him."

"Who?" Chase asked. He was looking out the door at the spot where he'd buried Astral.

Masters had no answer. "Did he kill Stevens?"

"Probably. I'll ask him when I see him."

"So you're going after him now?"

"Not directly."

Masters frowned. "But you just said—"

"I've got to close it all out," Chase said. "Go to the airport, get the bird ready, and I'll give you a call when I'm ready."

Masters nodded. "Roger that."

After Masters left, Chase went to his bedroom and pulled out a geographic map of the Boulder area. He called Thorne and wasted no time with pleasantries.

"Where did you meet Rivers in the mountains?"

"Eldora ski area. Next to the lake as you drive in."

"Do you have a night vision scope I can mount on an M-21?"

"Yes."

"Have it ready for me. I'll be by in an hour."

Chase clicked the phone off and looked at the map. That made sense. The ski area was closed for the season and no one would make the precipitous drive up there unless they had a very specific reason. There were thousands upon thousands of acres of wilderness in the Roosevelt and Arapaho National Forests surrounding Eldora. Tourists rarely went in that area, the vast majority flocking to the better-known Rocky Mountain National Forest to the north.

Chase sat on the floor, the topo map spread out before him. He was Rivers, looking for an isolated base-camp to operate from while he snuck into Boulder every so often, trying to track down Vladislav. Chase let go of his surroundings and enveloped himself entirely into the situation.

His eyes kept being drawn to the south and west of Eldora, to a black line crossing the Continental Divide. He knew that the only way to drive across the Continental Divide in this part of the Rockies was either I-70 out of Denver, which was south of Boulder, or to drive all the way up north to Estes Park and go through the Rocky Mountain National Park on Trail Ridge Road. Over fifty miles of impassable mountains in between. Except for this one black line. But it wasn't a road. He'd been there and knew exactly what it was; and he knew that Rivers would go there. They'd gone through the same training and a lot of the same experiences. Civilians wouldn't understand it. But it was the place because Rivers also had something special in his file.

The place was Moffat Tunnel.

Thorne had mentioned that Rivers had been a tunnel rat in the 101st Airborne during his one tour as a young private in Vietnam before coming back to the States and going into ROTC in college after the war. That took a weird mindset to be willing to crawl into a small, narrow dirt tunnel with just a flashlight and .45-caliber pistol in hand, searching for the enemy. Hell, Chase thought, compared to what he'd crawled into in Vietnam, the Moffat would look like the Ritz to Rivers.

Chase reached over and searched through the pile of magazines and books next to his bed. He found what he looking for-- a guidebook to the trails and parks of Colorado. It had a page on the Moffat Tunnel.

Just before the turn of the century, the Union Pacific had only two routes through the Rockies. One was way north of Denver through Wyoming. The other was a hundred miles south through Pueblo and across Royal Gorge. David Moffat, a local businessman, realized Denver was being bypassed. He got together the financing to try to build a rail line due west out of Denver. Construction began in 1905.

The line went from Denver into South Boulder, just a few miles from where Chase was sitting. Originally, Moffat ran the line over Rollins Pass, building a two-mile long snow shed over the tracks to keep it open the half of the year the pass was inundated with snow. Even with the shed, though, delays were common. Moffat even had the rotary snowplow for trains invented to try to keep his line running, but he realized he needed another answer. He died before he could implement the new solution.

In 1923, construction started at both ends of what was to be the Moffat Tunnel. Cutting right through James Peak it would reduce what had been a five-hour train ride over the pass in good weather to twelve minutes in any weather.

It took five years to cut, but eventually both side met up, only and the tunnel was completed. Over 6.2 miles long it cost 29 lives and millions of dollars to complete. It was still the highest rail line in the United States and the perfect place for Rivers.

Chase figured the Colonel would camp outside the eastern portal to the tunnel. The only people who ever went up there-- besides the trains-- were ice climbers in the winter and mountain bikers in the summer, both of whom had to brave a long unmarked, dirt road that switch backed off the Rollins Pass Road to the east portal

Chase knew the elevation and view would give Rivers extended warning of anyone coming on the road. If he sensed a threat, he could retreat into the tunnel, which reduced the bad guys to approaching from one direction and being easy targets.

To coordinate bringing people in both sides of the tunnel at the same time would require sending those coming in from the west on a three hour ride south, through Eisenhower Tunnel on I-70, then thirty miles north on a hard climb to the western portal.

There was a lot of land west of Boulder where Rivers could be hiding, but only a couple of places where he might be, and Chase was sure this was the one place he would be.

Chase put on his fatigues, combat vest, grabbed his gear and went out the back door. Louise was in the yard with Star scampering around her. She was watering his garden. She looked at Chase, noted all the gear he was carrying and the way he was dressed and turned the hose off.

"Horace."

Chase paused.

Louise pointed at the turned up dirt. "Your plants are growing."

Chase hadn't noticed, but now that he looked, he saw a few short shards of green poking through.

"Be careful, Horace."

"I will."

Chase had been so busy making calls and getting gear together, that he hadn't really thought about the entire situation much after making his plan. Chase knew if he thought about it too much the holes would start appearing.

"Five minutes," Masters informed him.

Chase sat back on his pack-- the rucksack flop as instructors in Ranger and Special Forces School called it-- and thought about something other than the flimsiness of the plan. Here he was, on board a chopper, weapon across his knees. Sylvie would have used the term déjà vu.

That was another bad thought. A dark place to send his mind when he was four minutes out from possibly confronting the most dangerous man he'd probably ever meet. A man who was trained in all the black arts like Chase, but had practiced them for real a lot longer; and in a lot more places. And who had slid over the edge from sanity. Chase believed Rivers had checked his conscience at the door when he decided to go after Vladislav and that made him unpredictable. Chase reached up and felt the green beret scrunched on top of his head. He hoped it would give him a few seconds.

"One minute. How you getting home?"

"I'll call you on the satellite phone. Can you set down somewhere and monitor for me?"

"Roger that. I'll just go back to the airport and camp out in the maintenance room. Just don't call me in to a hot LZ."

"There'll be one man left standing, one way or the other."

Cody pulled up the dark visor and his eyes met Chase's. "Good luck."

The top of James Peak loomed ahead. The storm clouds Masters had noted earlier loomed above it. Chase could see the rail line coming up a long spur and disappearing into the side of the mountain about six hundred feet below where the chopper was headed. He didn't tell Masters they were probably already in someone's rifle sights.

Masters did his usual expert job of standing off to the side of mountain, one skid on, one off. His head was turned left, paying close attention to where the blades were.

Chase opened the door and got out onto the left skid. He slid the door shut behind him, then jumped. His feet hit loose rock and then he slid about ten feet down the side of the mountain, underneath the chopper even as Masters banked away and flew off to the east. Chase came to a halt, the M-21 held out away from the body, the MP-5 having dug a gash out of his back.

Chase spit out dust and slowly sat up, feeling the rocks digging into his butt. He shook his head and then ducked as a rock about three feet to his left explode into fragments, peppering his side with rock splinters. The echo of the shot came a second later. Damn, he hated being right.

****

Rivers was looking over the M-21, which he had across his lap. The MP-5 and Glock were to his left. Chase was seated on the other side of the remains of a small campfire. Dry wood, which produced no smoke, was piled nearby, but the fire was long cold.

"Son, you're out of date with this," Rivers shook the M-21. "They got fifty caliber sniper rifles now that can blow a big hole through a man at a mile."

Chase spoke his first words since Rivers had appeared from behind a boulder, his AK-47 aimed at Chase's mid-section: "It's what I was trained on." Chase had simply put his hands up in the air, and Rivers had collected the weapons and walked Chase to his camp.

Rivers had made his home about twenty meters to the south of the east portal for the Moffat Tunnel. It couldn't be seen from the rail line, and he had an excellent view of the dirt road that ran up from Rollinsville for miles and miles. Very far in the eastern distance in the haze, Chase could even make out the Great Plains.

Rivers had a rucksack leaning against a log and nothing else. Chase imagined the old man took his poncho hootch down every morning, rolled his sleeping bag and put it in the ruck-- regardless of whether he was going anywhere. Just good old SF training.

He wore faded OD green jungle fatigues. A Special Forces patch adorned the right shoulder indicating combat service in SF. A CIB with two stars-- combat infantry badge, the stars indicating he'd fought in two wars beyond the first one that he had been awarded the CIB for-- was sewn above his left chest pocket.

The man inside the fatigues was old and tired. Not the young buck who'd been in the picture on Thorne's wall. The years spent in God-forsaken places around the world were etched on his face. He had a few wisps of white hair on his wrinkled skull. He was stick thin, as if wasting away. He should have been presiding over a grandson's birthday party, not sitting in the mountains adorned with the tools of killing.

His eyes, though, were icy blue and pierced right through Chase as he looked up from the wallet which he'd appropriated when he expertly patted Chase down, removing the knife hidden in the left boot, the garrote under the belt, and the back-up .22 caliber derringer Chase had hidden inside his boxers, right next to his dick.

"What kind of bullshit is a Federal Liaison Investigator?"

"I'm not here in an official capacity."

Rivers tossed the wallet into the dirt. "I'm assuming you earned that beret on your head. You wouldn't be stupid enough to come up here wearing it if you hadn't."

"I was in Group and Delta for ten years after being in the Infantry."

"Well, you can't be all stupid. I know no one could have told you I was here cause no one knows I'm here, so you figured it out." Rivers had the AK loosely cradled in his right hand, lying across his lap. He wiped his left hand across his forehead. Chase noticed that hand was shaking slightly. The one on the gun was rock steady. "But you're on the wrong end of the gun so you can't be all that bright either." He thumbed through the stuff he'd taken out of Chase's shirt pocket and stared at the picture. "Who is this?"

"My father."

Rivers nodded. "Bill Chase."

"You knew him?"

"Met him in-country," Rivers said. He looked at Chase and his eyes narrowed. "Interesting. They never found his body after his camp was over-run."

"I know."

"Last someone saw of him, according to the Medal of Honor citation, he was manning a .50 caliber machinegun, covering the withdrawal of the rest of his team and the indig's they were advising. Saved a lot of lives."

"That's what it says."

"Of course, there's shit it doesn't say," Rivers noted. "Like everything else, there's another level to every story."

"And what's the other level with my father?"

Rivers shook his head. "Got no time for that. Why are you here?"

"Vladislav."

The ice got colder in those eyes. "Go on."

"I know who he is. Who he's pretending to be. His cover. The name the CIA gave him." Chase was almost running on at the mouth, but he knew the look Rivers was giving him was the last thing a lot of people had ever seen.

"What is it?"

"Peter Watkins." Rivers didn't bother to ask Chase how he'd found the information. Chase knew it didn't matter to him now. Chase lifted his hand and Rivers eyes followed it as Chase slowly pulled out his satellite phone. "I have his number."

A small line furrowed between those deadly eyes.

"It ends up here," Chase said. "Tonight."

The line disappeared and Rivers slowly nodded. He put down the AK and reached for the phone.

Chase handed it over and then dictated the number. He really hoped Watkins was home because Chase wanted to spend as little time as possible on this mountain with Rivers.

Watkins was.

Rivers rattled something in Russian. Then listened. Several exchanges later, he turned the phone off and handed it back to Chase.

"He's on his way."

"Why's he coming?"

"Because he needs it to end too." He stood. "We got work to do."

"No, you have work to do," I said. "It's not my fight."

"So you're really not here in an official capacity?" Rivers asked.

"No."

"Then why'd you come?"

"So the body count in town stops where it is."

Rivers shrugged. He loosened the straps on his ruck.

"Why did you kill the baby?" Chase asked.

Rivers didn't even pause. "It was a mistake. That asshole drug dealer hid behind the crib. I didn't even know there was a kid in there when I hit the door, the lights were off and all I could see was the muzzle flash of his weapon. I returned fire."

"So that makes it OK? It was a mistake?"

"The baby was fucked up already. Both by its druggie parents and by Vladislav who'd just been there. I must have missed him by a couple of minutes."

Chase tried to fit those pieces. "So Vladislav tied the Barnes up and tortured their baby, then just let them go? Then you showed up and shot everyone?"

Rivers pulled out four green canvas bags that Chase recognized. Claymore mines. He'd memorized the specs on those when he was an eighteen-year old plebe at West Point. It was a fragmentation, directional mine. Seven hundred steel ball bearings packed in a curved, rectangular fiberglass case, with six hundred and eighty-two grams of composition C-4 explosive behind the spheres. Fifty meter kill zone in front, with a sixteen-meter danger area behind. It could be fired by hand using a clacker on the end of a long cord, or a trip wire could be rigged.

Rivers hands began pulling pieces out of each of the bags, checking them, unrolling wires, making sure there were no tangles. Chase knew Rivers could do that blindfolded because he'd been trained doing it blindfolded. Rivers used the testing clacker to make sure they were functional. Rivers spoke as he worked.

"I was looking for Vladislav. I'd tracked him to the Boulder area. I knew he'd be dealing-- what else could he do? The Agency gave him a new identity, a new life, but people don't change. Scum is scum. So I started working my way up from the bottom of the cesspool. I hit up dealers, showing them Vladislav's picture, threatening them to give him up to me. It wasn't working too well because they were more scared of Vladislav than they were of me. Plus, he provided their livelihood.

"Then the Barnes called me that night. Said Vladislav had just left. Said he was threatening to kill them. I headed over."

"Why was he threatening to kill them?"

Rivers inserted a blasting cap into the top of one of the Claymores, screwing it down, like other people might work on a bottle of ketchup. "They owed him money for a drug shipment. Except they claimed they never got the drugs."

Rachel Stevens' gym bag, Chase thought. That's what had started all of this. For Chase it had started two nights earlier when the Patriots had delivered the drugs to Vladislav and he'd been alerted to Wyoming.

"So you went over there and just shot them?"

"No. It was an ambush. The wife was waiting for me downstairs. She tried to get me off-guard with her feminine charms."

Chase felt sorry for Trina Barnes. She'd probably used her body all her life with success to get men to do what she wanted. She just hadn't known she was dealing with a single-minded psychopath when Rivers showed up at her door.

"When she realized I didn't want her body or her blowjob or any of her, she drew down on me and I shot her. I heard the husband upstairs. He was with the kid, except I didn't know there was a kid there. Like I said. Vladislav had been there not a half hour earlier. Working his magic on the kid to let them know he meant business about getting his money. The husband ambushed me in the kid's room. Fucking scum. I heard the sirens and left out the back. Disappeared into the dark."

"Why would they ambush you?" Chase was trying to keep up. "They called you to give up Vladislav."

"No, they called me to give *me* up to Vladislav. If they didn't have the cash, they must have figured they could use me as collateral. Vladislav knew I was looking for him. He had a bounty on my head. The Barnes must have hoped they could wipe out their debt with Vladislav and maybe even make some money by capturing or killing me and calling Vladislav back."

Double-cross and triple-cross. It was life in the world Rivers had lived in for over thirty-five years. Chase thought of Tim Barnes asking Chase to shot him, saying he was responsible. Rivers had shot the kid accidentally, but it had been Barnes' fault for hiding in that room behind the damn crib. At least he'd accepted that before he died. Except he hadn't had the guts to shot himself. He'd wanted suicide by police.

Rivers had all four Claymores rigged. He held one up, looking at it almost wistfully. "One time in 'Nam I saw an ARVN pull in his Claymore after we'd set up a night ambush that didn't catch anything. Instead of disassembling the mine like he was supposed to, he simply rolled the wire around the mine; clacker still attached, and stick it in his ruck. A couple of minutes later he did a rucksack flop, which depressed the clacker, and the mine blew him into two pieces. The price of stupidity."

Ah, the good old days of combat, Chase thought. He'd met many vets who would whisper over a couple of beers that whatever war they'd been in was the best time of their lives. When they'd felt the most alive. Chase didn't feel that way, he realized with a start. He thought of his mother's letter. Could a person have a new life if their old one was the wrong one?

The politicians and the CIA had ruined Rivers life for him. The wars his CIB indicated had to be three of the five most recent-- Vietnam, probably one of the Iraq invasions and Afghanistan. None of them particularly good wars. Afghanistan had been close with the connection to Bin Laden, 9-11 and the Taliban, Chase knew, having gone in with the first wave, but then it had gotten warped like everything else.

"What about the Patriots?" Chase asked.

"Vladislav used them too," Rivers said. "They supplied him."

"You dropped the dime on them that got that cop killed."

"That was a shame," Rivers allowed. "I didn't think that would happen. Figured they'd get pulled over, picked up. I tracked them in Boulder, hoping they'd lead me to Vladislav, but they were good. They did a half-dozen dead drops and I didn't know which one was the real one. I never got a line on the Russian. So when they left and headed back home, I called their plate in. Tried to at least bust that connection." Rivers had all the Claymores ready. "Who do you think is running those guys from the shadows anyway?"

Chase thought of Cardena. "The CIA runs the Patriots?"

Rivers shook his head. "Not run them. Influence and keep tabs on is better. There are always guys like the Patriots around. The CIA helps get those kinds of guys together. Organize them."

"Why?"

"The enemy you know is better than the enemy you don't know. Ever since Oklahoma City, everyone's been trying to get a handle on these militia people. The CIA's way is just sneakier and dirtier, as usual. They infiltrated and influenced the Patriots so they could keep a good eye on the organization and use it when they needed it. I wanted to help expose that. It's wrong both ways. It's wrong because it supports those assholes in the first place and it's even wrong about the assholes because it's setting them up. I don't like it when bad guys break the law and I don't like it when the supposed good guys break the law."

It all made sense to Chase in a perverse way: after all, how had the Patriots and Vladislav managed to hook up in the first place? Dialed 1-800-DRUGS ARE US? There was probably at least one, if not more, person in the Patriots on the CIA's payroll.

"What about York?"

"Who?"

"Jim York. The man who intercepted the drug courier to the Barnes. Did you pay him to do that to set the Barnes up?"

"I have no idea who you're talking about."

Chase saw no reason why Rivers would lie to him at this point. Had it all just been bad luck for Rachel? He'd thought that in the very beginning-- that Rachel Stevens had just run into the wrong person. Now it looked like that was true, but in a much more twisted way than he could ever have imagined.

Her death had trigged a landslide of events-- the Barnes not getting their product to sell. Then not having the money to pay Vladislav. The Russian then showing up and torturing their baby. The Barnes calling Rivers and trying to betray him to Vladislav but that going bad and Rivers taking out the family. And it looped back to Linda Watkins and her husband in that swingers club giving Rachel the product in the first place. And it was going to end tonight, here on this mountainside.

The tentacles the reached further out and further back to Afghanistan and Iraq and into the halls of the CIA and Gods know where else, Chase didn't even want to dwell on right now.

"And the woman? Did you cut her throat?"

"What woman?"

"Rachel Stevens. She was the drug courier for Vladislav."

"No."

Chase knew it was time for him to go. "Can I have my weapons back?"

Rivers was no longer interested in him. "Get your stuff and get out of here."

CHAPTER TWENTY-NINE

Chase left Rivers' camp in the same direction he'd arrived-- up slope and to the north and west. He walked until he went over the crest of James Peak, then he sat and waited for dark, before coming back over the mountain and settling down in his current position, which could overlook both Rivers' campsite and the road.

Rivers was nowhere to be seen, but Chase knew he was down there waiting.

Vladislav arrived an hour after nightfall. His four-wheel drive Land Rover stopped about a half-mile from the East Portal. There wasn't much illumination and Chase was glad he had the night scope he'd picked up from Thorne. Chase had tracked the headlights coming from over twenty miles away, far down the valley. He knew Rivers, two hundred feet below and a quarter mile south of Chase's location, had also.

In the night scope, the headlights were like two huge searchlights and when they suddenly went off, Chase had to wait a second as the computer in the scope adjusted. The scene that reappeared was as if he was watching through a regular four-power scope in daytime, except everything was in shades of green and black.

Chase's hands tightened around the stock of the M-21 as he saw that Vladislav had not come alone. Two other men got out of the Land Rover with him. Both had automatic weapons and they moved up the road warily, Vladislav following about fifty meters behind. Chase didn't know how much the Russian was paying those two, but he couldn't have paid Chase enough to take point into Rivers' camp. Of course, Vladislav had probably lied to them, telling them it was an easy set-up or, more likely, they owed Vladislav big time. They were bait.

Chase squinted. The person on point was a big man with a bushy beard carrying an AK-47-- the Patriot who had finished off the deputy lying in the road. Cop-killer. Chase shifted to the second man. He couldn't identify him, but he had little doubt he was the driver, the first shooter of the deputy. Vladislav would want men who had nothing left to loose, men who were facing the death penalty. So much for the Medicine Bow Mountains being sown up tight, Chase thought.

Chase watched them continue to move up the road as Vladislav slipped off among the pine trees and boulders on the uphill side. Chase caught his image intermittently among the rocks and trees. He moved stealthily, a bulky weapon in his hands. Chase recognized the silhouette-- an M-203. An M-16 with a 40mm grenade launcher attached below the barrel. Cardena had been right about the weapon of choice. A large canvas bag was slung over Vladislav's non-firing shoulder.

The two killers on the road lengthened the distance between themselves and that saved the trail man's life as the point man hit a Claymore's tripwire. The wire popped the firing cap, which ignited the C-4, blasting seven hundred ball bearings in a waist-high swatch across the road. Steel hit flesh, parted it, ripped through bone. The sharp crack of the mine reached Chase's ears as the two halves of the man's body hit the dirt road, blood and viscera oozing into the ground. Chase felt a moment's satisfaction.

The second man was frozen twenty meters behind the body. He yelled something, the sound very faint at this distance. There was no reply.

Chase checked for Vladislav, but he couldn't see the Russian. Chase swung the rifle back to the road. The second man was moving forward, stepping very carefully. Vladislav must have promised him a hell of a lot of money or threatened to turn him in. The man passed his partner's body, checking for another tripwire.

Rivers would have to clacker-detonate another Claymore to get the guy on the road or shoot him. Either of which would give his approximate location away. That was what Vladislav was hoping for.

Chase checked once more, but couldn't find Vladislav among the boulders and scrub pine south of the road.

The man on the trail reached the campsite. He slowly turned in a circle and then called out.

His hands flew up to his neck. He staggered, then dropped to his knees. He fell forward and was still. Chase had heard no shot and seen no muzzle flash. What the hell had Rivers used?

Vladislav must have been worried about the same thing, because Chase heard a flat thumping noise that he immediately recognized-- the grenade launcher being fired. Four seconds later, the round went off in the vicinity of the camp in a blossom of flame. Even as the explosion echoed across the mountain, there was another thump.

This went on for a minute with over twenty 40mm grounds being fired, before Vladislav paused. The sounds of the last grenade resounded across the mountains and after the echoes faded, silence reigned. He'd peppered the area around the campground. Vladislav's position had been secure because other than the sound, the launcher gave off no firing signature.

"Colonel Rivers!" Vladislav's voice was surprisingly loud in the sudden stillness. "Come out, Colonel. Let us settle this like men."

It was difficult to pinpoint where he was and Chase had no doubt the Russian had a big rock between him and the campsite. He could fire the M-203 over the boulder and continue to pepper the area with indirect fire as long as he had the rounds. Chase remembered the big bag he carried. He'd come prepared.

The thump of the grenade launcher began another round of firings. Chase counted twenty-one forty-millimeter rounds going off and he still had no idea where the Russian was firing from. Chase felt for Rivers, who might already be dead.

Silence once more.

"Colonel," Vladislav's voice was lilting, almost seductive. "Colonel. Colonel Rivers. Come out. I give you my word that I will not shoot you like the dog you are. I will give you a chance. A small chance. But a better chance than hiding in the rocks, waiting the next grenade to kill you."

Silence played out. Chase had the M-21 in his hands, his cheek resting against the wood stock. He could see his breath with each exhale. The night scope glowed green in his left eye. His hand was perfectly steady.

"Ah, Colonel! I know where you are. I was told about you. That you were a warrior. What kind of warrior you were."

Thump.

The 40mm round went off right in front of the dark black mouth of the east portal. Three more rounds were fired, each one getting closer to the opening, until the last one hit just inside. Then silence.

"You can run down the tunnel, Colonel. You can run away. Or you can come out. And be a man." There was a slight pause. "If you do not come out of that tunnel, I will have your brother's family killed. His two pretty daughters. Their husbands. The four grandchildren. You

277

know I will do that. I will end your bloodline's presence on the face of this planet.

"You called me and said you wanted to end it. Then let us end it. Here. Now."

Chase knew the man part wouldn't work. What would work on Rivers, though, was reality. There was no doubt in Chase's mind after listening to Cardena and seeing the DVD, that Vladislav would do what he threatened. Chase knew Rivers had seen the carnage in that village first-hand and probably much more of Vladislav's handiwork.

A figure appeared in the tunnel, limping forward on the tracks. Rivers' hands were empty and raised to his shoulders. Chase tensed, waiting for the shot that would kill the old colonel.

"Very good," Vladislav called. "Very good. Come ten feet more and then remain still, keeping your hands up."

Chase could see Rivers now. His stick-thin figure was slightly bent. Chase turned the focus on the night scope. There was something on Rivers' back, not a pack but something. His body was between it and Vladislav, who had suddenly appeared fifty feet down the tracks, walking up the grade to the portal.

The Russian held the M-203 tight against his shoulder, aimed directly at Rivers-- no grandstanding with it held loosely at his hip, aimed in the general vicinity. Vladislav might have been scum, but he was well-trained scum. Chase was surprised that he hadn't shot Rivers as soon as he saw him, but Chase sensed a certain degree of machismo, of wanting Rivers to suffer, to grovel, on Vladislav's part before he dispatched the old man. It was what a man who oversaw the rape and torture of schoolchildren would do. It was also a mistake.

Chase centered the night scope's cross hairs on Vladislav's chest. Chase's finger caressed the trigger and he began to get the rhythm of his heartbeat moving from the subconscious into his conscious. His breathing grew shallower, slowing his heart further.

He moved the crosshairs from Vladislav's chest to the bridge of his nose. Always go for the headshot if available had been the rule at SOTI training. After all, it was highly possible Vladislav was wearing a bulletproof vest.

He was walking along the tracks slowly, but he almost appeared to be standing still in Chase's sight. His time sense was slowing everything to a crawl. The space between breaths seemed interminable, between heartbeats several seconds long.

Chase felt the tiny sliver of steel under his left index finger, flat and cool on the skin.

He remembered what Thorne had said about Rivers. The look on the old colonel's face over the dead fire.

Chase relaxed his finger. He had to give the Colonel a chance at his revenge and he knew the old man wasn't giving up this easily. Chase blinked. Or was it that he wanted Vladislav to kill the Colonel and end that half, allowing Chase to kill Vladislav and make a clean sweep of it?

Vladislav was less than twenty feet from Rivers. He stopped the weapon still tight to his shoulder.

"Colonel Rivers. You should have left me alone. You should have taken your retirement pay and played golf. Or gone fishing. Who are you to come after me?" Vladislav's voice went up. "Your own government protects me. How did you ever think you would succeed?"

Vladislav laughed and Chase saw the dual M-16-40mm muzzles waver slightly. Rivers must have seen it also because he dove forward, arms grabbing over his right shoulder for whatever was on his back.

Vladislav fired the rifle, the round going over Rivers' diving form. The colonel had what had been on his back in his hands now and Chase recognized it just as Vladislav did-- a wooden crossbow hung from a sling. Rivers pulled the release and the bolt leapt forward as the Russian brought his weapon to bear on the prone old man.

The flint tipped bolt hit Vladislav's neck, slicing through the carotid artery on the left side. The M-203 dropped from stunned fingers. Whether it was the result of the bolt hitting or sheer shock at what Rivers had done, Chase didn't know. He didn't think Vladislav did either as his hands clawed at the bamboo shaft protruding from his neck.

He was trying to say something as Rivers got to his feet and walked toward him. Chase could see the mouth moving, but at this distance, he heard nothing. Vladislav went to his knees, and then rocked back into a sitting position, his hands still around the shaft, blood pouring over them.

Chase got up and began moving down the mountain as Vladislav's life flowed over his hands, down his chest. Rivers stood there staring at him, the years of hunting over, revenge completed. Chase thought they were speaking, or at least Rivers was, but he couldn't make it out as they were close together.

Chase was less than two hundred feet from the rail line, about sixty feet up when Vladislav died. His upper body slumped backward over his lower legs, a profane position but one he deserved.

Chase was watching, still making his way down, when Colonel Rivers' head exploded in a puff of bone, flesh, blood and brain. The echo of the shot raced by a split second later. Rivers' body fell on top of the man he had tracked for two years and finally caught up to.

CHAPTER THIRTY

Chase froze, becoming one with the mountain, muscles tightening, expecting the next shot to hit his own head. He remained perfectly still for a minute.

He heard a noise to his right, stone on stone, as a rock tumbled down the mountainside. He shifted only his eyes in that direction, knowing that movement would be picked up quicker than his still form in the darkness.

Someone was coming down the mountain above the south side of the rail line, about two hundred meters from where Chase was. Whoever it was had a long rifle in his hands. Chase very slowly lowered himself into a prone position, pointing downhill. The man reached the two bodies and bent over, checking to make sure they were dead.

It was Fortin. Chase recognized him as he stood up and ran his fingers through his hair

He slung the rifle over his shoulder just as Chase fired.

The round hit Fortin exactly where it was aimed-- in his left thigh, spinning him three hundred and sixty degrees before leaving him on the ground. He struggled to get the rifle off his shoulder.

"Don't even think about it," Chase called out as he stood. He had the night scope centered on Fortin's forehead. He was looking right at Chase, his eyes magnified in the reticules. Chase carefully made his way down slope, never removing the CIA man's head from the center of his sight picture.

Fortin remained still as blood pumped out of his leg and spasms of pain crossed the face in Chase's sight.

"Fucking Chase," Fortin acknowledged. Chase came to edge of the camp and paused, ten feet away. "I should have known you'd be too stupid to listen to advice. This isn't your fight."

With his right hand, Chase pulled the Glock out of its holster. Chase quickly exchanged the rifle for the pistol, never leaving the CIA man uncovered except for a split second.

He didn't make a move. Chase realized Fortin was confident he would walk-- or crawl, given his wound-- out of this. His next words confirmed that.

"Would you at least allow me to stop the bleeding? I don't think you hit an artery, but I'm losing blood here."

Chase didn't say anything, amazed at Fortin's confidence. Chase wondered where a man like him came from? What did it take to develop an ego like that?

Fortin must have taken Chase's silence as acquiescence and pulled a bandage out of a pack at his waist. Chase followed every move, the pistol centered on the CIA man's forehead as he bound his leg, ready to shoot if he made the slightest hostile move. He cinched down the bandage with a grunt of pain. Chase noted he wasn't wearing a bulletproof vest under his thin jacket and Chase shifted his aim toward the larger target of the man's chest.

"I'll let you walk," Fortin said. "This business here--" he nodded his head toward the two bodies a few feet away-- "is over. I'd call it pretty even."

"You'll let *me* walk?"

"You're not that stupid, are you?"

"You fund the Patriots?"

Fortin laughed. "Jesus, man. Get real. We try to keep a tight leash on them. You local yokels should be glad we take care of that."

"I'm not local. And the CIA has no legal authority to operate domestically."

"Oh, yeah, right. That's the FBI's job. And they've done so well at it. Ruby Ridge. Waco. Nine-eleven. Out-fucking-standing job." He laughed once more despite the pain from his leg. "It's not like they don't need some help."

"You called in that false report about the Blazer in Wyoming didn't you? To let those guys get away?" The answer was clear on Fortin's face. "And your people hacked that vehicle registration out of the Wyoming database. They killed a cop for God sakes."

"Hey, the two killers are dead down the trail there," Fortin said. "And right now we're keeping tabs on something going on in the militia movement that's bigger than that. Bigger than this."

Even if he was talking about another Oklahoma City, Chase didn't care. "And the drugs? The Patriots you supplied; who supplied Vladislav. Hell, you connected the two."

"Hey, if we didn't do it, real bad guys would."

"'Real bad guys'," Chase repeated.

"It's small time stuff. Less than ten percent of the shit that comes through the border. And it gives us great infiltration into the suppliers, into the terror networks, the financing, into really making a difference where it counts. And we turn the profits around to our country's benefit. If Congress wasn't such tight-asses we wouldn't need the money to fund our black ops."

Fortin sat up, testing his leg with a grimace. "Fuck, man. I can't believe you had the balls to shoot me." He shook his head, as if trying to accept that reality. "You split now, we'll call this over. I'll never see you again. You'll never see me. Hell, you can keep your fucking job."

"How did you know about this meeting?" Chase asked.

Fortin snorted. "We monitor all of Vladislav's phones—land line and cell. As soon as he got the call from Rivers, I had a chopper come get me, drop me on the other side of the ridge just after dark."

Just like in Wyoming, Chase thought.

"Rachel Stevens."

"Yes?"

"You killed her, didn't you?"

"That nut job was stalking her. She was a loose end that could've caused Vladislav's cover to be blown. And we still used him for odd jobs. She was expendable. And she wasn't a civilian. She was a player once she decided to carry that bag for Vladislav."

"Did she know what was in the bag?"

Fortin shrugged. "Who the fuck knows and who the fuck cares."

"I care."

"That's your problem," Fortin said.

"You called in the partial plate on York."

"Helped you out. He did steal the drugs off her. I saw that. Saw him drag her in his van. Then watched her get out without the bag and he left. Then I picked her up, closed her out."

"You were mirroring me in Wyoming."

"Bullshit." But Fortin's eyes shifted ever so slightly.

"You wanted me to take out the Patriots, and then you'd take me out, so there'd be no legal fall-out. They were cop killers and they killed a Federal Agent in their final gun-battle. That right, Hammer?"

Fortin didn't say anything. He carefully moved his hand toward his chest. "I've got a SATPhone here. I'm going to call for my extraction. It'll take them about thirty minutes to get me. That should give you plenty of time to get out of the area. I'll tell them I got hit in the shoot out."

"Why should I let you go?"

"You can't shoot me. You couldn't pull the trigger in Wyoming, there's no way you can shoot a fellow federal agent in cold blood."

Something on his hand glittered in the starlight. Chase squinted. A large gold ring on the middle finger. Chase had seen that ring before. In the video.

Chase pulled the trigger. The round hit Fortin in the chest, ripping through bone and muscle, right through the heart.

A surprised look coursed across Fortin's face. Complete amazement.

"Why?" The word came out of his mouth like an afterthought. Chase was thinking of the man whose head had been cut off by the guillotine.

Chase stared directly into Fortin's eyes, watching carefully. He blinked twice. Then he died.

CHAPTER THIRTY-ONE

Chase slowly walked into his apartment. He put his pistol on the kitchen chair and dropped all his field gear in the closet and secured it. He grabbed a beer from the fridge and went into the bathroom. He turned the shower on, and then stripped his dirt-encrusted clothes off. He stepped into the hot water, the beer in hand. Chase leaned against the tile, feeling the water beating him on the back. He took a deep drink from the beer.

It was the way he had always come back from training in the army. Hot shower, cold beer.

It had taken Chase several hours, working through dawn, to arrange the bodies in such a manner that someone doing a quick investigation would conclude that Fortin had been killed by Vladislav, as the Russian was dying from the arrow in his neck. Chase knew the CIA would be out there sometime during the day and they would close the book on it without looking too hard. As Fortin had said-- it had worked out pretty evenly. Chase didn't think anyone in the CIA would miss Fortin much. His death probably meant a promotion for whoever was going out there to sterilize the site. It wasn't like they were going to call in a CSI unit.

Then Chase had walked down the mountain into the long valley, putting many miles between himself and the scene until he found a place where Masters could land the chopper. He was real happy to hear from Chase. He picked Chase up and flew him back to the landing zone, holding back on questions that had answers he really didn't want to know. Chase drove home from the landing zone, finally arriving just moments ago, late in the afternoon.

The alcohol on an empty stomach and the hot water on his skin combined to make Chase dizzy. He sank down to the shower floor, letting the can fall, the golden beer swirling into the dirty water sluicing off his body and down the drain. He felt as if his head was going to float off his shoulders.

Chase stayed like that for a long time, falling asleep, until the hot water heater ran out. The cold splattering on his body brought Chase back. He reached up and slammed the knob off.

Chase staggered out of the shower and toweled off. He walked through the apartment naked, his feet slapping the concrete floor. He was lost, wandering, not knowing what he was looking for, if he was looking for anything at all.

Finally, he went into his bedroom and gathered clothes off the floor, pulling them on. Jeans. A t-shirt. Sneakers with no socks. He had no idea what he was doing or what he was going to do. He kept seeing Rivers' head explode, Fortin's eyes blinking.

Chase grabbed his Jeep keys and walked into the back. The new puppy must have been in Louise's house. He'd noticed she didn't leave Star out like she had Astral. She'd learned.

Had he? Chase wondered as he noted several sprouts of green in his garden.

Chase got in the Jeep and started the engine. He saw Louise come down the stairs with a large dog on a leash. It looked like a German Shepherd except it had short hair, more brown than normal for a Shepherd, and a broad chest.

"That's not a puppy," Chase said.

Louise seemed embarrassed. "I'm sorry, Horace. But a puppy—well, I don't think you could handle a puppy."

Great, Chase thought.

"She's Star's mother. Chelsea. You can take care of each other," Louise said. "She's a Shepherd-Chow mix. A very good dog. She can always find her way home according to my friend at the pound once she settles in. You need a companion, Chase."

She went around and opened the passenger door. Chelsea jumped in like she owned the Jeep and sat there, head as high as Chase's. She stared at him for a second, then looked forward, ready to go.

"Thank you," Chase said.

Louise put a hand on his arm. "You're welcome, Horace."

Chase paused, then reached out and pulled Louise tight. "Really. Thank you."

****

Chase stopped by Merck magazine. He took Chelsea in with him and the two pit bulls whimpered when they saw her. He told Thorne that Rivers was dead, but that the Colonel had gotten Vladislav before he died. Chase gave Thorne the Montagnard bracelet he'd taken off Rivers' wrist and told him where he'd hidden the crossbow in the mountains. Chase could have sworn he saw tears in that old man's eyes as he took the bracelet and the grid coordinates. Thorne didn't want to know any more than that and Chase didn't want to tell him anymore, so that worked out fine.

****

Chase stopped by the office, leaving Chelsea in the Jeep with the keys in the ignition. His job was no longer hanging by a thread. Wrapping up three murders and a big time drug operation in one fell swoop had given certain people amnesia about his little escapade at the bank. His badge was on his desk, waiting for him. He knew Jeffrey Stevens would be more than willing to forget about the letter and allow the whole thing to quietly disappear when he heard about what else his wife had been up to with Gavin. But Chase also didn't give a shit about his job, either with Boulder or with the feds either.

Chase was sure a psychologist would have had a field day delving into all the personalities involved in the case and their histories to explain why they had acted the way they had, but he wasn't a shrink. And the last shrink he had gone to had tried to kill him, so that wasn't an avenue he wanted to pursue. All he cared about on that end was that the case was finally closed.

The only regret Chase had was that Linda Watkins had gotten away. He would have loved to track her down at the Boulder Country Club. Right there next to the tennis courts that Linda would never come back to.

Porter walked in as Chase picked up his badge. "Hey, partner." A wide smile crossed Porter's face.

Chase nodded. "Partner."

"Good to have you back."

Chase was looking at the badge in his hand. "I'm not sure I'm back."

The smile was gone. Porter walked up and put a hand on Chase's shoulder. "It's your choice. But you're a damn good cop."

"I broke the law," Chase said.

Porter took a deep breath. "I been wrong about a lot of things lately. Maybe I'm wrong about that. You did what you thought was right?"

Chase nodded.

Porter stuck his hand out. "Whatever you decide, you know you can count on me."

Chase shook his partner's hand. "I know." He put the badge in his pocket and left.

****

When Chase walked out of the building, a black van was parked next to his Jeep. Chelsea was glaring at it. Chase pulled the Glock out of the holster as he approached and the side door opened. Cigarette smoke wafted out. Cardena waved for him to come in.

"Want a smoke?" Cardena asked as Chase got in the van and took the seat across from him, Glock still in hand.

"I'm quitting."

"Probably good for you."

Chase stared at him, smelling the nicotine. Realizing once more how stupid he had been. "You're not DEA."

Cardena chuckled. "That's a losing fucking war if I ever saw one. You can't stop demand. When you can't stop demand, you can't win. Prohibition didn't work, why does anyone think the war on drugs will?"

"So who do you work for? CIA?"

"Horace Chase, my man." The sound of a deep drag on a cigarette echoed in the van. "DEA. CIA. FBI. Fucking alphabet soups. I'm not even on the map. You get that? I try to keep things clean and keep them from fucking up too badly.

"The CIA should have never contracted Vladislav. Fucking psychopath. Fucking FBI of course should have never allowed nine-eleven, of course. I'll give your guys that. Spec ops Intel guys, reservists at that, weekend warriors, warned them about Al-Qaeda. But everyone was too worried about their damn careers and their little fiefdoms to do their damn jobs. I just clean up the shit they all leave behind.

288

"But let's not go there. I'm here as a courtesy to you. Because you finally did what needed to be done. You cleaned up the clusterfuck."

"Which? Rivers? Vadislav?"

Cardena lit another cigarette, chain-smoking. Chase felt the aching desire for one.

"Both," Cardena said. "Can't have that stuff happening here in the good old U. S. of A. The CIA should have just paid off Vladislav or put a bullet in his fucking brain. And eliminated Rivers before he even fucking retired."

"You got me this assignment," Chase said.

"Give the man a cigarette," Cardena said, holding out the one he had just lit.

Chase shook his head.

"Getting healthy?" Cardena asked. "Expecting a long and happy life? With the stripper? Like your mother?"

Chase just stared at the dark figure.

Cardena sighed. "Ok. Sorry. That was cheap. Your father was a fucking hero. Medal of Honor winner. And you did us right. Cleared a big problem up. Took you a while. Take some time off. Go fishing. Do something. Be happy."

"Fortin?" Chase asked.

Cardena shook his head. "Another dumb fuck. Good riddance."

"Why are you letting me live?"

Cardena actually looked surprised. "We're the good guys, Chase, for Gods-sakes." He paused. "You know. I'd really like you to work for us. Really. But. It just wouldn't work out."

"Why not?"

Cardena flicked the cigarette to the van's floor and ground it out. "You wouldn't smoke in the airport." He nodded toward the door.

As Chase exited, he heard Cardena say one last thing: "But you've got a special talent and we'll keep you in mind."

THE END

Bob Mayer

CPSIA information can be obtained at www.ICGtesting.com
Printed in the USA
LVOW081149120212

268260LV00005B/41/P